Vessel of Wrath

THE LIFE AND TIMES OF
CARRY NATION

Books by Robert Lewis Taylor

VESSEL OF WRATH

TWO ROADS TO GUADALUPÉ

A JOURNEY TO MATECUMBE

THE TRAVELS OF JAIMIE MCPHEETERS

CENTER RING: THE PEOPLE OF THE CIRCUS

THE BRIGHT SANDS

WINSTON CHURCHILL: AN INFORMAL
   STUDY OF GREATNESS

PROFESSOR FODORSKI

THE RUNNING PIANIST

W. C. FIELDS: HIS FOLLIES AND FORTUNES

DOCTOR, LAWYER, MERCHANT, CHIEF

ADRIFT IN A BONEYARD

Vessel of Wrath

THE LIFE AND

TIMES OF

CARRY

NATION

BY

Robert Lewis Taylor

THE NEW AMERICAN LIBRARY

ILLUSTRATIONS

following page 184

Vessel of Wrath

THE LIFE AND TIMES OF
CARRY NATION

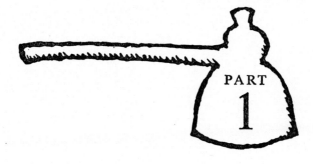

PART
1

THE INGREDIENTS

Chapter One

In the long and painful annals of good works, no name leaps out with more concussive impact than that of Carry Nation. Other women—taller, heavier, just as angry and dedicated to like missions of alteration—flitted across the scene and faded from the minds of a generally relieved public. Mrs. Nation is sharply remembered as the apostle of reform violence, prime dragoness on a field strewn with the bones of sinners. Doubtless she was fortunate in the choice of a symbol; at the height of her powers (regarded in some quarters as diabolic) she carried a run-of-the-mill hardware-store hatchet, through whose agency she was jailed with regularity on charges of common assault. She thanked God for these internments, feeling that they strengthened and purified, and the best photographic mementos of her career show her kneeling in her cell, Bible opened on a chair before her, bonnet tilted pugnaciously, her square face wearing a look of delayed-fuse retribution and her mouth opened (wrote witnesses) to pelt her captors with abuse from a deep reservoir of withering and improper rhetoric. Stated loosely, Mrs. Nation was against alcohol, tobacco, sex, politics, government (national, state and local), the Masonic Lodge, William McKinley, Theodore Roosevelt and William Jennings Bryan, in approximately that order. While it would be unfair to

Mrs. Nation's memory to limit her peeves to the foregoing, these had priority, and, of course, her greatest work, her costliest physical damage, was accomplished in the area of suppressing drink.

Curiously, Mrs. Nation's straight-from-the-shoulder methods had the effect of evoking protest from both her foes and her cronies, who felt, often, that she went too far. It was one thing to threaten a man with a hatchet; it was something else to hit him with it. She regarded the distinction as over-subtle. The enthusiasm of the Woman's Christian Temperance Union (with whose organization in Kansas she had busied herself) waxed and waned over the conduct of its sole member who supported parliamentary drill with hand weapons. After one of her raids on a Kansas town, a reporter described the Union's reaction as "emphatic coldness and disapproval." In retrospect, this attitude seems singular; the raid had been a success. During it, Mrs. Nation smashed one saloon's Venetian mirror with brickbats, flung stones through a second saloon's windows, leveled a half-brick at the head of a boy attempting to sweep up (missing by inches), ripped some candid and stimulating prints from the walls, powdered the bric-a-brac and glasses, separated the rungs from all chairs, drop-kicked a cuspidor over a pot-bellied stove and threw a billiard ball at what she mistakenly took to be "Satan" lounging behind the bar. (It was in fact the bartender, who dove to the floor and scuttled rapidly out of sight.) Before leaving, she begged to be arrested and then sang a number of hymns, only to express herself as insulted when a saloonkeeper said it was the worst atrocity she had committed yet.

As her rampages gathered steam, Mrs. Nation commenced the issuance of a weekly newspaper called *The Smasher's Mail*, which was published by a prosperous and compliant Negro named Chiles, who also ran a saloon. The starting-off copies sold for only a dime, but after a sensible reevaluation, Mrs. Nation dropped the price to a nickel. Chiles was the only publisher she could find. Throughout their association, which was scratchy, she essayed his regeneration; Chiles, in turn, made her a standing offer of free gin. In a general way, everything in *The Smasher* was libelous. Even her careful appraisal of President Roosevelt, as a "blood-thirsty, reckless, cigarette-smoking rummy," was thought to exceed fair criticism, and her ode to the Masonic Lodge was put down as an early sample of extremism. It was an order, she wrote, "whose members swear to have their tongues cut out, their throats ripped across, their hearts torn out and given to beasts, and their bowels taken out and burned to ashes." When President McKinley was assassinated, she withheld sympathy and laid his demise mainly to nicotine. "Government," she commented, apropos of little or nothing, "like dead fish, stinks worse at the head." In fairness, it must be said that Mrs. Nation stoutly operated a section of her paper, entitled "Letters from Hell," which, unedited, aired the views of the opposition. The selections were largely ribald, reflecting the rich, broad humor of the brawling West. A correspondent in Yazoo City, Mississippi appealed for help, saying, "Dear Madam: If you should happen to come across a bottle of good booze in your raids, I would appreciate it very much. I am a sympathizer in the destruction of good booze. It is impossible to get anything here but Blind Tiger." A triumphant saloon-owner in St. Louis wrote, "God bless you! You have increased my business 100 per cent. Hope you keep up the good work," and went on to speak of early retirement. Widely scattered bartenders announced almost simultaneously the creation of a new drink, called the "Carry Nation Cocktail," for which queues were forming early in the mornings. One man relayed his satisfaction that, with the drink, he had tapped a fresh and hitherto dormant layer of custom—"very young children of both sexes"— and he predicted wholesale defections from the more blue-nosed of the church groups soon.

Any reasonable historian must admire Mrs. Nation's armor-plated indifference to censure. At one point she was probably the most discussed woman in the world, and her detractors opened up with a vivid barrage of accusation. She was denounced as a quack, a humbug, a fourflusher, a felon, a bully, a busybody, a common scold, a secret drinker, a man in woman's clothes, a nymphomaniac, an Amazon-gone-amok, a sub rosa traveler in bar fixtures, a reincarnation of Lucrezia Borgia, a possible werewolf and a professional peddler of cheap souvenirs. (Mrs. Nation was, at this last stage, hawking miniature hatchets, wrought of pewter, and making a very good thing of it, but she either gave her money away or ploughed it into campaigns intended to stave off boredom for the saloon-keepers.)

Her opponents were even so unkind as to pounce on a trifling infelicity of mind that ran through nine or ten of the family. In letters and in her autobiography, *The Use and Need of the Life of Carry A. Nation,* which she revised seven times, the crusader discussed this touchy subject without embarrassment. The defect showed up in various ways, all of them interesting. An aunt, during certain lunar phases, made repeated attempts to clamber up on the roof and convert herself into a weather vane. A cousin, at the age of forty, unexpectedly returned to all fours, and was only restored to the vertical after heroic struggles by his minister (who gallantly assumed the nether position for his beginning chats). The above cases were short-lived aberrations only, and cleared up for good in time. Mrs. Nation's mother, on the other hand, suffered from the fixed delusion that she was Queen Victoria. Her predicament was well known in the neighborhood, and gave rise to household complications. Around the plantation home (in Kentucky) she preferred to be addressed as "Your Majesty," but nobody paid her regal homage except the Negroes, and that humorously. The records are inexplicit on the precise phrasing of their responses to inquiries about a missing sceptre (a recurring theme), but one may assume that they ran along the lines of "Ah shore ain' seed it, yore majesty. Not today, nohow. Might be yore majesty drapped it in de outhouse," the discourse accompanied by tolerant African chuckles. She also claimed that somebody had stolen her best royal carriage, and while several lacklustre searches resulted, it never turned up. She worried about trouble in the Sudan and appeared puzzled by the rather homespun appearance of Prince Albert. At the time of her death, uneasy over the success of her reign, she had made elaborate plans for abdication.

Carry herself had fallen prey to "visions" as a child, but in adulthood she was sane by any standards. Her visions involved, in the main, snakes, and were no more suspect than those of Joan of Arc, another thrustful member of the sex. Indeed, the two possessed shared facets, including an extraordinary skill with edged tools. It is impossible to dismiss Carry Nation as the product of mental weakness. In her time she was treated importantly both here and abroad, and women, long crushed beneath priapic male oppression, began sluggishly to realize their potential. In Britain, feminists of all hues fought to attend her meetings, which took on the sporting aspect of rugby and were reported with some jocularity by the austerest of journals. The *Glasgow Times* noted that she looked "remarkably fit" as she stepped from the train, and went on to say that "the cheery American's bright appearance provides an object lesson in support of her contention that the absorption of alcohol is not quite so necessary as many people maintain in counteracting the effects of our quick-change climate." A headline stated that "Mrs. Nation Carries Glasgow by Storm." The fairminded *Times* was perhaps trying to mitigate the crusader's imperfect reception in Dundee, where she was hailed by a blizzard of eggs and mushy tomatoes. The truth is that Dundee, swollen with municipal pride over its slogan of "the drunkenest city in Scotland," was not ready for Mrs. Nation, and it has become a little less ready in the succeeding decades.

She visited Yale in 1902 after an anguished appeal in the student newspaper: "Here are 800 shining young souls, the cream of the nation's manhood, on the broad road which leadeth to destruction. Assist us, Mrs. Nation!" On the campus, she consented to pose, flourishing a water glass, with a group of undergraduates who were represented to be viciously anti-drink, but when the picture was printed, her glass had somehow been transformed into a beer stein, and the students all held similar vessels. The photograph, with superimposed heads of distinguished alumni, today ornaments the Yale Club bar in New York.

Despite such mischievous setbacks, Mrs. Nation roared on, driving men from the near-religious sanctuary of the beer joint, implanting her new concept of physical supremacy, giving women heart. The idea germinated, grew and flowered, and in 1917, while the men were abroad fighting Germans and drinking French wine, American women plotted the unholy Eighteenth Amendment, ushering in home brew, bathtub gin, bootleggers, speakeasies, saxophones, flappers, Calvin Coolidge, gang murders and millions of ruined stomachs. On the local level, Mrs. Nation's effect was stunning. The season was the late 1890's, the place, Kansas. It would be difficult to imagine a combination less inviting for a woman to come between a man and his bottle. The fact that she was never shot is a tribute to the inborn gallantry of the western desperado. Among the thousands disappointed by the omission was Mrs. Nation herself. At the peak of her frenzy, she yearned for the martyr's crown. She often told friends that she aspired to a violent death. "Oh, I want to be shot!" she was quoted as crying. "How glorious to be a martyr to the cause!" A good many octogenarians still living in Kansas remain nonplussed why she was thwarted in this ambition. Allowing even for the westerner's mild bias against plugging women, the odds were solidly in her favor. It may well be that she simply had bad luck.

An argument could be advanced that the great days of Kansas were all but over. It is always mournful to see the chill of restraint placed on a region that has laboriously built up a distinction for wickedness. Babylon was possibly a nuisance to people trying to sleep, but the generality of its residents were happily absorbed in vice. The histories make no mention of a serious municipal problem with boredom during the heyday of Rome, and ancient, amoral Greece was a flowering garden of culture. Kansas, in the Eighties and Nineties, was in a class by itself. As the railroad terminus of the West, it annually received thousands upon thousands of Texas cattle driven up by hard, lean young men whose principal aim was to raise hell on arrival. Commonly they neglected to register at hotels; they expected to spend their scant sleeping time in jail, and they were accommodated. Nearly always their salaries from the grinding weeks on the trail were squandered, earsplittingly, in the first twenty-four hours. When the unbridled vigor of their celebrations finally achieved chaos, those multi-faceted enigmas of the wild West—the professional-gunmen-"marshals"—materialized like restless vultures. Enough romantic balderdash has been written (and broadcast and televised and released in motion pictures) about cowtown marshals to keep American youth misinformed in perpetuity. Actually it was often difficult to tell which side of the law they trod on; numerous citizens complained that they were more frightened of the marshals than the Texans. If the Texans shot up, or "hoorahed," a town, perhaps killing two or three women and a baby in the confusion, the bloodshed was accidental, and apologized for—handsomely; when a marshal shot somebody, there was a heavy flavor of hobby in it, or the act was performed to keep him from growing rusty. Off and on,

Dave Mather and Tom Nixon were the pious legal custodians of
Dodge City, but it may be definitive to observe that Mather finally
brought his marshalhood to a glorious peak by killing Nixon. Also
—not much stressed by today's minnesingers—it was Wyatt Earp
who, in "taming" Bat Masterson, wooed him away from outlawry
and over to the side of respectability. Previously, Masterson had
been little more than a drop-out from the school of hard knocks.

Wichita, which Carry Nation selected as the launching pad for
her first big explosion, had lately endured the ministrations of
Wyatt Earp and his brothers, the armed dentist Doc Holiday, and
Billy Tilghman, whose attitude toward crime was, charitably, permissive. Nearby Coffeyville basked in unquiet pride as the boy-
hood home of Billy the Kid, the child prodigy, who had killed his
first man at the age of twelve, and, small as the community was,
itself marked an important terminus, that of the malodorous Dal-
tons, who had almost robbed the First National Bank on October
5, 1892. It might be commented that, in not doing so, they provided one of the authentically fine photographs in the records of
frontier criminality. It shows Bob and Grat Dalton, Bill Powers
and Dick Broadwell lying propped against a board fence, apparently smiling in the hot glare of the sun; all look well relaxed, and
they were, being dead—shot full of .45-calibre slugs in an ambush
laid by the settlement's peaceful citizens.

From border to border Mrs. Nation's chosen ground was
crowded with men and towns of unexampled repute. "I'd like a
one-way ticket to hell," a drunken cowboy said in a whistle-stop
station of the Santa Fé Railroad. "That'll be a dollar-eighty and
get off at Dodge City," replied the unperturbed agent, adding another *mot* to the already impressive legend. Jesse and Frank
James, with their colleagues, the Youngers, and Mrs. T. S. C.
("Gotch-toothed Belle") Starr, were frequent vacationers in the
state, usually arriving at the line not far ahead of a posse, and
Quantrill's Raiders had sprinkled much Kansas land with the gore
of Jim Lane's Jayhawkers. The foregoing native sons and trippers,
though famous, seemed lacking in dimension by comparison with
the much-sung but more frequently cursed Wild Bill Hickok,
whose death has been lamented only because it occurred before
the spread of psychiatry. Presumably Hickok killed from mean-

ness; a friendly query about the weather might prompt him to bombardment. He had the disposition of a wolverine, coupled to a curious and becoming kind of modesty. Asked a not uncommon question of the day and place—obligatory by social usage in his circle—"How many men you killed, Bill?" he would reply, "Twenty-two," or "Thirty-six" (or whatever the score was at the moment) and add, with a deprecatory cough, "not counting Mexicans and Indians, of course." His friends who survived claimed that he killed in self-defense.

Against the force of such as these, Carry Nation's wrath was hurled with suicidal courage. Scientists have proved that human strength is not necessarily proportionate to heft. The Mad Barber of Mattewan offers an outstanding case in point. By every known measurement, the Barber was the most ferocious inmate some years ago at the excellent New York repository for the unhinged. He had arrived there, doubtless, after hearing one too many bad jokes, the shattered ruin of a neighborhood artist. As size goes in these days of professional football players larger than bison, he was a human shrimp, weighing 126 pounds in his *costume d'école*. But when the fit was on him, and it turned up pretty often, it required six burly guards to subdue him. Slight as he was, he tossed them around like confetti. It is the intangible that makes strength interesting. In one saloon, transported by whatever demoniac force possessed her, Mrs. Nation picked up a giant cash register and hurled it into the street. Awed onlookers said the feat would have been impossible for the average grown male; cash registers of the period were constructed with the specific purpose of being nonportable. Witnessing this, the bartender, who had drawn a pistol and was planning to shoot her (as he later acknowledged quite candidly), panicked, fired two shots into the ceiling and ran out the back door. Still under seizure, Mrs. Nation ripped a heavy steel door off a refrigerator, promptly clearing a room as she did so. "I figured she was aiming to haul the place down like Samson," a man said in court.

The sight of raw, unheeding purpose can alone have a quelling effect. Throughout her reckless career, Mrs. Nation addressed judges as "Your Dishonor," snatched cigars from the mouths of men notable for bile, called policemen, to their faces, "Whiskey-swilled, saturn-faced tosspots," cried out to jailers and their wives (whose aim, often, was merely to play graceful hosts) "Good morning, Ahab and Jezebel!" and challenged successions of bartenders to step around and mix it. On the surface, this last would seem to have been poor judgment. Most Kansas bartenders then were not actual gunmen, but they were forthright, ready fellows whose supplementary role as bouncers gave them standing as dangerous. The symbol of their authority was the bung starter, a handy tool for cooling hot skulls, which was beginning to take its revered place in informal brawling alongside the shillelagh and brass knucks.

In facing the worst of these roughnecks, Mrs. Nation inspired women to revolt on other levels. She was the first real catalyst, though scattered malcontents had begun to limber up. Her influence was, and remains, immeasurable. In America and abroad, in the 1800's, vast armies of females commenced to surge and mutter, declaring for freedoms as diverse as their traditionally whimsical natures. It may be that, like Spartacus, they'd only been biding their time. One Amelia Jenks Bloomer, a native of Homer, New York, collected a following and launched a campaign for universal pants. Women, all women, were to be stuffed into them whether they liked it or not. Great things were predicted for Victoria Woodhull, whose mother (in Ohio) was a professional swami and whose father had some local standing as a firebug. The daughter established a clairvoyancy parlor in Cincinnati and early secured the doddering Commodore Vanderbilt for a client. After placing salt cellars beneath his bedposts, as "health conductors," reportedly getting him on his feet in no time, she opened a New York brokerage office (with a leg-up from Vanderbilt) and made half a million dollars almost overnight, so to speak. Then she bought a newspaper and went in for all-embracing reform. Her influence was perhaps vitiated when the word got around that she was domiciled in Greenwich Village with a Colonel Blood, the ménage rendered more bizarre by the presence of an additional member, an amiable fellow whom she had married and divorced during her teens.

Margaret Sanger, a nurse with specialized interests in sex, undertook a program of birth control that would, in the mistaken opinion of the poor (who had few pleasures), not only have controlled the population but eliminated it entirely in time. One of her greatest coups was the enlistment as fellow lecturer of Emma Goldman, who, before, had been pushing anarchy as a vocation. Aside from these three specialists, a number of vigorous spirits announced themselves as fired up hotly about the ballot. By law, women were unable to vote, and, it was charged, they hoped to change all that and elect a string of handsomer and sexier-looking if bone-headed and weak-kneed presidents. Forerunner of this group was Fanny Wright, whose views in general set clergymen over the nation to grinding their teeth in rage. She believed in free love, sexual "equality" and a stimulating kind of education, possibly not involving downright pornography, that would assay out as the "regenerator of a profligate age." Young Miss Wright was well-equipped for her work, being "all woman" (a smitten historian noted), "with a beautiful, high-bosomed figure who carried her nearly six feet of height superbly, like a ship in full sail." She carried her high-bosomed figure into the ken of the aging Lafayette, who was traveling about the country sleeping in an incredible number of taverns, hotels and private homes, with the result that he lost his head, on the order of a rutting stag, and tried to adopt her as his step-daughter. At the last minute, his shocked kinsmen sailed in, fully, from France, and threw cold water on the connection.

In England, the cultured disciples of Sylvia Pankhurst, daughter of a rich and distinguished family, displayed new methods of gutter fighting in their quest for "suffrage," the uproar reaching its apex in the notorious "Mud March" of 1907. Japan, which had lagged slightly (its feminine contingent having been trained for the sensible purpose of pleasing men) at length brought forth a maverick, one Madame Kaji Yajima, who arrived in the United States bearing a petition containing ten thousand female signatures, all of them anti-sake, the Japanese national drink. She also bore a large sake bowl as a gift for some friends in Evanston, Illinois. Her actions grated nervously on the Japanese men, who stepped up their sake drinking and went so far as to suggest that some of the names were fakes, pointing out that the average Japanese husband, religiously attentive to domestic obligation, would have snatched up a bamboo switch and dusted any such blatant defector in the home. In Russia, Sophie Bardine entered the lists with a socialist tract that she claimed would arouse the peasants from their torpor. Her ambition centered on a wholesale uprising. She worked alongside peasants in factories and shared the warm rich intimacy of their hovels. But whenever she mentioned socialism, she came up against a blank wall of prescience; the peasants, foxy and dignified in the immemorial style of their class, made the curiously prophetic point that they would rather be poor and free than poor and ordered around by thugs. Miss Bardine wound up her crusade with a flawless record: of the several thousand peasants she had tackled, none bothered to read the pamphlet. Eventually she was jailed as a nuisance, conceivably at the instigation of peasants.

Thus the hyperthyroid sisters of reform were not always quickly successful in overturning a system of mores laboriously devised by men. It required a Carry Nation, with her crash program of mayhem, to advance the struggles—her own and others'—far ahead of any normal evolution. It should not be imagined, however, that Mrs. Nation squared away for the pure love of combat. She was a genuine and indiscriminate reformer, always ready, if necessary, to straighten out her closest friends. At one point in her career, in Medicine Lodge, Kansas, she joined the Campbellite Church, which was the region's class arena of worship; that is, though Christian, it devoutly attempted to keep out the riffraff. Among Mrs. Nation's first acts as a new member was to haul in a washerwoman who ranked as a social outcast. The congregation was stunned. Theretofore the penitents had been limited to the haut monde; anybody actually needing help was expected to sip at a lesser font. Mrs. Nation succeeded in ramming the girl down the throats of the elders, but they tossed out the unfortunate when her husband won a divorce on the grounds of adultery. Then, to complete the benison, the elders threw out Mrs. Nation, too. To everyone's embarrassment, she declined to abstain; on the contrary, she continued to turn up, bristling with fight, and converted the temple into a kind of Roman amphitheatre. She also brought along any number of townspeople who were emphatically not of the noblesse. In the words of a biographer, "When she went to church there, she often interrupted the services with audible and scornful comments, or with loud cries of praise and rejoicing." She tangled with the pastor, too, on all hymnal selections, the nadir of these spats occurring when, one Sunday, he called for No. 40.

"We'll sing No. 3," boomed Carry from the pews. " 'I Know Not Why to Me This Wondrous Grace He has Made Known.' "

"Hymn No. 40," repeated the minister, faintly.

At this point, Mrs. Nation burst into riotous song, aided by her cohorts, and the cleric, after emitting what sounded like a string of pithy lay expressions, retired to a neutral corner, where he knelt in prayer, and, no doubt, begged for a forgiving mind.

The truth is that Mrs. Nation was a marvelously complex and memorable person, touched by genius, and it was perhaps this ever awesome gift, the charmed circle of voodoo, big magic, that protected her during a career unparalleled for audacity. Her story is important. It reveals the essentially dissatisfied nature of women, and provides a sharp note of warning. Except for primitive tribes, whose wisdom is based on survival and therefore sound, only the Swiss have contrived to keep women workably enthralled. The suppressions have taken different forms. In Africa, females are frequently offered up in sacrifice and eaten, as a nourishing means of showing who's boss; in Switzerland women are denied the vote. Perhaps in consequence, the small Alpine state has stayed free of wars, politics, poverty and over-coiffured panelists; it is moreover the last responsible nation in which feminized western countries feel it safe to bank. To the regret of many, the question at large has two sides. The point has been made (by women) that it would have been virtually impossible, over the centuries, for men to reduce the world to a more pitiable level of chaos. Any colony of baboons, the dissidents contend, lives together in superior conditions of both peace and plenty. The Alexanders, Napoleons, Hitlers and Stalins will continue to rise and fall (goes the argument) and the merry slaughter is bound to proceed apace. It may remain for a reincarnation of Carry Nation, for some righteous ghost from the vintage where the grapes of wrath are stored, to establish the final supremacy of women. An examination of her life, and times, her successes and failures, follies and fortunes, might prove of value in the always difficult days ahead.

Chapter Two

If the human animal is in equal measure the product of genes and environment, Carry Nation had little chance to be normal. She was born, on November 25, 1846, in Garrard County, Kentucky, a district of ferocious and nerve-jangling piety. Not only had the first church in Kentucky been established there, but the western camp meeting, or revival—a form of deistic orgy featuring spastic seizures—was introduced into the area, around 1800, by the Mc-Gee brothers, who were divided in a sectarian way, one being a Methodist and the other (no less holy) a Presbyterian. Sociologists have tried without success to measure the effect on a frontier people of the old-fashioned camp meeting, which was so ably described by Mark Twain in *Huckleberry Finn,* wherein the seedy and counterfeit King took over the rostrum and after a brief but telling plea collected $87.50 for a group of pirates in the Indian Ocean (then stole a jug of whiskey from under a wagon on his way out). Passions inflamed by an excess of religion, including camp meetings, were in large part responsible for Garrard County's chief enduring fame, that of harboring the bitterest, goriest, most protracted and least sensible feuds on record. Any chance theological observation—about the celestial advantage of dunking over sprinkling, the probable dessert served at the Last Supper, whether

Adam and Eve had navels, the weather in Heaven, the number of angels able to collect on the head of a pin*—might touch off a thirty year row that involved fourth and fifth cousins, many with little more religion than a jackass.

The region was violent, an understandable condition when one reviews its history in the new republic. The Dark and Bloody Ground—premium land, filled with fine forests of beech and oak, elm, maple, hickory, walnut and magnolia; its streams running with fish; big game like buffalo, elk, deer, bear and "painter" roaming in numbers beyond belief; its valleys and glades cloaked with thick rich grass more nearly blue than green. The slow, desperate struggles required to defend this bought land from raids by the Indians—Cherokee, Iroquois and Shawnee—required a special breed of settler, people with a racial background of courage and combat, restless misfits to whom stagnation in the softening colonies of the east was a prospect as awful as death. In the main they were Scotch-Irish and English, with a handful of Germans and Scandinavians. Just above, in Illinois forts along the Mississippi, and at Kaskaskia and Vincennes in Indiana, the French, who had come first, were shakily established, trading, trapping, exploring, hoping for political resolutions that might give them peace. And in between, always, everywhere, were the Indians.

It has become fashionable to believe that in any dispute involving Indians and whites, the white man was an ogre and the redskin a noble and incorruptible dupe. Kentucky was legitimately bought from Cherokees, whose business sense may certainly be questioned, especially when one considers that they didn't own it. The handy nickname, "The Dark and Bloody Ground," arose from the tooth-and-claw fighting over Kentucky between Cherokees and Iroquois. At the time of the sale, the Iroquois let it be known that they regarded the transaction as sharp practice, and

* This last point, of some significance when one considers the incorporeal composition of angels, was discussed (without solution but with acrimony) at an ecclesiastical conclave of the Middle Ages. A similar subject of anxiety was recently argued before a solemn and august council of churchmen abroad— whether Today's Jews are responsible for the crucifixion of Christ. A question was raised, by outsiders, concerning the council's specific definition of "Today." "If I am innocent," it was asked by a well-known but perhaps irreverent Jew, "what is the standing of my great-grandmother, who died in 1867? And what about *her* great-grandmother? There may be discrimination here." To date no line of demarkation has been drawn by the deliberating body.

that they intended to lodge protests, in the general area of the head, with tomahawks and flint-tipped arrows. The Shawnees also demurred, and finally the Cherokees themselves, seeing which way the wind blew (away from them and toward their old rivals), decided to forget about the sale and join in the fray. It was more fun than working, and besides, they'd already spent all their money. In the end it was largely the Cherokees that Daniel Boone and James Harrod and George Rogers Clark tried to stave off, with unspeakable atrocities committed on both sides, during summer after hot summer of siege when grim little flocks of settlers were confined to stockades no larger than one of today's mansions. The white man's early sufferings in Kentucky have no counterpart in the winning of America.

Carry Nation's family, in Garrard County, were strongly religious and somewhat partial to brandy. The combination was not unusual in a region that made extreme levies on both soul and body. The crusader has written with candor, almost with relish, of the ceremonial pre-breakfast snort presided over by her maternal grandfather, James Campbell, who was, one gathers, the lordliest member of the clan. He was certainly the booziest. "Every morning," she noted, "my grandfather would put in a glass some sugar, butter and brandy, then pour hot water over it, and, while the family were sitting around the room, waiting for breakfast, he would go to each, and give to those who wished a spoonful of this toddy, saying, 'Will you have a taste, my daughter, or my son?' " When each had taken a nip (a "spoonful"), he drank off the rest, ate a whacking good meal, and went for a rather aimless ride on his horse, after being wrestled to the saddle by his colored servant, Patrick. A fair man, he devoted other hours to "toddies, juleps, cobblers and even rum," and appeared to enjoy them all. None of this activity, though time-consuming, interfered with his duties as principal deacon of the nearby Baptist Church.

Campbell was in fact a kind and unselfish fellow—a sporting man who loved hounds and hunting and hard riding—and had what was known locally as a "loose wrist" with the spirits, which were contained in barrels in a downstairs closet. On Saturdays he summoned his several slaves and ladled into each a pint of raw brandy. The granddaughter's autobiography does not make clear whether the Negroes had any choice in the matter, but it remarks again and again the household's high level of inter-racial affection, especially on weekends. An amusing story is told in connection with Campbell's baptism, which unaccountably took place in his middle age. He was entering the water, led by a triumphant minister, when his favorite hound, Sounder, uttered the dreadful view halloo from a distant wood. The communicant skipped out of the stream, made a running leap for his horse and was off like a shot, clad only in drawers and a sheet. In the style of many backwoods clerics, the minister had a species of Lincolnesque humor. "Well," he observed, after a brief interval of meditation, "we got him in up to his rump, by God [sic], so I reckon he's got partial protection."

Nearly all of Carry's family were people of substance. James Campbell was an authentic lineal descendant of the Dukes of Argyll, a fact that may have colored his outlook. It unquestionably affected his daughter, Carry's mother, who thought she was Queen Victoria. Her case, which might technically be described as galloping megalomania, was very singular, and, in a more scientific age, would have provided valuable notes for students of unbuckled reason. Her manner had always been grand, but after the birth of Carry it entered on a new phase, comparatively modest in view of her subsequent peccadillos. In this period of her development, she announced that she was a lady-in-waiting to the Queen, but she quickly succeeded to the throne in an overnight *coup d'état* that remained mysterious to all. Encouraged by an indulgent husband, she enveloped herself with the trappings of royalty. She was physically adaptable to the best, being statuesque—voluptuous, even— and, to one onlooker, "very handsome." Her costumes occasioned comment; indeed, it seems unlikely that Garrard County has ever seen anything similar since. Her gowns were fashioned of purple velvet, with a train, and on her head, even at breakfast, she wore a crown of crystal and cut glass. Her speech became fairly continuous, though lacking in certain essentials like subject matter, and her patience with commoners grew scant. At length she saw the family members, including her husband (the Prince Consort), only by appointment.

It is pleasant for the biographer to imagine acquaintance with Carry's father, a thoughtful but restless Irishman, George Moore, who must be suspected of sitting back unperturbed, interested, perhaps filled with inward mirth, a serious researcher anxious to see how far the imperious crank might go. After one audience with Her Majesty, he laid in an ornate rubber-tired carriage upholstered in crimson plush and drawn by matched dapple-gray mares with silver-mounted harness. Then, his dreamy Irish mind sporting among the rich potential of invention, he added a coachman wearing a high silk hat and a coat of black, purple-trimmed broadcloth. Behind the outrageous carrier trotted a Negro boy, in mufti, for the purpose of opening and closing gates; and a pair of uniformed outriders kept pace abreast of the windows. Even then Moore was far from finished. Selecting his choicest slave, a giant called Big Bill, he stuffed all that was possible of him into a scarlet hunting coat and sent him riding ahead with a brass hunting horn, to blast out visits of more than routine importance. On one occasion she set off to call on the King of Belgium but failed—could not, in fact, locate the palace—and on another she bawled out the Duke of Buckingham, who was hoeing a patch of onions. She knighted three or four farmers, one of whom struck back, and stripped an itinerant tinker of all his estates in Sussex. The man's first reaction was good-humored, not to say bawdy, but he later threatened to take her into court and get the property back.

"If I ever had an angel on earth, it was my father," Carry Nation wrote. "I have met many men who had lovable characters, but none equalled him in my estimation. He was not a saint, but a man—one of the noblest works of God." This regal eulogy from a woman who made a career of fighting the male sex, mostly in saloons and in the streets and with any available utensil, seems out of character, but her sincerity is shown by an action of her youth, a step normally regarded as outside the limits of childhood adventure. She borrowed a rat-tail file from a Negro shanty and tried to hone down her teeth to resemble her father's. The records state that his upper right incisor, canine and bicuspid were in truth somewhat eroded; his explanation, which sounded thin, was that the teeth had been "reduced in bouts with the terrible frontier cooking." A better guess is that the stem of an omnipresent corncob pipe had taken heavy toll. Moore was a trader, planter and slave owner, in easy circumstances despite heavy layouts to keep pace with the refined court circles in which his wife moved. Except for a couple of character flaws, he could probably have made himself rich. For one thing, he was an incorrigible migrant, not content to live in a fixed abode for more than a year or two. Any old move would do; shifting into an identical house across the county line might ease for a space his vagrant and frolicsome mind. He also had an uncommon amount of business bad luck that in retrospect approached carelessness. He was in the habit of driving hogs to Cincinnati, for profitable sale in the market, but on at least one occasion he sat chatting in a tavern so long that the hogs, tiring, all disappeared into the woods. Moore stated to companions that it was hard, that he'd always been good to those hogs and they should have stuck around to be slaughtered. Another time he was balked by political naiveté. He had taken a large drove of mules to Natchez, where he obligingly sold them "on time," but in the next few days Abraham Lincoln was elected president, throwing the nation into war, and Moore never collected as much as a down payment.

Perhaps no further point need be made that Carry Nation's forebears were out of the common run. Her mother was addled (with reference to the British throne) and her father was a prankster of devilish gifts. The union produced, in the child, passions extraordinarily warm. The world became familiar with her assaults on rum; regrettably overlooked—a prime reason why she remains in focus when so many public viragos blurred—was a bountiful wellspring of humor. She was given to the antic gesture, a rare and wonderful flair now suffocating beneath the leveling gray blanket of socialism. In her middle career she brightened people's lives, making a scrutiny of the morning paper cheerful rather than bilious. A great many literate persons found Carry Nation charming. In exchanges of wit, her retorts were quick and clear. Her tongue was, in fact, sharper than her hatchet. She could be urbane and epigrammatic, and her poise never faltered. On occasion, when it served her need for publicity, she descended to a fine broad base of slapstick.

Her celebrated visit to John L. Sullivan is illustrative of the imp that lurked beneath the mask of indignation. The champion was holed up in a New York saloon, training for a fight. During the course of an average day's workout, he drank several gallons of beer, frequently laced with whiskey to keep him from falling asleep. In the annals of relaxation, Sullivan was in a class apart. He fought best as his intake of poisons deepened, and his belly was a source of civic pride. Thus he had become an unfortunate symbol for emulation. Children not yet in their teens were swilling beer in the hope of gathering strength for the title, and Mrs. Nation decided to take a hand. But when she stormed through the saloon's front door, Sullivan retreated to the rear. In the presence of reporters, the crusader permitted herself a string of essentially masculine epithets and dared the giant to come out. Puzzled bystanders later agreed that the implication was strong that, in any bare-knuckle fight, she could beat him to a pulp. Sullivan, a gentleman behind the facade of beer fumes, declined to be drawn from his lair, upon which Mrs. Nation made the open declaration that he was yellow. The champion fought again, and fought well, but several observers noted a lack of spontaneity in his movements. A little of the spirit appeared to have seeped away.

One has only to read Mrs. Nation's autobiography to realize her astuteness. It is a remarkable work, concise, acid, attractively libelous, flinty in its attitude toward sinners, often self-damning though hinting at a close connection with Providence and showing throughout a neat gift for both narrative and description. Like some of Dickens' novels, it unfortunately became prosy and inconsecutive toward the end. In the sporting phrase, Mrs. Nation pulled no punches. Her humors however underwent mild alterations during the book's bumpy career. In her preface to the seventh revised edition, the author appeared to have settled on Free Masonry as the fundamental *bête noire* of the righteous. Her introductory remarks were offered as a rallying point, or reorientation, a fresh and restated "Yoicks!" for her colleagues, who she feared might hare off in useless directions. "At the age of almost sixty-four," she wrote, "I feel that my work is nearly done—one request I make of my dear sisters of the W.C.T.U. is to turn your powerful influence against 'lodgism,' especially against the paganism and idolatry called Free Masonry, in which are originated the roots of all kinds of lusts . . . I can with a clear conscience say that one of the most alarming compacts with immorality is the Masonic

Lodge. There is not one obligation which is not intended to gener-
ate a root of evil; there is not one obligation which is not in violation of God's law. This is the work of Satan from beginning to end.
There never was an organization of a Black Hand any blacker."

Any careful historian must record that Mrs. Nation's phrasing
—seen in some circles as intemperate, or vicious—was colored by
personal bias. During the last half of her life, she remained convinced that her first husband, Dr. Charles Gloyd, a career drunk,
was led down the garden path by the Masonic Lodge, and she was
furthermore miffed that the outfit laid on him a pledge not to re-
veal certain club vows, signals and curses. Try as she might, she
could never pry them out of him, but later on she somehow dug up
a *Manual of the Lodge,* by one Albert G. Mackey, and printed it
in her newspaper.

The Use and Need of the Life of Carry A. Nation, an autobiography of surprising depth and merit, is indeed a treasure trove of
the very personal, of sharp clues to the evaluation of America's
foremost lady hell-raiser. In its pages Mrs. Nation sets forth the un-
savoriest details in a career uniquely studded with buffet and humiliation. Her Table of Contents, besides numbering the chapters, ab-
breviates and describes the action contained in each, making the
book easy to read piecemeal and classifying the mayhem by time
and locality. The total effect is that of a herald announcing the
engagements at a medieval joust. Thus, in Chapter 17, we find:
"My Visit to Washington, D.C.—Arrested in the Senate Chamber
—Taken Out by Officers—The Vices of Colleges, Especially Yale
—Roosevelt a Dive Keeper" and again, in Chapter 19, a record of
profitable sightseeing in Illinois and Pennsylvania: "Dr. McFarland's Protest—Kicked and Knocked Down by Chapman of Bangor House—Meddling With the Devil—Timely Warning to Our
Boys and Girls—Brubaker of Peoria—Witchcraft—Arrested and
Put in Jail in Philadelphia—Third Time in Jail in Pittsburgh."

The first chapters of Mrs. Nation's autobiography have a strong
lyric quality, as she reminisces about her old Kentucky home, a
place of many delights, and a few abrasions, for a girl child of
sensitivity. The farm lay alongside "Dick's" River (now called Dix
River on the signboards) and had a hewed-log dwelling house of
ten rooms, weather-boarded and plastered, all but one of these or

the ground floor. For the day and place it was a structure of comfortable solidity, even of frontier elegance. The darkened parlor—kept closed off in that furtive, half-mysterious way that people linked to weddings, funerals, visits by the preacher and other melancholy events—had gold-leaf paper on the walls, a huge stone fireplace with brass "dogirons" several feet high and furniture of red plush, carefully shaded from the afternoon sun. "Standing on the front porch," Mrs. Nation wrote, "we looked through a row of althea bushes, white and purple, and there were on each side cedar trees that were quite large in my day. There was an old-fashioned stile, instead of a gate, and a long avenue, with forest trees on either side, that led down to the big road . . ." Near the river "the cliffs rose up hundreds of feet, with great ledges of rocks, under which I used to sit. There were many large rocks scattered around, some as much as fifteen feet across, with holes that held water, where my father salted his stock, and I, a little toddler, used to follow him. On the side of the house next to the cliffs was what we called the 'Long House', where the Negro women would spin and weave. There were wheels little and big and a loom or two and swifts and reels and winders, and everything for making linen for the summer, and woolen cloth for the winter, both linsey and jeans."

It is not strange that Mrs. Nation wrote with feeling of her childhood home, for never afterward, as the tempests of reform swirled round her, was she able to live in such a setting of pleasant drowsyhead. All the family, including the Queen (in a supervisory role), lent a hand in beautifying this already wildly flowering land: "To the left of our house was the garden. I have read of the old-fashioned garden, the garden written about and gardens sung about, but I have never seen a garden that could surpass that of my old home. Just inside the pickets were bunches of bear grass. Then there was the purple flag that bordered the walks; the thyme, coriander, calamus and sweet Mary; the jasmine climbing over the picket fence; the syringa and bridal wreath; roses black, red, yellow and pink; and many other kinds of roses and shrubs. There, too, were strawberries, raspberries, gooseberries and currants; damson and green-gages and apricots that grew on vines [sic] . . . At one side of the garden was the family burying ground, where the gravestones were laid flat on masonry, bringing them about three feet from the ground. These stones were large flat slabs of marble, and I used to climb up on top and sit or lie down, and trace the letters or figures with my fingers . . ."

Garrard County's superiority may have stood out more sharply in Carry's day than it does now. The division lies below today's rich Lexington–Blue Grass region of broad rolling thoroughbred farms with white board fences and thickly carpeted blue-green fields where the community, horse-wise and hopeful, collects each spring to watch the frisky, skinny-legged gambols of a new season's crop of colts, alerted by the carriage of a head, an unbeatable look about the eyes, a reckless sprint, the champion's separate manner, for reincarnations of Twenty Grand, Seabiscuit, and Native Dancer. In James Huneker's philosophic work, "The Pathos of Distance," the tragedy of coming close, just missing, of falling a few inches short of the best, is set forth with great poignance. Garrard County has patches of blue grass, but its hilly contours with their short fields make it subordinate to Lexington as horse country. The area still has a brooding frontier quality, as most mountain or near-mountain places do in the back lands. It may be that long shadows and brief sun have a sobering effect on man's spirits. The people of Garrard County are friendly but unfrivolous, mercifully sparing with those gleaming, shark-like, plastic-enamel smiles that Americans associate with cinema charm. Yet a stunning sort of blank-faced humor exists here.

After driving past "Belly Acres," a cafe, a writer on the trail of Carry Nation recently stopped for lunch—Sunday dinner—at a roadside lodge and ate "family style" for the first time in thirty years at room-long tables where the visitor sits down any old place and is enfolded with graceful ease into whatever group happens to be near. The patroness apologized for the meagreness of the fare, saying that a number of supplies had failed to come through from "town," meaning nothing in particular. In large white community platters and bowls along the table were fried chicken, baked ham, barbecued beef, chicken and dumplings, sugared beets, sweet corn, hominy (not grits), garden peas, green beans cooked with bacon, buttered carrots, applesauce, okra, boiled potatoes, yams blackened with burnt-maple syrup, slabs of beet-red tomatoes beneath white onion slices, hot biscuits and corn bread with sweet butter, and, afterward, pie and ice cream. Pretty, unsmiling waitresses whose gaze seemed extraordinarily level and warm kept glasses and cups filled with iced tea and hot coffee. The price was a dollar and a half.

Conversation was superficial, limited mainly to the business of eating, and polite somewhat beyond dinner-table discourse in the North. The dishes were moved about through an elaborate ritual of apology and exaggeration.

A woman at a far end said, "I wonder if I could trouble you to pass up that bowl of okrer. I don't want to do no more than sample it, but it'd be a crying shame to leave it sit untouched. I'll have it back before you can say Jack Spratt."

Man on her right: "I dislike to bother anybody at his food, specially when he's started off sucking hind tit, as the saying goes, but I've taken a hanker for another of them yams. I et one, and it's set up a holler for company."

Closer neighbor: "If you don't mind me seggesting it, I noticed you detoured and steered around that barbecued beef, sir. I realize this is a depressed area—sworn to, signed and sealed by the know-it-all federal government, over the people's dead bodies, mostly— but you won't be running any chances with that barbecue. None serious anyhow." As an afterthought, he observed that "I'd drive in to the Sheriff and give up before I'd play the buttinsky."

The above fragments were chosen quite selectively. Much of the conversation was perfectly grammatical and without idiom, but it was all on an articulate level of courtesy often approaching burlesque.

Across from the writer sat a fat, enormously cheerful woman and her husband, a tall, stringy, quizzical-looking fellow with an elongated neck and a turkey-gobbler's Adam's apple. After downing a meal that might have baffled a condor, he had the effrontery to look up and remark, "I wasn't hungry today, and I regret it. The food was tasty. No, I'm off my feed, and have been for a week or more. I slack off in the summer; it's the way I'm made." Nobody hit him, or even laughed, and his wife, falling into what presumably was a marital, or neighborhood, stance, said, "I couldn't hardly eat a bite. We could have set home and saved the money"; then with a kind of low wolfish growl she threw herself on a platter of pumpkin pie and destroyed three pieces.

Any visitor sooner or later divines that the Kentuckians of these parts, descendants of Indian fighters and feudists, can be among the first on whom to impose safely in friendship and the last with whom to take liberties.

Abraham Lincoln was born nearby. Signboards along the highway direct motorists to the site of the old log home, which has been converted into a shrine. Nobody has taken the trouble to mark out Mrs. Nation's birthplace. In the town of Crab Orchard, on the county's southern border, an octogenarian said he remembered hearing about a family of Moores "back in there," but he recalled only faintly, and with embarrassment, Carry's later world-wide notice. "Agin whiskey, wasn't she?" he asked with an acute look, and went indoors. The "William Whitel House and Recreational Area," where the first brick house built in Kentucky is preserved, is advertised as the sort of landmark that the local people can be proud of. Religion weighs heavy on the land, as it did in Carry's day. Along the roads joyless signs promise that "Jesus is Coming Soon," and one meets doleful queries of "Are You Ready?", the whole appearing to hint that the end of the world is just around the corner. The hamlet nearest the locale of Moore's old farm is named Preacherville, and everywhere, on colorful and impressive billboards, one is apprised of the "Book of Jehovah," an annual religious hootenanny, or pageant, for which the region is noted. The event is not dissimilar in scope and impact to Oberammergau's celebrated Passion Play, the populous German jamboree featuring somebody's notion of Christ. Garrard County's worship is predominantly Baptist, offering little hope of salvation except for those who tread the narrowest kind of path (and, to be sure, permit themselves to be ceremonially immersed). History is replete with incidents to prove that a Baptist at full gallop is a fearsome engine of piety. It seems likely that no other religion extracts such a full measure of self-abasement from its practitioners. At various times and places, a Baptist could be arrested by a deacon, then fined or imprisoned for riding a horse on Sunday; minor blasphemers could be administered forty lashes; dancing and card-playing were breaches of conduct on a virtual par with murder (and more opprobrious in certain cases). From the beginning to the end (often welcomed as a blessed relief) the congregation was threatened, warned, cajoled, made to feel dirty, cursed, shamed, intimidated, admonished, exhorted and given nothing to go on whatever.

The denomination has always been closely identified with snakes. It was a Kentucky Baptist minister who made himself into a national news story by wrapping what turned out to be several non-sectarian rattlesnakes around his head, to clear up a trivial point of dogma. Somewhat prematurely, they were given out to be converts. The gesture proved to be both foolish and unholy when one of the apostles backslid and bit him, causing his promotion to the Kingdom of Heaven two days later. There are times when any rational person must marvel at the weird and diverse monkey-shines committed by otherwise fine people in the name of one who at the very least was the most inspiring man yet to arrive by any route on earth. It is impossible not to recall Trader Horn's pithy observation: "And what is religion, Ma'am, but the leavings of superstition?"

Down the highway from smart-looking Berea to tired, dusty Crab Orchard, past patchy fields and tobacco in green rows and slopes wooded with walnut and black oak, with poplars along the streams, and unpainted old barns dangerously tilted or propped up with timbers, and white clapboard houses set as deeply as possible in the shade, past mules in muddy corrals, with sows lying here and there to keep them company, and, often, very steep, small fields ploughed and planted in crazy patterns, as if the farmer had gone to sleep behind his mule—southward from Lexington the country expresses its debt to Blue Grass, Horses, and Daniel Boone. By means of numberless place names—the Blue Grass Laundry, the Daniel Boone Tavern, the Thoroughbred Motel—today's visitor is invited to recall Kentucky's past and present glories. It is therefore surprising—depressing—that a conspiracy of silence about Carry Nation appears to lie on these hills. At the Dix River, a man past ninety—said to be the country's oldest white citizen, a remarkably spry and disingenuous old grizzle-beard with one gallus broken and eyes as candidly clear as a baby's—pointed the way toward Carry's old homestead, and said, "I hear they moved away some-wheres; heard it not long ago, right after the war." To a suggestion that, had she lived, Mrs. Nation would now be 121, he said sharply, "Die in an accident?" The day was Sunday, the river looked rushing green and deep, a few fishermen were scattered along the banks near an iron bridge. Asked if the stream provided good fishing, he said, "Finest spring run of white bass in Kentucky; she's famous for it." Sounded out, reluctantly, about their average size, he automatically set his hands in a measured space of perhaps two feet; then, meeting a frosty stare, revised it downward four or five inches, and finally, the resistance continuing, did it again, adding with belligerence, "Caught 'em so myself, and'll be happy to step out with anybody that wants to make something out of it."

"—on Dick's River," Mrs. Nation had written, "where the cliffs rose up hundreds of feet, with great ledges of rock, under which I used to sit." Children's memories tend to reconstruct early things much larger than life-size, and, usually, better than they were. As one pushes down the river bank through berry brambles and poplar sprouts and milkweed to the dismal dead droning and winding of midsummer insects—locusts and grasshoppers and cicadas— the cliffs still lean formidably out across the way, dozens of feet high, at least, with chalky white ledges to which teen-agers and younger swimmers climb and then jump off into the deep still pools where the river rests after the white-water rapids in the bends. It would be difficult to imagine a pleasanter spot in which a boy or a girl of spirit might grow up. A few foundations and some crumbling rocks are visible in an overgrown field where old residents say the Moores were supposed to live; but nobody seems certain. Surviving are only the outlines, no more than a few inches high, covered now with weed: a rectangle which appears small for a log dwelling of ten rooms; one still smaller that could have been Mrs. Nation's "Long House," where the Negroes spun; other remnants of indefinable shape; and, almost as she described the scene, a foundation at some distance behind the house where the overseer might have lived. Or maybe these ghost dwellings of a hundred years ago belonged to someone else entirely. No matter how cherished an establishment, its owners change every generation or so, families move away, records are lost, the jungle reclaims its own and the destroyer time dulls the importance of it all.

Mrs. Nation lived most of her young life with Negroes, her

mother being occupied with court affairs and her father often absent driving livestock in the general direction of the marketplaces. The child's experiences were scrambled. She was seven or eight years old before she had eaten a meal at "white folks' table." "I owe much to the colored people and never want to live where there are none of the Negro race," she wrote. And indeed, during all of her life, she enjoyed an uncommon intimacy with Negroes, championed them, treated many individuals on a level of equality and never hesitated to admonish them for what she regarded as transgressions. When her crusade against the bottle gathered steam in Kansas, leaving publicans staggering drunkenly in her wake, she undertook to document her outbursts with a newspaper and chose the Negro publisher named Chiles. There is evidence that each of the partners was fearful of being hexed by the other. Chiles was scarcely wiser than Mrs. Nation in Negro ways and folklore; furthermore, he knew it. He was a city man, reared without benefit of the shanty fireside's whispered conversation, ghost stories and handed-down legend from the dark continent. In her book Mrs. Nation has mentioned her familiarity with hexes, and told how to cast them, saying that certain persons (those within the cabal) "had power to put a 'spell' on others, would, if taken sick, frequently speak of having 'stepped on something' put in their way or buried in their dooryard." An intimate of Chiles, disturbed at the publisher's worn and jangled look toward the end of the sapping union, wrote that he "walked along real nervous, as if he's about to place his foot in a rabbit trap or a hole."

No proof exists that the reformer ever hexed Chiles, but she may have muttered a few low, aboriginal threats during times of altercation. Probably it would be difficult to exaggerate the influence of Negroes on the impressionable frontier girl in whom the passions of a violent people and uniquely original parents were rising in clamor of an outlet. Her principal nurses were Betsy, Aunt Eliza and Aunt Judy, who after their style tried to keep the child clean and trouble-free. Among other restraints, they prevented her from carrying any sharp tool such as a hoe or a spade or an ax (or a hatchet) through the house, knowing that the act would bring a dozen witches down on her head at once. The girl was also dissuaded from throwing salt into the fire, when she realized (at last) that the thrower must return soon as a dead person to pick it out. And she helped in the killing of any hens that made the fatal error of crowing, for such brazenness, unpunished, meant that somebody was selected for an early death. From several sources it is apparent that Carry, obviously affection-starved, yearned for her nurses' comforting presence later in life. "After I left Texas and went to Medicine Lodge," she wrote, "when I had a headache or was otherwise sick, I would wish that one of the old-fashioned colored women would rub me with their plump hands and call me 'Honey Chile', and would bathe my feet and tuck the cover around me and sit by me, holding my hand, waiting till I fell asleep . . . I felt lonesome without them."

The child's enthusiasm was less unrestrained about Aunt Eliza's husband, one Josh, an undersized jet-black Guinea importation who was "peculiar in the head," and bragged about it. The bonds of slavery chafed him only slightly; within fairly broad limits, he did what he pleased. His favorite expression, addressed to anybody handy, was "Get out of the way or I'll knock you into a cocked hat." He was immensely pleased with this mastery of the new language and occasionally aimed the phrase at Big Bill, almost always a mistake. The children, white and black, scattered when they saw him coming, crying many of those small, pointed compliments that are calculated to enrich the lives of the peculiar, and nail down their peculiarity, and even help it to spread. Spearhead of their attack was a jingle, authorship anonymous, that Josh pretended to find irksome.

> "Oh my gosh, here comes Uncle Josh
> He thinks he's smart, but it's all pure bosh."

In view of the merry warfare waged outside the house, it was unfortunate for Carry that, at night, she was obliged to sleep sandwiched between Aunt Eliza and the epithet-ridden Josh. Without going into details, the child made official representations about an alignment that she hinted was a continuing nightmare. Long afterward, her autobiography summarized the situation by saying, "Once when my mother had been away for several days and came home bringing a lot of company, I ran out when I saw the carriages driving up and cried, 'Oh, Ma, I am so glad to see you. I don't mind sleeping with Aunt Eliza, but I do hate to sleep with Uncle Josh.'" It need hardly be said that today's Freudian analysts, soaked in sex symbols and other nervous reasons why they became analysts, would pounce with shrill yelps and wrenching facial tics on this episode of the crusader's young life. Especially so in view of Carry's subsequent admission that she "was a great lover." There is certainly a mystery here. Her autobiography, a good and honest-sounding book, fails to specify her contention about romance, which is, of course, among the commonest boasts of egoists who have had no love experience at all. But her reference is puzzling, claiming as it does that love affairs played an important part in her development. She wrote that, "There are pages in my life that have had much to do with bringing me in sympathy with the fallen tempted natures. These I cannot write, but let no erring, sinful man or woman think that Carry Nation would not understand, for Carry Nation is a sinner saved by grace."

Uncle Josh may be discounted as the crusader's guide down the labyrinthine corridors of Eros. Peculiar in the head he unquestionably was, but not that peculiar. The white child needed only to mention any absent-minded departure from sound sleep by the Negro to bring him terrible retribution. (This besides instant punishment with skillet or poker from the competent and wiry Aunt Eliza.) In that time and place Josh would doubtless have been hanged first and a detailed inquiry conducted afterward. The action would not have indicated excessive cruelty in the Southern nature; rather, the system typified an attitude toward slaves, established by degrees, that saw them as several rungs down on the ladder of evolution. Mrs. Nation herself, while abundant in her praise of plantation life, including the treatment of slaves ("Happy indeed would the Negroes have been if all their masters had been as my father was"), was sufficiently honest to include a distressing scene in which her parents callously separated a couple while in the process of moving homes. (The woman belonged to a neighbor.) "After we got into the carriage . . . Tom followed us crying 'Oh, Mars George, don't take me from my wife.' My father said: 'Go and get some one to buy you.' This Tom did, the buyer being a Mr. Dunn. Oh! what a sad sight; it makes the tears fill my eyes to write it." And then, "I can't understand how my father could have allowed this." In all likelihood, Moore never thought about it at all, or, perhaps, no more than he might have pondered the sale of a choice and lovable stallion.

In that land of extremes, the incident does not appear especially incongruous when juxtaposed to Carry's account of one Newton: "A son of Aunt Eliza was named Newton. My father then had a mill and store up in Lincoln County, near Hustonville. Newton used to do the hauling for my father with a large wagon and six-mule team. He often did buying for the store and took measurements of grain, and my father trusted him implicitly. Once a friend of my father said to him, as Newton passed along the street with his team, 'George, I'll give you seventeen hundred dollars for that Negro.' Father said, 'If you filled that wagonbed full of gold, you could not get him.' A few weeks after that, Newton died. I remember seeing my father in the room weeping, and remember hearing the Negroes singing the chorus of a hymn."

Carry's amatory bouts may have been delusory, the products of fantasies indulged in when, among other occasions, she "used to climb up on top of the gravestones in the family burying ground and trace the letters or figures with my fingers." Scientists have observed that, generally speaking, the sex drive is usually proportionate to the creative impulse in the human. Beyond reasonable doubt, Carry Nation was a creative reformer, sublimely gifted in the variety and degree of destruction she was able to wreak single-handed. It seems probable that, as a child, she had difficulty controlling the swelling pressure of her emotions. Her life and explosions afterward could have been partly a sublimation of her sexual yearnings, which endured without appeasement through two marriages. Her later distaste at seeing a beau even kiss his sweetheart may have been a reaction from something intensely personal. There is no prude more tiresome than a reformed sinner. Mrs. Nation had five small brothers and sisters, and aside from these, she saw few other people except Negroes. By her account, she "followed the Negro men about in the fields and in the stables," and formed romantic girlish attachments to one after another. It must be doubted, though nobody can be sure, that her admiration ever ripened past the imitation stage. She aped most of their mannerisms. Taken all around, Moore's plantation Negroes left something to be desired as examples for a girl child of quality. Even so, Carry appeared to have been born with a running start on the worst of them. The implication shines out from the autobiography (and from additional sources) that the slaves pretty well took their cue from Carry, seeing her as a kind of girlish Robin Hood, engaged in felony and misdemeanor aimed to redistribute the plantation's wealth, or anyhow its loose bric-a-brac, edibles and petty cash. The bald truth is that, in the words of the Bard, the youngster had "a pronounced gallows complexion."

In later years an interesting sidelight on the young Carry was supplied by a Mrs. Witherspoon, a Kentucky neighbor, who wrote, "I went to school with Carry Moore during the session of 1857–58.* She was about 10 years old, I think, and I was several years younger. She was large for her age, had yellow hair and a fair complexion. She was inclined to be a tomboy, was very strong willed and absolutely afraid of nothing. She dominated the school, and was distinctly a leader of both the girls and the boys. Frequently she led us younger children into mischief. I especially recall the martial spirit, and how she used to delight in assuming the role of a conqueror. She would array herself and the other school children in paper-soldier caps, stain their faces with juice from the pokeberries that grew in the yard, and then, armed with a wooden sword, lead us into the woods to do battle against imaginary foes. Again, I remember her leading an exploration of a cavern in the neighborhood that the other children had always been afraid to enter."

In her maturity Mrs. Nation would often be praised for the candor with which she treated this hooligan phase of her life. Far from skulking behind silence, lies or evasions, she described herself as having been an accomplished juvenile thief. In these actions she was abetted by the nurse Betsy, who kept her trotting on errands for the purpose of abstracting "sugar, butter, needles, thread and other small articles." The trips were no burden to Carry, for, as likely as not, she had been planning similar outings on her own, to steal "powder, perfume, silks, ribbons and lace." Much source ma-

---

* Moore and some friends appear to have imported a "Professor Hanna" from Pennsylvania to teach a few winter terms.

terial suggests that the larcenous, or progressive, or motivated clique among the Negroes took pride in the child's skill, and felt that they had a foremost criminal in the making. It is always stimulating to watch a champion en route to the top. By her own admission, Carry had class; she was the toast of the plantation in the department of all-around mischief and bad conduct. In a subsequent divine flash of awareness, she finally saw that she had been "wilful, mendacious, stubborn, hard-headed, meddlesome and dictatorial." Her accomplishments in the field of lying set new goals for the plantation hands, and on Sunday visits to her aunts and her grandfather she always lifted whatever cash she could find in "boxes and bureau drawers." While others of the numerous clan were downstairs singing hymns, recounting hunting exploits and drinking brandy, the precocious toddler was upstairs quietly pilfering, for no reason except to gain status among the Negroes who praised her without stint for work well done. It is no exaggeration to say that Carry's influence in corrupting the slaves was extraordinary.

A contemporary was quoted in a magazine piece from the past, as saying that, "Along with her sisters and cousins she used to raid the attic where goodies were kept, until her mother, remembering why scarecrows were set up in the cornfields, hung an oil portrait of her own dead mother at the top of the stairs. The grim old lady had been something of a hellion when she lived with the family; now she glared down on the children from above. They tried to edge past but couldn't, until Carry, finding her father's fishing pole, poked out the portrait's eyes."

Both black and white playmates found her bossy in the extreme, and they deferred to her commands and exhortations. She sets forth as a sample of her incessant cruise-direction the mock funerals which she arranged over the cadavers of deceased mice, one-legged crows and mangy cats. Under Carry's direction the obsequies were turned into models of blasphemy. The child had a neat turn for mimicry; each step of the service was a burlesque on the tear-jerking bores bawled out by her elders on the otherwise festive occasions when somebody gave up the ghost. Carry of course did the preaching, and her remarks, plus a knavish and impious manner, earned her many a royal whacking from Queen Victoria, who may have felt, quite correctly, that she was trying to stamp out a dangerous uprising.

At church Carry sat in a gallery reserved for the slaves. There she was titillated to bursting by the hypnotic orgies of singing and shouting. She was made to feel vaguely indecent by the emotions thus released, and she wrote that, "The Negroes told me no one could help shouting. I did not wish the spirit to cause me to jump up and clap my hands that way, for these impulses were not in my carnal heart; so, for fear I should be compelled to do so, I held my dress down tight to the seat on each side, to prevent me from jumping up." Others of the slaves earnestly tried to reform the girl, who they felt was headed on the down slide toward perdition. They lectured her at length about "Judgment Day," a time of reckoning which they viewed as incomparably harsh and injurious, and the girl could see little profit in bracing up at the late age of nine. Nonetheless, in true evangelical style, the Negroes continued to push religion, to the point where the young miscreant finally began to have headaches, fits of depression and "visions." After a particularly soft, mournful, deeply religious African rendition of "Let Us Sit Down and Chat with the Angels," she withdrew to the graveyard, stretched out and had an authentic vision; then she chatted individually with several angels who showed up. Mrs. Nation later interpreted this phase as being the dawn of her young conscience. Even at the time, she spotted the symptoms as holy, for they were exceedingly painful, and residents of the area practised no other kind of religion.

Much of Carry's intercourse with the Negroes was comic, but she was also given immeasurable affection, profound and sincere if childlike feeling—perhaps more stirring than that of the undemonstrative white—and a genuine love of God. They protected her, made excuses for her, lied to cover up her derelictions and drew her close to the mystic and unobtainable secrets of their race. At night in a Negro shanty, huddled before the log fire whose charmed safety reached back before memory to instinct, they told subdued, cheerful, half-believed lies about witches and ghosts they had seen, frights they had enjoyed, blood that ran freely through their imaginations. "I would listen until my teeth chattered with fright, and would shiver more and more, as they told of the sights in the graveyards, the spirits of tyrannical masters walking at night with their chains clanking, and the sights of hell, where some would be on gridirons, some hung up to baste, and the devil with his pitchfork tossing the poor creatures hither and thither . . . Very frequently my nurse would hold me in her arms until both of us fell asleep, but she would hold me securely."

Thus the marked girl's life in Kentucky, a period of waiting, strong impressions, and unconscious preparation for the booming times to follow.

Chapter Three

After their long residence on the Dix River, the Moore family hopped, skipped and jumped from place to place in Kentucky, stopping off briefly near Danville and again at Midway, and then made a move, to Cass County, Missouri, that was to have a jarring effect on the soon-to-be reformer. None of the contemporary literature explains why Moore felt called upon to dislocate his ménage in this drastic fashion. The best guess is that he simply liked to move. Some men of the era enjoyed sitting around the general store to chew twist tobacco and discuss politics; others took to cards, or horse-racing, or chasing women; not a few chose religion, while the majority managed to combine the foregoing into one big hobby; Moore was happiest when the furniture was being piled into the wagons and carts. There is no evidence that sheriff's agents were close behind him with writs; as a rule, he was solvent, even affluent, but he elected to remain migrant. With his customary luck he managed to arrive in Missouri when trouble was breaking out between that slave state and Kansas, which had voted in favor of Abolition. Cass County being on the border, representatives of the two sides (armed bands) frequently rode rough-shod over Moore's property (again a farm) with the result that the immigrants were generally in process of placating either the Kansas faction, a group of desperados known as Jayhawkers, or the Missouri unit, a collection of thugs called Bushwhackers. Moore himself was an enigma to everybody. A fellow of absolute courage (and with a keen sense of the ridiculous) he described himself politically as "a union man but a southern sympathizer." This never seemed to clear things up for anyone, notably the Jayhawkers and the Bushwhackers, but they eventually decided to leave him alone. To the annoyance of all, he appeared neither grateful nor very much interested.

On the trip over from Kentucky—made partly by boat—his daughter Carry contracted a bad cold that developed into a prolonged and severe illness offhandedly diagnosed as "consumption of the bowels." The label alone was sufficient to frighten most children onto the critical list, and Carry had already been suffering, as stated, moody and introspective fits, the result of a well-founded suspicion that she had a criminal bent. In Missouri both her body and her spirits failed rapidly. During a year that she spent largely bedfast, amateur seers from the local minister on up through the members of her family to the slaves tried to revive her health by gloomy reminders that her condition had sprouted from Sin. Repeatedly she was assured that her chances of survival were miniscule. She was under sentence of punishment by a wrathful and implacable God. Even her father, who was on no more than nodding terms with Jesus, fell prey to the awful, self-satisfied predictions of the pious, and urged the wretched invalid to prepare her soul "for a possible flight to Heaven." Racked by remorse, which had the single beneficial result of obliterating some of the pain, the girl fought for her life. In the chronicles of frontier ignorance, the havoc worked in the name of religious salvation probably surpassed the damage from all other sources combined.

The dawn of penitence having broken, things moved swiftly for the indisposed child. It was thought necessary by the authorities that she get to a church as soon as possible, and after a few weeks, more dead than alive, she was conveyed in a carriage to a nearby Sunday School, where the minister gave her a booklet explaining that petty thieves were as monstrous as bank robbers in the eyes of the Lord. It did not explain the full cycle of larceny, wherein a sect called tycoons work up to the level of stealing whole corporations,

railroads, widows' savings, gold reserves and even nations, at
which point the behavior became honorable and, in fact, widely
admired. "I was greatly shocked to find myself a thief," Mrs. Nation wrote. "It had never occurred to me that I was as bad as that.
My repentance was sincere, and I was made honest by this blessed
book, so much so that after I grew up, if any article was left in my
house I would give it away, unless I could find the owner." Her
luck did not however stop with the one therapeutic experience in
the house of worship. A few signs of spiritual convalescence becoming manifest (though her physical health was rather worse), the
mountain was once again taken to Mohammed. An old-fashioned
fire-and-brimstone revival was under way at the Christian Church
in Jackson County—a "protracted meeting" thundered over by an
itinerant evangelist of exceptional powers. Within a day or so, he
had half the congregation groveling in the aisles, in abject apology
for everything, and the other half were wilting before the fury of
his blasts. In his workmanlike biography of Mrs. Nation, Herbert
Asbury states that "she was conscious of a strange exhaltation as
she listened to the throbbing music of the hymns." This was as
nothing compared to her emotions when the revivalist began to
speak, or rant.

The unsung catalyst was one of a thousand brothers who for
years afterward would exhort their way across the backwoods
American scene, shouting and pleading from platforms under canvas (or in churches of sufficient size), whipping up feelings, grinding out excitement, staving off boredom, the darlings of young and
old, addressing themselves to the most primitive of passions—the
desperate, jungle-old search for a court of final appeal, the total
love-worship of a deity willing to revoke unacceptable death. The
genesis in America of this formative means of entertainment came
about in the early 1800's, the dubious creation of Presbyterians
who quickly passed it along to Baptists and Methodists, almost as
if they were glad to get rid of it. What the Encyclopedia Britannica
has called "one of the most remarkable revivals of modern times"
became known as "The Great Revival of the West or the Kentucky
Revival." "Meetings were held in the woods and were attended by
great emotional excitement, people often falling unconscious, or
being taken with such strange exercises as the 'shakes' and the

'jerks', or the 'laughing' or 'barking' exercises." A writer of biographies who grew up in Southern Illinois, close to Kentucky and Missouri, recalls those staples of his childhood with such vividness that he still has to fight off the shakes after a lapse of thirty years.

As a general thing, evangelists were booked in during dull times, or after an unusual number of communicants had backslid for one reason or other. Summer was the best season for a successful all-out meeting; people heated up more easily in the higher temperatures. An up-to-date evangelist usually included in his retinue a male musician—a trombone- or cornet-player—together with a big-busted maiden to provide accompaniment at the piano. Among the trombonist's side-duties was the bawling of a sonorous "A-A-Amen!" after every second or third cliché during the "sermon." The girl's full and precise role was subtly left to the congregational imagination, which after a session or two was smoking along like a thoroughbred stallion. Any evangelist's message was bleak, not to say hopeless. That is, the sufferers were assured that they would probably wind up in hell, but they might just avoid it by walking, or crawling, or shaking, or jerking down to the front and declaring themselves to be 100 percent vile. Everything boiled down to that, a seeming oversimplification of God's earthly plan, as a few enlightened persons now and then surfaced to observe. A reiterated query from the pulpit was, *"Won't* you come to Jesus?" meaning the evangelist, and anybody who took the step was thereupon said to be "converted," or "saved," and could resume his old ways with a comparatively free mind. For those who relished an unaccustomed moment in the sun, the process offered rewards, and a sizable group found it convenient to yaw back and forth like a metronome, backsliding, being reconverted on the evangelist's next visit, then collapsing after he was gone. Keystone of the evangelist's style was a kind of calliope hysteria that served to warn people of a deadline approaching in about an hour. He shouted, threatened, begged, cried, foamed, raved, groaned, gnashed his teeth, waved his arms, got down on his knees and went into trance-like states, stunned by the diabolic mulishness in the pews. The swoons never proved permanent, though, or even crippling, and he was able to bounce up in a minute to help pass the plate. Allegations were made that some evangelists operated by a system of piecework, collecting so much a head for converts, not counting repeats—one ancient volume mentioning a scale of "a dollar for adult males, fifty cents each for women and children, and a nickel for idiots"—but the cases were thought to be rare. Evangelists came into the community for a fixed fee, which included lodging with parishioners, and took a bonus only if the meeting's crop had been spectacularly fine.

Crowning triumph of every revival was the evening devoted to Temperance. Religion aside, the mid-western area was ribald in its views and in general provided a regional school of humor. Indiana had supplied Booth Tarkington and George Ade; Ring Lardner came from Michigan; Mark Twain made his start at Hannibal; Kentucky and Illinois had contributed Lincoln, and there were others. In dealing with temperance the evangelist had two broad aims—his first a plea for hardened topers to swear off, the second an effort to extract a promise of total abstention from everybody in the house, or tent. The results in both cases were dramatic. "Folks," cried the deputy, on his knees, arms outstretched, face racked with anguish, "I know there's them amongst you that's had a mighty tussle with old John Barleycorn, starved for him, stole for him, wallered in the muck and mire, too hang-dog to hold up your heads, friends a-looking the other way when you pass, seen your wife and babies shoved from pillar to post, clothed in rags to the shame of blessed Jesus—*won't* you stand up and swear to throw down that bottle? Yes, throw it down for good and all, bury old John Barleycorn and come to the Lord with clean hands before the Judgment Day?"

It is embarrassing to record that, at this point, a group of boys of around twelve, sequestered alone in a kind of side annex because of past misdemeanors, immediately jumped up nodding and gave every sign of regeneration. They shook hands among themselves, tossed hymnals onto the floor in relief, expressed satisfaction that they were finished with whiskey at last, threw grateful looks at the ceiling and, finally, trooped down in a body to the front, whereupon they were promptly hustled out through a rear door, and afterward, at home, given a pretty brisk licking.

Most of the town drunks turned up on temperance night, and signed the pledge without argument, and many signed it seven or eight times. Not uncommonly, however, they signed names thought to be spurious, such as Kaiser Wilhelm IV, Phineas T. Barnum, Ali Baba & Group, and Jack the Ripper. Even so, respectable members of the congregation took the signing seriously, and moderated their drinking for long periods, of several weeks or more, and an occasional penitent quit for months. Invalids with stomach problems and women who opposed whiskey as part of permanent anti-fun campaigns against their husbands stepped up lamentations about the practice, so that the temperance drive, overall, was not without merit.

Evangelists were important in the period, especially so to Carry Nation, in that the dedicated toiler of Jackson County pointed her finally and irrevocably in the direction of her incomprehensible star. Desperately ill, she had just celebrated, or mourned her twelfth birthday. At the close of his sermon the evangelist launched the usual solicitation for converts, whereupon Moore paced to the front and engaged him in whispered conversation; then he pointed back at his daughter who, if not actually paralyzed, was in great and restrictive physical pain. The evangelist opened out his arms with a smile of terrible piety. The girl faltered, stumbled, burst into tears and struggled to her feet; then she dragged herself haltingly down the aisle while her father and the revivalist shouted in triumph. Mrs. Nation's partial account of this episode leaves the reader with a feeling of ambiguity. "At this [the searching look] I began to weep bitterly, some power seemed to impel me to go forward and sit down on the front bench. I could not have told anyone what I wept for, except it was a longing to do better. I had often thought before this that I was afraid of going to the 'Bad place'; especially was I afraid to think of the time when I should see Jesus come. I wanted to hide from Him . . . a cousin came up to me at the close of the sermon and said 'Carry, I believe you know what you are doing.' But I did not. Oh, how I wanted some one to explain it to me!"

If the confused and debilitated child thought that her ordeal had ended, she only betrayed an ignorance of the old-time religion. Two days later, as she tried to rally from her scourge at the church, she was plucked from her bed of pain and carried two miles to a stream fringed by ice. There she was hauled screaming into water

over her head, as a number of undoubtedly well-meaning clerics
bawled hosannas and a general thankfulness to God, or somebody.
Carry's "visions" of this period have been mentioned, and she
probably had several on the day of her immersion—of herself bast-
ing a string of skewered and roasting clergymen, along the lines of
the Negro tales back in Kentucky. But in retrospect she construed
the baptism as epiphanal, "for the little Carry who walked into the
water was quite different from the one who walked out. I said no
word. I felt that I could not speak, for fear of disturbing the peace
that passeth understanding. Kind hands wrapped me up and I felt
no chill." A good guess is that she was unable to feel anything at
all, especially chill or heat, for she was pretty much confined to her
bed for the next five years. If the dunking had been meant as physical therapy, its failure was complete; if it was aimed at spiritual
orientation, it succeeded well enough, because the girl, while an
invalid, became a converted invalid, determined to follow a course
of sanctimony and deprivation. Heretofore she had been accustomed to reading the New York *Ledger,* a popular and relaxed
weekly of the period, and had borne down with particular glee on
the writings of a Mrs. E. D. E. N. Southworth, who produced ro-
mances in which an occasional suitor caught stolen glimpses of a
well-turned foot. Carry now dropped Mrs. Southworth on grounds
of gross carnality. Specifically, the convert was miserable, both in
mind and in body, but she felt somehow that she was on the right
track. The only fly in her ointment was a family nuisance named
Uncle Jim, an unreconstructed fellow who had a nasty habit of
thinking for himself, rather than allowing "some bushwhacking
preacher" to set his intellectual pace. It was often necessary to explain to outsiders, in a lowered voice, that "Uncle Jim is not a
Christian," the announcement delivered as if the affliction were comparable to leprosy, or syphilis. He remained impenitent, deplored
by all. In his breezy fashion the reprobate strolled into the girl's
room one day and cried out, "So those——Campbellites took
you to the creek and soused you, did they, Cal?" (This last was a
nickname.) The dash of cold water on her evangelical fires daunted
the prostrate young apostle only briefly. In the inevitable course of
her messianic evolution, she soon felt ready to spread the gospel
herself, and, lacking a volunteer audience, she rounded up the

slaves (who had no choice) for an hour or so on Sunday after-noons. Leaning back against pillows, she either harangued them from her bed, or, in an unexpected burst of good health, lectured from a sitting position on the dining room table. This was a pointed case of chickens coming home to roost; in years past they had hurled religion at Carry; now it was their turn to be bored. Mrs. Nation does not give us a detailed account of the Negroes' reaction, but it may be imagined that they agreed solemnly, uttering such characteristic and sensible comments as, *"Ain't* dat de truf!" and "You sho is, Miz Carry; you the livin' spirit of Jesus. It stick out all over," etc. The race has usually found diplomatic and even en-joyable paths around the manifold irritations strewn along the way.

Meanwhile, Carry Nation, the girl of destiny, was handicapped in the pursuit of a temporal education. Her condition was such that she was thirteen before she could attend part-time at Mrs. Till-bury's boarding school in nearby Independence, a cultural mecca that later would house a large political library. Carry was an excel-lent student, and it's interesting to speculate on her probable course had she been given full, early access to the world of books. But her health forced her removal from Mrs. Tillbury's, so her father engaged, for a space, a private tutor who visited the farm two or three days a week. The unpleasant truth is that Moore had run into hard times. The swelling turbulence of the oncoming Civil War, notably in the border states, plus his lackadaisical business approach had caused a pinch in the family's fortunes. A decisive element was the attitude of the family's slaves, who heard more and more talk of war, and abolition, and began to smell the sweet scent of freedom, until at last they announced, through a spokes-man, "We quits." They declined any further to take their work seriously. No man to worry, Moore simply gave everybody orders to pack up—the family was heading south.

Moore had a theory that the slaves' cooperation would deepen as they receded southward from the sympathetic precincts of Kansas, but as usual in his planning, an unforeseen element in-truded. No fewer than ten—both black and white—of his populous caravan fell ill of typhoid fever only two days out from Missouri. For six weeks on the long, dusty, refugee-clogged roads (other people were also leaving the border states) the family prayed, doctored, scrubbed, rejected several suggestions having to do with witches and the distribution of chicken bones in the bottom of a pot and otherwise contended against the disease, which fortunately proved to be light though lingering. In Grayson County, Texas, Moore promptly bought another farm (he had not bought one in months) and was soon chagrined to watch most of his mules and horses die from a mysterious ailment. Presumably he took this as an omen, for he straightaway announced that the ménage would travel back up to Missouri. A beneficial effect of the trip down—a prime example of serendipity, or the finding of unexpected treasure while one searches for something else—was that the child Carry became miraculously cured of her ills. She was fully restored. An observer unfettered by prejudice against heathenism might wonder if the Negroes, Carry's stout supporters, had not worked up something special in the hex line and laid her indisposition onto the livestock. In any case, the girl, pathetically enough for the first time in years, wandered and sported out of doors, rode horseback with the rather fleeting friends made in Texas and returned to radiant health for the journey back. There is no reasonable way to explain Moore. Certainly he was not addled, as was his wife, but his actions at times resembled those of a man walking under water. His body moved slowly, deliberately, while his mind seemed to be occupied elsewhere. In this phase of Carry Nation's life, each of his decisions worked out to be a little feebler than the last.

On the trip back up, as when coming down, the principal members of the family rode in the regal conveyance that had been designed for Queen Victoria. There were other wagons, and carts, and uniformed outriders, and a straggling of animals, and considerable of the slaves on foot. A bewildering aspect of Mrs. Nation's autobiography, and other documents bearing on this episode, is that the Civil War appears to have started during their journey, though the fact is never set forth exactly. "We were often stopped on our trip by Southern troops, in the Territory and Texas, and then again by Northerners," she wrote. "We passed over the Pea Ridge battle ground shortly after the battle. Oh! the horrors of war." The picture of Moore and his incredible equipage plodding stubbornly northward through the Southern lines, through the Northern lines, over battlefields still smoking from combat, perhaps through stretches yet echoing to the explosion of shells, staggers the imagination. In the history of family travel, this off-hand ramble through rubble and concussion most surely must be viewed as unique. The astonishing thing is that the party got past at all. Mrs. Nation concludes her remarks on the ride by saying, simply, "We often stopped at houses where the wounded were. We let them have our pillows and every bit of bedding we could spare. We went to our home in Cass County, Missouri." Once again, the girl had stored up some persuasive impressions.

Back in Missouri she found the war raging with force, to a point where the Moores were compelled to leave their home almost im-mediately they arrived. The reason was bizarre. Colonel Jim Lane, of Kansas, "depopulated" a few Missouri border counties to keep the roughshod Bushwhackers from feeding on the citizens therein. With a sense of relief (his daughter felt) Moore freed his slaves, moved the family into an Army post at Kansas City and entered upon a changed life in which the old abuses, and the old graces, were gone forever. Several of his clan had freed their Negroes years before, only to keep them on as hirelings. Eventually most of these drifted away, uncomfortably bereft of the strong emotional ties that had bound master and peon together for generations. Sadly, the Moores watched their servants rush joyously northward, to the promised land, to reap the new, illusory freedom in which they met mainly indifference and unwelcome instead of the prom-ised Elysium. This was a period of harsh growing up for Carry. Since babyhood, she had found affection and full acceptance in the relaxed, sensible shanties of the Negroes. Now these undemanding foster parents had left, taking with them the riches of love and warmth and simplicity; little remained to fill the void. Carry's mother, whose head the crown had made uneasy for so many years, at last fell ill, too incapacitated to organize the simplest chores of the palace, and with the younger children trooping off to school, Carry "had the house work, cooking and most of the washing to do." * In her spare time she volunteered as lay nurse at a hospital, specializing in weeding the bugs out of the long and tangled hair of

---

* A few years thereafter Mrs. Moore died in the Missouri State Hospital for the Insane.

the wounded. She wrote with relish of this experience, saying, "I had a pan of scalding water near and would use the comb and shake off the vermin into the hot water . . . In health they [the men] were enemies, but I saw only kindly feeling and sympathy."

By good fortune for the heavily burdened girl, her father presumably blundered into a correct business decision a couple of years later, and Carry went off to a private school at Liberty (again in Cass County) presided over by a Dr. and Mrs. Love. She was ashamed of her untutored state, writing that "On account of ill health and the war, I knew but little." Still, she had continued to read books, of a generally antiseptic nature, had occupied her bedridden hours by writing sketches and, finally, had kept a diary, which afterward helped keep her, as the framework of her popular autobiography, *The Use and Need of the Life of Carry A. Nation.* Outstanding in her memory was a class in Smellie's Natural Philosophy, wherein the students divided ranks and argued the most trivial questions, the idea being merely to learn to argue, a course not usually thought necessary in Missouri. The girl's performance here is worth mentioning, because it represents the only recorded occasion when she became rattled in public. The problem up for discussion was, "Do animals have reasoning faculties?" Carry was dreaming of other matters when it was indicated that she would be among the affirmatives the next morning, and she arrived unprepared. When called upon to rise and shine, she drew a perfect blank, able to blurt out only, "Miss President—" (the class being operated like a formal debating society) and then, stricken, ran back to her seat, put her face in her hands and wept. "All burst out in uncontrollable laughter," she said. While the incident sounds trifling, it proved to be a turning point in her life. Phrased indelicately, she had Kentucky guts, of a sort that meant fight, never compromise, stand out for the right, don't appease, take an unpopular stand and ignore the critics, face up and recite the lesson, better dead than unread. Her face burning, she arose, stalked to the front and said in a shaky but aggressive voice, "Miss President, I am ready to state my case." "The moral force it required to do this was almost equal to that which later smashed a saloon," she wrote. Then she launched forth on an extemporaneous plea to prove that animals have the power to reason. Though her triumph was generally complete, several felt that the anecdote she selected was not entirely felicitous. But the girl had sprung from the western hills, and her tools were of the earth and its creatures. "I know animals have reasoning power," she began, "because my brothers cured a dog of sucking eggs by having him take a hot one in his mouth and it was the last egg we ever knew him to pick up." Skillfully she amplified the theme in detail, but the great majority of the young ladies were already persuaded; they'd heard enough. And never again in a career laden with trial and persecution did the debater find herself speechless in the face of a crisis.

Chapter Four

During the Civil War period, when Carry Nation was in her late teens, her reaction to the old ways of lying, thieving and careless living among the Negroes was complete. She still considered that she was "a great lover," but the emphasis now was on a suitor's spiritual qualities and education. In after life, she stressed the issue with such ferocity that the researcher is apt to feel that she protested too much. If she was telling the truth, and even her enemies (an ardent and cohesive group) never successfully questioned her integrity, she must have been one of the dullest dates in the Missouri-Kansas area. She declined even to join in a cozy exchange of personal compliments. "When I had company I always directed the conversation so that my friend would teach me something, or I would teach him," she wrote. Her mother and her aunts had trained her to sit, in the parlor, door open, poised for an emergency shout, at some distance from a caller. If one made a gesture to take her hand, he was shot out into the night like a burglar. "I would go to the country dances and sometimes to balls in the city," she admitted, "but my native modesty prevented me from ever dancing a round dance with a gentleman. I cannot think this hugging school compatible with a true woman." Oddly enough, it was only her native modesty that prevented her from joining the hugging; the Missouri church laid no restraints on hugging under the stimuli of fiddling and physical jerks; indeed, it counseled its parishioners to hug at will. In this, it was a step ahead of the Kentucky Chapter, which had been known to expunge from the lists a person breaking into nonsectarian song.

It is easy to reconstruct those painful evenings in the parlor: the starched and sweating suitor gazing across No Man's Land at the cerebrating nymph (and the photographs show her to have been lovely—soft-eyed, brown hair in ringlets, full-bosomed but with just a hint of Missouri's best-known product in the line of her jaw and mouth), and Carry surrounded by dismal-looking books as the props of Cupid's game. "I would read the poets," went the dry, sad tale, "and Scott's writings, and history. Read Josephus, mythology and the Bible together . . ." If the swain, emboldened by her beauty, made some reckless allusion to her lips, she might counter with a snarling passage from Josephus. And after that there was little left but the lemonade, cakes, a muffled curse and a bowed goodbye at the doorway. What was the girl's shock and surprise, then, to run up against a throwback, in the person of one Dr. Charles Gloyd, a physician, in the fall of 1865. This enigmatic young man had materialized from an outlying hamlet—in a region that the St. Louis radio stations still refer to unfrivolously as "Swamp-east Missouri"—to ask Moore (who seems to have had influence) for the position of county schoolteacher. It was a strange request for a doctor, but he maintained that he wished to "look around" for a year before deciding where to practice. Gloyd was as much scholar as physician, and spoke and read several languages. Granted the job as teacher, he made successful application for room and board at the Moores'. The arrangement ran contrary to the taste of Carry's mother, who considered the newcomer common, below peerage rank, emphatically not of the noblesse. All she had to go on was the fact that he was the only child of parents in modest rural circumstances, but she issued a royal ban against his speaking to Carry; also, the two were prohibited from being alone together in a room. The decree set up an awkward situation; the house was of limited size, and the young pair often had to skirmish, with quick dashes and sorties, to avoid finding themselves *tête-à-tête* in an unoccupied chamber.

Carry did most of the running. Gloyd took a determined attitude toward the Moores' oldest child from the start. He was an energetic follower of Shakespeare, whom Carry had missed in her pursuit of the Bible, Josephus and Mrs. E. D. E. N. Southworth, and by some low, smuggling device he started her reading his worn collection of the Bard. She approved of what she read, and the two started exchanging *billets doux* in the pages of Gloyd's book. The notes were dissimilar in tone, and we may imagine that when Gloyd deposited something as coarse as "How about meeting me tonight by the clump of alders south of the woodshed?" Carry probably replied with "I'm so glad you mentioned the passage in Act III, Scene 2. What ennobling, what *spiritual* language! Some of the words sounded new, but I feel that they must be beautiful all the same." However it went, Gloyd cornered his apprentice in the parlor one afternoon, enfolded her to his Shakespearian bosom, and gave her an emphatically unspiritual kiss. By her own account, the sheltered girl placed her hands against her face and shrieked, "I'm ruined! I'm ruined!" The report proving premature, she decided that she liked what had happened and permitted their acquaintance to ripen.

It is easy for the biographer to sound flippant in dealing with Mrs. Moore, Carry's mother. But her eccentricity was so wildly absurd, and its documentation so copious, that any attempt at a genuine portrayal rings farcical and contrived. During the major portion of her life, Mrs. Moore's ideas, in the aggregate, were worth slightly less than a bale of damp hay to her family. In the one solitary regard—that bearing on the impetuous Dr. Gloyd— her counsel savored of Solomon's. The Queen's instinct about Gloyd was correct, as she relayed it over and over to her daughter (and less frequently to her husband, whose mind was busy perhaps forty or fifty miles distant). Gloyd was a dud. He was considerably worse than a dud; he was an active drag on the energies of those about him. He was also to become a source of heartbreak and despair to his bride.

The courtship, overall, lasted nearly two years. In this time, Gloyd was attentive, constant, fitfully impassioned, with lapses in which he seemed curiously vacant, or unsteady. During these periods, Mrs. Moore made reference to the word "rum," which ironically had been a main fount of nutriment with her father (the descendant of the Dukes of Argyll). She also called into play the rather loose adjective "addicted," but her daughter, afterward, wrote that, "I had no idea of the curse of rum. I did not fear anything, for I was in love, and doubted him in nothing." On their wedding day, November 21, 1867, Gloyd was potted, to employ the slang phrase. Starting apparently quite early in the morning, he had consulted the jug with more than his normal zeal, and "his countenance was not bright, he was changed." This certainly was an extraordinary marital start for a girl whose name would ring down the generations as the symbolic destroyer of drink. It was very possibly here, as she stood arm in arm with her fragrant and wobbly betrothed, that her resolve—formed by the long-leashed pressures of disordered family, over-piety, a violent land, sex, jungle voodoo and hurtful remorse—was at last funneled into the single never varying channel. All unconsciously, as yet, her life was committed by the final ignominy of Gloyd.

"I did not find Dr. Gloyd the lover I expected," Mrs. Nation once wrote. "He was kind but seemed to want to be away from me; used to sit and read, when I was so hungry for his caresses and love. I have heard that this is the experience of many other young married women." The laggard had set up shop, or "practice," in a sense, in the Missouri village of Holden; then, to round out his household he had sent for his mother and father. Little need be said of them beyond the fact that they came. For several weeks after the ceremony, he moderated his drinking to keep pace with his wooing, and then, suddenly, the facade collapsed, as "Dr. Gloyd came in, threw himself on the bed and fell asleep. I was in the next room and saw his mother bow down over his face. She did not know I saw her. When she left, I did the same thing, and the fumes of liquor came into my face. I was terror stricken, and from that time on I knew why he was changed." Once his boozy secret was out, Gloyd abandoned all pretense. Having no drinking companions at home, he drifted off each evening to hold wassail with "the boys." It was in this stage that Carry conceived her bitter distaste for the Masonic Lodge. Gloyd was a strong Mason. He found fulfillment in the secret squat around the cauldron, the ritual, the whispered oaths, the striving for advanced "degrees" (the unlocking of doorways to the innermost jabberwocky) and the sacred and exclusive hand-clasp. But most of all, no doubt, he enjoyed the axis of masculinity against the encroachments of women, meaning his wife and mother. As to whether or not the brothers encouraged Gloyd to soak in alcohol—we have only Mrs. Nation's word, and here she was richly biased. It seems doubtful; the Masonic Lodge is not on record elsewhere as being a collection of drunks.

"These men would drink with him," his wife nevertheless wrote. "There is no society or business that separates man and wife, or calls men from their homes at night, that produces any good results. I believe that secret societies are unscriptural, and that the Masonic Lodge has been the ruin of many a home and character." Arguments could be marshaled against Mrs. Nation's logic. The calling of traveling salesman emphatically separates man and wife by day, and those of doctor and mortician by night. Gloyd was, as noted, a physician, but he allowed his practice to slide. "His sign in front of the door on the street creaked in the wind, and I would sit by the window waiting to hear his footsteps," complained his bride of a few months. It must not be thought that Gloyd was insensible to her suffering. Once in a while he might rouse himself from the brink of stupefaction and make noises of a feebly propitiatory nature, as one evening: "Oh, Pet, I would give my right arm to make you happy." Even his harried family were inclined to believe this, but it was a pretty long chalk from his right arm to the bottle, and it was the latter that he refused to give up.

Letters and notes from this phase indicate that Carry had begun to turn herself into a pest. Now pregnant and wrapped in a dingy shawl, she took to flapping around Holden at all hours in search of the errant Gloyd. Certainly she made life a nightmare for the Masons, who thought they had built an inviolable retreat, but both its front and back doors became subject to violent hammerings, over which arose, like the lodge's conscience, shrill demands for habeas corpus: Mrs. Gloyd wanted her husband delivered to the street, drunk or sober. At church her interpositions for personal attention grew to a point where the ordinary business of the congregation fell off sharply. Specifically, she wanted the preacher, and anybody else in good voice, to knock off what they were doing and pray for Gloyd. She collared individual Masons downtown and insisted that they drop Masonry for the salvation of Gloyd; people—her closest friends—began to flee when they saw her coming. Her father and mother at last got wind of her plight, and Moore drove to Holden in the Queen's carriage. He found his daughter "with insufficient food and clothing, and on the verge of a nervous breakdown through worry and constant weeping." Moore's solutions of problems had often been over-simple—as in the case of his aimless round trip to Texas—and his advice boiled down to, "Get your traps and put them in the buggy." Protesting, she was persuaded to return to the family home, now in Belton, Missouri, and Gloyd was dead within six months.

During her pregnancy Carry had been sick with apprehension that her offspring might be in some way marked by the father's intemperance. The child, a daughter named Charlien, was born in Belton, and the appalling misfortune that soon befell her is enough to make the bitterest cynic pause before ruling out the existence of supernatural forces, both malignant and benign. Several physicians have declared that no comparable case is to be found among modern medical records. In the anguished interim with Gloyd, Carry often said that, "One of my greatest sorrows was the rejection of Christianity from his life," and (Biblical to a degree) she kept repeating that "The mother of Samson was told by an angel to 'drink neither wine nor strong drink' [Judges 13:4] before her child was born." Since any argument that Samson turned out frail could only be regarded as silly, the bride made this quotation a reiterated theme of her rum-sodden honeymoon. Carry became obsessed by reflections on the drunkard's curse. Her instinct was curiously advanced, and she could have been on solid ground. The hidden powers of the occult—extra-sensory perception, the fear-haunted corridors of the mind, psychosomatic symptoms possibly linked to the divine—have lately been explored in special departments of perfectly sensible universities. The region has been called the last great frontier of medicine. In any case, whether Gloyd's inclination scarred his daughter, or whether Carry accomplished this unhappy feat by her brooding, is a question that might only be solved by an unlikely junta of earth-bound scientists and informed delegates from Beyond. But scarred she was, by something.

In Charlien's early childhood, her right cheek became badly

swollen. On examination, it was found that a large sore was eating its way through from the inside. Despite the application of remedies, which may have included aloes, swamp water, Dr. Frisby's Internal Combustion Bitters, eye of newt and black mamba, the child's condition worsened until at length her right cheek fell out, leaving the teeth bare. Of this step in her deterioration, the mother later wrote, "My friends and boarders were very angry at the physician, saying she was salivated"—a protest that baffles a writer of biographies whose grandfather was a doctor in that place and period and left a large library of medical tomes covering the range of then knowledge, half-knowledge and mumbo-jumbo. Charlien lay on the threshold of death for nine days, scarcely breathing, while Carry prayed, "Oh God, let me keep a piece of my child" and the neighborhood ministers helped matters little by advising, in their omniscient style, "Don't pray for the life of your child; she will be so deformed it were better she were dead." As between the two sets of opinions, Carry's was doubtless the stronger, and unexpectedly, defying explanation, the wound began to heal; it closed down to a hole the size of a quarter.

(It should be said that Carry does not emerge unscathed from the unsavory tale. She once bewailed, mildly at first, that "Charlien is not a Christian." Charlien's response, like many another's before and since, was to become considerably less of a Christian very quickly. "She owned to faith in God," her mother said, "but she refused to attend church or Sunday School, and would not read the Bible," a course that thousands of normal, intelligent, fully-weaned people might construe as normal. From this high level of debate, things degenerated to the physical. When Carry tried to coerce a study of the Scriptures, the girl had wild and rebellious tantrums, becoming so violent that it was necessary to confine her behind locked doors. Carry's answer, a partial hark-back to the Negroes' incantations, was to buckle down to something suitable in the hex line. She had been reading the Book of Job, an unhealthy action for any fanatic, and now she besought God to lay "terrible bodily afflictions" on her daughter. For whatever it's worth, the girl's swelling was first noted after the most frenzied of these outbursts.)

Besides the hole, another symptom remained for Charlien, that involving the closing of her jaws, which clamped tight-shut, as in the case of tetanus, and stayed that way for the next eight years. She was fed with difficulty through metal tubes, the insertion of which was made possible by the knocking out of several front teeth. Once again the researcher must admire the redoubtable Carry, who, though frequently wrong-headed and troublesome, showed humanity and mother-love in any real crisis, and whose stubbornness stands almost alone. She refused to give up. By desperate means that will be examined later, she accumulated cash, took Charlien to a celebrated Dr. Dowell, in Galveston, and for a space left her there among strangers, in order to speed treatment. After four operations the hole was closed in the girl's cheek, but her jaws continued shut. "I suffered tortures all these years for fear she might strangle to death," the indefatigable woman wrote.

At the end of Dr. Dowell's ministrations, which must have provided a preview of hell for the victim, Carry took her to Dr. Herff, in San Antonio, who "with his two sons" sawed out a section of Charlien's jawbone, in the hope of constructing an artificial joint. After this ordeal, the experiment regrettably turned out a failure (though it had been interesting to the doctor) and the jaws reclosed as tightly as ever. Other experts were called in at prices. No known sources explain how the pitiable child retained a vestige of sanity through those frightful years, but her outlook eventually gave cause for worry. The fact that she did not become a homicidal (or medicidal) maniac is a tribute to the hereditary fibre of her forebears. Carry's next visit on her trip down quack alley was to a Dr. Messinger, in New York City, who made himself a nuisance for a while and then began to mutter about "the pressures of other practice." This left Carry free to consult a Dr. Weyth, also of New York, who performed on Charlien what now would be called an operation of plastic surgery; that is, he cut off a flap from under her chin and folded it up (sewing it) to conceal the scar on her cheek. As to the jaw, it remained fixed.

Charlien, while not herself an organized worshiper, had no objection to her mother's devotions, and she wrote from one of the torture chambers, "No one but God can open my mouth, Mamma; ask him to do it." "There was a Catholic woman, Miss Doregan, who boarded with me," said Carry, "who had a store around the corner from the hotel, and I could think of no one who had as much faith as this woman. She said she believed that God would heal my child according to prayer, so I went for seven mornings before breakfast to this saint of God. She taught me many holy truths and explained the Scriptures to me. I learned from her a prayer that we said in concert . . ." From her convalescent post of the moment, Charlien periodically wrote, "Keep on praying," and a little later she announced that she had letters of introduction to a Dr. J. Ewing Mears, of Philadelphia, an explorer on the upper slopes of surgery. Exploring being costly, as Mears outlined it, she added that she needed four hundred dollars. Moving quickly, Carry went into a long session of prayer, which proved financially sterile; then she borrowed the money and sent it immediately to Charlien, in Philadelphia. This done, she boarded a train with the few dollars she had left, but when she entered Charlien's hospital room, the girl was preparing to leave. "I cannot describe the meeting," wrote Carry as she went ahead and tried: "She was packing up her clothes. I said, 'Why are you doing this?' Then she told me this pitiful story: 'Mamma, you did not send me any money, and the Doctor and nurse seemed dissatisfied, so I took most of my clothes down to a soup house and pawned them, that the woman might give me a room and soup until I could hear from you.' "

Certain elements of Carry's story seem fuzzy. In the process of revising her autobiography seven times, she made alterations that obscure clarity. Facts came and went; the fine, monarchical detail about her mother, for instance, is missing in the later editions. Dr. Mears must have operated on Charlien, but there was a mysterious hullabaloo about the section of jawbone, with teeth, that Dr. Herff was supposed to have removed in San Antonio. Mears said it was still present; Carry stated, and was willing to swear, that she had seen it out. Meanwhile the child's jaws had been pried apart half an inch. In view of this, Carry decided to release her hold on the disputed member and declare the whole thing a Miracle: "I placed my hands on each side of her face and said, 'Now chew. Well, this is just like God; he has not only opened your mouth, but has given you a new jawbone. My darling, you know that the bone from this side was taken out.' 'Yes,' she said, 'I told Dr. Mears that, but he said it could not be.' " Mears finally expressed himself as being prepared to go along with the miracle, but he never quite cleared up the matter of the missing four hundred dollars.

In the following six weeks, Charlien visited the doctor, who continued very painfully to open the aperture between her jaws. Outside of office hours, she was taken by her mother to see the sights of Philadelphia, and later, when Carry returned to Kansas (where she had at that time a considerable program of smashing laid out) Charlien went to Vermont to visit her father's kinfolk. It would be pleasant to record that Charlien, wholly cured, lived happily ever after, but the grinding years of mental and physical anguish had taken their toll. Though improved, her jaw never healed fully. She was married, to an Alexander McNabb of Richmond, Texas, but her reason tottered and in 1904 she entered the State Lunatic Asylum in Austin. Horrified, Carry rushed to Texas and worked her release, over McNabb's Scottish protests (the place being free). As the unhappy years rolled on, the wretched girl was in and out of other, private institutions, took to drink, became cured, developed "chronic mania," suffered a relapse and made what her mother declared was an authentic recovery in 1910. Throughout the expensive period, Carry footed the bills. In the crusader's will, drawn up later, she stipulated that the income from her "estate" (real estate valued at about $10,000 by a probate court in Washington, D.C.) be paid Charlien "provided she is not in an asylum for the insane." At the moment of death, the girl was at liberty and presumably received the legacy. No one could deny that it was richly deserved.*

---

* The principal was eventually meant to wind up in the hands of the Free Methodist Church of Oklahoma.

Chapter Five

On the death of Dr. Gloyd, his wife had a brief, bad interval of confusion; then she rallied to take a new grip on life. The fact is that, while the alcoholic swilled and languished, her sphere had narrowed to a point where she had almost forgotten how to function. Her days (and nights) had been spent dragging around town in the shawl, trying both to produce the body and talk somebody into mending the soul of her lover of the boarding-house phase. Carry was almost but not quite broke. Neither her records nor those of other family members present an accounting of Gloyd's neglected medical career, but we may assume that he had a few dollars owing from patients (Masons?) whose ills had healed in the natural course of events, together with, perhaps, a handful of suits for malpractice. But this is only speculation. Shifting into fact, we find the reviving widow shaking off the daze, taking stock, planning her future moves. The day was not far distant when her force and distastes would explode on a stunned world, and now, for the first time, she showed her mettle. She led off by peddling Gloyd's surgical paraphernalia as well as his medical textbooks, which, considering Charlien's subsequent experience, might better have been burned. Then her father stepped in and gave her several town lots; these she sold, adding the money to her proceeds from the scalpels, leeches and volumes of medical beliefs.

With the cache Carry built a three-room house, entrusting Charlien to "Mother Gloyd" (who also had been lately widowed) and left to attend the nearby Normal Institute of Warrensburg. Photographs show that the squared-off look of determination had hardened slightly; the expression of maiden softness and expectancy had begun to fade. Her aim was to support her family (of three) by teaching, but after she won her certificate and got a job in the Holden public schools, she went to the mat with a school-board posturer over a technique of incredible triviality. It was to be the precursor of many struggles in which she preferred to sacrifice everything rather than budge. In her reading class, Carry had been following the natural course of using the everyday, working short "a" in such sentences as "I saw a man." But (by double coincidence) a Dr. Moore waltzed in and demanded that she stick to the letter of the law and use the long A, as one might say Amen, or A-man, as the case actually was. Moore could reasonably be described as a typical early egghead, that is, a mediocre but noisy fellow with insufficient intelligence to evaluate what he had learned. His species would eventually blow up, breeding like maggots, until they would rule the nation, providing a ripe compost of misinformation—a small minority of "professors" not capable of earning more than plumbers who nevertheless brandished on all public questions an oracular blueprint of what not to do for survival. With Carry, Moore came a cropper. Being aware that grammar is what a literate and commonsense person chooses to make it, she held fast. But in a sense he had the last two words (long A), for she threw up her badly needed job.

All but impoverished, at liberty, seething with indignation, the reformer-to-be now set out callously to snare a man, a second husband, and if convenient on this round a non-dud. She left the final choice to Providence, putting the matter thus, "I resolved then to get married. I made it a subject of prayer and went to the Lord, explaining things about this way. I said, 'Lord, you see the situation. I cannot take care of mother and Charlien. I want you to help me. If it be best for me to marry I will do so. I have no one picked out, but I want you to select the one that you think best.' " If her supplication bore overtones of an ultimatum, it could be laid to her distracted state of mind. In the light of developments, even the most devout could scarcely be persuaded that Providence had consented to shoulder the responsibility. Approximately a week from the moment of her decision, Carry was walking down the main street of Holden, eyes at the ready, and spied a distinguished-looking man standing in a doorway. He turned and lifted his hat, and the next day he wrote her a letter, begging her to enter into a correspondence. He described himself as David A. Nation, a Civil War veteran who had several professions.

The result was disaster. Nearly everybody who came into Carry's life appears to have been far, far out of the common run. At the time of their collision, Nation was "acting" as editor of the Warrensburg *Journal* while his "actual callings were successful attorney and minister of the Christian Church"; the reader may take his choice, or flip a coin. It will be recalled that the whiskey-logged Gloyd, when he met the Kentucky maiden, was a doctor temporarily functioning as a schoolteacher. Her mother was a housewife playing at being a Queen, and her father was a gentleman farmer with a taste for unprofitable travel. It might be said that, by this stage in her career, only the Negroes had been real. Nation was nineteen years older than Carry, and "my friends in Holden opposed this [marriage] because of the difference in our ages. . . ." A widower, Nation had a family of his own, and probably felt that he clinched the better of the bargain; after all, he was acquiring a foster mother and first-class housekeeper. From his history and appearance, the dispassionate examiner must agree with Carry's friends that she might have shot a little higher. Nation's record of professional successes had thus far been nugatory, and his looks were spookish; they bordered on the frightening. Of the latter, the best that normally polite persons could say was that, "Well, he is certainly *not* handsome." One writer stated, with restraint, that his aspect was "imposing if not startling." A sharp photograph survives of Nation in the moon of his second wooing. It reveals what on first glance appears to be a shifty Old-Testament prophet dressed in a high-crowned black hat and a funereal, ill-fitting mail-order black suit. He wears a long white beard that straggles down offensively over his cravat, his eyes have the self-righteous grimness of a man about to set up a lynching and his mouth is a down-turned crescent of autocracy, bitterness and disappointment. In sum, he looks like a dead (or nearly dead) ringer for the kind of New England cleric that scored such triumphs in Salem. In a pinch, he might have been regarded as a good catch for an unemployed witch; how a buxom young widow of breeding could have viewed him seriously is beyond comprehension. But Carry wanted him, married him (in 1877) and in doing so hammered the last nail into the coffin of her hopes for a life of fulfillment and domestic felicity.

Perhaps the best thing to issue from her second union was a name-change that Carry eventually saw as a portent. In the family Bible she had been inscribed "Carry Amelia Moore" (after the christening) but her father absently wrote it later as "Carrie." After becoming Mrs. Nation, the reformer saw that the combination—"Carry A. Nation"—indicated the high chore for which she had been singled out by God. In the succeeding years she derived further hints from both the words and the initials. "C. A. N." meant, of course, that she must not fail; "C. A. Nation" signified clearly (to her) a republic free of booze, and there were other signs to which she alone had the key. In 1903, Carry applied to the courts and gained permission to change her name legally to Carry Amelia Nation, a brand that she stamped indelibly on the consciousness of her generation.

There is something almost Grecian in Carry Nation's tragically wrong moves that led rung by rung down the ladder of catastrophe. The offstage chorus of lament is always present in her chronicle, and she herself finally came to understand a part of what had shaped her, saying, "I think my combative nature was largely developed by living with him [Nation] for I had to fight for everything that I kept."

She kept very little. By another jolting coincidence, she shortly found herself embarked on a second fizzle of a trip to Texas. The one with her father could be classed as a tourist's delight as set against the unrelieved disaster of her jaunt with Nation. No documents from the period tell us why Nation, so generously endowed as editor, lawyer and theologian, required to seek a broader scope for his talents, but he talked his bride into "pooling" their resources, with which sum they bought seventeen hundred acres on the San Bernard River, in Brazoria County, Texas. In only one

sense did this add to his lustre: before, he had failed in three areas
of male endeavor; now he branched out and became a well-known
unsuccessful farmer. It had been Nation's idea to grow cotton,
about which he knew nothing, but as he blundered from one error
to another his disposition soured. He picked a quarrel with a
neighbor—the wrong neighbor—who presented a strong rebuttal
by throwing all of Nation's plows and farming tools into the river.
This was a handicap, but there were worse ones coming. During
the spring, eight of his nine horses died (the horses of everybody
Carry had connections with seemed to die in Texas) and a farm
hand hired by Nation decamped with the establishment's loose
cash. At this low point, the bridegroom decided that his true vocation was the bar, so he went into nearby Columbia, leaving Carry
to worry about the cotton, and took to loafing around town trying
to drum up a lawsuit. (He never succeeded.) Meanwhile, back on
the farm the situation degenerated to the starvation level. For a
month, Carry and Charlien and Mother Gloyd and a step-
daughter, Lola Nation, lived on "side meat" (fat bacon), corn
meal and sweet potatoes; they had neither bread, milk nor butter.
Not only the children but Carry fell ill, and in the deepest winter of
their discontent, Nation sent word that he was having a pretty
rough time; he needed money.

Arising from her sick bed, Carry prepared a meal with the last
of her provisions: cornmeal mush and two or three sweet potatoes.
Then she loaded the emaciated group onto a buckboard and
headed for town. From all accounts, it is clear that the Nations
might actually have starved to death had it not been for a saintly
Irish ditch-digger named Dunn. Dunn was one of those extraordinary mortals, a true rather than a fashionable Sunday Christian,
who thrive on selfless acts of Samaritanism. After Carry had failed
to find a job, she cast an appraising eye at the dilapidated Columbia Hotel, as a possible focus for her energies. The hostelry was
little more than a way station for rats, mice and bedbugs. Carry
surveyed it carefully, noting the punched-out windows, the peeled-
off wallpaper, the plaster cracked, the unemptied pots, the livestock and rich deposits of guano on all the floors. Even with her
frail grasp of finance, she sensed that her principal need was capital. The sole voice of sympathy in a chorus of suspicious nays was

the ditch-digger Dunn, who stepped forward with his all—$3.50. Using this, Carry went into business (as tenant-operator). She spent $2.50 fumigating, making curtains out of sheets, and pasting newspapers on the walls and broken windows; then she blew the other dollar on meat, rice, potatoes, coffee and sugar. She was not aiming at the carriage trade but mainly at transients who had a choice between the Columbia and sleeping in the park.

Columbia was a hamlet of five hundred souls, to use the term loosely, and the terminus of a railroad with the unlikely name of Columbia Tap. A Mr. Painter, conductor of the line's only train, came forward to board with Mrs. Nation almost at once; and soon afterward he brought in a family named Oastram, who had drifted south to buy a plantation. When Mrs. Oastram forked over an advance of ten dollars, Carry and Charlien rushed upstairs and wept, Charlien crying, "Now we can buy a whole ham!" Carry did the cooking. She also did all the other dining room work, washed the tablecloths and bed-linens, and did the laundering for the boarders. Her day commenced about an hour before dawn and wound up a little after midnight, the late hours being spent at tubs in the basement, where she always had company, because fumigate as she might, she never got rid of the rats. Mrs. Gloyd and Lola cleaned and made the beds, and Charlien did the buying. Nation's role in the ménage was ambiguous; in essence, he sat behind a desk in the hotel lobby, thoughtfully pulling at his beard, his expression fixed in a kind of threatening legalistic scowl. Probably he was used as a dummy, for window dressing, to give the place class. Certainly he had all the best of it, for he dined with the guests (while his family ate nothing but leavings for months) and in between times strolled around the town, still snooping for litigation (though he had no office and would doubtless have proved befuddled had a suit turned up).

It is not surprising that Carry's health and morale began to crack under the strain. She gave way to insomnia, nervousness and the morbid and hysterical fits of her childhood. But her distractions now went further. Her memory, once sound, waxed and waned in accordance with the prosperity of her tumbledown inn. Often she was quite literally unable to recall her own name, an embarrassing state of affairs for a *maîtresse d'hôtel* who, by the nature of her work, must sweep up to new arrivals and cry, "Why, how do you do. Welcome to the Columbia Hotel [perhaps aiming a shrewd kick at a mouse]. I'm—" then the blank look of horror, a howl like a wolf, and flight. Her behavior was not capable of exaggeration. "Her supplicating cries could be heard a block away," wrote a reporter, and the building was said to "tremble" as she skittered about the room, "advancing on her knees." "During these severe afflictions," she later wrote in a near-biblical vein, "I began to see how little there was in life. I wondered at the gaiety of people. It seemed as if a pall hung over the earth. I would wonder that the birds sung, or the sun would shine. I might say that for years this was my experience." Had it not been for a religious horror of suicide, she might well have put a period to what she now saw as an intolerable prison sentence. Significantly, during the long, desperate watches of her nights she developed the habit of sitting and staring from her bedroom window at a saloon across the street, wondering how the marriage to Gloyd might have thrived without alcohol, her anger mounting, the need for action slowly building.

Events moved swiftly now. Carry began to have profound and disturbing dreams, (and "visions"), of which for the first time she decided to take vigorous note. She chose to evaluate them in terms of remedies necessary to put things in order. An exception was a recurring dream that she had about a pair of snakes; in this, one was large, fat and poisonous, the other nothing very special in the snake line, being scrawny, torpid and, on the whole, harmless. The dream might have passed unremarked except that the venomous snake had a mannerism of striking at her viciously, while hissing in an unneighborly way, and signified its intention of retiring her from the hotel business. Carry always awoke from this ordeal shaken in body and spirit, having spent the night dodging, ducking and uttering nightmare shrieks. Her performance was, curiously, not unlike that of the late Gloyd when the fit was on him. In her waking hours she wrestled with the portents of the delusion, and came to a startling and rather political conclusion. The ugly snake represented the Republican Party, she felt, for no good reason that any responsible person has yet deduced, while the listless one represented the Democrats. She filed away her findings, determined to examine the matter later.

Carry's life was further complicated, in 1881, by a move away from Columbia, where she had kept abreast of the rats and little more. With her husband (still muttering about lawsuits) and retinue, she moved to Richmond, Texas, in Fort Bend County, to take a more promising job. Now she had charge of a cheerless wooden hotel of twenty-one rooms, with six cottages, the whole calling for an increased output of hard work; however, she had a chance to make some money. It was here that Charlien, after the long years of torment, married and, sure enough, moved into Carry's hotel with her husband. Thus there were six persons for the crusader to feed, clothe and house. Of some slight help was the arrival of her father who, down and out at last, turned up to help wait on tables, chop wood, run to the store, run up and down stairs (and eat). He died there, in his new harness, and was given a decent burial by his beleaguered daughter. On the whole, Carry's contacts with the male sex were enough to send the mildest of women smashing through centers of masculine recreation. Her assignment was staggering, but she tucked into it with such vigor that visions engulfed her completely. She accepted these as being sendings direct from the Lord, and told friends that "from henceforth all my time, means and efforts should be given to God." She promptly became the greatest nuisance in the history of Richmond, a Texas town that had seen troubles, and went around confronting everybody on the streets, to demand, "Do you love God?" Many of the answers were indecorous, along lines of "Why, shore, chicken, but I've got room for you, too." The astonishing number of improper suggestions she received must stand as a tribute to the virility of the modest cattle state. A Negro who delivered eggs to the hotel fell into the habit of dropping his burden and bolting, avoiding the morning evangelism with the fleetness for which the race is noted.

But it was at the Methodist Church that Carry made her presence felt most keenly. In brief, she kept the place tied in knots. Technically a member of the Christian Church, she had taught Sunday School at Columbia's Methodist Church and had taken a fling at the Episcopal as well. Both engagements left the congregations on the brink of civil war. In Richmond, the Episcopals showed her the door because she threw out the church's catechism. The Methodists, in total uproar, expelled her for being over-religious; they also felt that the pastor should be permitted occasionally to open his mouth, an impossibility when Carry was around. What's more, they said she was leading their children away from the true (or Methodist) dogma. When they refused her the use of their pews, she organized a non-denominational Sunday School of her own, with the financial support of a saloonkeeper named Frost. She held classes in the hotel dining room, somewhat to the discomfort of the guests, and if the weather permitted led her communicants to the graveyard, where they arranged themselves for lessons, psalms and fist-fighting among the headstones, socles and chains. From childhood she had been partial to graveyards, and the instruction went well. In both a doctrinaire and a racial way, the group was heterogeneous, including Catholics as well as Protestants, along with a scattering of Negroes, Mexicans and Apaches. Carry's conduct at length grew so irksome that a merchant friend stopped her downtown and said, "I have something to say to you, Mrs. Nation."

"Do you love God?" she countered, this now being her generic phrase for "How do you do?" "Hello there!" "What's new?" and the like.

"That's exactly what I mean," replied the merchant soberly. "Your friends are becoming uneasy about the state of your mind. You are thinking too much on religious subjects, and they asked me to warn you."

Her answer was to laugh in his face.

Two of Carry's last acts in consolidating her position as Richmond's village idiot should be mentioned before proceeding to the circumstance that removed her from Texas. They are difficult to appraise, as they appear to border on the supernatural. Both, however, were verified by independent witnesses and must be viewed as essentially correct. In the first of these, she stepped in uninvited to tidy up a ruinous drought that Ford Bend County had suffered for years. Some measure of the crisis may be seen in the fact that the Methodists lifted their ban on Carry temporarily, to let her relay signals, or demands, from the church. Working fast, she formed a committee that generously included the minister's wife, two other women (rather docile by nature) and herself. Then she announced that a church prayer meeting would be held to "offer supplications for additional moisture." It is not precisely clear what Mrs. Nation meant by the phrase "additional moisture," unless it referred to tears shed by the minister's wife, who promptly began to weep, saying, "I have read of so many thunderbolts lately that I am almost afraid to pray."

Over this feeble and self-interested protest Carry rode without pause, and the devotions got under way. It was remarked that Carry did most of the praying, and her manner was observed by a Mr. Jackson, who afterward transcribed his sensations for one of the county papers: "She [Mrs. Nation] had a style not usually noticed in entreaties before the Lord; aggressive, not humble, her eyes wide open for one thing, and her bonneted head waggling back and forth as though she'd lost patience with everybody in the Celestial Organization." Presumably Carry's attack gave no offense, at least in official circles, for nothing erupted in the way of thunderbolts. She adjourned the session, as she told the crowd, for the purpose of going outside to check the Heavens, and her narrative takes up the story: "After the meeting we were standing on the platform in front of the church when a sprinkle of rain out of a cloudless sky fell on the platform and on the shutters of the house. This was nothing but a miracle, and was very astonishing to us all. The next day clouds began to gather in the sky and the moisture started, at first, to fall like heavy dew. There was no lightning or thunder, but the rain came down in the gentlest manner and continued in this way for three days." To signify her thanks, Carry took an orphan girl and a pauper old man home to her hotel and supported them for the rest of her stay in town. As for Richmond, the cries of gratitude (and surprise) at first were clamorous, but as the miracle-worker noted, a trifle sourly, many soon began saying, "Oh, well, we probably would have had rain anyway." Carry was undisturbed; by now her experiences with the human race convinced her that a cloudburst of ten-dollar bills would have netted her little but the usual criticism and abuse.

In the second incident, the miraculous element is not quite so evident, but the coincidence was singular. It was in March of 1889, late at night, that one of her roomers, an elderly ne'er-do-well, went on record with a series of groans and idiomatic expressions indicative of a bellyache. Carry had been accustomed to handle all complaints of her tenants, including the medical, and she arose, lumbered down to the kitchen and heated a mustard plaster, which she slapped on the victim's stomach, presumably getting his permission first. When she headed back toward her room, "there seemed to be a light shining behind me, which would come and go in flashes, as I ascended. I looked everywhere to see where it came from, but discovered it to be an unnatural manifestation." She interpreted the glow as a vision, in the shape of a warning, and assured her family that trouble was coming. Next night at precisely the same time, Richmond awoke to an enormous hullabaloo: half of the town was on fire. Understandably, Carry's guests commenced a wild scramble to gain the street, dragging whatever belongings, including their own, they could grab. One aristocratic dowager in reduced condition even succeeded in finding two Negroes to help cart out a set of costly personal furnishings. Her actions were memorable, for she kept pointing at Carry, who had seated herself in one of the lobby rockers, and saying, "That woman has lost her mind." Several guests repeatedly urged Mrs. Nation to flee before it was too late; she replied that the Lord had signaled her to hold fast. One commonsense fellow, semi-dressed, rushed back in to cry, "Are you insured?"

"Yes, up there," said Carry, pointing to heaven.

As the fire approached with a roar, and the heat increased, and the panicked crowds stepped up their wails, Carry selected a psalm book and began to bawl out her favorite hymns. The people outside could hear her above everything; they were insistent on the point in an investigation that followed. At a moment when it seemed that Richmond must surely lose its most controversial worshiper, either a freak of nature or a Divine agency moved in to stem the tide. The house next door burned to the ground, and there the conflagration stopped. Two guests opened the hotel door to cry, "You are saved!" and Carry gave them a benign smile. Years afterward she wrote, "From that day to this, I have never had any fear of fire."

It was the usually torpid Nation who caused his family's departure from Texas. Of late he had lain fallow, in a potentially litigious way, but now he tapped one of his dormant professional skills and became a sporadic correspondent for the Houston *Post*. For some reason, he selected politics as his milieu, and got himself into a marvelous amount of hot water. In Fort Bend County, as in much of Texas, a pair of high-tempered factions were disputing one of the touchiest questions of the day. The Jaybirds held out for white supremacy at all levels of public service, while the Peckerwoods, mainly Republicans, thought that a few Negroes might hold office without destroying the social structure. It is difficult to fathom from Nation's reports exactly where he stood. In their turgid, preachy, super-verbose style, they managed to convey that everybody concerned should probably be shipped elsewhere and resettled. The tone of his pieces had the effect of endearing him to nobody. In fact, Nation's unpopularity with the Jaybirds was matched only by the contempt in which he was held by the Peckerwoods. Both sides were to suffer from his irresponsible maunderings, but the Jaybirds managed to get in a few licks first. Nation came home one midnight, having been down to "meet the trains" (this was something he appeared to do for recreation) in a condition that might be described as the last extreme of journalistic unfitness. "Wife, get up!" he cried. "I have been beaten almost to death." Numbered among the Jaybirds were several brothers named Gibson—sporting types, rough-and-ready fellows who loved a quarrel. Encountering Nation waiting for Old 99, or the Long Horn Limited, possibly with his watch in his hand, playing engineer, they asked him to seat himself on a cotton bale and develop his stand on the Jaybirds *vs.* the Peckerwoods. He lost the match, for in the rebuttal the Gibsons all jumped on Nation and dusted him off with canes. He had exaggerated the degree of his plight, but he expressed an anxiety to leave Texas when he started to get letters, of atrocious literary merit, which forecast his premature burial if he continued to hang around.

Historians have marveled that Nation's scribblings, however gross, could have given offense. Texas journalism was uniquely, uproariously offhand. "The fearless journalist was the editor and his own reporter," said the *Southwestern Historical Quarterly* in a roundup of the situation. "He developed in the Wild and Woolly West, and he backed up his paragraphs with a six-shooter . . . usually he was slightly built, but he feared no man." A new editor of the Houston *Post,* in 1800, greeted the town thus:

TAKE WARNING:—The *Post,* following the example of some of the leading journals of the West, has employed for the use of this office, an ex-prize fighter, who is in excellent training and carries two-hundred pounds of solid flesh. This gentleman is under contract to settle all disputes and to soothe any excitable party who wishes to raise a row with any member of the editorial staff. If a man comes scooting out of the office like a roman candle with his pants kicked up under his hat and both ears chewed off, the law can't touch the *Post* for it, as the public has been solemnly warned!

The birth of *El Progresso,* an Arizona paper, was described more concisely (and perfectly straightaway) by a competitive organ of the area: *"El Progresso* made its appearance in Phoenix yesterday. The name of Enrique Garsias appears as editor, Mr. Joe Redondo is the fighting editor, and Mr. C. Aguirre, printer." In El Paso, people were only casually interested in a newspaper statement, "There has not been a natural death in El Paso in some time." As abrupt as they were, editors could be complimentary, often lending a hand to some worthy local enterprise. "The Riverside Restaurant," said a San Antonio paper, "is cool and clean and there are no flies in the soup." For all their forthrightness, some of the pioneer western papers seemed sensitive, the Dallas *News* commenting that "A little chisel-faced skunk was at one of the bars a few days ago and said he didn't care a damn for this paper."

Papers carried on elaborate long-term feuds, the parry-and-thrust generally being skilled enough to produce gunfire somewhere along the way. When the Gatesville *Post* asked, "Are we right in the suspicion that the Fort Worth *Gazette* is the owner of a patent hog-cholera cure?" the *Gazette* replied, "Yes, and we might inquire after your health."

Good news-writers of the era strove for eloquence, even if it involved subjects normally regarded as delicate. The suicide of a leading San Antonian was recorded as follows: "Texas is today shrouded in sorrow at the unexpected demise of our esteemed fellow citizen, John Eccles, Esq., who in a moment of hallucination gurgled a considerable quantity of tinct. opii., and from that mo-

ment took no abiding interest in the ordinary events of the day."
Eccles' obituary, routine to Texans, was so irreverent that it drew
a rather waspish editorial from Harper's *Monthly*.

Viewed candidly, the reporting might have been called slipshod,
but few papers were too petty to correct minor errors. The account
of a railway mishap was re-grouped to everyone's satisfaction in
San Antonio: "The *Light*'s report on the Sunset train tragedy at
Valentine on Saturday was based on hearsay evidence and was
therefore a little inaccurate. The tragedy occurred on a train coming east instead of going west. The murderer's name was Taylor
and not Johnson or Day. And he killed his victim by stabbing him
with an eight-inch dirk, not by shooting him. Taylor isn't dead,
either, though reported so, but is fatally injured, and if not dead,
soon will be."

As to Carry Nation, San Antonio's journalism treated her visit,
in 1908, with almost exemplary decorum:

"At exactly one o'clock the International and Great Northern
pulled in at the depot from Guadalajara, Mexico. Stepping off the
train with a firm step and a determined mien was a woman severely dressed in the fashion of the day. She was about five feet tall
[?] and was carrying a large suitcase. In her piercing eyes was the
fire of battle.

"She boarded a streetcar with her traveling companion, a man
named Hill, who had been discovered wandering aimlessly around
Mexico. She was taking him to an institution in Missouri. At the
old Bexar Hotel she registered. This is what she wrote: 'Mrs. Carry
Nation. Your Loving Home Defender, Medicine Bow, Kansas.'

"The 'Kansas cyclone' had hit San Antonio."

Somehow or other Carry managed to swap her Texas property
for a place in Medicine Lodge, Kansas, and the family made ready
to move. But Nation had sowed the wind, for the Jaybirds and the
Peckerwoods, armed and having a gorgeous time, met in downtown Richmond and shot it out in "broad daylight." Five men
were killed, which may have been a good thing, since it certainly
eased the tension, but one of them was Henry Frost (a leading anti-
Peckerwood), the saloonkeeper who had underwritten Carry's
venture with the graveyard devotions. The Nations tarried long
enough to see him planted at the site of her old tutelage; then they

boarded a train for the North, Nation having accomplished the demise of his wife's main support in Richmond. Charlien and her husband remained, and Mother Gloyd decided to stay with them for awhile. She died in the next few months; aged eighty-six. In the new land, Nation fell back to the last of his prepared positions. Farming had collapsed, law had missed fire and journalism had all but proved fatal. In Medicine Lodge he was to assume the ministry of the First Christian Church, launching one of theology's bleakest chapters since the days of Peter the Hermit. Nation was a vapid, forceless man, but it is hard to understand why he endured the Amazonian browbeating now given him by Carry. True, he was nineteen years older than she, but in a knock-down, drag-out fight he could probably have whipped her. Nevertheless his demeanor in the pulpit of the First Christian Church was that of a human rabbit.

It is not easy to describe Carry's management of the preaching Nation in a spirit of pure sobriety. A number of accurate sources have set the scene; yet the facts sound farfetched. Perhaps the nearest parallel to Carry in this phase is the modern boxing manager with a totally helpless, submissive and boneheaded prizefighter in tow. Wearing a depressing black frock coat, at around 180 pounds and carrying an oversized Bible, Nation usually ascended to the dais on his own. There his autonomy ended; indeed, the initiative had passed from his hands somewhat before. Carry had undertaken to choose his text, implement it with wrathful and bloodcurdling anecdotes—principally involving liquor, tobacco and sex, but with any number of adverse references to specific persons in the audience—then to edit and rewrite the sermon two or three times. At the moment of delivery, she seated herself conspicuously on the front row, in the role of prompter, or critic. It is a recorded fact that Nation rarely got out a sentence without some noisy and helpful assist from Carry. If he seemed to be speaking slowly (and many wondered that he was able to utter more than strangled cries) she boomed from the pews, "Speed it up, David. You're dragging." She told him to raise his voice, lower his voice, clear his throat, blow his nose, clutch his lapel, walk to the right, kneel briefly, pull his beard and make gestures such as "Stop right there and point at the Heavens!" All this was perfectly audible—

that is, pitched in a key far louder than the sermon—and it transcended the bounds of embarrassment. The congregation assembled in the shamefaced but determined humor of carnival-goers viewing a monstrosity with diverse genitalia. Nation's Sunday morning burdens all ended on the same note. When Carry suspected that he was winding down, she bawled, "That will be all for today, David"; then she hied herself to the rostrum, banged shut his Bible and led him out of the building, almost but not actually by the ear.

Chapter Six

"I soon saw that I was not popular with the church at Medicine Lodge," Mrs. Nation wrote in her autobiography. She very seriously understated the case. By "church" she meant all the churches in Medicine Lodge, for she was soon spread pretty thin there in a religious way. Her first choice of membership was, of course, the Christian, or Campbellite, whose flock her husband was shortly to address, at second hand, with difficulty, and in interrupted spurts, each Sunday. Before many weeks had passed she and the incumbent minister had squared off over a peculiar point of dogma. Carry put in a claim for a special level of privilege, approaching sanctification, or sainthood, on the basis of two religious visions she had suffered in Texas. The church heads wanted proof, making the seemingly valid claim that, according to Christian Church by-laws, only the Apostles had thus far been honored. Carry countered with an irrelevant assertion that the minister spent most of his off hours visiting the town druggist, a "heathen who peddled whiskey in the back end of his shop." The doctrinaire skirmishing and infighting that Mrs. Nation conducted in this period, when her wrath was gathering for the grand, the epic, the world-shaking assault on liquor, are all but impossible to follow. It is known that, during a tented revival, her attention shifted briefly to the Free

Methodists, a small but rackety splinter group of the Methodist Episcopal Church. The split, important in its way, was caused by the new outfit's acceptance of a "second blessing," something, if only small—perhaps a mishap to a detested neighbor—in the way of a divine manifestation, which Carry claimed to have collected in abundance.

It might be thought that, with two Kansas churches on her hands, Mrs. Nation had found religious satiety, but she branched out with an odd experience during a visit to her home by the Baptist minister. Except for a scattering of Negro sects, with handles too complex to unscramble here, this completed the representation in Medicine Lodge; Carry had touched all bases. With the Baptist minister, and his daughter, she was seated "reading the Bible, praying and meditating," when a snakelike fork of lightning ripped loose out of an unclouded late evening sky, illuminating the out-of-doors. She acknowledges that the revival had just concluded, and she was still a-tingle from the emotional points made by the Free Methodist evangelist. Directly after the lightning, she discerned "the dim outline of wings pressed against the window pane." A less excitable, or less godly, person might have said, "Look at that whopping big bat!" but Carry cried, "Just now, blessed Father, give me the witness!" At that juncture, she said, she heard a faint fluttering of wings and felt what she called "Divine electricity" pelting down on her head. She promptly went into an "ecstasy," probably of the sort that many Americans now get from benzedrine, or dexamyl. A discordant note in this sonata of the miraculous is that the Baptist minister, and his daughter, arose and headed for the street. One writer said that "the amazed Baptist preacher and his daughter stole softly from the house"; a better guess is that they left without delay, for Carry had gone berserk. Flinging a weatherproof shawl over her head (the rains had come at last) she raced outside and ran along pounding on one door after another, shouting that the Lord had paid her a visit and demanding that everybody give thanks. As nearly as may be ascertained, nobody did, and a good many slammed doors in her face, offering vulgar and irreligious suggestions as they did so.

Carry's popularity had declined to a state wherein few doors were left open to her. But the rebuffs served to stiffen her will, and on the occasion of the wings and the electricity, she sprinted back home to find "every word and every letter" of her Bible surrounded by "a bright light." Feverishly she thumbed it through, noting that the obscurest passages now emerged as crystal clear in her mind. As for the glow, it hung on for three days, which might be described as the nadir, the bottommost rung, of her husband's life. For three days Carry stayed in the basement, prostrate, while Nation was obliged to tackle the housework. He was not lonely, however, for songs, prayers, shrieks and stern supplications issued from his cellar, as Carry went through her knottiest spiritual wrestle thus far. Its apex arrived to a fury (in her mind) of thunder, lightning, high wind that bent trees double and a gaping rent in the earth's crust. In the center of this storm—the still and motionless hurricane's eye—lay a place of ineffable loneliness and peace, occupied by only two persons: Carry Nation and Jesus Christ. It was a long time coming, but she had finally achieved godhead. After this sublimest of visions, Carry's attitude in Medicine Lodge became so offensively self-righteous that her resemblance to the biblical vessel of wrath was complete. The wildness of mind, the fanatic fits and contortions, the seeming lunacy gave way to a quiet but deadly arrogance. She felt, looked and acted omniscient, and her impatience with mortal foibles far surpassed that of the Creator whom she professed to serve. ". . . She practically took charge of religion in Medicine Lodge," wrote a biographer in 1929. ". . . The ministers of the town avoided her whenever possible (though it was difficult), because she scolded them for their theological obtuseness and pointed out their shortcomings both as men and as preachers."

Carry was in the grip of a violent inner upheaval, her spirits whirling in a kind of Bessemer converter, preparing for the last great change, the resolution of her life's work. Despite the connection formed with Jesus, all was not yet clear to her. But the furnaces were fired, the ore ready and waiting. This religious frenzy passed to a secondary phase, no less painful to Medicine Lodge. She became obsessed with illicit sex, and appointed herself a vigilante committee of one, concentrating on parked buggies. If she had reason to suspect dalliance, she crept forward, her Kentucky woods training at the alert, until she had a glimpse of the interior.

Then, should her worst fears be realized and the buggy contain a couple happily necking, she leapt forward with warnings of hell and damnation. It should be mentioned that in this period Mrs. Nation had taken to carrying a wicked-looking umbrella, with a sharpened ferrule, and this she brandished on all occasions of malefaction. In town the conjecture was often made whether she would actually strike or stab a sinner with it; nobody appeared sure. Precisely why she was not horsewhipped or run over has never been explained. All Kansans are not mild, peace-loving creatures, as the admirers of John Brown will be quick to acknowledge, and the era was no time for a busybody to step between a man and his wooing.

Carry's attentions to women on the downtown streets were perhaps even more onerous. She stopped most females under the age of fifty for a session of earnest moral persuasion, of the most embarrassing sort. Principally, her message was—"Resist seduction, all men are monsters"—and the anatomical detail she offered up no doubt excited more than one virtuous maiden's imagination. Nation's attitude toward these public slurs on his sex is not known, but he must have cringed to hear the basic common interest of men and women so roundly abused. In 1901, after twenty-four years of mutually unhappy, not to say riotous, marriage, he divorced Carry, and proved himself something of a cad by publicizing a catalogue of needless complaints against the saloon-smasher and then, for a space, making himself a kind of career by discussing her with journalists, curiosity-seekers and even enemies of her cause. In the Topeka *Journal* of February 14, 1901, he hit the high spots of her rampages, the reporter noting that "All these things have stirred Mrs. Nation's husband to a high pitch of rage. His hands were clenched and his voice trembled as he talked with a correspondent today about his wife. 'I married this woman because I needed someone to run my house,' said Mr. Nation. 'She showed me that she had stern qualities and could manage things carefully and with economy. We went to Texas and set up in business . . . I attribute my financial success [?] largely to her. But she is so hard to manage when she wants to do anything! Once in Texas she talked of starting out on saloon crusades, and I told her to stay home. She gave me a piece of her mind and I got even with her."

In the interview, Nation neglected to say how he got even, but he may have given her to feel that he had formed an alliance with the Devil, for their disputes reached fine heights of invention. To the *Journal's* reporter, he spoke bitterly of "humiliations," saying that she once required his presence on stage during a woman's meeting, introduced him, and asked that he make a speech, but "Just as I was getting warmed up to my subject, she called aloud: 'Now, Papa, you had better quit and run for the train. I want you to go back home and take care of the place while I am away.' "

"Mr. Nation then related how his wife used to get up in the night and pray for the destruction of saloons," the reporter wrote, "and every time a tornado came along she would go into the back yard and pray that it would clean out every saloon in Medicine Lodge."

Carry was not insane during her emotional spasms in Medicine Lodge—indeed she remained sane, if forceful and fanatic, during the rest of her life—but she was approaching the menopause. Her viewpoint on sex grew warped and eroded steadily in the years to follow. But in Medicine Lodge, as elsewhere, her concentration on religion and then sex yielded to yet another phase, that of good works among the needy. It became her whim to badger the merchants and the wealthy in behalf of people whom she represented to be starving. It was true that drink had hampered eating for many in the town, and that others dined sparsely because of a resistance to work, but Medicine Lodge had some real hardship cases, too, and it was upon these that Carry focused her main attentions. When she went marketing she took a gigantic basket marked "For the Poor," and presented it everywhere with an impudent air of challenge. If a store-owner (possibly having loaded her up the previous day) refused assistance, she ran around the streets like a town crier, noisily lamenting his "stinginess" and threatening to invoke Divine retribution. She was a pest. In church on Sunday, she continued her slanders, asking the Lord to smite, say, "Abe Smithers, the parsimonious old hypocrite," and "Ned Bunker, a mean, swill-faced gouger of widows and orphans," standing up and shaking her umbrella and throwing a monkey wrench into her husband's sheep-bleats on the dais. Often, if the villains named were present, they quietly arose and left, while the remaining worshipers sat apprehensive that their turn might come next. Short of riding her out of town on a rail, there appeared no easy way to shut her up. Leading citizens of Medicine Lodge regretted that Carry's methods were so scratchy, for she contributed a lot of selfless and worthwhile service. Each autumn, for example, she filled her buggy with secondhand pants, roundabouts, frocks, old shoes and warm coats and drove over the county, making certain that no child was too meagerly clad to attend school. Most of her savings went for welfare, and at holiday seasons, such as Christmas and Thanksgiving, she threw open her home to anybody who cared to come in and eat.

Somewhere along this highway of self-denial, she became known as "Mother Nation," Medicine Lodge's "character," the good and wicked witch of the West, destroyer of serenity and boredom, keeper of the community conscience. A popular game in Barber County (wherein Medicine Lodge lay) was to speculate on what course she might veer off on next. The answer was not long forthcoming. After a few false starts, she decided to strike a blow against booze. The devil was prostrate, sex had virtually ceased to exist, and booze was about all that remained. In Kansas, after 1880, liquor could be sold only for "medical, scientific and mechanical" purposes. In consequence, the state having the relaxed western outlook, druggists equipped their shops with a rude plank, or bar, set up beside whiskey barrels to accommodate the legions of suffering who daily arrived for medical aid. From literature of the period one gathers that to secure a "prescription" was not difficult; rather, it offered opportunities for the region's thoughtful humor. A druggist first greeted any regular invalid with a solicitation about the nature of his ailment; then he heard something like, "Bubonic plague—it come on me right after breakfast." Here the proprietor's legal duty was to ask if the man had a remedial prescription, and a typical answer ran on the lines of "Why, yes, I've got two left over from the attack of leprosy I had last week." "If you don't have," the druggist might continue, "old Doc McpheEters left off six this morning for emergencies." The most preposterous device of the time, not uncommon, was the "refillable prescription for chronic alcoholism." Drugstore furnishings were standard; it scarcely ever occurred to anybody to object, or even to notice them. But it occurred to Carry, as she took it on herself to make a canvass of the places—drugstores and just plain "joints"— that sold liquor openly in Medicine Lodge. The job done, she arose in church the following Sunday and meticulously named the "offenders," a delicate move, for several were seated nearby, adoze after the medical, scientific and mechanical operations of Saturday night.

Not content with naming the fiends (as if they were not already known to everybody) Carry followed up by accosting them frequently on the streets. Her aim was to insult, with a variety of epithets that sometimes made sense and quite often didn't. "Hello, you rum-soaked Republican rummy" has been mentioned as having been among her favorites. Others were: "How do you do, maker of drunkards and widows," "Good day, you donkey-faced bedmate of Satan," and "Stand aside, you felonious purveyor of bottled drugs from Hell." The last of these, directed at the town's leading pharmacist, one of the most dignified, not to say pompous, men in Kansas, finally evoked a rumor that the city council had launched inquiries about a ducking stool, but nothing came of it; New England had perhaps cornered the market. At this rewarding stage of her life Mrs. Nation met a gifted and kindred though less violent spirit—Mrs. Wesley Cain, wife of the new Baptist preacher. Not the least of Mrs. Cain's possessions was a hand organ, which Carry immediately drew into use. The instrument was hoarse, and had an intermittent tone, and Mrs. Wesley Cain compounded its frailties by lapses in which she got her right index finger stuck in a defective valve. The two, Mrs. Nation and Mrs. Wesley Cain, formed a partnership that was aimed to eliminate all Medicine Lodge drinking, including that in the treatment of critical disease. First they held practice sessions to polish up a dual arrangement of hymns with temperance overtones. (Midway through the first of these Nation slammed out of the house without his hat.) When the partners considered them in shape (and reports claimed that both women were too easily satisfied) they spent a day praying and fasting. Then, on a Saturday afternoon late in the summer of 1899, they headed downtown into history.

If the success of a champion boxer may be laid partly to the wisdom of his preliminary choices, so must the brilliance of Mrs. Nation's mid-career derive from what went before. Medicine Lodge was an ideal arena for what might be called her out-of-town opening. Three whiskey drugstores and four regular joints brightened life for its residents, and turned like knives in the sides of Mrs. Nation and her sorority of shrews. With emotions of righteous anger, therefore, Carry and Mrs. Wesley Cain (the latter staggering beneath the burden of her dilapidated organ) strode down the main thoroughfare toward the boutique of one Mart Strong, jointist. Both crusaders wore "black alpaca dresses and their most becoming poke bonnets"; Mrs. Nation was carrying her umbrella, Mrs. Cain (as stated) the hand organ. In the course of their procession (remindful of the dead-march at the O.K. Corral) the morbid curious spilled out from store fronts and sidewalks to follow. Saturday was then, as it is now, market day in Medicine Lodge, and the crowd was in fiesta mood, if one may judge from a variety of encouragements which newspapers said ranged from "Sic 'em, you old bags!" to "I hope you get it in the neck, Carry Nation!"

Numerous accounts describe Strong's saloon as having previously been an orderly, cheerful mecca for the parched and the socially deprived. Before its rickety doors Mrs. Cain nevertheless unlimbered her hand organ, Mrs. Nation cried, *"Men and women of Medicine Lodge, this is a joint!"* surprising no one, and the two broke into song. Rather, they broke into two songs, for there was agreement among witnesses that, while Carry was singing, or squalling, "Who hath Sorrow? Who hath Woe?"—a leading anti-whiskey dirge—Mrs. Cain rendered "Nearer My God to Thee" on the machine. "Unmindful of the fact that Mrs. Cain played an entirely different tune," a reporter noted, "she [Carry] sang her favorite temperance song at the top of her voice." Characteristically, despite an animal chorus of derision from an estimated audience of two hundred, she sang the lugubrious tune on through to the final verse, which went:

> Touch not, taste not, handle not:
> Drink will make the dark, dark blot.
> Like an adder it will sting,
> And at last to ruin bring
> They who tarry at the drink.

When the last, split note died away, Mrs. Nation shouldered her umbrella like a musket, Mrs. Cain hefted the hand organ in the stance of a bomb, and they crashed through the swinging doors to an ardent cheer from the crowd, which now was panting for mayhem. Nobody among the onlookers left disappointed. The truth is that Mrs. Nation had misjudged Mart Strong, who, though courteous by nature, was a case-hardened loser in court and had the courage of his convictions. Carry and her colleague were scarcely inside the swinging doors when Strong skip-trotted out from behind the barrera like a Miura bull. Without ceremony, he seized Mrs. Nation and spun her around, after she'd chopped viciously at the air with her umbrella held in both hands; he yelled, "Get out of here, you crazy woman!" Then he tumbled her through the doors into the street. Mrs. Cain followed, unpropelled. Though repulsed, Mrs. Nation was far from daunted. A usually reliable source set the crusader's height at an even six feet in this period; her weight was 175 pounds, much of this muscle. The figures may be high. But she was in splendid shape, after the season of snooping for parked buggies (which involved quick sprints and footwork) and she backed off slightly, then launched another charge at Strong. On this round he caught her with a kind of football stiff-arm to the chest, which caused her to "bump" stern-to on the ground. Even Carry's wildest supporters scored it as a knockdown.

Things getting a trifle out of hand, Marshal Jim Gano, the usual Kansas officer of the era—soft-spoken but wistful about the chance to slap leather—spoke up from the crowd: "Now, Mart! Go easy, Mart!" The words were drowned in a species of wolf-like howls from Carry, on the ground, the noise finally revealing itself as a resumption of her dreadful hymn. At its conclusion she arose for the kill. In his intimate associations with lawmen, Strong had found no reason to fear them, and he abruptly shoveled Mrs. Nation with a thwack into Gano. The historian must admire Marshal Gano's self-control at this liberty. Eyeing Mrs. Nation, he said, with a sigh, "I sure wish I could take you off the streets." Carry then sailed into a memorable address that ranks with the more feverish babbling of Medicine Lodge's other nationally known citizen, Jeremiah ("Sockless Jerry") Simpson, the eccentric Populist (socialist) Congressman. Orating in his bare feet, as an inexplicable criticism of tariffs, he left posterity the ringing quotation,

"I can't have no drawers and ain't got no socks," the words presumably having some relevancy in the Congressman's mind.

"Yes," Carry cried. "You want to take me, a woman whose heart is breaking to see the ruin of these men, the desolate homes and broken laws, and you a constable oath-bound to close this man's unlawful business. Why don't you do your duty?"

The American psychology, a rather pulpy seed, has always been prone to irrational flipflops in favor of the underdog, and the sympathy of the crowd (swelled to five hundred) now shifted to Carry. The first signal was a reiterated chant, taken up by women, of, "Yes! Do your duty! Do your duty! Do your duty!" Strong was a scrapper but he knew odds, and he nipped back to his pothouse, banged shut the doors and persuaded those drinkers still on their feet to erect a hasty barricade of tables, chairs and barrels. So evident was his alarm that a handful of guzzlers sneaked out the rear exit, to be spied by Medicine Lodge's tardily-aroused females, who yelled, "Drunkards! Drunkards!" then tucked up their skirts and lit out in pursuit. Only one luckless farmhand failed to escape. In the semi-drunken act of climbing a fence, he snagged his jeans on a picket, was hauled down, dragged back and flung to his knees before Carry. Showing no mercy, she and Mrs. Wesley Cain lit into him with song and organ, a great many others joining, to the tune, "Yield Not to Temptation." During one lull, a wag crept forward and felt the farmhand's pulse, then sang out, "He's still alive, by gollies!" but Mrs. Nation took a swipe at him with her umbrella, and he scrambled back to safety.

The question has frequently been raised, What exactly sparked off Mrs. Nation's anti-liquor upheaval on this occasion? The answer is that she and Mrs. Wesley Cain, some months before, had commenced the organization of a Barber County Woman's Christian Temperance Union, modeled loosely after the national order, which was formed in 1874. Mrs. Nation was appointed Jail Evangelist of her group, a job in which she conveyed "religious and temperance propaganda" to the county lockup. The prisoners were a merry clique, and they all, without exception, whatever their crime, admitted that drink had caused their downfall. The artistic ribbing that Mrs. Nation took in this connection has been preserved partly by Sheriff Dobson, who told a Kansas City reporter, "She came to me and wanted to hold meetings in the county jail. I permitted her to go in and pray with the prisoners. Mrs. Nation is a very susceptible woman. She is an enthusiast, and is easily 'taken in.' One of my prisoners was a cowboy named Wash Philips. He was known as 'Red' Philips, and was in for cattle stealing. He was as tough as they grow. Mrs. Nation prayed frequently with Red, who would affect to be deeply interested. Mrs. Nation would tell me how happy she was to have converted Red. But Red would tell me that he was having glorious fun with Mrs. Nation, and his profanity in discussing her proved his non-conversion. She told me he was too good a man to keep in jail, that he was thoroughly converted and would never do wrong again. Red finally got out, and died with his boots on.

"Mrs. Nation gave me considerable trouble. She sometimes wanted to get into the jail to hold her services when it was not the proper time, and I had to refuse her. She would flare up in anger and upbraid me for my opposition (as she seemed to think) to religion. At other times when I would refuse her she would be as smiling as you please.

"Mrs. Nation is quite fierce when stirred. Her face, which has a benevolent aspect normally, becomes distorted with wrath, and she is not pleasant to look upon or to deal with when in those moods.

"She is a great talker—can talk your arm off if you let her. Back in Medicine Lodge she has been known always as a very determined woman. Whatever she believes in she believes with her whole soul, and nothing except superior force can stay her. She used to drive about the country collecting food and other supplies for the poor. She has done much good in that way, but when she sets out to get contributions she cannot be shaken off."

The raid on Mart Strong's had the effect of persuading the city fathers to close the place. The triumph was all Mrs. Nation needed to consolidate her thunders for new assaults. Her forays took on new verve and tone. Never was she so raucous in song, never Mrs. Cain's organ so busy. They held a series of street meetings, and, urged on by bystanders whose motives may now be seen as ambiguous, moved to choke off the town's remaining fountains of booze. It is conceivable that, to date in this narrative, Medicine Lodge has been presented as overly pliant, churchy and law-abiding. To leave such a mistaken impression would be unfair to Carry Nation's awesome courage. Apart from her, the town had other hellions, and other troubles. Dodge City in its heyday was hardly more abrupt in its methods. Nearby lay the vast, murky reaches of the Indian Territory, haven of outlaws and misfits, from which desperadoes frequently rode for the simple, recreational purpose of turning things topsy-turvy in Kansas. Many of the people with whom Carry tilted were as reliable as a grizzly with a toothache; she began to brace men on the streets—snatching pipes, cigars and Mexican *cigarritos* from their mouths—who would have shot a fellow male for a careless slip of the tongue. A leading antagonist was a combination saloonkeeper and poet called the Pilgrim Bard, who kept the Last Chance Tavern, a hellhole on the highway toward the Rockies (which were presumed to be dry). The Bard's musings have largely been lost to posterity, but we have the word of a Mrs. S. T. Roach, as captured by the Kansas Historical Collections, that "He was very prolific in his writings. Being almost altogether uneducated, a great part of his productions were of course worthless." The following selection, which he dashed off between ladling out beer and rescuing drunks from the floor, supports her contention: "Every bright and pearly dewdrop falls like a weeping angel's tear, and the ring dove's note on the zephyr's float, mourning for those who perished here, in the cold, cold waves and the darkness drear. The soil we tread is sacred as the soil 'neath the churchyard yew; while the household slept the dark waves crept. No farewell blessing, no fond adieu, closed those eyes forever to mortal view."

In a rough way, the lines were meant to commemorate Medicine Lodge's municipal cemetery, which the Bard's dive had helped fill, and while they are insufficient to disturb the ghost of Thomas Gray, they present the funereal vein of most local poesy in the era—hopeless and dripping with tears. By coincidence, another writer of the town was Carry's chief opponent in debate— one T. A. McNeal, to whom we are indebted for a vignette of the unpredictable sun-baked village. Medicine Lodge went in heavily for picnics that featured a program of games and speeches, along with lemonade and a barbecued steer, and it was McNeal's whim to place himself on the list just ahead of Carry, then to spin out his address until she was frothing with rage. It was during these intolerable waits that she conceived the habit of snatching firebrands from the mouths of tobacco smokers. McNeal had come to town from southern Illinois around 1880, invited to edit the Barber County *Mail*. The paper had developed a vacancy. The previous owner, a Mr. Cochrane, had been pursuing an editorial line that "a party of people in Medicine Lodge" found distasteful. The reason has been lost in time—something to do with a murder case—but when representations were made, without response, the logical frontier step remained: Cochrane must be tarred and feathered and ridden out of town on a rail. It is a curious truth that, through the rise of civilization, the best-laid civic plans fall apart over mechanical trifles. The French Revolution was slowed to a walk by a scarcity of guillotines, and the Romans had trouble stocking enough lions to eat the increasing supply of Christians. Now, at Cochrane's crisis, no tar was found in Medicine Lodge, and not one housewife stepped forward to offer up pillows. But the townsfolk showed their mettle when, after apologizing to Cochrane for an embarrassing breach of form (he appears not to have replied), they covered him with molasses and sprinkled him with sandburs. Then he was given the ride to which he was entitled.

The merit, the real historic value, of McNeal's account lies in his description of what happened next. The foregoing was, of course, routine; McNeal's view of the *Mail*'s new owner provides a sharp picture of a familiar regional type. After explaining that Cochrane had been "rescued by friends," and that he had nevertheless sold out, to an unknown quantity named Ezra Iliff, McNeal continues: "When I entered the *Mail* office on that windy March day, Iliff was seated at a pine table. In front of him lay his '.45' revolver, fully loaded. He filled my imagination of what 'Jim Bledsoe' * of the *Arizona Kicker* ought to look like. His hair, black and coarse as that of an Indian, fell down over his collar. His eyes, black and flashing, looked out from beneath beetling brows with hairs stiff and wiry and as long as the ordinary moustache. His dress was in keeping with his appearance. Around his neck was a red bandana kerchief. His dark gray woolen shirt, flaring open

* The reference is to Bret Harte's character, the engineer of the Prairie Bell.

slightly at the throat, revealed in part the muscular neck and hirsute breast. He wore the leather 'chaps' common to the cow men of that day, and his pants, stuffed in his boots, were held in place by a belt well filled with loaded cartridges. A woven rawhide quirt hung from his left wrist. The heels of his boots were ornamented with savage-looking spurs. He was booted and spurred and ready to ride. But he was not just then thinking of the range. He was engaged in writing a most vigorous editorial, as I recall, on the Hillman case."

The new owner, a little better armed, had simply taken up where Cochrane left off.

With such buckaroos as Iliff, Carry Nation feuded during most of her career. They were very dangerous men, a fact that appeared to whet her appetite, or pique her curiosity. Sheriff Dobson, in another interview, expressed the opinion that his principal nemesis had "a strong arm," and a contemporary journalist may have implied physical primacy when he wrote that "At no time during their matrimonial career did David [Nation] attain to a higher rank than second lieutenant in that household." Awestruck, a neighboring newspaper told the odd grievance of a W. C. McDill, whose experience with Carry equated her with the biblical David, with reference to the impertinent assault on Goliath. According to the piece, "W. C. McDill says that when he was playing a quiet game of whist in the office of the hotel in Medicine Lodge last summer, she saw them through the window and came in. The other boys saw her coming and hid their cards, but he sat there with a royal flush in his fist and wondered what was the matter with them, until the old lady entangled her fingers in his locks and asked him if he had a mother and if he didn't know it was dead wrong to play cards." The story has unique features, including the validity of a royal flush in a whist hand, and its aftermath involved the consulting of a local sage, Mr. Bramwell, Republican leader, about the question of Mrs. Nation's sanity. "She is eccentric in many things," stated Bramwell, after some thought, "but sharp as a tack, and anyone who undertakes to prove her non-compos will have an uphill job." From the reporting it seems clear that the technical point of sanity arose not from her interruption of the game *per se* but because she broke in when a player was holding a royal flush. Thus the genial Kansas philosophy before the reformers came.

An admirer of her later period called Carry "a tough old bird" but deplored that "she took terrible chances." And all down the line her muscular force was noted. In her mind, the foregone sequel to her liquidation of Strong's must be a march on one of the iniquitous drugstores. The episode was to have distinctive characteristics. Site of the inquiry was the pharmacy of O. L. Day, a prime target because Day had not even bothered to obtain an official permit to sell prescription whiskey illegally. The Barber County W.C.T.U. remained dubious about Carry's unholy row at Strong's; all the same, the members voted to close ranks for the assault on Day's. General-like, Carry chose herself and a Mrs. Noble, an amateur horse wrangler, for the role of storm troops, with the redoubtable Mrs. Wesley Cain (minus the organ) tapped to bring up reinforcements. When word came that a new ten-pound keg had been slipped into Day's back door, the battle was on.* The date was February 16, 1900, one memorable, but not memorialized, in Medicine Lodge history. Carry and Mrs. Noble crashed into the drugstore, and after a verbal skirmish in which Day was characterized as "a fool and a rummy," the women pushed past him to the back room, where the keg lay visible under his "prescription counter." "Women!" cried Carry, seeming to address Mrs. Noble, *here* is the whiskey!" Day explained reasonably that the keg contained "fine California brandy," costing seventy-five dollars, which was lying dormant until he obtained a permit, at which time he hoped to jack up Medicine Lodge's health. Mrs. Nation's reply was, "It's devil's brew to destroy the souls of men!"

The physical struggle was now joined. Carry leaped astride the keg, the ubiquitous Marshal Gano materialized from nowhere and Day gave her a push—a silly action for he was a frail man and Mrs. Nation swiped him out of the way with one arm. He landed in a corner, a painfully bruised druggist. Meanwhile Gano used the hiatus to place Mrs. Nation's head in chancery (to employ the jargon of the period); more familiarly, he applied a headlock, caus-

---

* To glean intelligence of whiskey-sellers, the crusader had formed a young espionage network not dissimilar to the later Nazi werewolves.

ing Mrs. Nation to cry out that "My neck's breaking!" whereat the faithful Mrs. Cain lit on the establishment with reinforcements. It was finished in a twinkling. When someone ripped away Gano's coat collar, he headed for the open air, all fight removed. "Roll out the broth of hell!" Carry cried, and the keg was kicked into the street. A woman who ran to a nearby hardware store and demanded a hatchet met unexpected resistance when the proprietor, a mule-headed man with a fine record of standing up to Amazons, replied that he was "in the business of selling hatchets, not giving them away." Though a teetotaler, he was loudly berated as a rummy, and the woman fled to a smithy across the street. The blacksmith stood petrified, or fused, while she snatched up his heaviest maul and delivered it to Carry. Then a great shout arose when Mrs. Nation smote the keg "with such force that the liquor streamed out many feet up in the air," as the Kansas *Journal* afterward stated. The shout came mainly from a swarm of low fellows who, in the style of looters at an important fire, arrived, running, with cups. "Form a line!" yelled Mrs. Cain. "Don't anyone touch these women! They are Christian women trying to save the boys of our state!" and the hopefuls were thus blocked off. Carry administered the *coup de grâce* by grabbing a broom, sweeping the freed booze into a gutter, and setting it afire. The mingled groans and huzzahs neatly divided the town, placing nearly everybody on record one way or another.

It would be slipshod to pass on to Carry's larger, out-of-town exploits without mentioning her encounter at the "restaurant" of Hank O'Bryan. His joint was the last in Medicine Lodge that she had to close forcibly—town officials shut down the rest. For some reason Carry tackled O'Bryan's alone, possibly because she knew the bartender, Black Jack Grogan, whose soul she had been trying to bullyrag into safe hands for years. Grogan was something of a comic, given to ornate gestures, and when he spied her coming in he sprinted across the shop and made a graceful dive for a window. Mrs. Nation intercepted him, clutching the tails of his apron. "You have a joint here," she said sternly. "No, Mother Nation, you are wrong," he was quoted as answering. She said, "I smell the horrid drink," then charged through several rooms and passageways to a cubbyhole at the rear, where sat a dignified-looking man, wearing a hat, at a table on which stood a beer bottle. He was a Mr. Smith, of Sharon, Kansas, who had ridden in for a quiet day's soaking. "I suppose you know you are going to hell," she remarked conversationally, and the authorities remain in disagreement about his reply. It was either, "Madam, won't you draw up a chair and join me?" or (studying the apparition) "I may have had one too many," depending on which fun-loving reporter the researchist favors.

"What was in this?" demanded the crusader, raising the bottle. The irrepressible Grogan was able to clarify the point, and he did. "Hop tea," he said. "Does Anheuser-Busch manufacture hop tea?" inquired Mrs. Nation, inspecting the label. "Now, Mother Nation, if you get me into trouble, I will do something desperate," said Grogan, and she replied, "I do not wish to get either of you into trouble; I wish to get you out." Then she opened her Bible to read a number of anti-drink passages and delivered a skull-cracking lecture, during the end of which Smith began bawling for more beer. But they were not yet done. Mrs. Nation thrust both men down on their knees (Smith protesting feebly) and resumed her prayers for an hour, or until Smith appeared on the verge of delerium tremens. Grogan, on the other hand, at last assumed a thoughtful expression and later moved to Wichita, opened a knick-knack shop and rose to a position of power in one of the city's hardest-hitting Sunday Schools. It may be that he'd decided to bore from within. We have only Mrs. Nation's word that Smith, of Sharon, degenerated from beer (or hop tea) to gin, whiskey, rum and brandy and, at length, "became a perfect wreck and lost his business."

Up to this point, Mrs. Nation could scarcely be said to have had the sympathy of Medicine Lodge. The celerity of its townspeople in crossing the street on her approach was matched only by the low esteem in which she was held by the churches. The aftermath of her Medicine Lodge raids changed everything. Both Carry and Mrs. Wesley Cain found themselves subject to reprisals by pro-liquor gangs that swooped down (after dark) for hit-and-run raids that left an untidiness of broken windows, smashed fences, killed chickens, littered yards and damaged outbuildings. Mrs. Nation's buggy was put out of commission and her harness all cut, a setback that merely provoked her to buy a sidesaddle, which she used on her horse, "Old Prince," for the rural visits among the penurious and the backslid. She was described as an unusual sight—175 pounds asymmetrically athwart the complaining beast, garbed all in customary black, her formal bonnet tied securely on, umbrella slung in a rifle-holster, and various baskets and packages fastened here and there to rings. She rode at a gallop, and took no nonsense from the horse, which was, or had been, male.

As well as possible, Carry staved off the guerrillas, and Nation himself infrequently appeared at a doorway, to voice some small threat of litigation, maybe supported by a mention of precedents. Finally she was visited by a Negro friend, a career bootlegger (it's odd how often Carry Nation's professional life became involved with Negroes) who warned her of a meeting he attended in which some men were making plans to burn her home. Thanking him, she expressed herself as delighted. Her specific reply, as reported in the autobiography, was, "You ought to know by now that such men as these will not prevent me from doing my duty. Besides, should my home be burned it would be a lecture in favor of my cause that would be worth more to me than the home." Nation filed a minority report, her hope for conflagration was noised around and the plot collapsed.

Nearly any sufferer—even a monster with a record of three child murders and a series of multiple rapes—finally wins the lachrymose acclaim of America, and Carry began to find herself lionized. She actually *had* turned Medicine Lodge into an alcoholic desert, pleasing many wives, and a large number of people theretofore indifferent to drink openly admired her courage. Another factor, perhaps decisive, was that the town had suddenly become equipped with a recreational facility. In a village where a dogfight was a conversational luxury, it was pleasant to watch a group of dowagers slugging it out in the street with bartenders. Even Mrs. Wesley Cain's organ, esthetically atrocious, came in for lefthanded compliments, her auditors taking the stand that really it could be worse. Boredom is doubtless the consuming dry rot of man, and Medicine Lodge, overnight, considered itself blessed. Thoreau's "lives of quiet desperation" no longer applied to the residents of Barber County; Carry never gave anyone a dull moment.

Elderly residents of the town recall her with pleasure. Mrs. Arthur Martin, wife of a state welfare executive, lived next door to the Nations as a child and found the experience rewarding. "I belonged to an out-and-out Prohibition family, and we all admired and loved Mrs. Nation," she said. "I can testify she was a very quiet, pleasant person to have about the house. She always asked a blessing at meals. Children were all drawn to her. She had a big purse full of nickels and dimes and always brought us presents from her various trips. The only time I ever saw her in action was when she jerked a cigar out of the mouth of Bill Horn, the old Medicine Lodge stage driver and a reprobate if ever there was one. He pulled her out of the stage by the hair and drove off without her. Except for that one instance, I remember her as a quiet motherly soul with a great fondness for children."

Mr. Martin's sister, Mrs. Riley MacGregor, considered Mrs. Nation a warm and generous and friendly woman in the Medicine Lodge years. "I can remember her coming to the fence between our place and hers and calling out to my mother, 'Sister Martin, come here, somebody's baked me a caramel cake and I want to give it to the children.' I used to run over to her house and ask her for hoe cakes; that's a hot corn pone, you know, split and buttered; Negroes used to bake them on hoes for their noon meal in the field. Mrs. Nation was famous for her hoe cakes. She used to rock me and sing to me. I had an extraordinary dislike of Mr. Nation. I can still remember puzzling over what the word 'pension' meant, because I once heard him say to her, 'Wife, my pension came today and you don't get a penny of it.' [Nation had been a Union Army officer, as explained, and was later a minor government functionary.] He was the minister in the Christian Church and he himself helped unchurch her because she befriended a girl with an illegitimate child."

Fortified with her new, respectable aura, Carry commenced to lay plans for a non-local foray. Throughout her life she had an instinctive sense of timing, and the signs now suggested that she was ready for larger game. A heartening element was that, recently, she'd been elected president of the county W.C.T.U. while retaining her portfolio of Jail Evangelist. For the first time, she felt certain of her organization's implied backing for any adventure, however exotic. Bearing these facts in mind, casting about for a spot hopelessly depraved, she chose for her attentions the harmless, half-asleep town of Kiowa, twenty-five miles distant, almost astraddle the Indian Territory line. In retrospect, one finds it hard to fix on the reasons for Mrs. Nation's selection, aside from the fact that ruffians drifted through the border sanctum, from one direction or another, for purposes only vaguely connected with good works. Kiowa's six unabashed joints were about the usual complement for a town of seven hundred, and none of these enjoyed a conspicuously lurid reputation. Carry herself, relating her story in court, disclosed that (before the assault) "I prayed to the Lord, and He opened the way for me. It came to me one morning before I got up." No responsible person can believe that Jehovah was so biased as to direct her to Kiowa specifically, but another source stated that "she was awakened by a musical voice which murmured in her ear, 'Go to Kiowa!' " Whatever the drill, she accepted the offstage voice as a mandate, and Kiowa emerged as its target.

Once again, no reason has been given why Mrs. Nation decided to go it alone. Her sisters of the W.C.T.U. now stood clamorously behind her, Mrs. Wesley Cain had shown a capacity for field command at Strong's and it would have been simple to recruit a task force in depth. Nevertheless, in the evolution of her scheme, or caper, she seems not to have considered the enlistment of subordinates. All tricky military operations call for fine-ground planning; on this occasion Mrs. Nation started at the grass roots and built with precision. Taking a burlap bag, she retired to an uncleared field and began to gather up rocks. When the job was done, she placed these in her buggy (now mended) together with half a dozen bricks found in her own back yard—part of a former outhouse reduced in a raid by habitués of a defunct saloon. The arsenal was complete, her spirits were never keener; Carry was ready for her first publicized descent on the national temperance scene.

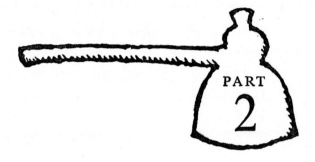

PART

2

FERMENTATION

Chapter Seven

The title selected by Carry Nation for her autobiography—*The Use and Need of the Life of Carry A. Nation*—was entirely suitable to the work. In the amusement and reproach that attended her struggle, most people lost sight of the hold that liquor had gained on Americans in the hundred or so years preceding the crusader's birth in 1846. It is not too much to say that the new western nation was a land cemented together by rum.

Dr. Karl Menninger, a founder of the famous Menninger clinic in Topeka, reminisced in a magazine piece about America's early liquor situation (and about Mrs. Nation) saying, "My grandmother was one of the many pioneer women who was stimulated to express resentment in the same way that Carry Nation did. She and a group of women smashed a saloon or two in the little farm town where they lived and where liquor was being illegally sold. Of course I got a somewhat prejudiced view of this as a child, but I do remember how helpless the pioneers felt in that little community when, for example, the only doctor available, a certain Dr. S., was a notorious drunkard and he would attend childbirth and serious sickness in a state of obvious inebriation. Other farmers would get gloriously drunk and beat their horses and their children and this would become public knowledge, and cause great indignation which was then transferred to these illegal liquor joints. I don't blame the pioneers a bit for feeling pretty damn mad about it. I have often explained to some of the many people I have brought to Kansas that the old prohibition sentiment wasn't as foolish as they may think.

"Drunken marauding was a pretty serious thing in those days. One must remember that the state was full of psychopaths and unstable characters who had failed in the East and had come out here to make a new start. They caused a lot more damage to life and property than did the Indians. It was tough going out here and the temptation to get drunk and forget it was pretty widespread, I have no doubt, but on the other hand, the sober, conscientious, hardworking, straitlaced folks who came out here to save the state from slavery must have been pretty disheartened to find that they had other things to combat besides grasshoppers, drought, slave squatters, Indians, chiggers and poverty.

"What I have always admired about Carry Nation was the fact that she couldn't stomach hypocrisy and I wish that there were more people today who feel the same way."

Spirits were often mentioned in the colonial laws under the affectionate term "the good creature of God." While this was (as far as is known) lacking in scriptural authority, ministers took it at face value and became perhaps the worst nuisance on the general intemperance scene. The Reverend Nathan Strong, pastor of the First Church of Hartford, Connecticut, an evangelist of remorseless piety, operated a distillery "within sixty rods of his church." He was not alone. It was common for clergymen to own interests in distilleries and taverns, frequently tending bar or handing out bottles in the off-hours when they were not publicly flogging the devil. The Reverend Leonard Woods, professor at Andover Theological Seminary, recalled a period when he could "reckon up among my acquaintances forty ministers who were either drunkards, or so far addicted to drinking, that their reputation and usefulness were greatly impaired, if not utterly ruined."

These were the leaders, the setters of the intellectual pace, guardians of the community morals. A Boston newspaper was quoted as saying that "a great many deacons in New England died drunkards," and Stewart Holbrook has related in *Dreamers of*

the American Dream that more than half of the clergy around
Albany, New York, were steady drinkers "and some were downright sots." More specifically of Albany, a Mr. Delavan complained by letter to Governor King that "fifty percent of the clergy
within a circuit of fifty miles" went to a drunkard's grave. Of the
city's twenty-eight clerics in 1820, only one could be persuaded to
speak up in behalf of temperance. The Reverend Woods, at Andover, was so far distressed by the indecorous cavortings of his guild
that he published a letter, in 1836, describing an ordination fete at
which "I myself was ashamed and grieved to see two aged ministers literally drunk, and a third indecently excited with strong
drink." Ordinations and funerals were slightly ahead of other
church functions in the orgiastic quality of their programs. The
Reverend I. N. Tarbox said in a lecture of the 1800's that "ordinations were seasons of festivity, in which copious drinking had a
large share, and an ordination ball often ended the occasion."
Herbert Asbury, a descendant of Methodist Bishop Francis Asbury, has added that the Reverend Tarbox "was being somewhat
conservative; in reality many ordinations were drunken routs, at
which everybody got well plastered. Funerals," Asbury went on,
"were likewise occasions of considerable jollity; once the corpse
had been disposed of, everybody pitched in to drink up the pota-
bles that had been provided." As a rule, these were considerable.
At one important Boston funeral (for the widow of a preacher)
the mourners required fifty-one and a half gallons of Malaga wine
to dull their grief, and at another, in Virginia, the liquor costs were
met by the expenditure of four thousand pounds of tobacco.
Twenty-four pastors in Hartford gave their colleagues something
to shoot at, in 1784, when they gathered for the ordination of a
new member and downed "3 bitters, 15 boles [bowls] punch, 11
bottles wine, 5 mugs flip, 3 boles toddy, 3 boles smash." Hartford
was a center of ministerial soaking, but great things were also
going forward in Massachusetts, especially in Woburn, where the
ordination of the Reverend Edwin Jackson shrank the ecclesiastical cellars by "six and one half barrels of cider, twenty-five gallons
of wine, two gallons of brandy, and four gallons of rum." A statistical study at elderly houses of worship shows that ordinations led
funerals by a nose, or snoot-ful, in the amount of spirits consumed;

a possible reason, with particular reference to New England, was that the church paid the liquor bills at ordinations and the family of the deceased got stuck for everything at funerals.

The Reverend Lyman Beecher, a progenitor of the American temperance movement, took a pastorate in Litchfield, Connecticut, in 1810, and soon afterward described an ordination at Plymouth: ". . . the preparation for our creature comforts, besides food, was a broad sideboard covered with decanters and bottles and sugar and pitchers of water. There we found all the various kinds of liquor then in vogue. The drinking was apparently universal. The preparation was made by the society, as a matter of course. When the Consociation arrived, they always took something to drink round, also before public services, and always on their return. As they could not all drink at once, they were obliged to stand and wait as people do when they go to mill. There was a decanter of spirits also on the dinner table, to help digestion, and gentlemen partook of it through afternoon and evening as they felt the need, some more and some less; and the sideboard, with its spillings of water and sugar and liquor, looked and smelled like the bar of a very active grog shop."

Litchfield County, Connecticut, is a hilly green region of prosperous hamlets with elm-shaded streets and dazzling white houses that look up to lean, unfrivolous church spires; its people are worthy citizens who absorb without question the Sunday wisdom of eager young (socially pure) clerics fresh from the seminary, throw themselves unsparingly into good works and, often, hug to their bosoms inherited nut-and-bolt wealth in a kind of nervous ancestral rite. They are dependable in personal crises. The community has changed little in the eight or nine generations since its founding. In 1830 it had a rude exposure to the limelight with a filing of the First Annual Report of the Connecticut State Temperance Society. The Society's catchiest item, from the county's viewpoint, was that "in one of the most moral and regular towns of Litchfield County, whose population is 1,586, the amount of distilled liquors retailed during the last ten years has been 36,400 gallons." There were other eye-openers. In 1827, "the village of Salisbury had consumed twenty-nine and one half gallons of rum for each of its thirty-four families." The figures were of course comparative. Nearby Hartford, said the report, annually sold 178,000 gallons of hard liquors. Perhaps in extenuation of Connecticut, the Society aimed its sights as well on Dudley, Massachusetts, where in 1829 the nineteen hundred inhabitants drank 10,000 gallons of rum; Troy, New York, with a population of ten thousand, put away 73,959 gallons; and, sure enough, Albany, the world capital of riotous clergymen, took all prizes with a consumption (again in 1829) of 200,000 gallons for the 20,000 inhabitants. As the report pointed out, this was an average of ten gallons for every man, woman and child.

The last-named figures do not imply that the adults necessarily drank more than the bare, statistical ten gallons each. In that heyday of American drinking, children hit it up pretty hard, as an early (1830) edition of the *Old American Encyclopedia* and other sources made clear. It was the custom—*de rigueur* in the South—for everybody to drink a glass of mint-flavored whiskey immediately upon awaking in the morning: ". . . no sex, and scarcely any age, were deemed exempt from its application." Crying babies were not a serious problem in colonial times; they were promptly dosed with enough alcohol to shift them into a state of glassy-eyed stupefaction, upon which the caterwauling dried up, to be replaced by pleasurable cooings or song, the intoxicated infant's version of "Sweet Adeline." All over the nation, the arrival of eleven A.M. was the signal for a reprieve from work and a half-hour's recourse to the jug. "Leven O'clock Bitters" was the designation of this happy interlude, which the males filled in with rum punch, hot or cold, and the ladies brightened with euphemisms like "Hexham's Tincture," and "Stoughton's Elixir," either potion containing enough alcohol to pickle zoological specimens. The lunch, or "dinner," hour soon followed, ushered in usually by whiskey-and-water flavored with apples, which the *Old American Encyclopedia* was candid enough to admit had a "curious flavor," but the complaint was unimportant because the punch absorbed shortly before had anesthetized the diners to a point where they could have drunk bilge water from a slave ship and not known the difference.

The midday meal itself was improved by generous intakes of whiskey-and-water or brandy-and-water, and, afterward, digestion was "secured" by unwatered tots of the foregoing. Except in special cases, all was quiet now until four o'clock when the parched populace broke loose with an "evening" counterpart of Leven O'clock Bitters. Supper was essentially a repetition of dinner, but with stepped-up amounts of spirits to ward off the nocturnal chill. Retiring for the night was almost unthinkable without downing some warm punch to induce sound sleep, and there were special cases where rum was hurled into a surprising range of emergencies. Rum seasoned with cherries drove back a cold; rum laced with milk, if taken in sufficient quantities, guaranteed an easy pregnancy (though not an absolutely normal baby); rum thickened by aloes was excellent for soaking a sore toe; rum with peppermint fought off measles; rum with seawater was a quick and powerful emetic (though seawater alone would probably have proved just as effective); in one area, a solution of rum and horse urine was regarded as a sure preventive of corpulence, the theory being, possibly, that a single treatment could kill the sufferer's appetite for a week.

Emetics ordinarily were not needed on the pioneer drinking scene. In a temperance tract of the early 1800's we get a picture of American "society's" dining salon, but the writing is disorganized, and the author was undoubtedly talking about taverns: "All tables were full of vomit and filthiness—there was no place clean." The tract goes on to say that "Old persons now living, who, in their youth, had large acquaintance with public men, can tell us how many eminent citizens, how many honorable judges, how many beloved physicians, passed in their latter days under a cloud which rested at last upon their graves; and the ecclesiastical and clerical records of every denomination show how common a thing it used to be for an aged and venerable minister of the gospel, as his natural force abated, to decline into habits which demanded his seclusion from the ministry."

Early taverns were places of paradise for the tippler of limited means. In his pamphlet called "The Drunkard's Looking Glass," the Reverend Mason L. ("Parson") Weems set forth a tavern bill, dated April 1, 1812, for a single day's sustenance by a Mr. Thomas C—:

3 mint slings before breakfast, 25¢	$0.75
1 breakfast	.50
9 tumblers of Grog before dinner, 12½¢	1.12½
3 glasses of Wine and Bitters, 12½¢	.37½
Dinner and club	1.25
2 ticklers of French Brandy, 25¢	.50
Cigars	.25
Supper and Wine	1.25
Total	$6.00

Now and then someone struck a blow at the reputed therapy of drink, but the opposition was slow to develop in America. Offsetting this, powerful singers stepped forward to sound the alarm in both England and Scotland, traditional sinkholes of drunkenness, and many of the best-known sophistries of the practice were attacked point by point. Dr. J. Livesy Preston was especially articulate on the subject of children, and issued a lively and informative list of specific dos and don'ts. Preston had already made his mark with "Advice to Females on the Subject of Temperance," in which he probed some delicate aftermaths of women swilling to excess in pubs, so that his words carried weight. Among other things, he said:

"Never give gin to destroy worms in children."

"Raw brandy in repeated doses can be injurious to the stomach-linings of children below ten years of age."

"Infants that are drugged with gin to remove wind and indigestion are sometimes even crosser."

"Never attempt to cure a cold by giving a child rum or warm ale."

"Discourage children from frequenting 'dram shops.'"

Preston's shafts struck at the heart of American pediatrics, and his meddling was resented. His tracts are interesting because they never seem able to stick very long to one subject. His advices to the young included the irrelevant but timely admonition, "Discountenance funeral drinking" (presumably aimed at adults, as children were not encouraged to get under foot at grown-up entertainments) ; then he wandered back onto the subject of women. Preston's principal reminder to the gentle sex, all the way down the line, was "Don't frequent Jerry shops with women's money clubs for social drinking." A "Jerry shop," in the England of the opening 1800's, was a species of inelegant, coeducational tavern, and a "money club" was usually a room with separate facilities, supported by subscription, wherein housewives of similar tastes could foregather to sip and gossip. It was Dr. Preston's feeling, based on experience, that the clubwomen nearly always established a warm peak of outlook and strayed into the men's precincts, after which their problem shifted from the alcoholic to the obstetrical. It was not true, as Preston hinted, that bar whiskey in Jerry shops was manufactured from "prussic acid, old boots and pigtail tobacco." The writer deplored the amenity, observed in England and America, of women having from two to eight ritual drinks of sherry when making calls on female friends, and he came out strong against one of the social grace notes of his day—the offer of a free drink to any wife who dropped by a tavern to collect her husband. The point was made that women appreciated this so keenly that many took to dropping in for their husbands five or six times a day, whether the men were around or not; and then, as the evening wore on, the husbands found themselves trying to collect the wives. In his views, Preston sometimes appeared to lack gallantry.

Other anti-liquor voices were feebly raised in protest, before the real start of an organized temperance movement in 1808. Both in England and in America it was felt that a curtailment of the retail trade might appreciably slow down the guzzling. Any number of alarmists hoped so in England, for Henry Fielding, in a pamphlet of 1751, gave gin as "the principal sustenance of more than a hundred thousand people" in London. The drink was so cheap, so successful in soothing proletarian complaints, that nearly every dwelling of the slums offered it for sale. Those establishments which aspired to the loftier title of "gin mill" usually displayed a beckoning sign: "Drunk for a penny, dead drunk for tuppence"; and, in the hospitable style of the region, provided free straw for collapsed celebrants to flop on. Curiously, the retail solution was raised in an early American medical tract called *The Influence of Ardent Spirits in the Production of Cholera.* After parading some impressive statistics tending to prove that "Persons who hurry into excess and dissipation become the first victims of cholera," the authors suggested that "Retail sellers furnish the grand incentives to the use of these liquors in our cities" and claimed that "Many who drink much are too poor to buy by the quantity and literally live, in relation to the glass, *from hand to mouth!*" In this line, the Methodists (well toward the front in American drinking) eventually went on record with one of the genuinely insipid resolutions in church history. It stated that none of the order's clergymen could retail spirits or malt liquors "without forfeiting his ministerial character among us." This was a setback, but the ministers were not inhibited from wholesaling liquors, and they continued to do so, while the Baptists, no less thirsty and even more bullheaded, continued until 1854 to expel any member who joined a temperance society.

An effort to circularize liquor as being concocted of poisons had little effect, and died early. James Gordon Bennett's New York *Herald* stated flatly that "Beer is largely adulterated. The brewers use *glucose, bad malt, cigar butts, resin, soap and leather scraps,* besides *cocculus indicus* and *drugs.*" (The italics are the *Herald*'s.) Any conceivable benefit that might have accrued from this palpable string of deceits was negated by Bennett's reputation as being an extreme, a dedicated, practically a gibbering bluenose; his readers declined to believe that a brewer had time to run around picking up cigar butts to put in beer, and one letter writer inquired sourly, "Is soap cheaper than hops?" A Reverend P. Coombe now leaped into the breach with a fighting brochure entitled "The Missing Link in the Chain of Evidence AGAINST THE LIQUOR TRAFFIC or a Terrible Revelation of Fraud, Drugging and Poisoning." Reverend Coombe (plainly out of step with his colleagues) did a masterly job of research, concentrating his wrath on the handbook of an F. A. Eichler, "Practical Distiller from the Kingdom of Saxony," then residing in Philadelphia, the city of brotherly love. Eichler sold recipes ("receipts") for faking, or imitating, nearly every kind of fancy liquor from vintage champagne to hundred-year-old brandy. He worked hand-in-hand with Philadelphia's best-known drug house, which stocked all the required essences, drugs, juices, berries, chemicals, oils, flavors and extracts. The published list, for purposes of advertisement, was a document to give any sane drinker pause, but readers were alerted only by the claim that "Eichler's Receipts will save you hundreds of dollars which you are now paying to others for preparing your Whiskies, Brandies, Gins, etc. . . . Liquors made according to these receipts so closely resemble the genuine that they cannot be distinguished."

The Reverend P. Coombe bounced back by analyzing two hogsheads of "Seignette" brandy, which had been ordered as authentic medical supplies by a druggist in Ohio. The brew proved so vile that the druggist, after tasting it, spat it onto the floor. On analysis (with the Ohio State Chemist in attendance) the Seignette was found to contain "sulphuric acid, nitric acid, nitric ether, prussic acid, guano pepper and an abundance of fusel oil." One part of the experiment remained obscure; nobody could explain it. When a steel knife blade was dipped into a tumbler of the brandy, the liquor "turned black as ink." On its removal, fifteen minutes later, the blade had a "thick coating of rust," and when this was scraped off, it presented a heavy copper veneer "almost as if it had been copper plated." There being no sensible chemical replies to these phenomena, the question was raised, probably by liquor agents— did the Reverend Coombe, the State Chemist and the druggist finish off one hogshead before analyzing the contents of the other? The incident was soon forgotten as people, undisturbed, resumed the drinking of Seignette brandy (including sulphuric acid, nitric acid, nitric ether, prussic acid, guano pepper and an abundance of fusel oil).

The Reverend Coombe himself became a little acid about Eichler's attentions to women, and conducted a campaign to halt the manufacture of "rare old European cordials" in Philadelphia barns and woodsheds. "Absinthe is one of the deadliest poisons," Coombe noted, "yet Mr. Eichler makes Absinthe Cordials for the ladies, as follows: 'Two ounces of essence of absinthe, four ounces of green coloring, one gallon of simple syrup, and four gallons of rectified spirits.' Here we have about five gallons of cordial with two ounces of *poison* and two gallons of *pure alcohol.* Rather strong, this for ladies." He explained that "rectified spirits" was a dressed-up name for the product of filtration, through a piece of cheesecloth or a bottleful of sand, to sift out the larger cockroaches and spiders, and had no medical significance. "Persico Cordial,

Eichler makes as follows," the Reverend continued: " 'Two ounces of concentrated essence of bitter almond (Prussic Acid), one and a half gallons of rectified spirits, and one gallon of simple syrup.' . . . Cherry Bounce is also made by Mr. Eichler, but here he is more moderate; he only puts two ounces of Prussic Acid in about seven gallons—not enough to kill, merely enough to perforate the intestines." Though his detestation of Eichler is clear, Reverend Coombe permitted a note of near-admiration to creep into his section on brandies, whiskies and gin (and Eichler did indeed offer hope for the large-scale drinker): "In this remarkable circular [Coombe wrote] we are told that half a pint of brandy flavor turns 40 gallons of rectified spirits into French Brandy, that the same quantity of concentrated essence of Holland gin turns 40 gallons of rectified spirits into Holland Gin. And, more remarkable still, *one-fourth* of a pint of the essence of Cabinet Whiskey, or of Irish Whiskey, or of Monongahela Whiskey, has the marvelous power of converting 40 gallons of rectified spirits into these respective drinks. If we are astonished at the power of Christ, who turned water into wine, what must we think of these men, who, without any miracle, can turn 40 gallons of whiskey into all these drinks, with a half pint of something else?"

It has been remarked as odd that America's Puritans did not act to curb the unrestrained wallowing in spirits. Their attitude is understandable when one considers that the prosperity of all New England rested on rum. For a century Boston distilled and drank more rum than any other city in America, and the Puritan farmers of Massachusetts, attentive to both God and success, though not in that order, commonly sold their wheat for rum, as being the more stable coin. Laborers received part of their pay in rum, and the work agreements of the area candidly specified certain days off from toil—"to get drunk," spelling the vacations out for all to read. The profitable, and incredibly wicked, "triangular" trade of New England operated as follows: molasses was imported from the West Indies and converted into rum by New England distilleries; the rum then was shipped to Africa for the purpose of buying slaves (from Negro dealers), and the unfortunate slaves in turn were sold to work in the West Indian sugarcane fields. It was a neat system, until the Negro dealers, sensitive to the emerging state of their fellows, grasped the fact that a first-class human beast of

burden was worth more than a gallon of last month's rum, whereupon they jacked the price up out of sight. Outraged New England
ministers and deacons voiced righteous dismay when the "nigger-
catchers" finally demanded two hundred gallons for any prime
specimen.

But rum was king for generations in New England, just as cotton was king in the South, or until New England, which had no
cotton, and no further use for the slave trade, realized the South's
gross immorality and stepped in to attack it with cartoon and nov-
elette. The Puritans passed laws curtailing every kind of pleasure
except drinking, and this they overlooked in the line of business.
The few meaningless gestures made were dismissed as jokes. Several
Massachusetts towns, unaffected by the rum trade, passed ordi-
nances imposing penalties for "repeated public drunkenness," but
the outer edge of offense was hard to fix. In theory, a drunkard was
compelled to wear, for awhile, either a white cloth containing a
red, painted "D" around his neck or a placard saying "DRUNK-
ARD" and pinned to his back. The trouble was, in an area and
period when nearly everybody was drinking all day, it required a
sharp (and sober) eye to select an exceptional case. Nevertheless,
an occasional nuisance was thus tagged, perhaps when crawling
down a principal street on all fours. To abet these paltry measures, Massachusetts belatedly passed a law (in 1838) that a retail
consumer of "ardent spirits" must buy at least fifteen gallons and
personally carry it away in one load. This was, briefly, a stumper;
it was awkward. The uninformed tippler who wandered into a
grogshop bawling for rum was asked if he wanted the whole fifteen gallons on a table or stacked outside, where he could handle it
less clumsily for removal. Before long the resourceful customer
simply drove in with a wagon, on which the ridiculous purchase
could be placed, and he thereafter drew on the cache at will, taking the liquor inside for mug-by-mug frolic. What remained after
the day's bout was ridiculously easy to sell back to the dealer. The
statute lasted two years before a resigned legislature repealed it,
and in that time only a few cases were recorded in which drinkers
sincerely tried to drink the fifteen gallons at once. These were
mostly drunk before they started, and none ever succeeded.

Meanwhile, rum was everywhere. A jug of rum flanked by a

pitcher of water and a bowl of sugar was a staple of colonial dining rooms. Many taverns sold no other liquor. Incontestably, pioneer America's favorite drink was "rum flip," a persuasive beverage that seemed to prod a person's reactions out of proportion to the actual alcohol imbibed. The brew was mixed of rum, beer and sugar, with beer the preponderant quantity, then stirred with a red-hot poker called a "loggerhead." The poker, iron-wrought, was made to glow in a fireplace, and when it had brought the flip to a boil, the evening was under way. Nearly always it proved rackety. A testimonial to the effectiveness of flip may be seen by the passage of "loggerhead" into the language under a slightly different meaning. The induction of sufficient flip often provoked a fight, and the opponents found it convenient to seize up loggerheads, with some notion of cracking each other's skulls; thus the term "at loggerheads."

Gin was the tipple of the lower orders, in America as in England. Costing only a few pennies a quart, it could be disguised in various ways; among the worst results was one called "Strip and Go Naked," which informal piece of behavior frequently took place after someone had drunk a pint or so. A lesser grade of gin (no mean feat) went by the name of Blue Ruin, and was regularly fed to slaves and servants; those who survived it over a period of years appeared to have a somewhat altered complexion, reminiscent of a drowned corpse that had lain too long in the water. An amalgam of Blue Ruin and a cheap rum known as Kill-Devil, regarded as the lowest rung on the ladder of drink, was relished by many who as children had been capable of swallowing pins, bolts, pennies and scissors. Soon after apple trees had been introduced into the colonies (which had none) the hardy old drink of apple-jack, familiarly described as Jersey Lightning, took its place beside the strong waters. Cider, too, turned out to be one of the principal boons of apple culture, its alcoholic nature, like that of applejack, having been discovered by some long dead and unsung hero (as the legend went) who noted that bees, recklessly loading up on fallen and rotting apples, had a tendency to skid, swerve, hop on one leg, and lie down to sleep it off.

Some picturesque variations on the foregoing—mixtures, dilutions, fortifications—were Tangle-Legs, Gullet Wash, Neck Oil,

Fogram, Hocus, Tape, Diddle, Bosom Friend, Barley Negas, Egg Flip, Military Cup, Sillibub, Roman Punch, Currant Shrub and Wine Whey. The colonists imported the staple wines of Europe— the still red and white wines, the sparkling wines of France, the German hocks and Moselles and Rhine wines, the madeiras, canaries, ports, malagas and sherries—or, at any rate, a crude approximation of the foregoing. It is a regrettable truth that some cynical European exporters have never been fastidious about the quality of wines which they shipped, and still ship, to Americans who, they have felt, would be equally content with colored bathwater or a good strong hair tonic. The genuine vintage wines have a curious way of reposing steadfast in the country of origin, only the labels managing to escape for the broadening experience of travel. As to the products of America's early vintner, it might be charitable to draw a curtain of silence over the whole subject. In brief, most vintages—the drinkable vintages—were bottled in the morning and drunk in the afternoon. There were few organized wineries; the settlers preferred to do the job themselves. A typical effort of the better class might involve a gathering up of two or three kegfuls of mulberries, an addition of sugar, a strengthening by several quarts of gin, with some yeast (for quick action) and an aging interval of two weeks. When the mess appeared to have fused, it was poured into bottles and the neighbors alerted. The conscientious vintner strove for strength, not bouquet.

Pennsylvania, already revered for the warming commodity known as coal, gave the world another important fuel in whiskey, the historic invention worked out by canny corn farmers who found that, while a horse could carry four bushels of grain laboriously over bad roads to market, it could tote whiskey distilled from twenty-five bushels. At one time, in the late 1700's, the Keystone State's government made the invigorating claim that "every family in western Pennsylvania operates its own still." The drink was comparatively easy on the stomach (and head), and the Continental Army issued it to soldiers as a daily ration during the Revolution. The results were debatable. A private of the 90th New York Volunteers, Z. Crooker, wrote during the war, "The evil effect of drinking has been brought with greater force to my mind in the short time I have been in the Army than ever before. In the causes of the arrest of privates, reduction of non-commissioned officers to the ranks, slanders and degrading reports running through the camps about commanders fighting and quarreling in quarters; about burglaries, contempt of superiors, etc., I find that, universally, drink is at the bottom of the whole." The authorities agreed, later, that beer might have been a less dangerous beverage for soldiers who many times had nothing to occupy their minds but the corrosive, rumor-ridden, hopeless waiting that forms the basic fabric of war. But beer was a scarce and indifferent refresher in America of the late eighteenth century. The great, even the competent middle-European brewmasters had not started to emigrate, and the American substitute was a creature of moods. The truth is that the frontier temperament was not fitted to the patient process of fermenting decent beer. As the stuff took shape, slowly, in orderly evolution, the rough and prankish (and usually drunk) puddler was apt to say, "Ah, the hell with it," and throw in several sacks of wheat, or hay, and maybe some left-over crab apples, along with gin, a couple of woodchuck pelts and four or five twists of tobacco. Unbelievable experiments were conducted to give the product flavor, and the final result lacked elegance.

By the time of Carry Nation's birth, in the middle 1800's, the fever of American drinking had abated slightly, though a serious problem remained. Swarms of Asians and Europeans had begun a restless drift to the new land, to assume positions among the police, to work the roadbeds of railways and trolley lines, to establish cheap and indigestible restaurants, to bake its bread and make the beds, to launder the nation's shirts, to catch its fish, to water the western lawns and photograph bridges, to cut its trousers and provide exchanges for the temporarily embarrassed—and from such modest beginnings to ascend to the reins of national management. These ambitious newcomers had in the main a history of alcoholic moderation, and, just perceptibly, they toned down the American spree. It is a subject for speculation, still today, why the streets of the Republic are cluttered by drunks while the populace of Europe rarely exhibits more than a rosy blush of induced superdigestion. A reporter who recently lived in both Spain and France looked in vain for the classic drunk on the streets of important cities, and the noisiest bars were free of the bellicose over-confiding nuisance that infests the American saloon. French children, who are given light wines at tables innocent of water, drink very little in their late teens, even at social gatherings among their friends. At college dances and frolics for the young Spanish, adult-like bars are always provided for refreshment during the evening. Students of both sexes sip the currently popular Spanish brandies—*Veterano, Soberano, Domecq, Magno* and the like (some sufficiently raw to have qualified for use in the American colonial days)—without the smallest discernible effect. The same facilities set up for an American teen-age house party might have seen, before the night was over, three or four fights, the downstairs windows smashed, a part of the rear wing burned off, a visit or two by State Police, automobiles crashed into trees, at least one critical injury, and a lodgment of various guests either in hospitals or hoosegows. It may be that, in America, the stern and incessant prohibitions have created a *desire,* an ungovernable lust to try the forbidden, while in old, wise, practical, wearily-civilized Europe nobody feels constrained, by Church or by parent, to think much about the matter one way or another.

But for Carry Nation, waiting at Medicine Lodge, her resounding future before her, there were no subtleties of improvements on the American drinking scene. She knew the awful record of her country at the bottle, and her eyes had shown her what she considered to be revolting examples at first hand. She, personally, was ready to "trample" out the vintage where the grapes of wrath were stored, and, at least at the start, she meant to do it alone.

Chapter Eight

It was around three o'clock in the afternoon (of June 6, 1900) that Mrs. Nation left Medicine Lodge in her buggy—deeply weighed down by rocks, brickbats and several throwing-sized bottles that she'd added at the last minute. She was headed for Kiowa along the parched clod road that wound among the white boulders, cottonwoods and sunflower patches of the "Medicine Creek bottoms." The day was warm, dust devils rose often to swirl in her eyes, and balls of tumbleweed—among the lonesomest sights on earth—bounced across the road on the high prairie stretches that today lie thickly planted in wheat and coby milo. The horse, Old Prince, was in a mettlesome state despite years of frenzied sorties among the Barber County poor, and his mistress, later, said that she "felt the strength of a giant."

Both the horse's and Mrs. Nation's spirits were dampened when they reached a small bridge about a mile out from town. They ran into a situation that has never since seen a counterpart in Kansas. A dozen or so man-like creatures with tails and cloven hoofs, and carrying three-pronged forks, boiled out from under the bridge to form a barricade across the roadway, dancing, grimacing, making obscene gestures and offering to whip the toughest pest that ever lived. Mrs. Nation instantly recognized them as emissaries from the infernal regions, dispatched to thwart the launching of her holy crusade. The horse, Prince (whose eyesight had begun to fail), merely reared, neighing in a well-rehearsed protest, at the sharp backward jerk on the reins.

Ignoring the horse, Mrs. Nation raised her hands in supplication, crying, "Oh, Lord! Help me! Help me!" and was gratified to see "the clouds part, and a dazzling beam of light shine through," after which she noted a towering figure astride a white horse and wearing a golden halo. Wasting no time, the visitor waved a regal sign, the clouds rolled back together, and "the diabolic creatures were no longer in front of my buggy. They were off to the right fleeing as if they were terrified . . . They were real devils, who knew more of what I was going to do than I did. The devil is a prophet. He reads Scripture. [Several nettled ministers later agreed that this broke new ground in theology; it had previously been held that the Devil was illiterate.] He knew Jesus when he was here, and he knows that I came to fulfill prophesy, and that this was a death blow to his Kingdom."

The encounter with Satan's agents gave a tonic boost to Mrs. Nation's feelings, and it was not without effect on Old Prince. Toward sunset, as she scanned the horizon for further demons, the pair hove within sight of a farm whereon dwelled "Sister" Springer, a fellow lodge member of the W.C.T.U. The place was about five miles from Kiowa, and Mrs. Nation had planned to spend the night there. But her triumph over Lucifer had so exalted her that she decided to leave things to Prince, just for the hell of it, in a sense. Abreast the Springer driveway, the horse leaped forward with a lurch, laid back his ears and bolted down the road toward Kiowa, in one of the few independent actions left in his locker. While the crusader took this as another sign—that the Lord wished her to hole up nearer the scene of tomorrow's struggle—cooler heads laid the eruption to a deerfly. Mrs. Nation arrived in town at eight-thirty and stayed the night with a Sister Parsons (also a sorority member) without, however, revealing the purpose of her mission. Her manner seemed subdued, almost abstracted. Next morning she arose early, ate a hearty breakfast and hitched up Old Prince; then she steered toward a popular wine-tub called "Dobson's," which was run by a brother of the sheriff. Evidence produced later showed that she had known, and threatened, Dobson for years.

In front of the saloon, Mrs. Nation debarked and carefully wrapped each rock, brickbat and bottle in newsprint. "I stacked up these smashers on my left arm, all I could hold," her autobiography relates, and she was ready for combat. The scene inside was routine for the morning hour; probably, it would not seriously have offended anybody else in Kansas. On one side of the bar, Dobson was whistling and polishing glasses; on the other, half a dozen men with important hangovers were bellied up for a reviver. This quiet pastoral was rudely interrupted by a shout of, "Men! I have come to save you from a drunkard's grave!" Everyone turned to stare at the large, motherly, black-clad figure who unexpectedly decanted half a brick and let fly at Dobson's elegant gilt-framed mirror, which crashed in splinters. "Now Mother Nation—" Dobson began, but his words were lost in the shower of missiles that followed the brick. Mrs. Nation later said that she first admonished Dobson as follows: "I told you last spring to close this place, Mr. Dobson, and you did not do it. Now . . . I am going to break [it] up." Nobody else on the premises remembered the words, but all were inclined to accept her other statement: "I felt invincible."

Taking careful aim, working with the seasoned deliberation of a major-league pitcher, Mrs. Nation peeled rock after brick after bottle off her arm in an enfilading fire that left the bar and the shelves behind denuded of everything but shards of broken glass. There was a uniformity of opinion that her accuracy was uncanny, bordering on the miraculous. Several men, pretty far gone in habitual drink, began to howl piteously while heading (with Dobson) for a corner, and above these battle noises rose an even eerier sound—that of Carry singing hymns, in the spirit of North Koreans blowing bugles during the human-wave attacks of 1950. Her selection was again the familiar "Who Hath Sorrow? Who Hath Woe?" a number that had already found its niche in the roster of Barber County's favorite curses. The bar stripped, Mrs. Nation now had a curious piece of good fortune, reminiscent of her vivid brush with the devils. A rocking chair stood near the bar, and in it, suddenly, was President William McKinley, gently rocking, looking on, his face wearing an expression of impudent superiority. The crusader went into what was afterward described as "a perfect froth" of rage. It was one thing to expend her all in a campaign that required genius in the planning; it was another to have it pooh-poohed by a seated critic who probably couldn't have hit a horse with a broom—and, what was worse, by a Republican. Mrs. Nation immediately bombarded President McKinley with a loud shriek and the last of her bricks, and was relieved to see him (and the chair) go down in pieces. "This meant," she wrote, "that the smashing in Kansas was to strike the head of the nation the hardest blow, for every saloon I smashed in Kansas had a license from the head of the government, which made the head of the government more responsible than the dive-keepers."

Her line of supply severed (for the astonishing armload of missiles was gone, and practically everything in the room destroyed), the reformer cried, "Now, Mr. Dobson, I have finished. God be with you." There was no reply; Dobson, crouched in a corner, was in a near-medical state of shock. His revival was accomplished by a rat-a-tat-tat and further explosions when Carry reached the street. She had apparently succumbed to the artist's urge for perfection, or closure, since she stooped over (in the presence of a congregating crowd), gathered stones large and small from the curb, and sent them sailing through Dobson's plate-glass windows. It was all he had left to smash. But Mrs. Nation's blood was now up, and turning wildly she sought further targets. A block down the street another saloon was administering restoratives to a select morning clientele, and thither Mrs. Nation directed Old Prince, having reminded herself that plenty of ammunition yet reposed in the buggy. She wrecked the place before anybody noticed that she had entered—smashed it to pulp; the proprietor told friends later he figured that the Devil had descended on his homey little pub, until he heard Mrs. Nation, in leaving, call out her accustomed, "God be with you!" At that point he became hopelessly addled, and himself snatched a rock from the floor to powder a window that had somehow escaped her notice.

In the third pothouse on her itinerary—called the Lewis Bar—Mrs. Nation let herself go just slightly. In the preceding visits she had confined her attention (excepting those involving President

McKinley—an excusable lapse, as he was openly scoffing) to inan-
imate objects: mirrors, glasses, chairs, windows, etc. At Lewis's,
she ran out of armament when the place was little more than two-
thirds down in ruins, and the logistic failure appeared to drive her
berserk. It was a minute or two before she spotted, and seized up,
the billiard balls from Lewis's recreation area, and as she did so, a
boy of about fifteen tried to scuttle from a foxhole near the bar to a
position of improved camouflage. Mrs. Nation fired a billiard ball
at his head, missing only by inches.* The try was so shrewd that a
biographer, who talked to observers, wrote that it "gently raised
his hair in passing." She took the miss sportingly, possibly because
some hearty sporting prints smiled down from the walls, but she
tore these away notwithstanding and ripped them into pieces.
Then she overturned several tables—swiped them aside with one
arm—kicked the rungs from a dozen chairs, pulled all fixtures
from their moorings, booted a cuspidor over a black iron stove,
and, as before, smashed the expensive front windows. The reformer nearly came a cropper with Lewis's ornamental *pièce de
résistance,* the long bar mirror, whose resistance was so strong
that it gave a mere glassy stare to a brick she had snatched up at
second hand. It was this rebuff that brought on another vision:
directly where the brick struck and bounced off, she saw Satan,
grinning, sticking out his tongue, waggling his horns, in general
making an ass of himself. Choking with rage, she determined to
dispatch him home, or, in the vulgar phrase, see that he went to
hell. The trick was turned by a billiard ball that Mrs. Nation
hurled through the mirror and its backing and into the wall behind. A neat spherical hole remained. Her "Thanks, God" was audible to all in the room. If this presumptuous address tended to
place God in the major-league class, it should be explained that,
beginning with Kiowa, the crusader began speaking of herself as
"God's right arm," and afterward, in terms that can only be viewed
as a demotion: "a bulldog running along at the feet of Jesus, barking at what He doesn't like."

Of her emergence from Lewis's, Mrs. Nation wrote in her auto-

* Some witnesses described this missile as a half brick; opinion was, in fact,
about equally divided.

biography what must stand as one of the most naive remarks ever recorded. "By this time the streets were crowded with people," she observed; "most of them seemed to look puzzled." Well they might. In the fury of her morning's smashing, Carry had soaked herself thoroughly in flying whiskey and beer; specifically, she stank to heaven. Her normally neat alpaca was limp with alcohol, her bonnet was atilt, her hands were filthy, her impressive bosom heaved, and she was sweating with exertion. As to the crowd, another witness saw it as "several-hundred persons pushing and shoving in the narrow street." These fell back when Mrs. Nation, uttering a rallying cry closely resembling "Ah-ah-aghhh!" lit like a hawk on the gutter rubble and completed the demolition of those few windowpanes still intact. Then she yelled, "Men of Kiowa, I have destroyed three of your places of business! If I have broken a statute of Kansas, put me in jail. If I am not a lawbreaker, your Mayor and Councilmen are. You must arrest one of us." Here the marshal obligingly stepped forward and took Old Prince by the bridle, while a member of the city council shouted, "Don't you think we can attend to our own business?"

Mrs. Nation replied (as she recalled it later): "Yes, you can, but you won't. As Jail Evangelist of Medicine Lodge I know that you have manufactured many criminals, and this county is burdened with taxes to prosecute the results of these dives. Now if I have done wrong in any particular, arrest me." She waited a moment and added, "Aren't you going to arrest me? Then I'll go home," but when she climbed into her buggy (now lighter) she found the marshal still attached to her horse. He indicated that Mayor Korn, waiting at some distance apart with a recovered saloon co-owner, wished to consult her. The equipage was led down the street with Mrs. Nation standing erect, like a French aristocrat in a tumbril, and rolling out another hymn (in English). She was in a particularly hopeful mood, she was to tell her sisters of the movement, because she felt certain that she would be thrown into jail and flogged, or even shot.

In a bitter humor, the saloonist demanded recompense, but he stated that the damage must be assessed by experts: the place was a shell. Drawing herself up to her full height—and several in Barber County were prepared to swear that this exceeded seven feet—

Mrs. Nation declined, saying, "I won't do it. You are a partner of the dive keeper and the statutes hold you responsible . . . Now if you won't arrest me I'll go home."

What followed could be laughable, but only if the temperance movement itself was comic, and no reasonable person can deny that its national ramifications assumed profound significance. Mayor Korn, the saloon-owner, and Mrs. Nation stood in one group, the city attorney and the council were huddled perhaps fifty yards away, while the town looked on, interested, farther down the street, near the wreckage. The trouble was that the officials could hardly prosecute without embarrassment almost certain to receive a full blast of publicity. (The liquor laws, and customs, were not reconcilable with enforcement.) Kiowa's city attorney, up to now the local embodiment of dignity, served as a liaison runner, scuttling back and forth with suggestions: trespass, destruction of private property, assault with a deadly weapon, disturbance of the peace, cruelty to a horse, attempted murder, etc. Perhaps for jurisdictional reasons, no charges were considered in connection with the attacks on Satan and President McKinley. Throughout this absurd rump session of the town government, Mrs. Nation managed to wring the worst from everybody by continuing to bray, "Who Hath Sorrow? Who Hath Woe?"

The situation was ticklish. By Kansas law saloons were illegal, but enforcement was onerous and it had become standard practice to wink at liquor sales, in both saloons and drugstores. No license was required, but "jointists" were hailed into court once a month and fined sums ranging from $25 to $100, depending on their volume of business. Through this compromise nearly everybody was kept happy except Carry Nation and the W.C.T.U. women whom she had fired up to take action. As the city attorney suggested, a lot of costly private property had indeed been destroyed, but "it was property being put to illegal use"—an utterance the county, state and national temperance groups would pounce on with grateful yelps for the opportunity, at last, of a complete public exposure.

Mayor Korn and his colleagues being essentially politicians, with the breed's high-principled lust for votes, they came to a baffling decision: nothing at all had occurred. "Go home," said the marshal, dropping Old Prince's bridle, and he turned away in disgust. The whole routine of his day, including whiskey-breaks at the saloons, had been disrupted and the town converted into a desert without an oasis. He appeared to be in an extraordinarily grouchy humor. One or two Kansas papers reported that, in a week or so, to save face, the Kiowa city council half-surreptitiously fined Mrs. Nation "a dollar and costs" (for disturbing the peace) but authorities now are divided on the point.

For years after her Kiowa visit—perhaps the town's high peak of excitement to the present—Carry's triumphal homecoming was recalled in detail. From early morning the telegraph wires between Kiowa and Medicine Lodge (as well as Topeka, Wichita and Kansas City) had run hot, and the Barber County W.C.T.U. was aligned in ranks at the Medicine Lodge city limits. The members were uniformly dressed, in war bonnets and black alpaca. As Mrs. Nation's buggy approached, they roared out a curious new hymn, "Peace on Earth, Good Will to Men!" but if anybody remarked the incongruity of their choice, it was drowned in the general hubbub. Some malcontent's allegation that, while this held sway, Mrs. Nation mulishly continued to sing, "Who Hath Sorrow" was never proved. The sisters fell into cadence behind her buggy, Medicine Lodge's remaining population—every man, woman or child not ill or incapacitated—trailed along, and the canonized booze fighter proceeded down the main street to the Post Office. When she marched up the steps (it was the only building in town with steps worthy of the name), an ear-splitting cheer arose, and a city official began a request that she recite her adventures. He had got out no more than, "We wonder if you—" when Mrs. Nation was swinging along at full throttle. All witnesses (including former dive-keepers with expert knowledge) agreed that she had never been in better voice. Her message was, in fact, so stirring that, as she proceeded, not only the W.C.T.U. but ordinary housewives who themselves didn't mind a nip now and then became worked up higher and higher, the fever rising dangerously, until at last they temporarily overstepped the border of sanity; whereupon, at Mrs. Nation's ringing mention of "BOOTLEGGERS!" the group dispersed in a wild medley of screams. It is the incredible truth that, for several hours, Medicine Lodge was turned topsy-turvy as the slavering females rampaged from door to door after bootleggers, a few of whom (suspects) were actually flushed out and chased pell-mell into the backwoods.

Carry's blow-up in Kiowa set off a deafening chain reaction of outcry. For weeks she was swamped with telegrams, letters, invitations to speak, one to play the lead in a stock company version of "Ten Nights in a Barroom," another (believed to be whimsical) to join a minor league baseball club, several to sign on as bouncer in out-of-state saloons (two of these offering her all the liquor she could drink, besides a salary) and one (perfectly serious) to wrestle a grizzly in Montana for a guaranteed purse of $500. She accepted a number of the first-named bids. In interviews for the big Kansas papers, she spread herself a little, adding posthumous grace notes to the already sufficiently lively facts of her exploit. To a Wichita reporter, she said, "It came to me one morning before I got up. And I didn't dare tell a human what I was going to do. I had bought four bottles of malt, from the joints, and had had it analyzed so that I knew what it was. I told my husband I was going out in the country on professional business. You know I am a practicing osteopath physician. So I went to the joint . . ." *
Years later the Kansas magazine, *Yankee,* carried a descriptive quotation by a veteran journalist, A. L. Schultz, who said, "I saw her once or twice then. She was no glamour girl, no Dolly Varden. I didn't feel attracted to her, and I'm a susceptible man. Perhaps I like the type that lean, and Carry was no leaner. She wore layers and layers of long full black skirts capable of concealing any sort of weapon—which they very often did. I reckon you might call her the motherly type gone wrong."

The state W.C.T.U. officers were among the few dissidents who considered Carry's violence extreme. Broadly speaking, Kansans stirred up such a hell's brew of moral indignation that further joints over the state were closed by wild threats, and those in Barber County especially took a pasting. For awhile, as the county women continued their romp, it was feared that they might get out

---

* Mrs. Nation may have confused this time with a previous occasion, in Medicine Lodge, when she claimed to have bought what she described as "Schlitz malt" from a drugstore, drank some, then ran to a congenial physician who permitted her to advise him that she'd been "poisoned." As to her occupation as "osteopath," she appears briefly to have announced herself as available for this work, though without much in the way of formal instruction.

of hand again and close everything, including grocery stores, and Carry's own actions were far from reassuring. Somehow she arranged that arrested malefactors such as bartenders, dive-keepers and building owners, instead of appearing before sympathetic town judges, were hustled to an outlying Justice of the Peace, one Moses E. Wright, a sanctimonious Free Methodist and friend (or captive) of Carry Nation. As to the state W.C.T.U., its president, Mrs. A. M. Hutchinson, journeyed to Medicine Lodge and rather acidly informed the local group that the Kansas W.C.T.U. "could not accept responsibility for the smashing at Kiowa." Carry replied with, for her, magnanimity, asserting that Mrs. Hutchinson was doubtless swayed by the fact that her husband had just been named resident physician of the State Reformatory—"a transparent bribe." She spoke of "Republican pressures," and said with a smile, "Many of the wives of these political wire-pullers are prominent in the Union." On receipt of her words, Mrs. Hutchinson abruptly returned home; she seemed inadequate to Mrs. Nation's style of jungle fighting. It was doubtless true, besides, that the state officials suddenly, and correctly, conceived the notion that Carry had grown beyond them.

Chapter Nine

Kiowa gave Mrs. Nation national standing, and world acclaim lay just around the corner—beginning with Wichita, marked down as the scene of her first big-city putsch. The incomparable gutting of the Hotel Carey bar would bring her praise and abuse (and immolation) unparalleled since the days of Jeanne d'Arc. But the Kiowa expedition had left a few trifling tag ends, not the least of these being a slander action leveled at her by Barber County's attorney, Sam Griffen, who said, in essence, that he was sick and tired of being called "a bribe-taker, a swill-faced rummy, a sink-hole of Republican corruption, and a low, gibbering creature of the liquor murderers." But the suit hung specifically upon Mrs. Nation's often-repeated charge (every two or three hours over a period of months) that Griffen was a notorious collector of bribes. "The papers were served on me, but I was not at all alarmed," she said, "for I thought it would give me an opportunity to bring out the facts in the case. I knew little about the tricks of lawyers, and the unfair ruling of judges."

In this line, Mrs. Nation's costliest knowledge-gap was the importance of securing legal representation. By the time she considered it, Griffen had thoughtfully hired all the lawyers in sight. To the crusader's dismay, these included A. L. Noble, the husband of her W.C.T.U. confederate, "Sister" Noble, who had done such a bang-up job at Day's pharmacy. Brother Noble cared little about noisy females who hypnotized his wife and even less about temperance; also, he had recently abandoned his strong Populist views on the promise of Republicans to throw him some business. Besides Noble and himself, Griffen had three others with various angles for wanting to join the show. Mrs. Nation was stuck with a G. A. Martin, whom she had uncovered in a brushy section of the county and whose license, he believed, was still valid. Martin has been eulogized by a reputable but realistic biographer who wrote that he "was incompetent and afraid." It seems useless to try and go beyond that pithy description. The question has arisen: Why did not David A. Nation, the cotton planter, preacher, editor, government appointee and barrister spring to the defense of his spouse? The answer is complex. For one thing, there is reason to believe that Nation might have been happy to see the rock-thrower confined. A dissolution of their contentious union hovered in the offing, and Mrs. Nation's bullying tactics had drawn on apace as her husband neared his middle seventies. Where once he could have downed her in a bare-knuckle brawl, she might have pulverized him without raising a sweat in 1900. "A lifetime of laborious physical toil had calloused and thickened her hands," wrote a biographer, "and had so hardened her muscles that she possessed unusual strength, as police officers and others learned to their sorrow when they attempted to handle her with the gentleness which they considered to be due a lady. Often the combined strength of several men was scarcely sufficient to control her, and she delighted in wrenching the arms of policemen and shoving them about." Another factor was Nation's ministerial manner; in any trial by jury, his exertions were often a godsend to the opposition. Moreover he had an unpunctual knowledge of the law, usually hitting on excellent points two or three weeks after the verdict, and his verbosity was soporific. Carry was not always at fault in crying halt to Nation's sermons; there appeared to be no civil way to shut him up. Finally, his physical presence was jolting. Of particular offense were his funereal adornments, centering on his beard, which was long, whitish-gray, bushy, uneven, wiry in texture and over-ample, flapping down like a nose-bag. The reformer's friends agreed that, as badly as she was represented, she could have done worse with Nation.

The trial, before eleven farmers and a reformed burglar, was conducted along extraordinary lines; non-resident lawyers agreed to this later. What it boiled down to was a simple battle of the sexes. At one time or another, every man in the courtroom had suffered the loss of a cigar or a bottle at Mrs. Nation's hands, and many had been selected for individual attention in church. Broadly speaking, the presiding judge ruled in favor of all exceptions by the opposition's attorneys and against Carry's (via the timorous Martin). "Judge Stevens and Judge Lacy, who were at the trial, told me they had never seen such determination on the part of any judge to cut down the defense as the rulings of Judge Gillett," Mrs. Nation wrote, adding that "Gillett read several pages of instructions to the jurors, telling them their duty was to convict and that the damages should be a large sum." She was inclined to ascribe the bias to Republicanism. Whatever it was, the jury found her guilty but refused to submit in the matter of damages, awarding Griffen a dollar. Understandably, he complained to friends that the amount made him look like a pipsqueak, but he eventually came through in western style by observing that he thought his character was worth "at least a dollar and a half."

Outwitted on damages, Gillett had his innings with the "costs." These amounted to $200, he stated, and he ordered Mrs. Nation to produce the money at once. Crusading is not a lucrative hobby. Missiles, inflammatory signs, bandages, hall rentals, etc. run into money, and she was obliged to confess herself stumped. Aside from her buggy, which the night riders had damaged, and Old Prince, who seemed less marketable than before the Kiowa raid, she had nothing to liquidate. To a reporter Nation once bragged that his wife's "good business sense" had made him $200,000 in Texas, but he appeared preoccupied before her present distress.*
A solution was found when the court attached Mrs. Nation's home; this lien would take her several years to retire. It should be remarked that the reformer's lifelong zeal in settling debts—hers

---

* The amount was exaggerated, but Nation did in fact pocket the fruits of Carry's enterprise.

and those of her intimates—was admired by her worst enemies. Beginning with Gloyd and plodding on through the irresponsibilities of father, daughter, nieces and others, she smoothed out a trail of obligation at the strict rate of 100 cents on the dollar. It sounds unlikely, but Carry was a little harder on herself than on anybody she ever met.

"In two weeks from the close of this trial, on the 27th of December, 1900, I went to Wichita, almost seven months after the raid in Kiowa," Mrs. Nation wrote. "Mr. Nation went to visit his brother, Mr. Seth Nation, in eastern Kansas, and I was free to leave home. Monday was the 26th, the day I started. The Sunday before, the 25th, I went to the Baptist Sunday School, then to the Presbyterian for preaching, and at the close walked over to the Methodist church for class meeting. I could not keep from weeping, but I controlled myself the best I could."

The cause of Mrs. Nation's dolor, during this encompassing circuit of worship, was her conviction that she would not survive the impending Battle of Wichita (whose shots were to be heard round the world). Nevertheless she bent her energies to the improvement of the faiths involved, doing so in her familiar nosy way, and said, "I gave my testimony at the class meeting; spoke particularly to members of the choir about their extravagant dress; told them that a poor sinner coming there for relief would be driven away, to see such a Vanity Fair in front. I begged them to dress neither in gold, silver or costly array, and spoke of the sin of wearing the corpses of dead birds and plumage, and closed by saying, 'These may be my dying words.' "

As this last piece of nonsense smote the air, a Sister Shell (by chance a fellow member of the W.C.T.U.) blew up. She was crowned in the usual number of bird feathers for the era and season (which was winter) and had on besides a sprinkling of the accursed silver and gold; in short, she was dressed for Sunday. She said, very tartly, "Now what do you mean by 'my dying words'? You never looked better in your life!" There followed a testy argument over Carry's humanitarian preference in costume, several of the ladies squaring off at her for the first time. A letter from a Sister Ennis to a friend in Joplin, Missouri, detailed the sarcastic flow of discussion. The point was made that, if they abandoned all gifts from the bird and animal kingdom, they'd be pretty hard up for covering. Leather shoes, of course, would go first, "perhaps to be replaced by Dutch clogs—awkward for riding horses"; bone buttons were out (clothes could be fastened together by twine, or wire); the abandonment of wool would mean light cotton substitutes and imprisonment indoors from about November to April; and no whalebone meant no corsets, leaving women "as shapeless as mashed potatoes"; as to silver, and gold, and gay plumage, two women had the temerity to suggest that "men liked them," and they meant to go on wearing them with or without the endorsement of Carry Nation.

Hewing to custom, Carry remained unperturbed, and began thinking about the grand assault on Wichita. For this outing—one still discussed with animation in Kansas—she effected several innovations. The history of warfare being a record of crash programs in science, Mrs. Nation refined her art (saloon smashing) to meet the demands of changing terrain. For one thing, she phased out rocks, bricks and bottles; like the catapult and flint-tipped arrows, they had served their purpose and gone to pasture in museums. Instead, she chose an iron rod a foot long "and as large around as my thumb" and (when Nation had cleared the house) one of his heaviest canes. Rocks could be used only once, as she put it, while an iron rod and a cane were suited to repeated attacks. "I took a valise with me," she said, having pondered the chance of a stopover in jail and wanting some toilet articles to brighten up her cell. Finally, she added recreational reading in the form of the family Bible. But Mrs. Nation's widest divergence was the course of her pre-fight training. For Kiowa (she told a reporter) she had spent half an hour in a vacant lot, firing rocks at empty tins and bottles (and one cat). The night before her departure for Wichita [the day was Christmas, and one cannot help but wonder what effect the holiday had on her lonely and over-excited mind] she dressed herself in a garment she made out of sackcloth and sprinkled fireplace ashes on her head (this last after unfastening her long thick hair till it fell in a shower down her back). Then she took to the Scriptures and thrilled, as before, to find each letter luminous with golden light. Spurred by this manifestation, she commenced to clip-clop about the house on her knees and at an early hour in the morning she made a rapid ascent (still kneeling) from the basement up to the attic.

Obviously Mrs. Nation was ready. Anything further would have been in the way of over-training; something might have snapped. As the sun rose, she exchanged her seance attire for the regimentals that would see her through all the succeeding and violent crises of her life. She wore the formidable black alpaca dress with the big black-pearl buttons up one side, a white bow at her throat, multiple petticoats, a dark poke bonnet tied by silk ribbon under her chin, black cotton stockings with knee, toe and heel reinforcements, and a cloak of navy blue serge. (In summer, she laid aside the cloak, for a white linen duster.) Thus memorably garbed—in a field uniform soon to be established in American folklore—she boarded a Santa Fé train for Wichita and the pivotal test of her career. She went with full knowledge of the odds—one against many, Wichita's late fame as a gunmen's preserve, liquor's entrenched position. As the accurate Kansas City *Star* commented afterward, "Mrs. Nation is by no means an ignorant woman, and she is far from demented." At fifty-four she was in fact at the height of her powers, and she had determined not to waste another minute of the years she had left.

The period in Kansas history was outstanding. A good many things were going on, echoes from the fading frontier and heralds of the oncoming machine age, curiously blended. The Topeka *State Journal* had just run a story, with pictures, about Terry Stafford and "the only automobile in Topeka," a creation he had built in his machine shop. Stafford's car was driven by a "compound gas seven-horsepower engine," could speed at twenty-five miles an hour and averaged twenty miles per gallon of gasoline. But the Crosly Brothers Dry Goods Company, in the same city, preferred to take no chances, ordering a new electric van. The Wichita *Eagle* had predicted a cold winter because "the seed on the buffalo grass is very thick, and this sign is as sure as sunrise." The Reverend Peter Anderson, whose devoted congregation had sent him from Abilene to Alaska as a missionary, returned with $200,000 he had "made in the mines" and was buying land in Dickinson County (all thoughts of the Lord apparently shelved for the moment). On November 10, tiny Washburn College's football team defeated the University of Kansas by the humiliating score of 29 to 0—this despite the fact that Lawrence W. Boyington (of Cornell) had just been hired as football coach by Kansas at the princely sum of "$400 a year and expenses." The cornerstone of the "Carl Browne Flying-machine Factory" was laid near Fort Scott, the day's activities including a sealing of Browne's sketch in the stone itself and speeches that predicted flights of "up to 200 miles eventually." Simultaneously, the Kansas Anti-Horse Thief Association had concluded its annual meeting in Wichita, taking the sensible line that, while automobiles might come and go, horses (and of course, horsethieves) would lope on forever. The Pottawatomie Indian School at Nadeau opened with a "barbecue [beef], a dance, games, and races"; and the government made its "final payment" to Chippewas and Muncies at the reservation near Ottawa; for the valuable lands, "all Indians 18 years and over received $419.48."

A student of Kansas happenings in the era can get the feeling that no problem, no situation, no human behavior is ever entirely new. In September of 1900 the organized "wheelmen" of Salina made vigorous declarations to prosecute carriage drivers who, "refusing to give half of the road," ran down bicyclists "in the heavy traffic." Toward the year-end, Kansas had 115,177 government pensioners on the state rolls; this represented an increase of 7,000 in the twelve months, according to the U.S. Pension Commissioner's happy report. The head of Bourbon County's experimental "Freedom Colony"—an unqualified fiasco—was making pro-socialist speeches over the state, in an effort to widen the failure; and Eugene V. Debs, the tail-end socialist candidate for President, spoke at Topeka on the "Ethics of Human, Social and Political Rights." Miss Lizzie Wooster, popular authoress of state textbooks, had just been invited to Harvard "to assist in instructing teachers from Cuba"; and Frank Rockefeller, of the Standard Oil Company, bought a 14,000-acre ranch near Belvidere. Then, as now, frictions between the Left and the Right (or Middle) continued while the economic, cultural and charitable life of the community steadily progressed. In October, Kansas corn had taken the grand prize at the Paris Exposition; and twenty-eight carloads of cattle, averaging 1600 pounds each, were shipped from Barnes to

Glasgow, Scotland. Barnum Brown, of Carbondale, returned from a two-year trip to Patagonia, where he collected geological specimens for the American Museum of Natural History in New York. Lester and Johnny Reiff, Wichita jockeys, were successfully riding in England, one having captured the $50,000 Prince of Wales stakes. A relief train carrying food and clothing was made up and sent to Galveston, where a hurricane and tidal wave had killed more than 6000 persons.

Best-selling books of that year, as Carry Nation rode the Santa Fé's green plush seats toward Wichita, were: *Alice of Old Vincennes,* by Maurice Thompson; *The Lane That Had No Turning,* by Gilbert Parker; *Eleanor,* by Mrs. Humphrey Ward; *Tommy and Grizel,* by James M. Barrie; *The Reign of Law,* by James Lane Allen, and *The Mantle of Elijah,* by Israel Zangwill. Temperance, one way or another, occasionally made headlines unassisted by Mrs. Nation. A Dr. Cunningham, editor of the Parsons *Daily News,* was convicted of criminal libel for calling an Oswego man a drunkard; and a hundred convicts at the State Penitentiary, finding liquor cut off, solemnly signed a pledge of abstention.

Carry arrived in Wichita at seven P.M., registered at a dingy hotel near the railroad station, then decided to reconnoitre the joints. Altogether she visited fourteen, peering into them briefly, in a few giving friendly warning to the bartender not to open next morning if he valued his chattels, and, at the Hotel Carey, suffering the experience required to hone her tired mind and re-focus her venom. The Annex of the Hotel Carey had been praised from coast to coast. It contained the finest bar in the West, after the oriental splendor of the Alcazar Saloon in Peoria, Illinois, whose floor and bar-rail were wrought of marble and black onyx. The Carey was finished off, ceiling and walls, with blocks of fine gray stucco that once had provided the décor of some buildings at the Chicago World's Fair (of 1893). Its bar was more than fifty feet long, gracefully curved, made of gleaming cherry wood rubbed, always, to a high polish by proud attendants who felt that there was no place like a home-away-from-home. The brass rail, the cut-glass decanters, the enormous museum-piece mirror, the cherry tables—all were spotless. Even the fat brass spittoons were kept lustrous as ship's bright-work, and many a tired whiskerando, re-freshing himself from the trail, trimmed his beard by the anamor-phous image in a spittoon (or gobboon) that he lifted to a table. The place was artistic and homey, having the air of serenity often sought but seldom caught by a big-city club. Mrs. Nation, at first serenely looking in, saw the chandeliers as "crystallized tears"; when she saw the lifesized painting (over the bar) of "Cleopatra at the Bath" (formerly called "The Temptress of the Nile" for pur-poses of display at carnivals, honky-tonks, and peep-shows) she went up like a rocket.

In its account of Carry's preliminary snoop at the Carey (and her reverberant call of next day), the Kansas City *Star* (a family paper) glossed over the art work, describing it as "a large painting, valued at $100, representing Cleopatra preparing for her bath." It was rather more. The oil was the masterpiece of an impecunious art student named John Noble, who afterward became well known, his principal hand-up being provided by Mrs. Nation on the morning of December 27, 1900. By his own account, he had labored over his conception of Cleopatra for nine months, which would reckon out his pay at eleven dollars a month, no great sum even at a time when art was indifferently regarded. All the same, he had done a good and complete job. The Temptress sprawled entic-ingly nude on a couch, her most debatable feature being a neat but unobtrusive swatch of pubic fuzz, not unlike that which had helped lift Goya's Naked Maja to the genius level and almost got the artist skewered. Cleopatra's Roman and Egyptian handmaids were com-parably festooned (by Nature and by Noble) and a pair of over-sized eunuchs busily keeping off the flies wore only the usual, or less than usual, breech-clout, or medieval codpiece. The painting was critically acclaimed in the peep-shows, but Noble's health had cracked under the travel and he gratefully unloaded the picture on the brothers Mahan—Thomas and John—who owned the Carey and sold wholesale liquor on the side. The purchase had proved an inspiration. Wichita was then, as it is now, an artistic garden-spot, and the Hotel Carey's clients flocked to the bar in droves. Their appreciation of the expert and aphrodisiac scene hanging over their heads was so overwhelming that often, during wistful lulls, they had to be reminded to buy a drink. Cleopatra was a civic rallying point.

Her first sight of the fully accoutered Temptress caused Mrs. Nation to recoil as if struck. Then she emitted what some witnesses described as a "screek," and others as a "shrill, thin 'Yawk!' " Whatever it was, she recovered and strode angrily to the bar, where an innocent-looking youth was polishing glasses (breathing or spitting on them, for cleanliness, then giving them a final swipe and high shine). In her rattled condition, the intruder shouted what all agreed was a perfectly pointless question: "Young man, what are you doing here?" The fellow had been day-dreaming, and he must have misunderstood her presence, for he said, "I'm sorry, Madam, but we don't serve ladies." Where before (on seeing the painting) Mrs. Nation had been speechless, she now burst forth with a torrent of invective. *"Serve me!"* she cried at last. "Do you think I'd drink the hellish poison you've got here? What is that naked woman doing up there?" Witnesses later applauded the youthful bartender's poise; the naked woman was obviously taking a bath, or preparing to, but he replied, "That's only a picture, Madam."

"It's disgraceful," Mrs. Nation shrieked. "You're insulting your mother by having her form stripped naked and hung up in a place where it is not even decent for a woman to be when she has her clothes on!" The suggestion that he was insulting his mother (who was not in the saloon) appeared to deflate the young man. He shrugged, made a brief but courtly bow and retired to the rear, leaving the field to Carry. Finding herself alone at the bar (several men sat drinking at tables, and one, half-rising, made a tentative gesture to buy her a drink), the crusader had to do something or explode. With a yowl she snatched a full bottle from the bar and crashed it in splinters at her feet. Then she turned and fled into the night. There was no time to waste. She half-walked, half-ran back to her hotel and began the task of reshuffling the arsenal. All of a sudden, outraged by Cleopatra's secondary sex characteristics, she'd decided that an iron rod and a cane were inadequate to Wichita's corruption. Taking the cane, she "put a heavy iron ring on the end of it," and, from the street, selected "some of the nicest rocks, round with sharp edges."

Then she considered things set. Shortly before eight the next morning, Mrs. Nation headed toward the front, fire in her eye, a flowing cape concealing her engines of war—looking to an awed spectator like a "one-woman caravan"—striding ominously toward the Annex. She was armed and ticking. Carry's ability to transport, concealed, such a whopping amount of equipment has been questioned by authorities, but the mystery has never been solved; hints point to the existence of large pockets sewed inside the cape. (She was known as an accomplished seamstress.) Lacking these, if one considers the cane, the rod and the rocks, she could scarcely have hoped to add brickbats without hiring a cart. The best guess is pockets, not much smaller than knapsacks.

As on other occasions, Mrs. Nation spent the battle-eve night walking around on her knees, somewhat to the discomfiture of an insomniac salesman housed below. Now slept the crimson petal, now the white, but the crusader stayed up till dawn. During her tramp to the Carey, refreshed, she limbered up by taking deep breaths and swinging her meaty arms, and she bulled into the establishment straightaway, not bothering to paralyze with her version of the lion's roar—that is to say, for once she sang no warning hymn. "She stood there in the entrance," went a magazine account, "a six-foot, 180-pound female with broad shoulders and hips. Her thin lips were pursed under a flat round nose, her black piercing eyes glared furiously at the scene before her—a scattering of males imbibing at a luxurious curved bar of cherrywood. Reflected in a huge mirror behind the bar was an enormous nude painting, 'Cleopatra at the Bath,' an original by artist John Noble. Not only was Cleopatra completely naked; so were her handmaidens, and the two huge eunuchs who fanned her were clad only in loincloths."

From the entrance Carry shot a second look at the voluptuaries —it was enough to propel her into action. To report the quickly unfolding violence, it is perhaps best to give a synthesis of eyewitness accounts. In matters of detail, different people saw different things; all agreed on the tornado's basic course. Behind the gleaming board—Wichita's pride—stood bartender Edward Parker, on the morning or therapy shift. Before the cherrywood lounged seven men clutching medication. All were in advanced states of disrepair. As they faced Parker, the Temptress and the mirror, their first intimation of trouble was the whizzing sound of a viciously thrown rock that zipped into the undraped apostles of sanitation, leaving a hole three inches south-southwest of Cleopatra's left knee. The rock broke the painting's glass screen and passed on through the canvas and the frame. The first missile was followed by another that unaccountably went wide; it represented one of Mrs. Nation's rare mechanical breakdowns—a wild pitch—and would haunt her for years. "I wish I had thought and thrown another at the face of the picture so it could not have been repaired," she was quoted as lamenting afterward from her temporary domicile in the Sedgwick County Jail. But she had other fish to fry. Her basic motive, she said, was to wreak damage "as expensively as possible." Thus it was that her third rock shattered the elegant Venetian mirror that reputedly had cost the Mahans fifteen-hundred dollars. There was no question of mending this second *objet d'art;* it was picked up by a dustpan and a broom.

The triumph provoked Mrs. Nation to her first utterance of the attack, an oddity from anybody's viewpoint. "Glory to God! Peace on earth, good will to men!" she cried, and hauling out her rod she took a horizontal swipe at the bar. Here the drinkers scattered; the woman had obviously passed out of the bric-a-brac stage and was ready for mayhem. One man dove over the bar to join Parker, who was describing short circles on all fours, like someone demented; three made it to the rear exit (two of these tumbling over chairs en route) and the others took refuge in corners, pulling down tables for shields. They were just in time. The crusader's past rampages never even approached the frenzy seen in the Hotel Carey during the next half-hour. At the last minute, Mrs. Nation had tied the iron rod and the cane together, bow and stern, to make a deadlier cudgel, and it was this instrument that she used in the events that followed. First off, in the words of a biographer, she "brandished it wildly about her head." Then she ran up and down the long bar slashing at everything she could reach: glasses, bottles, decanters, small, friendly signs such as "In God We Trust—All Others Pay Cash," the fittings on the bar, the cherrywood itself (hacking out deep dents), a chandelier, some cigar butts, the brass rail—everything in sight. Parker, a man with normal curiosity, partly arose at one point, perhaps to see if the ceiling was falling, and Mrs. Nation grabbed a beer bottle and shot it at his head. Like a prairie dog tentatively erect, he scuttled back into his lair, but it had been a very near thing; the bottle broke against a shelf and scattered its contents on his head.

A previously serene resident of the hotel said later that he "thought Judgment Day had arrived." He and three cronies (playing Seven Up in the lobby) scrambled downstairs to the Annex, but they scrambled back up even faster. A single look proved sufficient. Carry was flying around the room, whacking right and left at chairs and chandeliers, the place was knee-deep in glass, the bartender had gone to earth under the taps, Cleopatra was wounded and leaking oil, the mirror had disappeared, and over all rose a rich, anesthetic miasma of spilled whiskey and beer. The scene was altered only in its outlines upon the arrival of Detective Park Massey, who had responded to strangled cries of *"Help! Help! Police!"* from all quarters of the hotel, including several opened windows. On his entrance, said the Wichita *Eagle*, Mrs. Nation had her iron rod–cane in one hand and "a great brass spittoon" in the other and was hammering like a maniac on what remained of the bar. Nothing else of importance stood intact to be smashed.

Everybody agreed that Massey conducted himself like a gentleman and that it was a tactical error. One newspaper suggested that the Police Department could more humanely have dispatched a lion tamer to the Carey, and a second spoke of equipping the constabulary in plate armor. When Massey took Mrs. Nation gently by the arm, saying, "Madam, I must place you under arrest," she wheeled and tried to crush his skull with her rod. It whistled over his head as he ducked, looking startled. "Arrest *me!*" the crusader cried. "Why don't you arrest the man who runs this hell-hole? Don't you know this is against the law? Can't you smell the rotten poison?" She belligerently ordered Massey to sniff, but he declined, saying only, "You are destroying property, Madam. I must arrest you." Very gingerly the detective removed both the rod and the spittoon from Mrs. Nation's hands—later to be offered as the silliest evidence introduced into Kansas courts in years—and ushered her toward the door. The Kansas City *Star* noted changes in the Annex's geography, reporting that "The bar proper was divided from the small ante-room opening upon the street by some stained windows, but only a few bits of broken glass remain."

Headed out, balked of further demolition, Carry finally exploded into song. Many wondered how she had kept it bottled up so long. Her choice this time was "Am I a Soldier of the Cross?" prompting whimsical answers from the crowd (which felt not) and she delivered a peroration before leaving. "They are going to put me in jail!" she shouted, and after a chorus of general satisfaction, she promised that "I'll make it hot for the other saloons when I get out. I came here to stop the joints and I am going to make trouble." She continued to belabor the hymn while in transit down the sidewalk toward Police Headquarters.

"I was treated very nicely by the Chief of Police, Mr. Cubbin, who seemed to be amused at what I had done," Mrs. Nation reported in her book, but she could not resist adding, "This man was not very popular with the Administration, and was soon put out." She made no mention of Cubbin's sporting offer—that he'd turn her loose, scot-free, if she agreed to board the first train for Medicine Lodge never to reenter Wichita for any purpose. Mrs. Nation's response, said reporters in attendance, was to laugh immoderately and vow that, if released, she would "wreck every saloon in the city." Sighing, Cubbin locked her in the strongest room at Headquarters and sought advice from higher-ups, including the county attorney. As in Kiowa, Carry presented a problem. It was difficult to proceed against her without proceeding against the illegal saloons. (Cubbin had, by the way, expressed shock and surprise that a "joint" was operating in Wichita. The fact had theretofore escaped his notice. He didn't get down much to the Carey, he implied, and then only in the area of the lobby.) In Mrs. Nation's room, which socially was a cut above the cell, one of the new-fangled telephones hung on a wall, and with this she went to work trying to reach Governor William E. Stanley, who then was in Wichita, his home. In the presence of a warder stationed alongside to prevent her from kicking down a door, she first tried the Governor at the Hotel Carey Annex, and after other mock-serious tries, equally insulting, she got through to his residence, where a secretary informed her that Stanley had "nothing to say." "This is the man," Carry recorded in contempt, "who taught Sunday School in Wichita for twenty years, where they were letting murder shops run in violation of the law. Strange that this man should pull wool over the eyes of the voters of Kansas. I never did have any confidence in him."

The county attorney, Sam Amidon (an anti-feminist), stepped forward boldly to announce that, as he meant to prosecute Mrs. Nation, he had ordered her arraignment before Judge O. D. Kirk of the City Court. The proceedings began unpacifically. When the judge inquired whether Carry was ready for trial, she refused "to have anything to do with this court" until Amidon discarded his cigar. "It's rotten and the smell of it poisons me," she explained. Amidon arose in a rage and hurled the offending weed into a cuspidor. Mrs. Nation pursued her advantage by asking that the charge (signed by the Mahans) be altered from "malicious destruction of property" to "destruction of malicious property." Hardly any official sympathy was won to the crusader's cause by her insistence on addressing the judge as "Your Dishonor." Neither did she win friends when she grabbed an enforcement agent by both ears and waggled his head back and forth briskly. This was a mannerism Mrs. Nation had lately cultivated around policemen; whenever convenient, she seized a minion's ears, if they stuck out far enough, and gave him a shaking up.

The reformer then voiced an opinion, to Judge Kirk, that Amidon was "the friend of every jointkeeper in the city," and after Amidon had leapt up to retort that, "I have no use for spotters!" the Judge shouted down her reply, which several feared might take the form of a thrown chair or a desk. The Topeka *Capital,* reporting the rackety and much-enjoyed hearing, noted that, "Mrs. Nation's bail was fixed at $300, and her friends immediately arranged to secure bond. She refused to accept the privilege however. She said: 'Don't bother about the bond. Maybe they will get enough of this after a while.' " The first person to get enough was Judge Kirk. With a look of profound relief, he set her trial for January 5 (1901) and remanded her to the Sedgwick County Jail. In the course of an average day's sitting, he was accustomed to deal mainly with peaceful and penitent drunks; his brush with an anti-drunk had left him emotionally drained. Carry took note of Kirk in one of her forthcoming and numerous "statements." "Yes, when I was first arrested I knew it was not legal," she told the Kansas City *Star,* "but I was in the hands of the police force here, who, to a man, are perjurers. It gave me satisfaction to tell them so. The poor old trembling white sepulchre of a police judge looked conscience-smitten and only said, 'It is getting too warm here.' "

The uproar stirred the lately serene Wichita to a ferment of excitement. People stood on corners discussing the events of the night and day, often taking nips from bottles, and wondered where the storm might break out next. Heightening their speculation was the fact that each incoming train bore a load of Mrs. Nation's faithful, from both the Temperance union and the growing branches of its offshoot, the Home Defenders. "The W.C.T.U. is taking great interest in the case," said one paper. "Mrs. Lillian Mitchener, state president, has arrived here and will assist in the prosecution of the saloon men. Large delegations of the members called upon Mrs. Nation today and sang and prayed . . . It is believed by politicians that another liquor war has begun and that the saloon wrecked by Mrs. Nation is just a starter.* She agrees to this view of the case." The crusader might have been dismayed, but wasn't, by a paragraph concluding a round-up account in the *Capital:* "Hundreds of people filled the Carey Hotel saloon today and last night to see the scene of the wreck. The painting has been removed from the wall and will be repaired as soon as possible. As a result of people visiting the saloon, its bartenders are overcrowded with work and liquor is being sold tonight as fast as it can be drawn out." Over the state it was reckoned that Mrs. Nation had done more for whiskey in twenty-four hours than the lobbyists had accomplished during the past year.

Carry was finally lodged in a wedge-shaped steel compartment of the County Jail's proud new "rotary" cell-block (a kind of revolving cylinder) from which she lost no time in issuing a windy statement to the press. In some quarters this was denounced as impertinent and in others as gibberish. "I wish to say [it went] that owing to the fact that the governor could not release me, as there was no cause of action against me, as I destroyed nothing that law of Kansas calls property, and knowing that a court that, in open violation of the law, would try to protect the lawbreakers,

---

* Turbulence had earlier marked all the events leading to the passage of liquor legislation in Kansas.

would, in the nature of things, extend no clemency to me, I sent repeated messages to Governor Stanley, asking him to write me an answer or call or see me, or ask me to come to him. He refused. I find I am on the wrong side of the question to get a favor from the Chief Executive of Prohibition in Kansas." There were three other long paragraphs, from which the public gleaned that she was operating "in defense of humanity," that "these murder shops are grinding up 100,000 boys annually," that Mrs. Nation was "posted on the law in this matter," that she intended to "make it so hot for the officials that they will be glad to let me alone," and that, furthermore, "I will keep my movements under cover."

The last avowal puzzled the authorities, for everything Carry had done to date in her life had been accompanied by jangling fanfare. In any event, the declaration rang hollow when it appeared that she had no intention of keeping anything under cover even in jail. She had entered the building with a kite-tail of reporters to whom she gave revised statements every ten or fifteen minutes. The truth is, she turned the place into a bedlam the second the gates clanged shut behind her. A lack of rapport was immediately noticed between her and the collection of rustlers, pimps, drunks, brawlers and high-spirited cowpokes currently in residence. Smoking was, of course, a prerogative of her colleagues, who lounged within view, and smell, in the cylinder's other cages. Mrs. Nation ordered these normally good-humored inmates to douse their cigarettes. When they refused, she fell onto the floor, groaning and wailing, then commenced to shout out hymns. Penologists have agreed that the male group now took the indicated course: they all lit up tobacco and earnestly tried to choke her. "Mr. Simmons was the sheriff," Mrs. Nation wrote, "and he told the prisoners to 'smoke all you please,' that he would keep them in material, and he kept his word." Her ire centered on her next-cell neighbor, one John the Trusty, who favored an antique pipe that "stank worse than old rubbish burning." The Trusty, working hard, laid down smoke like a destroyer. "Oh, the physical agony!" she recorded, among a good many other things.

Mrs. Nation was no more than uncomfortably settled when a delegation of supporters stormed in to express solidarity. It was headed by Mrs. Mitchener (the then W.C.T.U. state president) and the hymn-singing that followed had the toughest of the prisoners groveling for release. One man offered a bribe to Jailer Dick Dodd, admitting that he had no money but promising to obtain some from a bank, any bank, the minute he got out, and several swore on their honor to go straight. Nothing prevailed against the female wrath. "Take your consecrated hatchets, rocks and brickbats, and everything that comes handy," cried Carry as they left, "and you can clean this curse out! Don't wait for the ballots! Smash! Smash!" It was long after midnight before they broke away, bearing the remembrance of their leader's shouted admonition to Dodd: "You put me in here a cub, but I will go out a roaring lion, and I will make all hell howl!" Here she heard the mutter of slow, bitter cursing from her neighbors, and she said, "What do you boys mean by asking God to damn this place? I think He has already done so, and I don't want any more damns here. Get down on your knees and ask God to bless you." Needing sleep, they relapsed into silence, and Dodd, ingeniously attaching a sign saying "Danger—Keep out!" to the main gates, turned in at last. The women continued to improve the night, however.

The reformer's mood lifted as she eased into the routine of Sedgwick life. Her single attempt at a jail-break failed when she tried to wrench all her iron bars out of their cement base. She made them rattle, but dislodgment appeared unfeasible. In anticipation of jail she had brought her own tea to Wichita, and this the authorities brewed for her in an effort to keep the peace. It is not known whether she offered any to "the boys," but one may assume that she did, for their relationship took a surprising new turn. The oaths quieted down, and within a week was heard the first tentative masculine piping of hymns. These increased in both volume and frequency, to the point where Dodd eyed the piebald group with speculation. They seemed to be overdoing the music, which was "led by a graduate of the Boston Conservatory" who had added drunk-rolling as a hobby. Any close follower of Mrs. Nation's life might set her down as the most gullible reformer in history. The simple fact is that, while she disapproved of nearly everyone, she disliked nobody. She would have found decent motives in a cannibal. "There were limits to her narrowness," observed a discerning piece years later in the *American Mercury*. "A Southerner, she was without the Southern rancor toward the Negro. She had high regard for the Jews, and except for Christian Science, which she dubbed witchcraft, she was tolerant of other creeds. And though she would have elected a Kaffir President on the Prohibition ticket, this same zeal for her cause led her to discover much sham and corruption in politics and to form shrewd judgments thereon. The disparity between the public utterances and private views of Great Men did not escape her, nor did the loftiness of office dazzle her."

But the horseplay of scamps (for whom she showed special fondness) often did dazzle Mrs. Nation, and she took the hymn-singing by Sedgwick's outlaw brothers as a touching and genuine tribute. "How are you, boys?" she cried one noon at its height, and they replied, meekly, "We've all been converted, Ma'am." To prove it, they jointly, and after much effort, composed a nine-stanza ode to the crusader, entitled, "Solemn Thoughts." There is reason to believe that the scapegrace crew became emotionally involved in their labor. Muffled sobs were heard during its birth-pangs (which went on for three days, involving large numbers of erasures, additions, editing, wholesale elisions and last-minute alterations) and these became very pronounced toward the end. Fragmentary reports have been handed down about the gestation period of these verses, but the signs point to an unusually troublous period at Sedgwick. Progress of the work was uneven, marked by that hyper-sensitivity which sets the artist apart and stamps him as an ass beyond the bounds of mortal conduct. Such phrases (between the wire cages) as "Now look here, Bill Downs [a noted rustler], you can jest hand over the pencil; you've had your brand on that pome long enough"; and "Me, I'm for knocking out 'Wine it is, the drink that led them'—call it whiskey and give the little lady her due"; and (to the rather parsimonious jailer) "I'm telling you, Dick Dodd, you wait till I get out of here. If you don't ante up some more notebooks, by God, I'll—," etc., etc. While this proceeded, Carry read her Bible out loud, as usual; oblivious.

The ode in its conception had been ribald, but a more wholesome spirit prevailed for the final version. Criminals are the only true sentimentalists, being extremists at both poles of their nature. Tears more frequently dilute beer in saloons than in parlors. "Solemn Thoughts" had literary merit, its rhythms patterned loosely after Coleridge and its reflections, both brooding and noble, distinguished by genteel omissions. For example, attention to chronological fact had been thought unnecessary in Stanza Six, in the contention that, "Each one rose from out his slumber, Listening to her songs of cheer, Then the stillness rent asunder, With their praises loud and clear." The precise Sedgwick-jail reaction had been, of course, an attempt to murder her by asphyxiation. The poem in its entirety went:

SOLEMN THOUGHTS

'Twas an aged and Christian martyr,
    Sat alone in a prison cell,
Where the laws of state had brought her,
    For wrecking an earthly hell.

Day by day, and night she dwelt there,
    Singing songs of Christ's dear love;
At His cross she prayed and knelt there,
    As an angel from above.

In the cells and 'round about her
    Prisoners stood, deep-stained in sin,
Listening to the prayers she'd offer,
    Looking for her Christ within.

Some who'd never known a mother,
    Ne'er had learned to kneel and pray,
Raised their hands, their face to cover,
    Till her words had died away.

In the silent midnight hours
    Came a voice in heavenly strain,
Floating o'er in peaceful showers,
    Bringing sunshine after rain.

Each one rose from out his slumber,
    Listening to her songs of cheer,
Then the stillness rent asunder,
    With their praises loud and clear.

Praise from those whose crimes had led them
    O'er a dark and stormy sea,
Where its waves had lashed and tossed them
    Into Hell's captivity.

Wine it was, the drink that led them,
    From the tender Shepherd's fold,
Now they hear His voice that calls them,
    With His precious words of gold.

Like the sheep that went astray,
    Twice we've heard the story told;
They heard His voice; they saw the way,
    That leads into His pastured fold.

Carry had the common touch. No matter how great a nuisance, she was always enjoyable except in the high frenzy of her fits, and she had a rare gift of placing herself on a footing of camaraderie and humor and real understanding with all classes of people. As she ended her first week at Sedgwick, she had achieved a position not unlike that of house-mother in a college fraternity. She was pleased with the poem but had no compunction about citing its confessional to the authors as evident proof of their folly. The give and take of banter occasionally worked its way into print, the Topeka *Capital* reporting that she said, " 'Boys, it looks pretty hard to see an old woman like me behind the bars, but I am here for the purpose of saving young men from destruction.' The boys laughed at her remarks," the story continued, "but she warned them that it was no laughing matter but a serious duty she owed to womanhood and rising manhood." The *Capital* was one of the few to describe her accommodations, saying that "She occupies a large cell. Sheriff C. W. Simmons is in [overall] charge of the prisoner and has done everything to make her as comfortable as possible. Mrs. Nation's cell contains a toilet room and bath tub. She brought with her a pound of tea." In no time the cell, including the lavatory, was ankle-deep in telegrams, cablegrams, letters, hand-delivered notes and donations. Carry's daring had stirred, even aroused, the world. It seemed that many women and a surprising number of men had thitherto felt deeply, if silently, on the subject of drinking; now their long-suppressed rage gushed forth in a flood of congratulation.

"The boys" lent a hand with the avalanche, helped sort it, commenting on this missive and that, agreeing that rum was a destroyer and hoped they could get out to enjoy some soon. Mrs. Nation overrode their advice about an announcement by Walter L. Main, a prominent circus owner in Cincinnati, that she would join his show next season. "Her services have been secured," the Topeka *Journal* quoted him as declaring. "She will talk for fifteen minutes in front of the menagerie tent." Impartially, the paper carried Mrs. Nation's sulphurous reply: "I had a lawyer write me yesterday telling me I could sue Mr. Main for $100,000 if I would give him [the shyster] half and I told him to go ahead." The boys had seen the offer as an opportunity in a million. They were likewise baffled when she rejected an Illinois distiller's request to name a brand of liquor in her honor. "We aim to call it Crusader Rye, Ma'am," it said, the dispatch phrased in cultured but colloquial English, "and I apprehend that it will take its place on the shelves beside the family favorites." A percentage of Mrs. Nation's mail was abusive, not to say threatening. "Poor old Granny Nation," wrote a man in a one-sentence blurb that Mrs. Nation handed to the press. "You are in a fine pickle, ain't you?" A Mr. Lippincott, saloon-owner of Chicago, invited her to his city, but his plan was to "throw a rope around one foot, tie the other end to a beer wagon, and haul you over the streets so the people can see what the cat drug in." Weighed against these were the bright spots, the nickel-and-dime contributions from Saturday night widows, the pleas for physical assistance, the expressions of hope. All over Kansas special meetings were held by churches and W.C.T.U. groups and collections taken to advance the cause. The United Brethren Church in Winfield forwarded a purse containing the unwieldy sum of $7.38; it caused Mrs. Nation and, dutifully thereafter, the boys to break down and weep.

Meanwhile the Kansas newspapers kept the presses hot firing out editorials, for, against and in the middle. Except for the organs of Olympian detachment (relieved by humor) such as the Kansas City *Star,* the editorials were richly partisan. Carry's strongest supporter was the Wichita *Beacon,* edited by Henry J. Allen, who later became governor, a pious fighter against sin in the aggregate and liquor specifically. The *Beacon* managed some admirably adroit prose in encouragement of Mrs. Nation without actually endorsing her violence. The paper's viewpoint was prophetic of a continuing trend, in America, that hopes to summon Utopia by the rubbery device of turning the other cheek. The *Beacon*'s message was, in essence, "Bravo, Mrs. Nation! We're with you all the way. You have struck an unprecedented blow at the evils of drink. Your work has opened the eyes of the world. We only wish you could have smashed the Hotel Carey Annex by prayer in Medicine Bow." As sonorous as it sounded, the *Beacon* served up no formula for accomplishing the same ends by meditation. The Wichita *Eagle,* on the other hand, liked neither Mrs. Nation nor her methods nor anything she had done since about her third year on earth. "Mr. Dodd frequently brought me the papers," Carry wrote, "and nearly every time the Wichita *Eagle* would have some falsehoods concerning me, always giving out that I 'was crazy,' 'was in a padded cell,' 'only a matter of time when I would be in the insane asylum,' that I used 'obscene language' and 'was raving' . . . This Wichita *Eagle* is the rum-bought sheet that has made Wichita one of the most lawless places in Kansas." The paper was edited by Victor Murdock, who afterward turned politician and went to Congress. His distaste for the crusader kept the *Eagle* digging into her past. "All sorts of stories are coming to the surface about Mrs. Nation since her actions here," it noted. "The people of Medicine Lodge, in fact all of Barber County, were not surprised at [her] outbreak in Wichita. Away back for years Mrs. Nation has shown similar activities in the county seat town. In the boom days she made it a practice, it is said, to visit the prisoners in the county jail and pray with them. The prisoners didn't enjoy it as a rule . . . The Medicine Lodge people say that Mrs. Nation was always given to singing hymns on the street and campaigning single-handed and alone in various ways. People who know her expect her to soon end her campaign in Kansas, and tackle, in a demolishing way, some of the large Eastern cities. They describe her temperament as one of exceptional versatility; she is easily thrown into a rage, which will turn quickly and with preposterous contrast into a smile, and her smiling condition is as quickly turned into a rage . . . It is anticipated in the city that Mrs. Nation will return to Wichita again to continue the crusade already begun here. It is also reported that preparations are being made for her reception, but all sorts of rumors are prevalent on the street."

The staid Kansas City *Journal* finally erupted with an editorial in a spirit of exasperation, under the heading of "A Time to Stop It." It made the point that, "The friends of Carrie [*sic*] Nation should, if possible, persuade her to desist, because if she keeps on she is going to get hurt. Thus far she has been fortunate in assaulting only saloons whose proprietors are unwilling to do her injury, but this immunity cannot continue. The men who engage in the saloon business are not usually the kind that will put up with this sort of thing patiently. Mrs. Nation will presently run up against the wrong barkeeper.

"It is true that the Kansas liquor seller is engaged in an illegal business, but he feels that if the officers of the law permit him to keep open saloon, no private individual has a right to interfere. He has invested his money, he pays a licence fee in the form of monthly fines, and he is not disposed to witness passively the destruction of his property. It appears that Mrs. Nation has gone her limit in Wichita. It would not be safe for her to make another assault in that town . . . As a matter of personal safety, if nothing more, Mrs. Nation should be taken in charge by her friends and kept quiet. If nothing can be done through persuasion, she should be placed under bond to keep the peace, or be locked up."

The object of these dubious encomiums shouted with glee when she was unexpectedly endorsed by William Allen White, Kansas's most melodious thrush, already a national literary figure, who wrote in his Emporia *Gazette,* "Fight the devil with fire. Smash the joints with hatchets. Drive the jointists from Kansas. They have no rights that a white man is bound to respect. Hurrah for Carry Nation!"

Chapter Ten

Wichita's divided opinion on its noisiest visitor soon boiled down
to the question, Is Carry Nation crazy? Heated arguments took
place all over the city. The authorities, in the dilemma already
noted, sniffed carefully to see which way the wind blew. The news
leaked out that many officials were on fire to commit the trouble-
maker to an asylum. Like most politicians, however, they were
even more anxious to avoid letting their principles rob them of
votes. The verdict at last took shape at the listening posts: Mrs.
Nation had the sympathy of the crowd. Also, some prominent attorneys were muttering about beginning agitations in her behalf.
The vengeful chess-move that followed is believed to have no
counterpart in the records of either reform or politics. An elderly
lunatic named Isaiah Cooper, plopped into the cell adjoining Mrs.
Nation's, piously declared himself recently exposed to smallpox.
Instantly, the jail was sealed like a sardine can—"quarantined," in
the sense that no prisoner could leave and no visitors were allowed, while the sheriff, the jailer and the other employees continued their normal movements to and from the city. The *Eagle*
pounced on the opportunity to remark that "Wichita has discovered a new way of treating cranks which beats going to court, and
that is to quarantine them." From her cell, Mrs. Nation issued a

rejoinder that "The Health Board belongs to the Republican whis-key ring, and is in a conspiracy to make me insane."

Like the machinations of other devious politicians, the quaran-tine backfired in the faces of its sponsors. To start things off, it reacted like a draft of 100-proof rum on the W.C.T.U., which hired a physician and dispatched him to jail with a court order. He took soundings on Cooper and reported that the lunatic was in top shape, physically, and that indications of smallpox were missing. When Judge Kirk stood firm, intoning that he had "no power to break a quarantine," the W.C.T.U. engaged not one but three Wichita legal firms and raised a howl for habeas corpus. The truth is that the ladies were in a thoroughly nasty mood. Their principal mouthpiece was confined, Wichita saloonkeepers were crowing over the stepped-up flow of booze and, perhaps decisive, all the excitement and good fun seemed in danger of dribbling away. Moreover, Carry's support had now become national. The Topeka *Capital* carried a Chicago story that said, "Mrs. Lillian M. Ste-vens, national president of the W.C.T.U., thinks that if anti-saloon laws cannot be enforced when on the statute books, force may be used to compel the resorts to close. Of the action of Mrs. Carrie Nation, who wrecked a saloon in Wichita, Kas., Thursday by hurling stones into the mirrors and decorations, she said: 'Kan-sas is a prohibition state, and the laws should be enforced. If no other means were possible, I believe Mrs. Nation's course was jus-tifiable.' Miss Eva Marshall Shontz, national president of the American Young People's Christian Temperance Union, applauds the action of Mrs. Nation. She said: 'I have recently returned from Kansas. While the state is fifty times ahead of Illinois, the liquor traffic demands that the governor bow down before it, and he does bow down and refuses to have the laws of Kansas enforced. What could that woman do, if she wanted her home protected, but take the law in her own hands?' "

The solidarity of Mrs. Nation's backing was dramatized when her husband unexpectedly sprang, or hobbled, to her defense. Na-tion was aging and, several thought, had grown hypersensitive about his wedded status. He found himself in a position where no suitable answers appeared to cover queries like "Good morning; how's your wife?" Replies such as "Cramped," or "They let her take exercise in the yard today" placed a strain on his miniscule good humor. Over the tumultuous years Nation had chosen to remain quiescent while his wife ran the public range of her emotions; now he joined the W.C.T.U.'s legal staff in presenting her plea for habeas corpus to the Kansas Supreme Court; the petition was, in fact, offered in his name. "The Carrie Nation case has reached the capital," said the Topeka *Journal* with relish. "The petition which is made in the name of David Nation is rather spicy. It charges that Mrs. Nation is held in the county jail, 'imprisoned, confined, detained and restrained of her liberty.' . . . [It] goes on to state that she was arrested for unlawfully and maliciously breaking, smashing and injuring and destroying a picture in the business house which was run by T. H. and J. P. Mahan and states that, in default of bail, she was locked up in the city jail. The petition also states that the authorities had quarantined the jail, because they said that there was smallpox there, and that it would be dangerous to the community to release her. The petition denies that there was any smallpox in the jail but says that the smallpox scare was used simply as an excuse. . . . It also states that the picture which she destroyed was obscene."

With the tide of sentiment swinging adversely, the authorities decided on a move that exceeded their quarantine in stupidity. Time and the destruction of records have obscured the officials' real aim, but they very evidently hatched a plot to sneak Mrs. Nation out of the jail's back door by night. The popular notion—one shared by the crusader—was that they planned to haul her across the state line and shoot her. Another body of opinion held that she would only be kidnaped and placed in an asylum. A minority felt that, unable to beat her, the politicians had hoped to join her, in a temporary way, by freeing her in advance of the law. The fell scheme (of whatever sort) was foiled by no less than John the Trusty who, having outgrown his urge to eliminate Mrs. Nation by pipe smoke, now claimed her friendship. During her incarceration she had bought food—mainly fruit and butter—for the boys and had lent John four dollars to give his wife, who had no means of support while her husband enjoyed his role of Trusty (the first position of eminence to which he had succeeded).

Late at night Jailer Dodd sidled up to Carry's cell. He asked her if she'd like to be freed, then advised her to get ready—a cab would be waiting in an hour (at the rear door) to take her "to the home of a friend." It was here that John the Trusty showed his mettle. Risking the perquisites of his privileged station, he approached Mrs. Nation to whisper, "Don't you leave this jail. There is some plotting going on, and they mean mischief." The reformer never questioned his veracity; she had spent her career fearing the worst, and her assumption was that the foe (in the main, Republicans) had organized a lynching bee, or, in the local idiom, a necktie party. Mrs. Nation's unexampled courage has often been sung, and no better sample could be found than her behavior now at what she considered to be death's door. She was not frightened; she merely determined to sell her life dearly, taking along as many Republicans as convenient. From John she obtained a length of stout wire with which she trussed her cell door to the adjacent bars, and to legs of her cot. Also, she removed one cot leg. Thus fortified and armed, she sat awake all night, "waiting for someone to come in my cell to drag me out. With the cot leg I was going to strike their hands if they attempted to open the door. I know what it is to expect murder in my cell."

Somehow the plotters suspected Mrs. Nation's alertness and let the evasion drop. And soon thereafter other occurrences took place to her advantage. On January 12 (1901) the Kansas Supreme Court ruled that she must be given bail, which now was set at $200. The quarantine was tacitly held to be false, and the charge of malicious destruction of property was dismissed altogether. In dropping it, County Attorney Amidon tried to get in one last lick by declaring that "my solicitude for the crusader's mental welfare is so great that I cannot conscientiously bring her to trial. Her mind," he went on, "would be unable to stand the shock of further confinement." Ignoring Amidon, Carry granted an interview to the Kansas City *Journal* in which she summed up for the defense: "I wanted the case to go to trial, and was in hope I would be convicted so that I could carry [it] to the Supreme Court. This would bring the matter more prominently before the people." Then she continued, after a pause [said the *Journal*]: " 'There will be an opportunity for that to be done, though, a little later.' "

Of significance in Carry's dismissal was the testimony of her brother, Jud Moore, a Kansas City dealer in livestock, who said, "I went to Wichita to see my sister while she was in jail there. I found the jail quarantined because of smallpox and no visitors were admitted. I went to a saloon keeper, out of curiosity, to see what he would say. I did not tell him at first that I was Mrs. Nation's brother. I asked him about Mrs. Nation and he said, 'We have put her in jail and sent a smallpox patient over there so as to get a quarantine on the jail and keep her there.' I did get to see her finally," Moore continued, "and had a talk with her. I asked her if she wasn't afraid of getting hurt. She replied: 'Why, brother, these whiskey sellers are the 'fraidest people you ever saw. All I have to do is walk in the front door . . . and they tumble over themselves getting out the back.' "

Amplifying his remarks, to the *Star,* Moore spread himself slightly. As Carry Nation's brother, son of the late Queen Victoria, scion of a family gifted in discourse, he offered hereditary tidbits of information. The interview ran to about two thousand words, from which the public learned, among other surprises, that Carry (and Jud) "had a favorite sister who married a cattle dealer worth $150,-000 and every dollar of this was spent in whiskey drinking." The statement was so odd that a subscriber worked out an estimate that, to drink up $150,000, the cattleman, if he had lived to seventy, must have consumed 2,143 gallons a year (at the going price), including his infant years, or about six gallons a day. "It seems unlikely," wrote the subscriber. Jud described his sister as "headstrong," adding that she always had been, and passed the opinion that she was "not crazy," after which he concluded on a note of moderation, saying, "My position in this matter is that my sister has gone far enough for the present."

Presumably, Carry never read the interview. She was busy giving out interviews of her own, none of them containing any faint trace of compromise. On the contrary, they bristled with fight. "I guess I will accept bond tomorrow so I can get out and smash some more of these joints," she told the Topeka *Capital.* "I think my staying in jail did much good toward arousing public sentiment . . . as I received hundreds of letters from people endorsing my actions. I think some more of these joints need to be wrecked. . . ." On the morning she emerged, the street outside was filled with weeping, singing and cheering women (as well as a scattering of weeping, singing and cheering drunks) but she paused only to make a brief, ominous speech. If the city had yearned for a moratorium on violence, its blood must have run cold after Mrs. Nation's words at the coming-out party. As a preliminary, she assured the throng that "God intended to make me a sacrifice as He did John Brown." This allusion to the state's other monomaniac sparked off a cheer, plus a few mouth-fizzles among the drunks, but her next sentence drew a blank. "I intend to get right to work smashing more Wichita joints, but first of all I've got to horsewhip Sheriff Simmons and Sam Amidon."

This last sounded to many like an assignment of unworkable size. Both men were sinewy, and neither had ever been inclined to take much nonsense from anyone. The newly revived Nation was skittering nervously in the background; now he creaked forward in an effort to cool his wife down. She brushed him aside as usual and bawled, "God's work has only begun! Show me a joint!" The psychology of mobs has always been of outstanding interest to head-doctors. While a collection of worked-up females can hardly be taken as the norm, their reaction followed a not uncommon pattern. From starting mildly off in a spirit of gratitude for victories over the male, their blood warmed, they considered the matter, and ended by reversing themselves to undertake a clamor for gore. Nation's disregard for his personal safety on this occasion was widely applauded. The unfortunate Daniel, trapped in the lion's den, was in no deadlier peril than Nation as he interposed himself between his wife and her scramble (aided by the storm troops) to gather rocks for an assault. By some miracle he soothed her without recourse to a whip, or a chair or a pistol full of blank cartridges; then he led her off down the street. And afterward he hustled her to the outlying village of Newton for a recuperation with friends.

It proved brief. On January 21, a date sung and cursed in the annals of temperance, Mrs. Nation reappeared in Wichita to be feted at a special muster of the city's W.C.T.U. After the passage of some routine resolutions against whiskey, men, etc., the guest of honor was tapped for an impromptu speech which proved so inflammatory that the room began to hum in suppressed excitement. A kind of Amazonian unrest stirred the group as Mrs. Nation reached new heights of slander until at last, in what later was called "an aboriginal seizure," she shrieked, "Who will be a sacrifice unto the Lord?" In retrospect it was never made clear whether anybody really understood what she meant. The obvious interpretation was that she had solicited volunteers for a human death offering to the anti-whiskey gods. Even so, nearly everyone on hand leapt up to cry, in effect, "Me! Me!" The crusader pursued her advantage with a ringing shout of "Praise God, women! We may all die for the cause!" Then, with the quick, sure generalship that had marked her previous campaigns, she selected as first lieutenants Mrs. Lucy Wilhoite, Mrs. Lydia Muntz and Mrs. Julia Evans—all well-tested standouts in courage and muscularity.

Sternly, Mrs. Nation ordered her listeners to kneel in prayer. During this (and it went on awhile, to the popping of middle-aged joints) she instructed the Lord to give all four ringleaders "the strength of giants." But she recalled that Goliath's giant strength had failed against the puny David and his homemade sling, so she acquiesced when somebody suggested that the Evans family had a cellar piled high with potentially dangerous implements. Shortly thereafter, the meeting adjourned, the apostles of good works emerged from the underground storehouse with what a contemporary biographer described as "iron bars, chunks of scrap iron and stones." But the prize catch, the weapon that may have surpassed David's sling, the symbol of wrath and destruction destined to endure, was carried by Mrs. Nation herself. When she walked out of the Evans' basement clutching a hatchet, her career had achieved its final sense of identification. The hallmark of her place in history was established at last; thenceforward she would seldom be photographed without the avenging tool.

Posterity was far from Mrs. Nation's mind on that crisp winter's day in Wichita. What she did have in mind, aside from a possible temporary blood clot, was smashing. "Wrap weapons in newspapers, all!" she barked, and when the job was done, the procession took to the streets. The women were noisily singing "Onward, Christian Soldiers." Mrs. Nation, naturally enough, strode in the van, wearing her habitual black regimentals, now draped with

cobwebs after her exertions below stairs. Occasionally one arm
(that lugging the hatchet) would go up as she made signals indi-
cating a turn to the right or left. Experts in drill have deplored the
fact that the crusader never provided herself with a whistle. Nothing else, it was felt, could have extracted such a full flavor of comi-
cality from her bulldog advances across the American scene. By
now, of course, she was recognizable to Wichitans. Her face had
become a newspaper staple on a level with the truss ads and the
blurbs for Lydia Pinkham's elixir. Thus the procession picked up
strollers, people standing in front of stores, defecting workers and
even dogs, who sensed another historic thunderclap in the making.
The joyous queue strung out for half a mile, excited members
shouting to friends, "Come on! It's Carry Nation and there's going
to be hell to pay!" while a mischievous element attempted (with
success) to scramble the battle hymn.

By chance the first important saloon encountered by the guerrillas was that of James Burnes, who had a reputation as being kindly
and chivalrous. Seeing the remorseless oncoming column, he
rushed to the entrance, arms outstretched, and cried, "Now ladies
—" then he jumped back when Mrs. Nation took a murderous
slash at him with her hatchet. En route, she had been hefting it,
swinging it, trying its edge, and she found it admirably suited to
her style. She warned, "Don't come near my hatchet! It might fall
on you, and I won't be responsible for the results!" Then she took
another swing, the blade whistling close to Burnes' chin, and cried,
"Get out of my way, you rummy! How dare you interfere with
God's work?" Here as on other occasions the bar-loungers took a
single look and rushed pell-mell out of the back, three of them
hanging up for a moment in the doorway.

Burnes surveyed the situation and flung himself onto the floor.
He pulled down a table for a shield, and peeked out furtively to
watch the awful carnage that followed. Spectators found it hard to
believe that the group had not been trained by a high officer of the
regular military, so precise were its maneuvers. The delegation
marched in in single file, holding aloft the borrowed weapons and
singing the threadbare bore, "Who Hath Sorrow? Who Hath
Woe?" This done, the Mesdames Nation, Wilhoite, Muntz and
Evans wheeled into a column of fours, facing the bar; then Carry

did a present-arms with her hatchet and cried, "Smash, women! Smash!" "A hail of stones thudded against the bar and sideboard, and with squeals of joy the crusaders fairly flew at their work of destruction," wrote a correspondent. For some reason Mrs. Evans devoted herself to cigar cases, lashing them with an iron bar until she cut her wrist severely, a fact that she ignored until later when a surgeon called at the jail to stitch her up. Mrs. Nation chose her milieu in the field of plate-glass windows, all of which she shredded. She now attacked and repulsed an "impertinent" row of slot machines. Behind the bar, Mrs. Muntz and Mrs. Wilhoite worked terrible havoc among the decanters, bottles, glasses and bric-a-brac (becoming thoroughly soaked in the process). When Burnes first surfaced, sliding back the table, it was to see Mrs. Nation chucking whiskey bottles at his mirror like an amateur pitcher throwing baseballs in a carnival. "Not even the small windows in the large refrigerator were spared," said the *Star* in its awestruck account. "Presently," said another source, "when nothing remained to smash, they stood in line in the center of the room, while little rills of whiskey and beer seeped from the piles of wreckage and flowed gently over the broad toes of their shoes, mute but fragrant reminders of an unusually fine stock of liquors."

A lesser reformer might have been content with this stunning access of damage; Carry was warming up for the day. The four left gracefully, Mrs. Nation again crying the inappropriate "Peace on earth, good will to men!" and her followers adding "A-a-amen!" and "Praise the Lord!"—"quaveringly," as one writer put it. When they cleared the dry waterhole, a bystander asked Burnes, curiously, "Why didn't you knock that woman down?" The publican's reply may some day be inscribed in bronze, as a memento of the old gallant West. "God forbid that I should strike a woman!" said Burnes, one hand placed minister-like in his vest, his eyes uplifted, both feet awash in two inches of free-running whiskey.

The next establishment to claim the women's attention, a short distance down Douglas Avenue, was run by a different breed of man. John Herrig, owner of the popular Palace Café, a saloon, had often expressed his aversion to feminists of any sort and to Carry Nation individually. He considered her "a pesky nuisance that long since should have been put under observation." As a result, he had taken certain precautions upon hearing the outrageous powwow up the block. Over-hurrying, Mrs. Nation's demolition squad myopically piled into Herrig's locked front door, a setback that appeared to drive the crusader briefly out of her fevered wits. In the words of the much-hated (by the W.C.T.U. people) *Eagle,* "With one blow of her hatchet, Mrs. Nation smashed the glass in the door. Mrs. Evans struck the other large glass to the right. Mrs. Nation repeated her blow, and the glass was entirely out of the door. But they were not in the building yet, nor was the door open. The fact that the glass was out offered a suggestion. Mrs. Nation started to climb over the woodwork on the left side of the door. Mrs. Evans immediately began to climb over on the right side."

Thus bracketed, Herrig's had no more chance of standing than the Alamo. For anyone by chance unfamiliar with the physical layout at Herrig's, it should be explained that a lounge, or ante-chamber, stood apart from the barroom and contained a large part of the goodies—liquor stocks, beer kegs, cigars—which accounted for the Palace's discriminating custom. Five minutes after Mrs. Nation and staff piled into the anteroom, nothing worth mention-ing remained intact. "The entire stock of liquor was ruined, as was the show case," reported the *Eagle,* which had one of its best hawks on the scene from the start. "Mrs. Wilhoite smashed a large mirror on the left side of the room. Then the women met in the rear of the room and scattered blows on the diamond-shaped mirror . . . After this was finished, Mrs. Nation was looking for more worlds to conquer and immediately started for the barroom."

At this dramatic moment she encountered the first dangerous opposition of her career. (Other, and rougher, opponents would follow.) Herrig, very quietly, showing the deadly calm that marked any frontier gunman's exploit, stood behind the locked barroom door holding a cocked revolver. He doubted, he said later, that Mrs. Nation would be brash enough to force an entry into his inner sanctum. This misapprehension was laid to rest when the crusader's number-ten right foot burst through a lower panel; her hatchet blade followed through one of the upper panels. Here Herrig stepped out and placed the mouth of his gun at Mrs. Nation's temple. There was disagreement about the exact phrasing of his polite but meaningful words; most accounts had them as "Leave this instant or I shall blow out your brains." Not only Mrs. Nation but her disciples took a close look at his face and decided that the party was over. They skedaddled. It was the first occasion on which the reformer had quitted a field under fire. To her credit, it would be her last.

When the quartette stepped outside, Mrs. Nation appeared dazed. The shouting, pushing crowd that had collected seemed disappointed by her expression. Then a roar went up when she shook off her confusion and made a recovery. She cried, "Women, to the Hotel Carey!" The crowd surged and broke, then scattered down Douglas Avenue toward Wichita's recreational showplace. Deprived of a murder, the people hoped at least for another round of smashing. Not all the spectators accompanied the grim and (again) singing group on its way. What one paper saw as a "wild melee" of stragglers turned back in a frenzy of looting and souvenir-snatching both at Herrig's and at Burnes'. Bits of glass, rocks, iron bars, broken cigars and remnants in whiskey bottles fell to the horde, and several persons sank to all fours to sip in the fragrant puddles.

The crowd in attendance on Mrs. Nation had to settle for mayhem alone at the Carey. "From Police Headquarters every available policeman was dispatched to check the threatening riot," a reporter noted. Before the saloon door, when the women arrived, stood Detective Sutton and Patrolman Pryor, who signaled to turn them back. Sutton, moreover, recklessly seized Mrs. Nation's arm. Instantly, she whacked him a glancing blow with an iron rod. The action overstimulated a nearby youth to cry "Hooray for God and Carry Nation!" and to hit Detective Sutton in the face. Patrolman Pryor then knocked the attacker down, and out. This was the sort of thing everybody had come for and, by one estimate, "three-thousand persons, with more arriving every moment, milled and yelled in the streets." There followed an exceedingly satisfying "struggle," with the redoubtable Mrs. Wilhoite—a standout—darting in to jab with her left hand, then crossing beautifully with a ballbat supplied by an *agent provocateur* in the rear. Mrs. Evans, with her slashed and streaming wrist, whaled away with a piece of scrap iron; and Mrs. Muntz cleverly used her head, to butt both officers in the stomach. It was entirely futile; the reformers were overpowered and hustled off to jail, with a lively proportion of Wichita strung out a few yards behind. The day was developing into the finest Wichita had known since Wyatt Earp's running gun battle (also on Douglas Avenue) in 1874 with cronies of the incomparable Shanghai Pierce.

Those interested in Carry Nation's life should realize that, in Wichita, the reformer had a sophisticated audience. In matters of violence, its crowds were hard to please. The attention paid Mrs. Nation was a rare compliment from a people who had known and enjoyed the toughest citizens in a country as hard as stone. In a biography of Wyatt Earp, Stuart N. Lake entitled his busiest chapter, "Wild and Woolly Wichita." Hub of the community life was the great iron triangle hanging outside Judge Jewett's office on Douglas Avenue. Its purpose—and it had been used often— was to warn townspeople to arm themselves for battle against the hundreds of restless cowhands who usually were camped beyond the town, across a "toll-bridge." Trained sociologists, assisted by a mortician with a gift for mathematics, might possibly have determined whether the Texans who drifted across the bridge after entertainment—meaning whiskey, women and fracas—were tougher than the Wichitans who received them. Fights developed over the smallest points of protocol. The feud between Rowdy Joe Lowe (with his wife, Rowdy Kate) and Mr. and Mrs. Red Redfern is a case in point. Rowdy Kate may have given first offense by a rather jingoistic remark (to an acquaintance at Douglas Avenue's Horse-Thief Corner) that she operated "the swiftest joint in Kansas." The statement was thoughtless; many felt so, and Mr. and Mrs. Redfern, who ran a similar rat's nest, took umbrage at what they regarded as misleading propaganda. One thing led to another (as things will in the busines world) until Rowdy Joe and Red Redfern agreed that the question of who ran the swiftest joint could be determined by a street duel. Rowdy Joe showed superior management when he appeared with a sawed-off shotgun, while Redfern continued loyal to the old-fashioned six-shooter. As the debate progressed, Rowdy Joe sprayed Redfern with a lethal dose of buckshot and regrettably blinded an onlooker for good measure. It speaks well for young Wichita that Marshal Earp promptly ar-

rested Rowdy Joe, but the restaurateur was released when everybody concerned (except the onlooker) held that the victim "could
not prove legitimate business in the line of fire."

Wichita's roaring saloons of the Seventies were not the Hotel
Carey and Burnes' and Herrig's but the Douglas Avenue House,
the Occidental, the Texas House, the Southern and the Empire.
Prominent among their patrons was Shanghai Pierce, who rivals
Carry Nation for the honor of Kansas' worst-behaved visitor.
Pierce was six-feet four, weighed 230 pounds and had a bland if
bizarre outlook except when in drink, which was generally. He was
a Texas cattleman who kept a Negro servant by his side leading a
pack horse that staggered beneath a load of silver and gold (for
stock transactions on the spot). Pierce lacked the curse of modesty, and once spent ten thousand dollars for a forty-foot bronze
statue of himself, in full range rig, which he put up at the gateway
to his Rancho Grande. He seemed mainly to deal in sums of ten
thousand dollars. He offered one of these to the Nebraska legislature for an exclusive right to organize monte games on trains
within the state's borders. Turned down, and in a fit of moral indignation, he revised his tender to deal "only against such passengers as professed to be clergymen or missionaries." Wichita conceded that Pierce's herds had partly been rustled and the brands
altered to suit his convenience. However, his reputation was so
fearsome, and he brought Wichita such golden freshets of cash,
that the subject seldom was mentioned. If it was, the cemetery
usually gained a new headstone.

When word came to Earp one afternoon that Shanghai was
drunk on Douglas Avenue, and threatening to shoot everybody in
sight, the marshal made a tricky and dangerous arrest somewhat
eased by the fact that Pierce could see little more than the blurred
outlines of buildings. Released, the miscreant coralled forty of his
cowpokes, the triangle rang out strongly at Jewett's and Earp, to
prevent wholesale slaughter, persuaded everyone that he could
handle the matter alone. There unfolded a thunderous and prolonged gun battle between the cowhands, in the center of Douglas
Avenue, and Earp, popping out of alleys at the rear of stores. Its
reverberations, some say, may still be heard on quiet Wichita days.
An enduring western legend was written when Earp scooped up a

double-barreled shotgun, crashed through a store window, and brought his weapon to bear beneath the noses of the forty mounted revelers. They backed down, dropped their revolvers, and marched off to jail, where each paid a stiff fine of one hundred dollars. Shanghai Pierce, ever courtly, apologized with such grace that his return to favor was complete, so that his rustled cattle continued strong in demand. As for Earp, it marked the upsurge of a reputation that grows yet apace.

Wichita had been a proud and attractive town in the Seventies, sufficiently noisy to satisfy exacting emigrés from Texas and the Indian Territory. It had not yet become eunuchized by the time of Carry Nation, as she was to learn from the events that succeeded her second arrest at the Carey. Detective Sutton and Patrolman Pryor (both battered around the edges) escorted the crusading band to Headquarters, where Chief Cubbin—still in an unaccountably genial mood—released the attack cadre of four on its grudging promise not to uproot anything important "until noon tomorrow." All factors considered, the ultimatum was surprisingly mild. Another reformer might have made it a week; Carry's blood was up, as we shall see. Mrs. Evans' blood was both up and out, spilled generously from her cut wrist over the Headquarters floor, and her husband, a doctor, checked in to effect repairs. He did so in what one paper reported as "a lowering and unsympathetic humor."

What Mrs. Nation soon saw as a very hasty promise to Cubbin rankled all afternoon in her bosom, as she lay up at the residence of friends. Toward dusk she was seized by an uplifting thought, where shortly before she had been seized by policemen who had appeared to cast her down. During Carry's previous residence at Sedgwick, she had received letters from women in the nearby hamlet of Enterprise. All told substantially the same story: their husbands were deep in thrall to the whiskey kings—not only the wives but their children were starving, threadbare, cursed, beaten with regularity and otherwise shamed. As her pledge extended no farther than Wichita (Mrs. Nation decided) she brightened up to toss her hatchet, several iron bars and a scattering of rocks into her valise; then she steered off quietly toward the depot. In the years since, the Wichita railroad stations have been made models of peace and comfort and decorum; on that January 21, 1901, all hell broke loose on the platform. In the afternoon county authorities (still her worst nemeses) had issued a warrant for Carry's arrest, and the wily Sheriff Simmons had managed to cross her spoor. It proved to be the hollowest triumph of his life. When, at the terminal, he grasped her sleeve to say, "Madam, you are my prisoner," she screamed "Ahab!" and smacked him resoundingly in the face. A crowd quickly gathering, she grabbed Simmons by both ears and shook him in the style of a terrier worrying a rat. He was said to have "struggled bravely," but he was diminutive, and when police came to his aid, Mrs. Nation was "literally dragging him about the waiting-room by the ears." The Topeka *Journal* reported that "Mrs. Nation caused a new sensation last night by slapping Sheriff Simmons in the face, taking hold of his ears and giving him a rough handling generally . . . the Union Depot was full of women who began screaming, and tremendous excitement eventuated as the sheriff, who is a very small man, struggled with his powerful antagonist."

Again Mrs. Nation was waltzed off to the Sedgwick County Jail. The experience, though annoying, was in no way traumatic: the place had begun to feel like home. She was no sooner established than deputies dragged in a struggling Mrs. Wilhoite (the lioness of Herrig's) and Mrs. Evans, with her bandaged arm, spilled out of the dragnet a few minutes later. A certain mystery developed about the conspicuously absent Mrs. Muntz; it was cleared up when a deputy explained that the apostle had taken it on the lam. Fighting a rearguard action, Mrs. Muntz lit out for the bush, planning, one imagines, to pursue a scorched earth policy and dart in and out on guerrilla-like forays. (The authorities never did manage to grab her.) The remaining weird sisters fell tearfully on one another with cries of "Hallelujah!" and "Glory to God!" They were first placed in the same cell and given a cot each, but they joined voices in such wrenching hosannahs of psalm that Simmons expressed fears for the building. His wife, a quiet, demure lady, walked up to remonstrate and received raucous shouts of "Jezebel!" and "How's Ahab's health?" for her pains. There was only one solution, and Simmons took it, probably recalling the workout given his ears. Carry and Mrs. Wilhoite were placed in cells of the rotary, where Mrs. Nation renewed old friendships among "the boys."

Meanwhile Wichita had gone mad. Gangs of fired-up partisans roamed the streets, guzzling, replaying the day's events, discussing what might be done to insure freedom of drink, making plans that augured no comfort for the captives. Balancing these off, the W.C.T.U. and other female cliques gathered in upwards of a dozen places to pray and plot against Satan's creatures. "During the evening, as public excitement subsided, public indignation took its place," reported the *Eagle*, "and there has never been a time when Wichita sentiment was so unanimously afire with adverse criticism . . . A short time after the saloon episode there could be seen crowds on the streets talking excitedly of the affair. It was not confined to men alone, for here and there were little groups of women watching the proceeding with as much interest as men." Women notwithstanding, it was the uninhibited and the sinful who prevailed on the downtown streets, and inevitably, as befitted the frontier taste, someone sang out to urge that the reformers be tarred and feathered, or lynched, or maybe both. The signal had been flashed, and all aroused hands joined forces for a stampede toward the jail, shouting, breaking bottles on the sidewalks, dispatching agents after tools for the punishment. Men "moved restlessly back and forth in front of the prison" and cried, "Lynch them!" "Tar and feather them!" and "Who's got a rope?" When the mob arrived, by coincidence, Carry and Mrs. Wilhoite were singing "Nearer My God to Thee"; they had indeed never been nearer. The plan's miscarriage has been laid to a lack of responsible leadership on the part of the lynchers; there was bitter criticism all the next day. Had Carry been in charge, another pretty deed would doubtless have been added to the West's record of peremptory justice. But when nobody appeared capable of giving a decisive order, an unexpected mantle of common sense settled over the crowd. Its nearest approach to a commander said, "Boys, I've parched my gullet. I move we haul back and get a drink." With a whoop (and no discernible lessening of zeal) the group wheeled and tore off in the opposite direction. Several men expressed disappointment but no hard feelings; on the whole they were a sporting and fair-minded lot.

Next afternoon the crusaders were arraigned in District Court and released in bail of a thousand dollars each. The sums were supplied by temperance enthusiasts. Dr. Evans refused to go bail for his wife; she was a nuisance, he stated, but he modified this to speculate that she had been "hypnotized by Carry Nation." The last-named had just announced her idiomatic intention of landing "all spraddled out" on Kansas City; she told a *Star* reporter: "I hope to be able to fill my engagement in Kansas City Saturday, but if I am not, just tell them that I am unavoidably detained." Her attorneys went on record as saying that they "were taken completely by surprise by [her follow-up] action," and the adverse editorials began to pile up. The *Eagle*, sour as always, reprinted a sympathetic blast from the Lawrence *Daily Journal,* to the effect that "It would have been wiser for the Wichita authorities to take Mrs. Nation before the probate judge on a charge of insanity . . . She wants notoriety; she wants to be talked about and be looked upon as a martyr. Her first talk was about being burned at the stake. . . ." Even the *Star,* goaded to impatience, published an appreciation of "Colonel" Murdock, owner of the *Eagle,* whom it presented as a gentleman of the old school: "It is the idea of Colonel Murdock that the sole mission of women is to make the world bright and cheerful for men; that in the lowly walks of life it is her sphere to wash and fry meat, and that as she advances in the social scale she should adorn the home of luxury with her grace and loveliness. To have this cherished ideal shattered by a virago with a literal axe in her hand is, indeed, a crucial trial."

Word of Mrs. Nation's freedom had no sooner gone out than the saloon men girded to defend their lives, their property, their sacred honor. They could scarcely be blamed, for their insurance companies had responded to the crisis by canceling all coverage on bar fixtures. The sentiment (so often expressed by large, selfless institutions) was that "We are very anxious to protect you but not if you need protection." Thereupon the saloon people hired what might be described as roving goon squads that ranged the rialto armed with pistols and clubs. Here and there they met to discuss plans of attack on the crusader—whether to kill or maim, the comparative merits of head and stomach wounds, etc. Meanwhile Mrs. Nation confounded her enemies (as usual) by returning to the railroad depot. Nobody yet had fathomed her iron-jawed adherence to a single idea. Once again she was headed for Enterprise. America has probably never since produced a flintier symbol of purpose than Carry on her tramp from the Wichita jail to the station. Remnants of the mob had stayed close at hand all day, hoping that the lynch group might cohere. Now, when she strode out, carrying her valise, all formalities complete, these strung along behind, bawling like maniacs. The crowd grew during her progress until, as one writer saw it, "most of Wichita went with her." The streets became clogged, some bolder spirits rushed forward to make hit-and-run attacks, and extra police stormed in to clear a passage. They were ineffective. Had it not been for a unit of the Salvation Army (holding an empty street-corner meeting) Mrs. Nation might actually have been strung up. The squad— twenty private soldiers and a noncommissioned officer with a whistle—closed round her and then led the way, drum booming, horn sounding, to the depot. Indomitable in the face of danger, Carry again drowned out lesser sounds with shouts of "Hallelujah!" and "Glory to God!" Dispassionate observers felt that she had little or nothing to crow about.

The waiting room resembled a scene from Dante's *Inferno*. Even with her military escort, the crusader could find no ingress until she was taken in hand—lifted bodily—by a sad-faced, moustachioed giant wearing a large black sombrero. Her curiosity piqued, she yelled (perhaps thinking that, in mufti, he was with the intelligence branch) "Are you one of the Salvation Army?" "No, Madam," he replied; "I am only a tin-horn gambler." When he deposited her on the lower step of a coach, she conveyed her gratitude by assuring him that he was "certainly going to hell." The man merely sighed, touched his hat, and stepped back. He was just in time. A blizzard of eggs, presumably gathered along the street, raked the car with noisy poppings. "But the window fell down," Mrs. Nation wrote, "and I did not get a spatter." Her ill-wishers followed the eggs with rocks that broke nearly all the windows on that side of the coach. These had one desirable effect—they assured the reformer of privacy. Disinterested passengers in her car leaped up and fought their way in a wild rush to far sections of the train. As for the engine crew, both members had

seen enough. Tossing aside his timetable, the engineer lunged forward on the throttle and the train moved out, smelly, punctured,
congested in spots but still luckily mobile. Mrs. Nation was at last
en route to Enterprise and the first corporal penalty of her career.

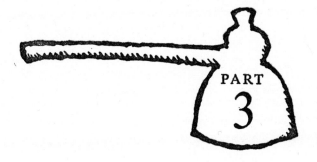

DISTILLATION
and
RAW SPIRITS

Chapter Eleven

Mrs. Nation's second Wichita raid sparked off her first important notice in the eastern press. The New York *Times* of January 22, 1901, gave her nearly a column on page one, under the heading, "Mrs. Nation Begins Her Crusade Anew." No source was credited by the *Times* for its account, but a number of details turned up that most Kansas papers had overlooked. "In the barroom three policemen met Mrs. Nation, and she struck at Detective Sutton with a poker," the story went, and it laid heavy stress on the matter of Sheriff Simmons' ears. Throughout, the tone was muted, subdued, awestruck, as if the editors prayed that the tornado might not touch down at New York. In this they were destined to disappointment; the smasher would frighten the city out of its wits in less than a year.

Carry's headline was the second-boldest on the *Times'* front page, principal attention being given to another woman, regrettably not in the ascendant, who for four decades had been a world symbol of peace. It would have been impossible to find two more dissimilar representatives of their sex, this despite the fact that Mrs. Nation could validly claim many years of spurious relationship with the invalid. Queen Victoria (the original) was dying in Osborne House, at Cowes, the then super-fashionable English spa on the Isle of Wight. The Queen's death, like her life, was proceeding serenely, and a good many foreign dignitaries arrived by the moment to help usher her out. Chief among these was Emperor Wilhelm of Germany, who was soon to become known more familiarly (and melodically) to his hosts as Kaiser Bill, with hopeful suggestions about hanging him to a "sour apple tree." The Kaiser mooned around, appearing doleful, and may well have made a few sketches of bridges and fortifications in preparation for the unimaginable holocaust he let loose, or permitted to be loosed, thirteen years later.

The *Times'* front page was absorbing in general. "Anarchist Scare at Yonkers," a third headline announced, but it developed that the uproar centered on peanuts. A Greek-American named Masuras changed his testimony on the witness stand. Previously he had stated, after rushing into police headquarters with a gash under one eye, that Anarchists had ordered him to "kill a prominent American." Under pressure, he said that Yonkers was in the grip of a "peanut trust," thus making things difficult for him (Masuras), an independent vendor operating on a coveted corner where the citizens appeared to be peanut-starved. The authorities promised to try and break the terrible peanut trust. The Fifth Avenue Coach Company, in a progressive humor, was leasing three of the new omnibuses for experimental purposes on its main routes, while the New Haven transit companies were abandoning their try at motor-driven vehicles "because of a lack of business sufficient to pay expenses." The directors failed to see any future in the machines; what's more, they (the machines) seemed over-fragrant.

"Venezuela Charged with Blackmailing" described a situation that has remained a staple to the present; the old story—trying to expropriate the gringo's property. In 1901, however, Washington officials took retributive action and meant it, not reversing themselves and apologizing the next day, with promises to free the serfs (whether they liked it or not), establish the Indian population in penthouses, punish the country's best brains, send down ten billion dollars and scuttle the United States Fleet.

The impeccable Tammany Hall was making its usual noises on page one, in this instance advancing a slate of typically shifty and unsuitable political spongers for the offices of President on down.

Asked who might be the "reform" candidate for Mayor, a spokes-
man replied, in good Tammanyese, "There's only one that knows,
and he ain't going to tell—the Lord." By and large the interview
lacked punch. Stocks were "irregular," and the weather promised
"Fair and Colder." Cost of the paper, on that cold, fair, wonderfully free day in New York, was a penny.

Mrs. Nation was excited by her attentions in the *Times,* and by
the news that a non-seeded Scotch-Irish poet, Patrick Crowley,
was preparing a biography of her in verse. When it came out, her
fans received it with mixed emotions. For one thing, Crowley un-
gallantly refused to take any responsibility for her, describing his
work, in an introductory paragraph, as "The story of a sincere
woman with a laudable hatred of the abuse of alcohol, which carried her to extremes." In Crowley's view, his subject had "all the
characteristics of the reformer, and reformers are frequently extremists. Obviously a little mad, one cannot give unqualified ap-
proval to her actions." Poets are not required to be grammarians,
but Crowley's grammar, in that last sentence, makes it unclear
whether it was he or Mrs. Nation who was mad; either way, the
biography disappoints. It is one of those books which, once you've
set it down, is almost impossible to pick back up. The narrative
pace is marred by the fact that the quatrains never seem to scan,
though they come through ringingly with some astonishing rhymes.
The slender volume, published by Arthur H. Stockwell, Ltd., at
Ilfracombe, sold well at one shilling, sixpence (then about a quarter) among a clientele whose appetites were perhaps whetted more
by a hatred of booze than an inborn love of books.

The uneven texture of the work proved an irritant to biblio-
philes who had been looking forward to a treat. Crowley got off to
a smooth-running start when he wrote that

> "Kentucky was her native State,
> She cradled on a scraggly farm,
> In eighteen forty-six, and Fate,
> Decreed her ways should rouse alarm."

but there was open criticism of a paragraph dealing with Gloyd.

> "A baby in due time arrived,
> For Carry. She had failed to save,
> Drink sodden Gloyd, who headlong dived,
> Wildly raving to an early grave."

The objection was raised, did Gloyd really dive? And if so, was he wildly raving? His relatives, among others, thought not. The group was represented, in a loose sense, by a first cousin who sought to extract damages, getting nowhere (the transatlantic barricades were too formidable for the emerging American system of jurisprudence).

Crowley's treatment of Mrs. Nation's Kiowa venture indicated a knowledge of the facts largely denied to witnesses on the scene; however, the rhymes were sound.

> "Ammunition she found handy
> On a pool table—sixteen balls.
> These she flung at the gin and brandy
> Bottles in shelves upon the walls.

> "The bartender, retreating, ran
> Directly in the line of fire
> Of one swift-flying ball. The man
> Collapsed before he could retire."

Dealing with Mrs. Nation's visit to John L. Sullivan's saloon (made after the Wichita raids) Crowley allowed both his facts and his rhymes to go pretty much to pieces.

> "They said that Sullivan thus spoke,
> And many heard the threat: 'Be sure
> If she comes near my joint, I'll poke
> Her head into a smelly sewer.' "

Sullivan was miffed by Crowley's easy assumption that the grand old fighter caved in, and the verses did indeed take an unequivocal line.

"On the door banging, Carry cried,
  'You rum-soaked coward, open!' Peeping
Through a slit, a barman inside
Explained that now John L. was sleeping.

"Triumphant, Carry faced the crowd
  And snorting in derision, said:
'He is afraid of me.' A cloud
  Had fallen on the champion's head.

"In the ring or elsewhere, never
  Had John L. Sullivan moved faster.
The only fight he refused ever
  Was this, for him a dire disaster."

The question of good taste arose in a section pertaining to a "purple-faced" policeman who was attempting, with some exertion, to stuff Mrs. Nation into a van, after she had shredded a tobacco shop in New York.

" 'Your days are done, rum-sodden beast.'
  And then in prayerful tone she said:
'Thank God, that's one good thing, at least,'
  Six weeks from then that cop dropped dead."

The consensus was that the principle of *de mortuis nil nisi bonum* should have applied here, and, more important, many devout persons were disturbed that Carry had put prayer to such a base use as the felling of a policeman. The action was on the level of African savages stricking pins in a replica doll.

With Crowley's offering, and others, Carry Nation enlarged the already swollen abundance of temperance literature. For awhile it had been uphill work; the practitioners had been bucking a backlog of approbation by classical *belles lettres*. The genius Keats, for example, had made things difficult by inquiring, in a kind of multi-stanza-ed pub-crawl:

"Souls of poets dead and gone,
What Elysium have ye known,
Happy field or mossy cavern,
Choicer than the Mermaid Tavern?"

A student of the new, opposition strain, excavating the seemingly endless such reels from the musty stacks of libraries, is awed by the aroused army of people who have sung in mournful numbers about drinking. Desserts piled high with whipped cream, chocolate and meringue may offend the body as grossly as alcohol, but passionate writing on the subject is hard to find. It has become fashionable for tax-hungry agencies to belabor tobacco firms, which have a weak and timorous lobby, but no government—federal, state or local—would impose punishments on the lobby-powerful dairies, whose products have been singled out for attention by the heart doctors. And the clergy, so shrill against stimulants, have remained curiously silent about desserts.

American temperance literature had its genesis in the person of one Timothy Shay Arthur, a journalist dedicated to getting ahead. In a sense, Arthur blundered into the saloon theme and thrilled to find it a bonanza of popularity. Thenceforward he pursued it with gusto, usually somewhat fortified by beer, wine or whiskey. At a point in the middle 1800's he had half of America weeping (often into beer) over the heart-wrenching plaint of little Mary as she sang, in the immortal *Ten Nights in a Barroom,* "Father, dear Father, come home with me now; The clock in the steeple strikes one." Only a case-hardened hater of children, such as, perhaps, W. C. Fields, could deny that Mary had a legitimate beef. Her situation verged on the intolerable. In the play, which ran for decades everywhere in the country—in theaters, barns, churches, even saloons—the toddler visits the Sickle & Sheaf bar with some hope of rousting out her father, Joe Morgan. She finds him slumped over in a chair, embalmed. Taking his hand (which actors in the part made shake so severely as to rattle glasses on the shelves) she gives vent to the song, now established as a dubious sample of American folklore.

"You said you were coming right home from the shop
As soon as your day's work was done.
Our fire has gone out—our house is all dark—
And mother's been watching since tea,
With poor brother Benny so sick in her arms,
And no one to help her but me."

Mary's appeal fell on deaf ears—Joe was out, cold, thus enabling her to come back later in the play and sing a second verse. By this time the girl's plight had radically worsened. Benny was dead, gone to his reward without even the comfort of a diagnosis; the mother, freezing, was ready for an institution, and Mary herself was only moments away from the Reaper. Slade, the saloon-owner, falls into a fit of rage over customers who neglect their families, seizes a beer mug, winds up and flings it in the general direction of Morgan, killing Mary. Sophisticated audiences expressed the opinion that she was well out of it. Even so, Morgan took a hitch on himself, threw off the shackles, and never touched liquor again.

With morality tales like these, Arthur became the idol of the temperance set, the second most popular writer of his age, close behind Harriet Beecher Stowe, instigator of the Civil War. *Ten Nights in a Barroom* was published in 1854, and the dramatized version, accomplished by a William W. Pratt, Esq., appeared soon afterward. The success of both was so explosive that Arthur remained quiescent until 1872, working in his church, penning religious essays, discreetly tippling on the side. When, in the year named, a publisher bore down on him, appealing to his conscience with a reminder that saloons were on the rise, he shook off his lethargy and produced *Three Years in a Man Trap,* a novel of moving spleen. It was a hard-hitting denunciation of saloons (which Arthur in fact never frequented, doing all of his drinking at home) and provoked a landslide of curiosity about the recreational centers under discussion. Many persons thitherto indifferent to saloons began dropping in to see if all those high jinks really took place. But there was action on the other side of the fence. Not long after *Ten Nights* materialized, New Hampshire passed a law prohibiting the sale of liquor; with its formalized desiccation, thirteen states and one territory, including Kansas, had some kind of drinking laws that were violated with good cheer and impunity, apart from visitations like those of Carry Nation. However, some unsung horticulturist has noted that every rose has its thorn, and the most plausible reforms are subject to violent reactions. While *Ten Nights* was booming at its noisiest, and after *Three Years in a Man Trap* had appeared to give it support, every dry state except Maine repealed its prohibitions, and even Maine cut back to a "license system."

This came as a blow to Arthur, who drank some wine and thought the problem over. He let his ideas ferment. The saloon vein having conspicuously petered out, he switched to a general assault on poverty, especially in the cities, with a novel called *Cast Adrift*. It not only caught on in the book shops but received important critical attention, being compared favorably with the worst of Dickens.

Arthur's genius lay in the fact that he had no knowledge whatever of saloons, or of slums, either. Even so, his influence remained potent for years. The truth is, few temperance writers ever got within sniffing distance of a bar; reform literature in general was built on a foundation of sand. A valid though heretical case could be made that the sainted Harriet Stowe was indeed a prime mover in causing the Civil War, and her total experience of the South—a complex of ignorance that endures to the present—consisted of one day's visit to friends in Louisville, Kentucky. To consider that the slaughter of friends and relations was preventable is a shocking betrayal of America's woolliest-headed taboo, but if Mrs. Stowe had taken up skiing, or necking, and if Abraham Lincoln (another gifted writer) had been less intent on declaring a century's culture changed Right Now, slavery might have vanished with no more dislocation than took place in England. Carl Sandburg has made the point that Southern states might never have seceded had Republicans not insisted on the extremist Lincoln as their candidate. Moderation is a two-way street.

But reformers are usually in a hurry, and the temperance group set the dizziest pace of them all. It was hoped that *The Drunkard,*.

or, The Fallen Saved, a distraught "moral drama" in five acts, might provoke a frenzy of bottle smashing in the 1850's, but people weathered it with admirable calm. The play opened in Boston, then a bibulous center, and ran for 140 performances, establishing a record for the place and time. When audiences began to lose interest, Phineas T. Barnum brought it to New York, to a rackety backdrop of tub-thumping, and set it rolling in the Moral Lecture Room of his American Museum. Barnum had only recently turned moral, having signed the pledge (in a public ceremony popularly seen as a humbug) and vowed to abandon other sources of entertainment. There is no anti-alcoholic quite as strident as a reformed drunk, and Barnum's moralistic disdain grew into a municipal burden. Considerable evidence remains that the showman actually did quit drinking, for good, while continuing to function as a professional mountebank and cheat.

Two thousand persons nightly jammed the Moral Lecture Room to view the unrelieved sinkhole of misery set forth by *The Drunkard,* and at the end of each performance the now saintly Barnum, wearing an unctuous look, ushered everybody into his museum to see (for an additional fee) "the cherry-colored cat," which turned out to be a black-cherry-colored cat, and his eighteen-foot Feejee mermaid, which was a small, bottled article of inexpensive manufacture, believed struck off somewhere in the inscrutable East. Barnum had an overall success, and a few problems, with *The Drunkard.* Editor Horace Greeley, a sturdy critic of chicanery, visited the play and loosed several gratified editorials in his *Tribune,* hoping that the drab and lachrymose mask might restore the public to a "sound and promising condition of moral healthfulness on the subject of Temperance."

The play did not in fact have precisely that effect in New York. Barnum's main problem with it consisted in the outpouring of males between acts toward saloons around the corner. It made no difference that *The Drunkard* was hard to swallow without a bracer; as a newly converted prude, the showman sensed inconsistency in the moral atmosphere of his evenings when seen as a whole. It was noble to bring people a powerful assault on drink, but was it persuasive if they attended it while intoxicated? After a wrestle with his conscience (and a regretful look at the till), he declared against issuing return checks between acts. For awhile the crowds diminished only slightly; most men had responded by bringing flasks. Barnum then announced from the stage that facilities for signing the pledge had been established at the box office. Anybody so minded, and he hoped that everybody would be minded thus, could drop by and swear off, in writing. Several persons complied.

It must be recalled that the period marked a flowering of the elaborate practical joke, an obvious outlet at a time when over-religion had stigmatized fun of nearly any sort. Two retired New York tycoons named DeVoe and Lozier had lately announced, and sold to the public, their intention of sawing off most of Manhattan Island and turning it around. Lozier explained to the curious, and they were legion, that he had the support of Mayor Stephen Allen (who must either have been in a coma or out of town). Owing to Wall Street construction, Manhattan sagged at the Battery end, said Lozier, so he and his philanthropic partner had decided to saw it off at Kingsbridge (the northern end); then they could float it out past Ellis Island, swivel the cumbersome real estate, and restore it to a safer position. Accordingly, they somehow obtained several hundred-foot saws with teeth three feet deep, two dozen oars 250 feet long, 300 sawyers and 200 men to row the island across the harbor. Both Lozier and DeVoe were at the site for eight weeks, toting ledgers, hiring, firing, giving orders and looking exceedingly solemn. But when the great day came, the partners checked in absent. Approximately a thousand workmen arrived to begin the remarkable incision; the philanthropists, somebody finally learned, had gone to Europe, where they stayed till things cooled down.

Barnum made himself famous through a conviction that the public enjoyed being gulled, and *The Drunkard*—entirely serious—was one of his lesser triumphs. As the play continued its run, and New York audiences appeared to see it as a comedy, Barnum took to delivering windy temperance talks from the stage. *The Drunkard* began to lose its grip on continuity; there was no means of determining when the fever might seize him. Also, for his reform work he employed the old circus device of planting shills in the audience. These were to ask questions he had hit on as being both pertinent and catchy: "Mr. Barnum, how does alcohol affect us—externally or internally?" His reply was rendered in an evangelical, sheep-like bleat: "E—ternally."

Another affecting voice in temperance was that of Mrs. Nellie H. Bradley, whose plays fell short of the smash-hit levels established by *Ten Nights* and *The Drunkard* but quietly brought liquor to the attention of thousands, including many initiates, for three decades after the Civil War. Critics held that her genius reached fruition with *Wine as a Medicine,* rating the work (which bowed in 1873) even over such of her previous triumphs as *The First Glass, The Young Teetotaler, Reclaimed,* and *Marry No Man if He Drinks. Wine* had as a subtitle *Abbie's Experience,* and Mrs. Bradley, in the view of one dissident, often seemed hard-pressed to make the experience sound disagreeable. The theme did not strike a wholly new note in the annals of toping. A betrothed girl of quality suffers an onset of ill health—or fit of the vapors—and is attended by an offhand physician who slips her a bottle of medical wine, a practice both standard and respectable. It promptly revives her, and gives her the strength to demand another, a trifle larger. By the time her friend Emma Marsh arrives, she (Abbie) is pretty far gone down the rosé path. The duties of friendship prompt Emma to say, "I hope you will not be offended by my plain speaking, Abbie; but I fear you are cultivating an appetite which may cause you sorrow."

It could be expected that Abbie was innocent. As there are no guilty criminals in prisons—they've all been framed—few alcoholics admit to a fault beyond "social drinking." (Case histories abound. A noted suburbanite, popular around the country club bar, whose social drinking was increasing at the rate of about three ounces of whiskey a year, at last began to feel continuously poisoned and wondered if he had contracted an organic disease. A diagnostician who checked him carefully over made a reluctant report to the sufferer's wife: "I'm sorry to tell you this, but your husband is an alcoholic." Confronted, the man took it decently, squared his shoulders, returned to his job, paid his medical bill and changed doctors.)

Mrs. Bradley's plays lasted because her characters made classic points, relevant to drinking in any age.

A.—Emma! I really should be offended, had anyone else hinted the possibility of such a thing; but I know your motives are kind, and your words prompted by friendship. To relieve you of any anxiety, I assure you I can give it up at any time with perfect ease; but I am equally sure it is beneficial, and for that reason alone I continue to use it.

Emma has a hard, stubborn streak, and she bulls right along in the same vein.

E.—I think you said a wine-glassful was the prescribed quantity; that glass (pointing to it) contains at least four times as much as the largest wine-glass. Why do you increase the quantity to so great an extent?

A.—A wine-glass holds so little Emma, and I was very weak then, and of course could not use it as freely as I can now.

Still attentive to friendship, Emma warns Abbie two or three more times and then marries her fiancé. In the play's middle, Abbie goes completely to pieces, still on medical wine, and manages to corrupt her younger brother, Lennie, who, in a memorable scene, makes known his debauchery to his mother, while Abbie stands aside, holding an empty bottle and watching with sisterly pride and vexation.

L. (laughing)—Indeed I'm *not* drunk; only a little funny; and I think, instead of scolding, you ought to thank me for keeping *you* sober, for that wine would have gone to your head instead of mine if I hadn't been so fortunate as to appropriate it. Sis, how can you carry such a great chignon? Ain't it heavy? (Catches at it; she evades him, and he snatches off his mother's glasses.) I feel uncommonly jolly today.

Successful temperance plays of the period had the affected characters sober up permanently toward the end. *Wine*'s shift of climate is startling to readers (or audiences) who had become resigned to Abbie's entertaining lapses of decorum. After a scene in which she comes home dragging a drunk by one hand and holding a "satchel-ful" of wine in the other—to announce her elopement with a nonentity—even the most hopeful had begun to write her off as a loser. But her bridegroom (perhaps seeing her clearly for the first time) shudders with revulsion, and we have an interlude that shocks one with its similarity to the present. On any day, in a million homes, at a million parties, the same, sad dispute proceeds apace.

> S. (Claude Stanton, the new husband) aside.—Heavens! what a future is before me. Scarcely has my honeymoon begun, and my wife is again, and for the third time, intoxicated!
>
> A (offended).—I think it is very unbecoming in you to refer, in so pointed a manner, to *my* taste for wine, when you know well that you always drink *three* glasses to my *one*.
>
> S.—But remember, Abbie, three glasses do not affect me as powerfully as *one* will affect you.
>
> A. (scornfully)—Why don't you speak in plain English, and say that it takes three times the quantity to make you *drunk* that it does to make *me* so?

In Mrs. Bradley's touching last scene, Stanton emerges as a tower of strength, Abbie falters then promises "all you require," and the frolicsome Lennie winds up as the greatest surprise of all. His speech brings down the final curtain:

> L.—I say Amen to that [total abstinence] and hurrah for the temperance doctors; for I intend to be one myself, and then you may look out for a crusade against all kinds of liquor as medicine, from port wine down to plantation bitters.

It may be important not to treat *Wine as a Medicine* flippantly because of its stilted speech and archaic construction. Its message was uncomfortably apropos in the period. As already suggested, American and English women had fallen into the habit of sipping wine both as tonic and as the glue of social connection. The delusion had somehow been spread (probably by liquor sellers) that to consider wine and drunkenness as related was beyond the bounds of gentility—even when the gentlest guests at a morning sherry-sip were snoring under the table. To confound the problem, aristocrats viewed the temperance movement as a convulsion of the vulgar. In their embarrassment, the gentry stepped up the consumption of spirits in a desperate effort to preserve the graces.

It would however be hard to prove that temperance writers had a marked effect on reform. Their moral was so ridiculously over-stated that it appealed only to the securely converted; the great middle-group of undecided usually found themselves bored stiff or doubled over with laughter, or, at the worst, thirsty.

In her maturity, Mrs. Bradley's thoughts turned to the young, for whom she rattled off a seemingly endless series of anti-drink playlets. *A Temperance Picnic,* which opened to mixed notices in 1888, has been mentioned as being the most ornate and least digestible of the group. Mrs. Bradley's synopsis, description of the cast and suggestions for costumes would alone have shot most self-respecting children off to the pool hall; by mischance for them, they were dragged to the presentation under duress by parents.

The work was among the first racist documents to deal with the subject of infant intoxication. Kindly old Mother Merryheart, "familiarly known as the Old Woman who Lived in a Shoe," had suffered a setback before curtain time when her twelve-year-old son, Charlie, cleared off to become a drunk. Some un-kindly old critics took the line that she had driven him away with her syrupy attention to good works. However, instead of mourning, she simply stepped up her exertions in behalf of the underprivileged, these taking the form of hauling to the forest (and her "Shoe") a Chinese boy, a young Negro, an adolescent German and a wee Irisher, among others, the group being progeny of drunken fathers and itinerant mothers. The play's text does not make clear in which woodsy region of America this assortment was available, but there may have been a kind of United Nations for juveniles operating in the period. "To contribute to their pleasure," says Mrs. Bradley's synopsis, "Mother Merryheart has arranged for a picnic, and has taught the younger children a quaint little conceit about 'water spirits,' 'wood nixies,' birds, etc."

Everything was going well, despite a tear-jerking song that Mother insisted on bellowing, and the Chinaman had presumably adapted himself to the nixies and water spirits, along with the im-probable nosegay of Occidentals, when who should stroll into the dell but Wandering Charlie, smoking a pipe and carrying a half-concealed flask. He seems sleepy, or maybe one over the mark, and flings himself down for a nap, on which the nixies and water spirits whirl into a frenzy of excitement. Briefly, they douse him with spring water, inside and out, to mumbled incantations understood only by the shaman of the tribe. The effect is extraordinary. Charlie, converted instantly to sainthood, leaps up and bursts into song—one that he and his mother finish *en duet*. It has to do with how grateful he is for all that spring water.

Relief was expressed that Mrs. Bradley, no doubt with an effort, refrained from injecting a nationalistic flavor into the final exercises, perhaps having the Chinaman publicly eat a bird's nest, the Irishman imitate a leprechaun, Fat Fritz sing something from the beer gardens, and the colored lad do the double-shuffle. For a racist creation, the play was admirably restrained.

Mrs. Bradley was not alone in her ministrations to the young. Powerful voices had arisen to help her spread the word. In Boston, Dr. Charles Jewett issued "The Youth's Temperance Lecturer," a kind of indoctrinational primer for the uninformed. Jewett was a realist and had the good sense to say, in his preface, "I anticipate for it rather a cool reception from the sellers of intoxicating drinks, as well as from distillers, brewers, etc." His judgment was sound; the tract aroused a furor of interest and indignation. Perhaps not since the days of the Tea Party had there been such consternation in Bean Town. An early effort by distillers to buy up copies and burn them was foiled when Jewett's wily publishers ordered an immediate new printing.

Apprehension over Jewett died away fast when the returns began to come in. Chapter One was indeed alarming from the liquor sellers' viewpoint. The booklet was illustrated, with surprisingly good sketches, and the first of these showed a human derelict in shocking disarray leaning grotesquely against a barrel. "Little readers," advised the text, "look at this picture of a man, with his ragged clothes, worn-out shoes, and old slouched hat. What a sad plight he is in! One eye, you see, is shut up, and the other is but half open, while, with his bottle in his pocket, he is leaning on that large cask. It is the picture of a drunkard."

So far, so good, but there followed a wonderful series of drawings, beginning with a home-sized still, that would have made the production of alcohol smooth sailing for a chimpanzee. If the sketches were crystal-clear (and they were) the supplementary directions were masterly. Reading the pamphlet, one cannot avoid wondering what was in Jewett's mind, and some influential Bostonians reflected along the same lines. "The articles which are used to make people drunk are Distilled Spirits, such as Rum, Brandy, Gin and Whiskey," the section began. "Next we have wines, of which there are many kinds; then Beer, which is sometimes called Ale; and Cider. I will now tell you how these drinks are made."

In his subsequent description (and drawing) of the still, Jewett explained the "worm," which passes "through a tub of cold water," converting the steam to liquid; then he galloped on over the final stages to ingestion. Within a week after the primer hit the streets, most of Boston's copper tubing had disappeared from the shops, and any number of little readers were busy in basements. The concentration appeared to be on Rum, for which the doctor had also supplied a poem, in case his other directions proved unclear.

> "They put molasses many an hour
> Into vats and let it sour;
> When it is as sour as swill,
> Then they put it in the still.
> Under it they put the fire,
> Till it burns up higher and higher.
> Now the poison, hot and strong,
> Trickles through the pipe along,
> Till it drops into the cask.
> Little readers, do you ask
> Why they turn molasses sweet,
> Which is given us to eat,
> Into Rum? I'll tell you why;
> 'Tis that foolish men may buy
> And drink the poison stuff and die."

Many agreed that the last few lines rang a little hollow; the excitement lay in the brewing. Numberless homemade stills were broken up over the city, and the popularity of Jewett, with his no-doubt high intentions, died down to a general sigh of relief. There

The child of destiny aged six,
with her mother, "Queen Victoria."
(from Carry Nation's autobiography)

Carry's father, George Moore,
a movable Irishman
of wit and forbearance.
(from Carry Nation's autobiography)

The crusader at twenty-six,
wedded to an alcoholic,
storing the grapes of wrath.
(from Carry Nation's autobiography)

The unmemorable David Natio
with customary suit of solemn
black and look of scalding piet
(Kansas State Historical Society)

The human tornado sweep
through saloon Kansas:
an Enterprise bar in
ruins after "hatchetation.
(Kansas State Historical Socie

Wichita's pride—the Hotel
Carey Bar with its oil
of the naked Temptress—
ravished in a smash-and-run raid.
(Kansas State Historical Society)

"I CANNOT TELL A LIE--I DID IT WITH MY LITTLE HATCHET!"
Mrs. Nation's Reform Crusade in Kansas, as the Globe Artist Understands It From the Press Dispatches.

(Culver)

Confined in the friendly
Wichita jail, home-away-from-home
for the reformer.
(Culver)

Carry in full war rig,
at the peak of her career.
(Brown Brothers)

Coming-out party at a
small, local jail: Carry
faces some bibulous frontiersmen.
(Kansas State Historical Society)

Mrs. Nation rounds out her
education at Yale, victim
of an undergraduate prank.
(Bettman Archives)

A New York paper's
indelicate view of
a Carry Nation spasm.
(New York Public Library Picture Collection)

MRS. NATION'S CLIMAX.

Carry's theatrical billing—
clear, curt, copious.
(Kansas State Historical Society)

Fresh, sober faces from the Nineties
Carry leads a meeting
in upstate New York.
(Kansas State Historical Society)

Carry the platform draw— misspelled and misunderstood.
(Kansas State Historical Society)

Ribald saloon men await an invasion, with its stimulated sale of spirits. *(Kansas State Historical Society)*

Thorn-covered cottage of Carry and the beleaguered Nation. *(Kansas State Historical Society)*

International symbol of
direct action; the
battle-hardened reformer
in her twilight years.
(European Picture Service)

was talk that the community's brewers intended to honor him—
with a purse or a life's supply of their products—for the exhaustive
and valuable research he had done for his section on European
hop fermentation, but nothing ever came of it. He may well have
declined.

A defect shared by these earnest reform workers was a goggle-
eyed view of human nature, and particularly the nature of children. It was no time at all until young readers had devised a game,
that promised to sweep the nation, called "Go Out in the Yard and
Play Drunk." The child who could best mimic the posture of the
inebriate, as gleaned from artists' guidebooks, for example, was
declared to be the winner. A faked drunken stance thus threatened
to become permanently admired in juvenile circles. From there,
anxious parents feared, it was but a step to the saloon for a realistic
collection of the attitudes. Fortunately, as in the case of Jewett, the
fever subsided.

The *chef d'oeuvre* of Julia Colman (popular authoress of *Catechism on Alcohol*), called *Temperance Manual for Teachers,*
—published in New York in 1885—was a prime sample of reformers' vulnerability. So far as is known, Miss Colman was neither a physician nor a nutritionist, yet her work (in the form of
questions and answers for children) is one of the loftiest pieces of
medical pontification extant. What seems more piquant, the questions presupposed an equally high knowledge of science by the tots
under inquisition.

Q. Why do we believe that it [alcohol] does no good?

A. (theoretically by a child of nine): Because when the system throws it out, it is alcohol still, just as it went in; which shows
that it has no use for it.

Q. Is there no food in porter, and ale, and beer?

A. There is not; and if the alcohol were taken out, no one
would drink them.

Q. Why, then, do people grow fat who take them?

A. Because the alcohol puts so much impurity in the blood
that it cannot all be worked off, and so it is tucked away in corners as dead matter or fat.

Miss Colman's long asides were intended to help orient the ju-

venile mind. These sometimes shaped up as what the critics protested were pretty far-fetched parallels. In Chapter Nine, the childhood preoccupation with animals, especially vicious animals, was
noted in her memorable analogy of the Bear: "We might call alcohol a bear, and suppose the bear should get into the house where
papa and mamma and all the children are busy about their work.
Do you suppose they would all go right on with their work, papa
writing an article [no reason has ever been found why Miss Colman lumped all husbands as article-writers] and mamma getting
dinner, and Jennie sweeping, and Walter cleaning out the cellar,
and let the bear range around and do as he liked? No, indeed!
They would start right up to drive him out the quickest way possible. They would drive him from room to room, just as the alcohol
was driven from stomach to liver, and from heart to lungs, and
they would pitch him out where there was the most convenient
opening, whether it was door or window. He came in by the stomach door, and if they could drive him out again that way they
would do it; but if they found it more convenient to send him out
by the window in the lungs, out he would go that way. . . ."

By this time, it was claimed by the unkind, the average confused
youngster may have been deluded that somebody, probably Miss
Colman, had a bear in her lungs, with no immediate hope of getting it out, and one child, questioned by unconvinced parents, felt
that the animal had entered the house in the first place for the
specific purpose of bumming a drink. Besides, it was said, the author's remarks about bodily openings were in bad taste; "apart
from authors like the Frenchman Rabelais, the subject has always
been considered out of bounds," stated a New York newspaper's
roundup of new temperance material issued by the National Temperance Society and Publication House.

An English sociologist once deplored that most reform literature has been produced by women. Risking his life, he dared to
point out that females have a distressing habit of thinking with
their emotions rather than with their brains. His sole exception
was the Englishwoman Sarah Stickney Ellis, primarily a writer on
female education, who, as a reformed wino, took up the subject of
temperance. She described "a mysterious sinking" to which she
had been prone, especially in her cups, causing her greatly to

increase the dosages of wine, which made her sink deeper and added "a kind of whirl" (not uncommon in such cases), which symptoms disappeared when she quit drinking altogether. She was one of the few female writers who ever had genuine notes on the problem. In America in the 1800's emotionalism all but ruled out the trivial question of research. It is safe to contend that nearly all the spotless women who wrote temperance arguments never saw the inside of a saloon; moreover, they knew nothing about liquor. Carry Nation was, of course, a-typical. Her nocturnal prowlings in search of the whiskey-drenched Gloyd, gave her an insight into drinking perhaps denied to any other reformer of her age.

The suggestion has been made that Harriet Beecher Stowe started the Civil War after a twenty-four-hour visit to Louisville; her hysterically applauded jousts with slavery obscured the fact that she had written some equally untutored treatises about booze.* Mrs. Stowe was born in Litchfield, Connecticut, the daughter of Lyman Beecher, a dedicated striver against drink. By trade he had been a minister, working out of Boston, but he seized the opportunity to become head of the newly founded Lane Theological Seminary at Cincinnati; his move to Litchfield, a place of great physical charm, was to ascend the pulpit of the Presbyterian Church there. Beecher became locally famous for his Six Sermons on Intemperance, which were issued in book form and reduced drinking for a time among the New England clergy. (The Reverend Lyman Abbott, a temperance historian, claimed a wider influence for Beecher's multiple thunders, saying that "In ten years the consumption of strong drink was decreased more than one-half per capita"—though not making clear whether this falling-off was limited to ministers, or to New England's laity, or to itinerant tinkers, or what.)

Nearly all of Beecher's seven children made their mark. The best-known of them, aside from Harriet, was the Reverend Henry Ward Beecher, who became the brightest luminary in New York's

---

* *Uncle Tom's Cabin* was translated into twenty-three languages, many of them serving lands where slavery and oppression existed at their worst. Nevertheless the play evoked pity from all; an Indian Brahmin might read it with tears coursing down his face, then kick an Untouchable away from the common, or clean-folks', well. (Despite India's currently favored position, the custom has not yet been altered.)

theological heavens. He was a tireless espouser of causes, a champion of both temperance and emancipation, among several dozen other things, and a remorseless enemy of Sin. In the Plymouth Congregational Church of Brooklyn, his best friend was Theodore Tilton, who had a voluptuous wife of a religious ardor outstanding even in the flock presided over by a figure whose mortality was thought by some (mostly females) to be a matter for awed speculation. Beecher seduced Mrs. Tilton about as soon as possible, giving rise to the best-relished scandal and law case of the century. Friend or not, Tilton expressed himself as displeased. His suit for alienation of affections indicated that he preferred to keep Elizabeth's white body for his own use, which was essentially secular. For her part, the strayed lamb explained that Beecher had unfairly crept up behind the shield of the Lord, performing the whole operation (which needed frequent re-doing) in a spirit of pure salvation. Beecher's conduct through the trial was declared to be singular. In court he was rebuked for making jokes on the witness stand; outside, he caused the luckless Tilton to be fired from his editorial job, dishonestly accused him of immorality with a pair of famous suffragettes, and accepted $15,000 worth of Northern Pacific Railway bonds from Jay Cooke for the open purpose of "influencing the public mind to favor the new railroad." Beecher's tilts with Mrs. Tilton lost him his pastorate (which carried an annual salary of $20,000), but he continued to shed lustre on reform by lecturing at halls where women (presenting a strong case against suffrage) smashed in doors to hear the "Minister Plenipotentiary" whom editor Henry Watterson had just called "a dunghill covered with flowers."

From childhood, Lyman Beecher's daughter Harriet had been busy with pen and pencil. She was regarded as a typical intellectual-in-the-making, and first gained notice, while in a class of her father's, with an anonymous essay taking a bold negative on the proposition, "Can the Immortality of the Soul be Proved by the Light of Nature?" (Such questions perplexed New England thinkers in the era.) "Who wrote this?" demanded Beecher, uplifted, and Harriet, admitting her guilt, said afterward that it was the supremest moment of her life. Her career was, however, to have many such moments, or near-such-moments. Her temperance novelettes, done largely in the Fifties, never really caught on, and it was understandable that she should switch to a theme of broader appeal. *The Coral Ring* had followed close on the heels of *August Howard,* both published by Glasgow's Scottish Temperance League and priced right, as used-car dealers say, to sell for a penny.* *The Coral Ring* concerns itself with the plight of a Colonel Elliot, who took a little wine, not especially for his stomach's sake but because it seemed a cheerful and civilized thing to do. Mrs. Stowe (in adulthood she married an invalid pedagogue whose health became progressively worse with the proliferation of his wife's novels) has her heroine rescue Elliot from this dilemma —described in the book as being "on the verge"—by means of a coy parlor trick, a thoughtless vow, spoken in jest. Trapped, he signs the pledge, but the action appears to leave him joyless, as the remark of a friend—one of the old wine-sipping crowd of hellions —might indicate:

"What's the matter with you, Elliot? You look solemn as a hearse."

Mrs. Stowe was an important force in American life, even as her brother had been in the life of the Tiltons, and the quality of her prose remains interesting to true lovers of literary mysteries. *The Coral Ring's* opening lines will be sufficient to set the pace:

Chapter One

"There is no time of life in which young girls are so thoroughly selfish as from fifteen to twenty," said Edward Ashton deliberately, as he laid down a book he had been reading, and leaned over the center table.

"You insulting fellow," replied a tall, brilliant-looking creature, [Florence Elmore] who was lounging on an ottoman hard by, overcome of Dickens' last work.

"Truth, coz, for all that," said the gentleman, with the air of one who means to provoke a discussion . . .

"Pshaw, it's one of your fusty old bachelor notions."

---

* It is odd how frequently, and positively, Glasgow turns up in the temperance fight. Its love of whiskey then was challenged by only its sister metropolis of Dundee, and, more lately, Evelyn Waugh, in defining Hogmanay for one of his fictional characters, explained: "People being sick on the pavement in Glasgow."

Etc.

If the book had a flaw, it was that it failed to go on, after the historic signing, and tell how long Elliot managed to remain alive and well, without wine, in a company of such conversational dynamism.

Temperance poetry and songs in Carry Nation's time were not regarded as influential in weaning drunkards away from the jug. Probably because the messages sported in such rarified cerebral heights, their aim appeared more literary than evangelical. As in today's intellectual journals, the contributors seemed to be writing for each other. In "Women *vs.* Rum," by S. Adams—an epic a little longer than "Endymion" and a thumping critical success— the plea was so obscured by high flights of diction that its impact was scarcely felt in the saloons. From its start:

> "In Eden's pure and hallowed bowers,
>   All robed in green and decked with flowers,
>   Our mother Eve in bliss reclined,
>   A perfect type of womankind."

it proceeded to contend that the serpent was actually a tool of the wine merchants. Barring possible involvements with hard cider, or applejack, there exists no biblical precedent for Adams' rhymed suggestion that the first honeymooners took to the bottle. One or two critics, while acknowledging a skilled pen, spoke up briskly at what they considered to be unpardonable anti-liquor license. Even the reference to Eve's décor, as being a robe of green besprinkled with flowers, came under attack: the clergy's position had theretofore been that she was naked; the assumption was, in fact, pivotal in the legend.

In Carry Nation's girlhood the best-known—certainly the most notorious—of the temperance hymns was a corruption of "The Star-Spangled Banner," which offended practically everybody. Its impertinence was held unpatriotic, and its language was so gross that the words stuck in the throats of all but the most rabid fanatics.

> "Oh who has not seen by the dawn's early light,
>   Some poor bloated drunkard to his home weakly reeling,

With blear eyes and red nose most revolting to sight;
Yet still in his breast not a throb of shame feeling!
And the plight he was in—steeped in filth to his chin—
Gave proof through the night in the gutter he'd been,
While the pitiable wretch would stagger along,
To the shame of his friends, 'mid the jeers of the throng."

In later stanzas the epithets coarsened as the wretch's plight grew worse; his wife was dragged in, her face "furrowed with suffering" when she saw her "loved lord like a wild demon rave"; the author spoke of "foul curses and pollution"; and then, in a crowning burst of impudence, the last line rang out serenely:

"O'er the land of the free and the home of the brave."

For fear of physical reprisals by listeners, the song was not much sung.

Every action is said to have an equal and opposite reaction, and a whole new literature—in defense of drinking—was uncorked by the challenging temperance works. Any objective critic, even one softened by wine, must concede that its quality suffered by comparison with the output of sanctimony and rebuke. It seemed to lack fire; genius appeared to have seeped out of the genre with Keats. It may be that passion, half-asleep in the glutted, burns more brightly in the deprived. For one thing, the new vintage was not a product of natural fermentation; much of it came to maturity after low and moneyed coaxing by the whiskey interests. Needless to say, there were exceptions. Dr. Oliver Wendell Holmes, the poet, physician and educator, raised the hopes of beleaguered tipplers with a resounding tract praising alcohol "both medicinally and dietetically." The doctor had lately come out against Calvinism and had thus gained the enviable status of Controversial Figure. Such of his poems as "The Chambered Nautilus" and "The Wonderful One-Hoss Shay"—free of religious or alcoholic bias—

helped reduce the anti-intellectual suspicions of the commonalty, and he is presently remembered by *Who Was Who in America,* among other guides, as one of those public voices "ahead of their time."

Springing to Holmes's support were further literary doctors, including several in England who staggered beneath the weight of royal and academic distinctions. Sir James Paget, Bart., F.R.C.S., D.C.L., L.L.D., F.R.S., President of the Royal College of Physicians, made the acute diagnosis that, "The stomach of one man is offended and irritated by wine and his digestion impeded, whilst the appetite of another is improved and his digestion facilitated. The former is better without alcohol, and he comes into the category of fools if he takes it; but the latter has no claim to the character of physician if he abstains at the bidding of a fanatic or a mere theorist." Rounding out the group, a horse doctor named C. Gordon Richardson, Lecturer on Chemistry in the Ontario Veterinary College, struck sharply at the teetotalers, but his prose was so technical and polysyllabic that his enemies professed to believe he was advocating strong drink for horses. His treatise was dismissed as impractical, one acid-penned fellow (American) scoring the telling point that "You can drive a horse to firewater, but you can't make him drink."

Pro-liquor advocates knew no regional or ideological bounds. Such an oddly assorted pair as Abraham Lincoln and Jefferson Davis spoke out with like eloquence on the subject, perhaps the only one on which they ever agreed. Of early attempts at legalized teetotalism, Lincoln wrote, "Prohibition will work great injury to the cause of temperance. It is a species of intemperance itself, for it goes beyond the bounds of reason in that it attempts to control a man's appetite by legislation, and in making crimes out of things that are not crimes." Jefferson Davis (a devotee of mild stomachics) waxed loftier yet when he wrote that "To destroy individual liberty and moral responsibility would be to eradicate one evil by the substitution of another, which, it is submitted, would be more fatal than that for which it was offered as a remedy. The abuse, and not the use, of stimulants, it must be confessed, is the evil to be remedied." Both men, in their ways, were striving to keep government from running the lives of men.

The liquor people seized with glee on the death of a Mrs. Sarah Roll, of Livermore, Kentucky, who was bitten by a snake while gathering kindling and died for want of whiskey in a community of local option. Several staff poets at distilleries undertook to sing her requiem, and her sacrifice might have become a *cause celèbre* had the word "copperhead" been less unwieldy in the poetical sense. Detractors suggested the substitution of "asp," claiming literary license, but the Egyptian complexion of the latter made the idea ludicrous.

While S. Adams ("Women *vs.* Rum") had turned the Garden of Eden into a bacchanal, another author of the period, Barry Gray, with sympathies at the opposite pole, also put Adam and Eve on an alcoholic footing, but with his (Gray's) lyric endorsement. He saw them as indefatigable mixers of mint juleps, and wrote, in his rural episode called "Out of Town":

"I defy any man, I don't care who he be, who grows mint in his grounds, to resist on a summer's day the delights of a mint julep. It is the only drink which might have been made in Eden. I can imagine how Adam and Eve, walking in blissful innocence across the dewy fields in the early morning, conversing of love, were arrested in their way by the delightful perfume which was exhaled by the humble plant upon which their virgin footsteps trod. . . ."

Gray went on to describe the excitements through which the couple stumbled in their evolution of the drink—their attempt first to brew mint tea, the discovery that cocoanut milk "ferments while lying in the sun," the triumphant wedding of the two ingredients, the wholesale swilling that followed, as Adam remarks to his mate: "A jewel to the lip!" It was expected that temperance groups would protest, but to their cries were added those of the feminists, for Gray fell into the mystifying habit, during his narrative, of referring to Eve condescendingly as "Mrs. Adam." He made the further mistake of observing, about Adam, that "he knew one or two more things than Eve." Raucously assailed, the author retreated into a work of such milky goodness (the unlikely conversion to Baptistism of a consumptive juvenile delinquent) that his popularity suffered a sharp slump.

The literary war between the soaks and the prudes, the drinkers and the non-drinkers, might charitably have been described as a draw when the hatchet queen burst into print, in 1906, with her clarion autobiography, *The Use and Need of the Life of Carry A. Nation*. Its circulation was quickly so wide, and its plea so urgent, that the enemy's gun fell silent for a space. Like her deeds, her words brought the world to full if reluctant attention.

Chapter Twelve

Mrs. Nation's arrival at Enterprise, on January 23, 1901, was inauspicious for one who almost single-handedly had stampeded a western cow-town twice in the space of a few days. She climbed down from her coach at seven A.M., noted with satisfaction its egg-spattered and rock-punctured side, ignored the indignant looks and comments ("Well, I never!" "Ought to be locked up!" "Crazy as a loon!") of fellow passengers who had found sanctuary in other cars and proceeded without escort to the home of friends—specifically that of C. B. Hoffman, Sr., the father of Enterprise's mayor. This was an anomalous position for Mrs. Nation, and for the Hoffmans, for her standing among Kansas officialdom, with special attention to its sheriffs, was no better than that of an unconvicted rustler.

Hoffman's residence had previously been noted for a certain serenity of spirit that had made it the envy of his associates in the turbulent and addle-headed Populist party. Within a few hours after Mrs. Nation's appearance, there had boiled into the parlor (and other rooms) any number of W.C.T.U. members spoiling for a row. As they sought preliminary refuge in prayer, Hoffman sought refuge in the cellar. He had built it as a hedge against tornadoes, and the belief of a reporter that he had gone down to pray for a tornado was thought to be a flippancy from one carried away by the artistic horizons of his trade.

Hoffman was burdened with other problems; his wife had long been a mainstay of the local temperance union. While he was still in the cellar, probably looking for a secreted and well-deserved bottle, he heard a wild thundering as of many hooves. On inquiry he found that the women, led by Mrs. Nation, had bolted for the First Methodist Church, where an emergency meeting was in progress. According to the Kansas City *Star,* the crusader "asked to be allowed to speak to the congregation." She had not taken into account the spirited Reverend Vincent, who stepped forward boldly and declined, adding (again from the *Star*) "I do not approve of your method of carrying on temperance work." The minister, in turn, had not reckoned on the immovable will of his opponent. Mrs. Nation coolly went over his head and demanded a spot assemblage of the board of trustees, which was held, rather embarrassingly, off to one side, while Mr. Vincent stood with arms folded, trying to gaze unconcerned out of a window. Meantime, Mrs. Nation also waited, standing, and removed from her reticule the recently acquired hatchet, which she examined with interest. She hefted it, and cut a few swaths in the air. The board's decision —quickly reached—was unanimous in the affirmative. Then she made what must have been a stunning address (which she was capable of doing when aroused), and to his everlasting credit, the Reverend Mr. Vincent told a reporter, later, that "It was the best temperance talk I ever heard." "She quotes Scripture and Shakespeare with equal facility," said the Kansas City *Star,* awed.

Grave events followed with dizzy speed. With Mrs. Hoffman and her reinforcements strung out behind, the reformer began a sort of portentous dead-march down the main street, hatchet held "in the crook of her arm," singing "Am I a Soldier of the Cross?" The saloon people had thrown out pickets, and these scampered back to the establishments of John Schilling and William Shook (the only two in town deserving of the name saloon) to report that the first shock wave was due momentarily. Both places had been locked and their shades drawn; the owners stood across the street, not without apprehension. It is fair to say that the remaining ambulatory residents of Enterprise were in close attendance along the curbs. Mrs. Nation's principal cohorts in the fantastic succeeding events were Mrs. Hoffman, Mrs. L. A. Case and a "mysterious heavily-veiled woman" whose name was never secured for posterity.

Before Schilling's lounge, Mrs. Nation rattled the doorknob (which somebody said had the added effect of rattling the whole building), pounded on the wooden panels with both fists and then, on receiving a whispered briefing, whirled to shout at Schilling: "Open this door, you rummy! This is God's work!" By refusing to assist in destroying his own property, Schilling presumably aligned himself with the Devil; more accurately, he shrank back into the crowd and made himself as small as possible. In the words of an able biographer, the crusader then "overwhelmed him with selected characterizations which drew shouts of laughter from the crowd." Mrs. Nation's language, under stress, leaned to the Anglo-Saxon, the good short words, a hark-back to those dim Dukes of Argyll whose peons had no wit for refinements beyond the needs of belly, work and procreation. But she herself did not escape unvilified. Of the towns that Mrs. Nation had so far smashed, Enterprise was, at that point in history, easily the toughest. The guilty reactions from the old, riotous days of the cattle terminals—Wichita, Abilene, Dodge—had no counterpart here; the village was choked with roughnecks. A group of shouting youths commenced to tell the crusader what she might do with her hatchet, and it is distasteful to note that the suggestions, while interesting, were not only coarse but impractical. Undisturbed, she fell on the door with the instrument.

Crashing through, in order, were Carry and the veiled mystery woman; fanned out behind in a protective crescent were Mrs. Hoffman, Mrs. Case and a rear-guard unit. Mrs. Nation went to work methodically and, following custom, first destroyed the expensive bar mirror. Next to go were all the bottles and decanters. Her blood now thoroughly up, she broke the locked refrigerator, twisted off its door and hurled it across the floor; panting, eyes ablaze, her garb a drenched and disheveled ruin, she dragged a dozen heavy beer cases into the center of the room and smashed the bottles one by one. She attacked the furniture, took note of some posters, "cut gashes in the bar" and saved the windows until the end. During this orgy of demolition, the veiled mystery woman had not been idle. It is easy to fall into the trap of comparing this willing newcomer unfavorably with the seasoned veteran who led her. The mystery woman acquitted herself well. No doubt a novice at trespass and misdemeanor, she had a tendency to lag behind, to smash again what Mrs. Nation had already smashed with completeness—her saloon initiative had not matured though it gave rise to no serious criticism—yet her contribution was invaluable if only for the sharp, seemingly involuntary "yoicking" that escaped her lips as she plunged hot into the fray. The speculation was raised—was this perhaps a visiting Englishwoman of caste to whom the pleasures of the chase, the skirmish with fox, hound and whippers-in were instinct to her background? Asbury's *Carry Nation* says in a footnote: "According to a letter from Enterprise, published in *The Outlook* of January 23, 1901, the veiled woman was not a member of the W.C.T.U. or of any church, but was 'simply a brave woman who believed in trying the new method of closing the joints, which law and persuasion had failed to close.' " Whoever she was, she had nothing to be ashamed of. A large drawing of the interior devastation, reproduced on page one of the Kansas City *Star* of January 25, 1901, showed a scene of incredible wreckage. The chamber resembled one that the Jukes family might have inhabited for ten or fifteen years.

Marshal W. R. Benham, alerted, dropped the task that concerned him in his regular employment as fireman at a nearby mill and rushed forthwith to Schilling's. To get in, he had to climb over debris that freshets of beer had washed up in the doorway. In a loud voice, he ordered Mrs. Nation to retire; in a slightly louder one, she said, "And who are you?"

"I am the marshal," he replied, trying to look official despite the residue of coal-smoke and ashes that seemed to hint at a different calling.

Mrs. Nation took him at more than face value and cried, "You are a murderer and perjurer protecting this unholy traffic!" Then she swung her hatchet in a menacing arc. One thing led to another; the marshal, briefly losing command, called her a "hoodlum"; she cleft the air near his chin, to a snarling quotation from Job, and he pushed her in the chest. It touched off a magpie cackle of protest— "Brute!" "He struck a woman!" etc. (the laments not taking into account the fact that Mrs. Nation had tried to cut off his head with her ax)—and the two wound up glaring and breathing heavily, nose to nose, in the street. A few minutes later, Mrs. Nation was led off home to Hoffman's, and the crowd dispersed. The last words hurled at her retreating back were from Schilling, who shouted an odd threat, "My wife will settle with you!" Maybe because of this, she insisted on returning to the front immediately after supper, and therein lay her undoing.

In her book, Mrs. Nation gives as the reason for going back downtown a desire to explain her actions to the people. She had only just started to do so when "a furious woman" rushed out of a niche in the walls and struck her two staggering blows in the face. It was Mrs. Schilling, wife of the unhappy publican. The blows were shrewdly delivered, and Mrs. Nation stumbled forward slightly, making the instinctive motion to clinch and hang on. But Mrs. Schilling had taken to her heels, and the crusader lit out in what proved to be futile pursuit. When she returned, she appeared in no way dismayed. She stormed into a butcher shop, ordered half a pound of sirloin and directed the clerk to tie it over her left eye. Then she resumed her harangue on the corner, "ignoring the jibes of the crowd and the meat juice which trickled down her nose." Her oration must surely have represented the oddest spectacle that Enterprise had thus far seen or ever would see. Mrs. Nation was one of those rare humans without self-consciousness and it disturbed her not at all that, when her head tossed about, as she scored off this jointist and that official, the beefsteak flapped like a castanet. She was oblivious of everything except her attack, and this eventually prevailed (as usual) to the point where the crowd was wildly cheering. "Half the women of Enterprise then pledged themselves to help smash its saloons," a reporter noted. This was well and good, but Mrs. Nation had never been one to shirk an advantage. "And we'll smash the saloon-*keepers* as well!" she shouted. A few women muttered dissents such as "Shucks, I thought we were going to keep this thing reasonable" and "Murder ain't tolerated here." To these, the reformer cried, "I want to suffer! I am ready to die for the cause! I am merely an instrument in God's hands!" Nobody seemed overly convinced, and the session dissolved.

Next morning Mrs. Nation led a prayer meeting of fifty women out of church and off in the direction of town. She looked refreshed in her poke bonnet, brushed and pressed black alpaca, and a choicer cut of steak strapped more stylishly over her eye. Loudly (musically) rejoicing, she led her flock into the street, where grim retribution finally overtook her. Arranged in battle line, facing the temperance-ites, were Schilling, a group of the toughest hooligans in town (complemented by some strangers on the order of gangland's imported torpedoes), and, most sinister of all, the fist-worthy Mrs. Schilling and three other women (also strangers), wearing long black capes and veils. The crusader at last had met her first organized opposition, and the cohesion of its movements attracted favorable comment in low quarters. A whistle sounded and a hail of rotten—conspicuously rotten—eggs sprayed Mrs. Nation from head to foot, persons nearby, it was reported, being "almost stifled with their noisome smell." Though inured to punishment, she dropped her hatchet, and at this instant the dragon-ladies threw aside their cloaks to produce "whips, heavy rawhide thongs and stout sticks." The beating that the saloon smasher then suffered exceeded the aggregate of all the attacks she had made to date against men. She was viciously flogged on both face and body, and she took it with characteristic pluck; indeed, she struck the first assailant who reached her so heavily as to knock her down, from which position the surprisingly young and attractive virago scuttled sidewise away, like a crab. Another woman, as Mrs. Nation also went down, seized her and jerked out a thick tuft of hair, which she held up and waved in triumph, like an Indian lifting a scalp lock. When the crusader crawled into the gutter, the ravening beldames followed, not only using their whips, thongs and sticks but kicking her as well. With blood streaming down her face from half a dozen welts, she cried, "Women, help! Will you let me be murdered?"

To one sympathizer, at least, her anguish sounded like that of Christ as he called from the cross "Father, why hast thou forsaken me?" It is depressing to note that, during this prolonged melee, Mrs. Nation's timorous faithful remained stolidly rooted, but one woman, bolder than the rest, finally sprang into action (at a point when it appeared that the crusader *was* about to be murdered) and snatched up half a brick. Mrs. Nation's book quotes this good Samaritan as crying, "If anyone strikes that woman again I will hit them with this." (The autobiography also identified her as "the mother of the saloonkeeper's wife," but other sources disagreed.) In any case, the utterance acted as a catalyst on the frozen temperance-ites, who now swooped in to the attack. The enemy faltered, retreated a few paces, broke ranks and fled in a rout, greatly to the dismay of Schilling, who with his whistle had been exhorting the mercenaries from a command post safely toward the rear. The publican should be mentioned in dispatches here. It is not too fulsome to say that Schilling represented the highest type of coward, the flower of western knavery. He had never been known to fight a man, and, when the going got rough, he did not flinch from importing women to flog a woman. Nor did his consistency waver at any turn. The youthful and voluptuous troupe, placed under arrest and, later, fined a few dollars each, turned out to be prostitutes brought in from Topeka and Kansas City. All told, Schilling was out of pocket a considerable sum. Not only was he obliged to reimburse the whores for two days' work—no mean amount, for the ladies were at the top of their profession—but he had to fork up their fines as well. This in addition to outlays for whips, thongs, capes, a whistle, transportation and pre-battle hooch. Of some assistance was a purse of thirty-two dollars which the saloon-owners of Topeka collected and sent along to Mrs. Schilling, together with expressions of their highest regard.

As for Mrs. Nation, her plight was sorry indeed. A writer summed it up well by saying that "Her hair was down and some of it was missing, her poke bonnet had been trampled in the dust, and her dress was offensively odorous from the remains of the rotten eggs. Her face was cut in half a dozen places, and the eye which Mrs. Schilling had struck the day before, and which had been responding satisfactorily to the curative influence of the raw beef, was again puffed and purpled, and the chunk of meat with which it had been bandaged lay in the dirt of the gutter. She was dazed and weak, and would have fallen again had not friends helped her into a buggy." Schilling, like all mortals, had his weaknesses and presumptions; a biographer would be dishonest to deny that Mrs. Nation also had hers. Climbing into the rig, she turned and uttered a remark that must forever stand as the epitome of gall: "There is a spirit of anarchy abroad in this town!"

The stricken gladiator was conveyed to Hoffman's, and a physician hastily summoned. After a survey, he declared that Mrs. Nation needed restoration, with more beefsteak, as well as rest—"in bed for several days." She was up and laying plans before he had reached the sidewalk. Meanwhile a curious sequence of events was unfolding downtown. Once over their inertia, her band had clamored tooth and claw after Mrs. Schilling and the daughters of joy, chasing them through the streets until they reached, and scrambled into, the Schilling domicile. There the reformers quickly piled a variety of debris before the doors, against any chance of evasion. Thus corralled, the malefactors were found by Marshal Benham, who muscled his way in to make the arrests.

Violence has long been known to be the most contagious of ailments. It is seldom that *one* fight breaks out on a corner; persons of totally detached interest are apt to leap in and join this side or that. No doubt some low, murky atavism lurks in the average man, causing a yeasty stinging sensation to develop in his bowels as he watches combat begin within arm's reach. In Robert Ardrey's scientific study, *African Genesis,* it is proved that man is a killer by instinct, and little lately has happened to raise hopes that the trend might be reversed. During the rest of that day fights broke out all over Enterprise. Up and down the streets, argument, name-calling and fisticuffs commanded everybody's attention. All stores were closed in deference to the carnival of riot; casual strangers tore off their coats to do battle over nothing; temperance was largely forgotten. After dawn had broken the next morning, its citizens seemed disinclined to look one another squarely in the eye. Their expressions were sheepish, with overtones of mystification.

It was soon after dawn that Mrs. Nation, wearing her head-lamp of meat, returned to the streets. She herself was technically under house arrest, an annoyance that prompted her to get out of the house pretty fast. (She was subsequently acquitted, after a two-hour trial, on a charge of breaching the peace.) Overnight her costume had undergone repairs, being cleansed of both eggs and blood, its rents sewed up, the pleats pressed and its shape generally improved. She hastened to the two sites of her tirades, found the saloon doors closed—and looking somehow reproachful—then threw herself on her knees, while a weary and lacklustre crowd again commenced to gather, with no great show of interest. During the night, Mrs. Nation had decided to take on Abilene, one of the two or three rowdiest places in the outstanding history of Kansas. She so announced to her listeners, and word immediately went out by telegraph. The Abilene saloon-owners started operations to button up in advance of the storm. One man called in carpenters to erect a heavy oaken barricade over the lengthy front of his place. Others had the fixtures, including the bars, removed to stables in outlying sections. The only jointist who showed real originality brushed out the word "Saloon" on his windows and substituted the inexplicable "Modiste," placing an aged and motheaten tailor's dummy unconvincingly in the entrance.

The preparations were wasted. During the afternoon the reformer received a telegram from the nearby village of Hope, which she reported as follows: "Come here and help us break up dives." It was signed, simply, "Temperance Committee," and a hard-bitten campaigner like Mrs. Nation should have suspected a ruse. But she changed her plans in all innocence, giving Abilene a reprieve, and once again left for the station.* Even in largely cowed Enterprise, pockets of resistance yet remained, for she was pelted (by men) with eggs at every corner of her route.

In later years Hope did not spring eternal in Carry Nation's breast; instead, the town stands nearly alone as one of her significant failures. It was also the scene of an uproar almost too ludicrous to be believed. Her autobiography takes note that, when she debarked from the train, "I saw some suspicious men keeping in the dark. I got into a hack and went to a hotel. I went up to my room, which was very small. It had one window which was raised an inch with a lath under it, and I thought it strange at the time that the landlord should have let the window down, but I was very tired and dropped asleep almost as soon as I touched the bed."

Mrs. Nation's book was written several years after the event, and it is interesting to note how her memory was at variance with, for example, that of a *Star* reporter who stayed close to her side

---

* A *leit motif* of the crusader's life was "leaving for the station"; it usually followed a belligerent address of intent, and it must have been, at the least, monotonous. For one thing, no research has yet developed that she ever, in all her career, rode in a Pullman. Night and day, asleep and awake, she bumped along in the coaches.

throughout. "Mrs. Nation left Enterprise for Hope late last night," he wrote. "She had received a telegram from Hope: 'Come here at once; two saloons here—The Woman's Temperance League.' . . . Mrs. Hoffman, wife of the richest man in Enterprise, went with her to the train. A big crowd followed, hooting and throwing eggs at Mrs. Nation.

"With her little black satchel clutched in her left hand, a thick black veil down over her bruised and blackened eye, she grabbed the hand-rails of the car as soon as the train stopped and clambered aboard. On the car platform she wheeled around and waved her hand at Mrs. Hoffman.

" 'Goodbye, Mrs. Hoffman,' she cried. 'Keep up the good work; don't let them open the rum holes again.'

"She sat down alone in the front seat and began examining her dress in the lamplight. Her black skirt was smeared with broken eggs. She wiped the smears with her handkerchief, smelled it and, raising her eyes and looking upward, said, solemnly: 'Thank you, Lord.'

"A reporter for the *Star* was standing in the aisle beside her seat . . . 'What feature of the demonstration are you thankful for?' asked the reporter.

" 'I'm thankful that the eggs were not rotten,' she answered. 'Just imagine what a fix I would be in if those eggs were rotten or if they had struck me in the face. As it is, I can easily wash it off in the morning. It's only on my skirt. Oh, the good Lord is with me . . .'

"When the train reached the prairie town of Hope at midnight, Mrs. Nation looked around for the committee of women she expected to meet her. Not a woman was there. An omnibus stood in the background, its lanterns blinking dimly in the darkness. A crowd of men and boys jostled each other looking to see Mrs. Nation. She got off quickly, asked the bus driver about the hotels and said in a loud voice: 'Take me to the dollar-a-day house; that's all I can afford to pay.' The crowd ran after the vehicle and thronged the hotel office to see her, but she went straight to bed."

As nearly as Mrs. Nation's hotel-keeper could place it, the hour was approximately two A.M. when the first explosion of the Great Nicotine Conspiracy boomed out to rock his establishment. A notion had been circularized by the press that the reformer reacted unfavorably, dangerously—some hoped fatally—to whiffs of tobacco smoke in her presence. She was "allergic to" tobacco (in the frightful jargon of the video commercial). There was the disgraceful incident of the rustlers and pimps, in jail at Wichita, who had sought her demise from cigar fumes exhaled by John the Trusty, in the days before he became a man and a brother.

Around two o'clock, at a point when Mrs. Nation had been deep in slumber, she leaped out of bed with a shriek that bounced even those guests sodden with drink to their feet in alarm. Her enemies, she cried, were trying to asphyxiate her by blowing cigarette smoke through the keyhole of her door. There may have been some truth in the claim. A trickle of smoke seeped through, and the atmosphere showed a light blue color. Mrs. Nation's wits, knife-like at the early hour, quickly divined that the tobacco was merely a cover for gases of a more noxious composition; she wrote, afterward, that "the room was full of the most poisonous odor, as of cigarettes, and other smells." Like the man in the Christmas poem, she sprang to the window and threw up the sash; then, in a vision, she suddenly understood that two men were crouched in the hallway, bent on mischief. "I knew that there were persons at the door puffing the poison in," she wrote.

"I see you sluggers on each side of the door," she cried in a ringing tone [the dialogue verbatim from her book]. "You villains, you have tried to murder me by throwing poison in my room and now you are trying something else."

By this time, needless to say, the grotesquely costumed clientele of the hostelry was opening doors and voicing complaints, such as "I checked in here to get a night's sleep, by God!" and "Why doesn't somebody shut that old hag up?"

In an interview, Mrs. Nation stated categorically that a man called from beyond the barrier, "There is a mob here after you."

"You are a liar," she replied with typical candor.

"There is a committee wants to speak to you."

"You are telling lies in order to have me open my door."

"He left [she said] and went down below, and for ten minutes there was a great tramping of feet and I could hear the landlord pretending to disperse a crowd."

The hotel owner, in nightshirt and cap, seemingly agitated, came shuffling up to plead for restraint, and the hubbub quieted down. What was the truth? It is difficult to assess the precise events of that night. Most writers have treated Mrs. Nation's ordeal seriously; one or two lapsed half-heartedly into the whimsical. The best guess is that pranksters were simply having some fun at the reformer's expense. On the other hand, it is possible that a paid lynch mob was forming and the tobacco used as a means of persuading her to open up. Her influence was beginning to be felt, and the "interests"—pinched—may have decided on drastic measures. The persons involved with illicit liquor, gambling, entertainment, have never been of absolutely first-rate quality.

Mrs. Nation did not loiter in the hotel; the place lacked the resort air that she may have hoped to find. Early in the morning, groggy from her involuntary debauch with the weed, she dressed and sailed out into the street. There she met a boy with whom she had an exchange that has long puzzled Kansas historians.

"Are there any Christians in Hope?" she inquired.

"No, ma'am," the lad replied, "but there are some in the country."

The answer implied, first, a desperate and unusual situation in what looked like an average plains village—partly corrupt, largely God-fearing; and, second, an acute understanding of Hope's adults by a brilliantly precocious child. The boy hadn't a word to say for urban Hope, he'd spotted a few decent people in the country.

Mrs. Nation was obviously taken aback, for her autobiography drops the subject and sees her on to the depot, where she ate an indigestible breakfast. Thus fortified (and noting that the customary curious were beginning to gather, as they might watch a caged gorilla ingest a banana), she could not resist announcing a temperance meeting half an hour thence in front of the smoky hotel.

It failed to develop the excitement that had distinguished her previous efforts. A discordant note was immediately struck when a saloonkeeper rushed forward with a pistol and promised to shoot her if she "flirted near" his place. This might have given a lesser feminist pause, but Mrs. Nation walked up to his face and bawled, "I am not afraid of your gun. Maybe it would be a good thing for a saloonkeeper to shoot Carry Nation. It might be the means of causing the people to smash the dives." The man thought better of his threat and beat a retreat, seeming apprehensive that she might seize the gun and shoot *him*. Then she read her telegram and recounted in detail her experience with the smoke-blowers. As she made points, reiterating her purpose, a few women uttered faint "Hallelujahs!", though keeping a wary eye on their husbands.

The fundamental weakness of the session could perhaps be found in the artistic ribbing that Mrs. Nation began to absorb from the unregenerates in the crowd. Far from disputing her remarks, they over-piously agreed with everything she said. "A-a-men, Sister!" and "The lady's right—saloons have got to go!" were shouted with transparent falseness every three or four seconds, to an accompaniment of hoots, honks, whistles, Bronx cheers, nose-blowing and horse-laughs. The sum of these might eventually rattle a robot, and she threw up the meeting as a bad job (or "Hope-less," as one reporter had unavoidably put it). Punctilious to the end, the saloon-men, hats in hand, carried her bag while escorting her to the station. "With much ceremony, they put her aboard a train," another writer observed. The men appeared broken up at the thought of her departure, and one or two removed neckerchiefs to swab piteously at their eyes. She was given a rousing "Hoorah for Carry Nation!" as the train pulled out. For once, the crusader looked thoughtful when she resumed her increasingly familiar squat on the sooty green plush.

Chapter Thirteen

Once again the crusader's exploits were viewed with consideration by the New York *Times,* which might be said to have represented the eastern press in assessing her importance. Beneath the front-page heading, "Mrs. Nation Horsewhipped," the paper devoted half a column to her struggle at Enterprise, while directing its main attention to the "Proclamation" of England's new king, Edward VII. Victoria was dead, and the western world was beginning a new era. Apologists for Mrs. Nation's "methods" could perhaps have found solace in parts of the British story, and in another that the *Times* dutifully printed. There were elements of uncomfortable similarity, pointing up the moral (long suspected) that human nature, and people, are basically the same everywhere. "The officials purposely arranged the function an hour ahead of the time given in the public announcement," said the news from England, and added, "About 10,000 soldiers, Life Guards, Horse Guards, Foot Guards, and other cavalry and infantry regiments, had been brought from Aldershot and London barracks after midnight." Sadly enough, the plans could almost have been prepared as a blueprint for a successful presidential visit to Dallas. The overseas correspondent further noted that "Soldiers and policemen formed a solid lane down Cheapside, where the pageant passed. The people behind them, crowding for a sight over their shoulders, were of all classes, from prosperous brokers to East End costermongers. The mass was subdued and remarkably orderly, an impressive contrast to the usual London holiday crowd."

"Lively Riot on Broadway" was another front-page report, at the top of a column, that emphasized the universality of Enterprise's purgative day of combat. "A little after midnight this morning," said the *Times,* "there was a free fight at Twenty-ninth Street and Broadway which kept all the policemen in the neighborhood working hard for over half an hour before order was restored . . . Four men were observed arguing together, and they were soon surrounded by a crowd of curious people. A moment later the four men began to fight. They finally struggled over toward a cab, and one of them fell inside it. Several bystanders had commenced to take sides in the fight, and in a few moments it became general. By the time the policemen on foot appeared at the scene there was a crowd of over 500 people, most of them fighting and shouting as loudly as they could." The *Times* article went on to make the baffled observation that, under questioning, practically nobody knew what he was fighting about. As the senselessness of the melee grew more pronounced, all the cabbies in the area unexpectedly jumped on the police, who until then had comported themselves with decorum. A good many trivial injuries, with a scattering of cracked skulls, were carted off to hospital, and a general air of jubilation pervaded the Daly's Theatre district (focal point of the fracas) for the rest of that night. Came morning, as at Enterprise, the residents seemed preoccupied, with small, tuneless whistlings and starings off into space. The fever had subsided.

Thus Mrs. Nation, and Kansas, were not alone in the occasional violence of their conduct, and there was a marked absence of the holier-than-thou attitude which the *Times* had not quite managed to avoid in the earlier dispatch from Wichita. Mrs. Nation, at least, had an underlying cause; the New Yorkers were simply fighting for the right to fight. If the latter could claim any small facet of superiority, it was that the crusader had by no means reached a level of satiety. Undoubtedly, she alone of those involved in the tale of two cities felt no slight twinge of remorse. The *Times* was quick to point out that, as the Kansan hullabaloo died down, Mrs. Nation announced her intention to quell Kansas City, beginning "the usual operations there." This proved fallacious. She was befuddled when she left Hope behind, and her ideas about further assaults did not crystallize until after she reached the hamlet of Ottawa, where she rested at the home of a W.C.T.U. friend and lectured to a large turnout at the First Baptist Church. In the main, she said, she was able to give Ottawa a clean bill of health, but in any case she hadn't time to go into the matter fully. Her destination was the home of a brother, in Louisburg, and on her arrival there she did little more than receive callers and weigh a succession of plots. In one interview granted to a reporter who brought credentials in the form of a temperance pledge signed when he was nine—thought to be forged—she made the surprising admission that Kansas City might possibly be "too much for a single woman to straighten out alone." It was, therefore, almost a foregone conclusion that Mrs. Nation should settle on the capital city of Topeka as the target of her next attack. The place was usually referred to—by newspapers in other Kansas cities—as "a cesspool of corruption." The opprobrium was occasionally altered, for the sake of variety (and literary excellence) to "a sinkhole of corruption." The capital's thirty-five thousand inhabitants sipped at the founts of forty joints, none of which flourished in the open; the owners kept ice boxes and plank counters in cubbies partitioned off within larger rooms, like Chinese boxes.

Topeka's reputation was not entirely fair. A paradoxical, nearly unheard-of, situation existed there. The town had an honest man, Frank M. Stahl, as chief of police; later on, in fact, he became a vociferous force in the Anti-Saloon League and the Kansas State Temperance Union. It was Chief Stahl's nervous habit to swoop down periodically on the joints and dump out their whiskey. The saloon people and the politicians had made spirited attempts to reason with him, to tutor him in the police methods of frankly iniquitous centers, but he continued stubbornly trying to uphold the law. In this, he complained of non-cooperation by state and county officials. Stahl was a nuisance, but the joints, despite him, kept popping up like toadstools. Kansans are dedicated people, not easy to swerve from any course, and for every two saloons closed, exertions were made to open three more. Topeka's illogical notoriety arose, actually, not so much from a proliferation of the joints—for their lot was a hard one—but because the city happened to be the state capital, with such a spot's inevitable stench of political graft, deals, dishonor, compromise, cronyism, self-serving and stupidity. But the temperance bloc was inclined to lay the whole mess to booze, and Carry Nation, arriving at 6:40 P.M., January 26, 1901, on a local train of the Atchison, Topeka and Santa Fé, was welcomed by at least part of a surging crowd, as a kind of female Moses, girded to lead Topeka out of the wilderness.

She had telegraphed ahead, and the Reverend S. C. Coblentz of the United Brethren Church, hatless, wearing a look of holy deliverance, was at the depot in the role of formal spokesman for his group. He never got a chance to open his mouth. The crusader was instantly overwhelmed by a swarm of reporters who hustled her into the waiting room, where she unsuccessfully struggled to address a crowd of several hundred. Her unusual décor was believed to detract from the good impression which she might have made had she not, someplace en route, availed herself of a fresh cut of beef for her eye. As the Bible has noted, the world seldom produces one of God's creatures completely without vanity; Mrs. Nation was such a one. Friends were forever telling her, discreetly, that carelessness of attire was a liability to the cause of prohibition. In response (aside from washing her person constantly) she might so far bend as to take off her bonnet and whack out the dust. This was her conduct in the field; at home she was spotless. A *Star* reporter at those long-ago Topeka scenes wrote later for *Commonweal* magazine, "The first thing I noticed when I saw her was how terrible her clothes were—quite worn out. She had on a shiny black dress with a fringed gray shawl; her black bonnet hadn't even a feather on it . . . Mrs. Nation's shoes seemed pitifully thin and worn as she went sloshing around in the drifts, raiding saloons. Everything she wore, though, was clean and mended, and her humorous face had something of the shine of her clothes, as if it, too, were being perpetually scrubbed and polished."

A celebrity trying to lecture from behind a piece of raw sirloin cannot be taken seriously, and Mrs. Nation failed to sway the humor of the crowd, which included a claque of uncommonly gifted hecklers. When several of these—"pretty far gone in drink," according to a witness—became menacing, the crusader was hurried into the carriage of Reverend Coblentz, who had thrown down his notes in a rage and replaced his hat, for the evening was chill. No newspaper account of Mrs. Nation's Topeka arrival tells whether an attempt was made to restrain her at the Coblentz home. The Kansas City *Star* said only that she was back on the streets "within an hour." The crusader's movements on that evening were dazzling in their unpredictability, and they left Reverend Coblentz older—his face "seemed drawn and sallow." Instead of storming the joints frontally, Mrs. Nation proceeded, with the familiar jeering queue, to the Topeka *Capital,* the city's leading journal, and demanded the services of "an escort to the dives," implying that everybody on the paper was a party to subterfuge and disorder. An editor referred her to the police station, apologetically making the point that the *Capital* employees had other fish to fry. The crusader's reception at police headquarters convinced her for all time that Topeka was a cesspool (or sinkhole) of corruption. The desk sergeant to whom she spoke (awaking him from a nap) indignantly "declined to act as an escort or guide," said the *Star*. She expressed shock and dismay that the lawmen wouldn't join her to survey the hellholes under their protection.

The fact is, Mrs. Nation had no need of official escort, for by the time she left police headquarters she was attended by most of the reporters in Topeka. At their suggestion she went directly to the saloon of Bert Russell, across from the Hotel Throop. There a surprise awaited her.

Russell's recreational center was labeled, in green letters on the windows, "Billiard Parlor," a testimonial to three rickety pocket-pool tables used as a digestive between drinks enjoyed by guests who trod a path to the "back room." The establishment, a haven for quiet soaking, was situated on lower Kansas Avenue (the city's main thoroughfare) between Fourth and Fifth Streets. On her appearance at the threshold, one of the players shouted, "Hey, Bert! Shut the door! Here comes Mrs. Nation!" By this time, of course, her picture was as well known to Kansans as those of President McKinley and Jesse James—better-known, for the views of Mrs. Nation showed her holding aloft a hatchet while neither of the others was identified with a specific stage property, if we except Jesse James's gun. "She walked boldly into the place," wrote a reporter, "and at once began a lecture against the 'evil of selling liquor.' " She had barely started the preamble to her address (which was uniformly offensive) when a man sitting in a chair, smoking a cigar, seemingly oblivious, arose abruptly and "gathered Mrs. Nation in his arms." It was a Mr. Ryan, a large, cool-headed fellow, and he carried her outside and plopped her down firmly on the sidewalk. In retrospect, one cannot help admiring the common sense of Ryan's direct action. Except for Schilling's tarts, nobody had presumed to repel her physically; she posed, always, a problem. She was a challenge to the highly refined chivalry of the West. Ryan's antidote did her no harm, it saved Russell's furnishings and it had the effect of driving Mrs. Nation into a frothing tantrum. She bounced up and cried, *"You scoundrel!"* said the *Star;* "then she spent three minutes abusing Ryan," who stood by calmly, finishing his cigar, an effectual barrier against further intrusion.

The *tête-à-tête* represented one of the few times when Mrs. Nation appeared at a loss. She simply ran down. It is unrewarding to revile a totem pole, and Ryan was outside the perimeter of her barbs. In the words of a reporter, she gave up and "made a dash across the street to the 'Senate' saloon." This place, in its line, was the pride of Topeka, with fixtures and appointments as fine as if Police Chief Stahl had been a full-fledged crook. It rivaled Wichita in the elegance of its décor—a rich, comfortable sanctum much frequented by the state politicians who had outlawed liquor. Here Mrs. Nation suffered further frustrations, for she found the door locked, the windows boarded up, and furniture piled high as a barricade. From inside rose an inelegant chorus of boos, cat-calls and windy political threats. "Open up, you cowards!" the *Star* quoted her as crying. In the years since then, nobody has presented any good reason why the Senate should have complied. The owners had everything to lose, and nothing to gain. Newspapers later agreed that the crowds now surging in the streets numbered about two thousand. "There was an incessant and boisterous yelling," went one account. "Those walking by Mrs. Nation's side experienced difficulty in hearing what she said, though she talked at the top of her voice."

A roar of delight went up when somebody shouted that the cru-

sader, stung, intended to liquidate the next joint visited—the
"cigar store" of a Mr. Myers, a few numbers down Fourth Street.
Here she ran into more serious physical opposition. No sooner had
she entered, skipped by a row of patently dummy cigar cases and
begun her prepared speech on Motherhood (while heading toward
the busy pine board in the rear) than a small, furious woman
clutching a broom handle exploded from nowhere and bonged her
a ringing blow on the head. Then she rained additional blows on
Mrs. Nation's head and shoulders, the last whack cutting a deep
gash behind one ear. "Keep out of here!" screamed the assailant,
who would variously be referred to as Myers' wife, Myers' mistress
and a rather murky salesgirl of non-existent cigars. Whatever she
was, her strength and hustle were awesome; she was a genuine
crowd-pleaser. "At the first blow, Mrs. Nation bent forward," said
the *Star,* and another source, after explaining that both her bonnet
and her sirloin were dislodged, delicately observed that when she
stooped to recover them, Mrs. Myers "smote her upon that portion
of her anatomy which chanced to be uppermost."

Seizing her blistered posteriors, Mrs. Nation "set off down the
street at top speed." This was a full retreat, a rarity during her
career, but it should be described as strategic rather than cow-
ardly. For the hasty outing she had brought neither hatchet nor
stones nor half-bricks; she was entirely unarmed. Myers' defender
had all the advantage, and Mrs. Nation retreated, then pulled up at
a corner to re-group. When a man made a gesture to staunch the
blood from her wound she whirled as if to strike him, and he
jumped back. Friends in the throng pressed her to retire—the battle was going sour—but she cried, "What does a broomstick
amount to when one has been used to rawhides, rocks and eggs?
Where's another joint?" The journalists gleefully pointed out a
nearby "Chili Parlor," where the crusader met yet another surprise. Her face flushed with dreams of demolition, she swept
through the door to be greeted by a proprietor of Continental
charm. He was honored by her visit, it was a red-letter day in the
history of Moe's Chili Parlor and he begged the privilege of con-
ducting her on a guided tour of the shop (which was meager).
Chatting, smiling, inventing frilly compliments, he demonstrated
here an urn filled with beans, there a potful of peppers, hot ta-

males, cracker bowls, hot sauce from Texas—in the end he offered her a slap-up feed on the house. Mrs. Nation was no fool, and, though softened by these attentions—the first such of her campaigns to date—she ungenerously poked about in corners, knocked rudely on the walls, and looked out back. Then, balked, she resorted to what many have referred to as the gamiest example on record of her disinclination to admit defeat. She fell on her knees and prayed that the Almighty would forgive the proprietor for "tempting American appetites with foreign dishes."

As Mrs. Nation's Topeka evening built in excitement, she escaped lynching by a margin so narrow it might have reformed a horse-thief. The crowd of two thousand had been swelling in size and in hostility, and, as at Wichita, the peace-keeping machinery threatened to collapse. First signal of real trouble was, again, a vintage egg that came looping out of the shadows to splatter on a wall beside the crusader's head. It was followed by a shower of rocks, which had the effect of convincing her (aided by pleas from friends) that the neighborhood was drained of entertainment. Reporters hustled her through a restaurant, out of the rear door and up an alley; but the mob, screaming for blood, picked up the trail and came boiling along behind. The journalists shouted suggestions that Mrs. Nation scramble into a cab and head post-haste for the stockade of Reverend Coblentz, but she insisted on hot-footing it to the *Capital*. For some reason—not encouraged by the editors —she had selected the building to serve as her downtown command post. There she found safety of a sort, for the paper dispatched its special officer, George Luster, to the door with a drawn revolver. The crowd fell back, and Mrs. Nation promised to denounce it as soon as she caught her breath. "She sat down for a brief rest," reported the *Star;* "then she said, 'I want to have that woman who hit me arrested,' rubbing the black eye she brought from Enterprise and examining the cut received in Topeka." Another source noted that "when a comfortable chair was procured she seated herself very gingerly": soon afterward she observed chattily that "Hell seems to be howling tonight." Then she spoke with bitterness of the police, who had told her at one point, "Can't keep a crowd like this back," a laconic utterance later criticized by the press.

A Mr. Lerrigo, secretary of the local Y.M.C.A., appeared to be in the editorial office during this scene, for he was quoted as protesting when Mrs. Nation arose to "visit the city attorney."

"T'ain't safe for you to go on the street," said Mr. Lerrigo, putting his concern ahead of his grammar. "The crowd has made threats of lynching you."

"They won't do that," said Mrs. Nation quietly, and she stepped toward the curb in the face of uniformly negative advice. Her brashness placed a strain on Luster, whose background and qualifications have unfortunately been lost to posterity; certainly he must have been one with the Earps and the Mastersons, for his admonition, when the crowd surged toward the reformer, was "I'll kill the first person who offers resistance or interference to this woman." The *Star* reported that, "The crowd resented this, and the leaders advanced regardless of the threat. Mrs. Nation saw that trouble might result, so she hastily entered [a] carriage and was driven to the Columbia Building, where the deputy city attorney, D. H. Gregg, was waiting." None of the news stories explained *why* Gregg was waiting, at this late hour on a blustery winter's night, but we may presume that he was summoned by the forces of anti-booze. To find him waiting and to reach him, however, were different matters. Topeka's cow-town gorge, always high in that era, had arisen in earnest, and the cries of "Get a rope! Get a rope!" had never rung out more joyously. Luster had done his job at the *Capital* and was out of the picture. Now a second, similar agent stepped in to mop up. T. D. Humphrey, custodian of the Columbia Building, was described in the accounts as "a desperate man," nobody bothering to make clear whether the moment had rendered him so or whether he was desperate by nature. A reasonable deduction would point to the latter, for he leaped toward the mob with a howl, "brandishing" *two* guns, thus removing much of the glitter from Luster. Humphrey not only stampeded the lynch faction down a hallway to the street but, after a second's thought, went ahead and kicked out eight or nine policemen as well. Even Mrs. Nation complained about his methods, but he paid little attention; he seemed to be having a good time. The threat of a necktie party resolved, she signed a complaint against Mrs. Myers and announced, to everyone's satisfaction except Humphrey's, "This ends my work for tonight."

The least interesting event of Mrs. Nation's next day was the arrival, from Medicine Lodge, of her beleaguered spouse, David A. Nation, who lately had tried to register mild demurrers at what he viewed as the public and vulgar aspect of their union. Ordinarily he did this from a distance, the complaints taking the form of whiney interviews given out to reporters whom he naively embraced as sympathetic. "At times I think she is a little daft about this saloon smashing business," he told a correspondent. "She will fast for days, until I have to make her eat or she will die. She claims to have visions of the Lord, and lots of times I have arrived home to find her talking with an unseen being, who she claimed was Christ . . . When she smashed the saloons at Kiowa she came home all covered with blood, and I thought she had been shot, but she had only cut her hands on broken bottles. I wanted to send for the doctor, but she said the Lord would heal her wounds, and sure enough in a day's time there was not one scar left."

In the reports, Nation's fire was scattered; it is hard to correlate the weird agglomeration of his complaints. The barrister-cleric-editor-farmer represented himself as being too infirm to practice law and was angered that his wife had consequently reduced him to the status of stenographer, causing him to handle "about 200 inquiring letters every day." On the positive side, he paid her high tribute as cook. Of the three or four meals a month which he was currently receiving at her hands, all were expertly prepared, and he referred the reporter to neighbors for confirmation (which the fellow was impertinent enough to walk across the street and obtain). In closing one interview, Nation reflected that, "I think her head is being turned by all this notoriety. I have warned her not to talk so freely about her plans and they would carry better, but she seems not to listen to me as much as she does to some of those temperance cranks in Topeka."

Mrs. Nation huddled with the Topeka temperance cranks on the Sunday morning after her nocturnal spasms, and received commendation from all the splinter groups. A delegation arrived from the Kansas State Temperance Union—sometimes jealously unsympathetic—and the W.C.T.U. waxed effusive in its praise. While a crowd stood outside the Coblentz home, awaiting further violence, a Salvation Army brass band marched up and serenaded her "with sacred songs and music." On a passing of the tambourine, which netted $1.80, a slug for a honky-tonk melodeon and two suspender buttons, the leader appeared nettled, but he gallantly continued the recital without any noticeable alteration of the beat. The Topeka *Capital* then circulated a querulous editorial, saying, "The newspapers are full of items about Mrs. Nation; and rumors of what she says, what she is doing, and what she proposes to do are telegraphed all over the country. Why does the woman occupy so much public attention? Is her action of any real importance?" The answer was, at the moment, evident throughout Kansas. At a temperance meeting held that Sunday in the Reverend Coblentz's church, it was announced that the Abilene authorities, fearful of subjugation by Amazons, had boarded up all the joints in Dickinson County; and at Wichita, as the tide of protest mounted, 200 women met in the Salvation Army barracks and announced that, unless immediate steps were taken to close the saloons, the city's streets would "run red with blood."

A spirit of revolt had seized the state, and Mrs. Nation was no woman to let an opportunity slip through the fingers of her hatchet hand. On that same Sunday, she spoke, rabble-rousingly, at two temperance meetings and was instrumental in choking off support from a second member of her family. It is impossible not to feel sorry for David Nation, though his candid motive for wooing the crusader could scarcely have been more knavish: "I married this woman because I needed some one to run my house." But he had bought a new blue-serge suit for his trip from Medicine Lodge, and his aim was to stand at her side (he was sick of opening letters). At the second temperance session, held in the United Brethren Church, he tottered to the podium and attempted to get off a few remarks of a generally anti-whiskey nature, but he was squelched with humiliating promptness. A paper estimated that he delivered four whole sentences;* another said he was extinguished "long before he had reached his peroration." At his wife's "Sit down, Papa. You've talked long enough," he showed, for the first time, signs of dangerous bile. One writer said that "he was observed to glare at her and mutter incoherently into his flowing beard." In his eye was the unmistakable look of a man starved for divorce, and the re-

---

* Nation's sentences were verbose, "virtually interminable"; his address may well have run to half an hour.

buke no doubt marked the turning point in what proved to be the couple's unhappy division.

By coincidence the State Temperance Union's annual convention was set for the succeeding day, Monday. Mrs. Nation declared that she would make a speech calculated to "arouse the delegates and send them afield with hatchets." It was too much. Union leaders issued a kind of papal bull in which they disavowed her sanguinary aid, and went so far as to say that her presence would not be tolerated on the platform. The *Capital*, smarting from its undeserved night of siege, said, quickly, "The logical effect of Mrs. Nation is anarchy pure and simple." The suggestion should have jarred, but didn't, a woman who had found Enterprise to be in just such a state. The meeting had little more than begun when Mrs. Nation, accompanied by the Reverend Coblentz and a bristling contingent of woodsmen, marched down the aisle, creating all the uproar possible. Luckily for the crusader, the delegate then on the stand was Mrs. C. B. Hoffman, her trusted crony from Enterprise. Mrs. Hoffman cast aside her notes, threw up her arms, and plunged into a wild eulogy of Carry Nation. One Thomas H. Bain, an influential worker in the group, attempted to reverse the flow of sentiment, but he was hissed and booed and barely escaped the assembly hall with his life. The women of Kansas were ready for the holocaust, the days of violence and bloodshed, the destruction and city-wide riots that waited just around the corner.

Chapter Fourteen

Led by Mrs. Nation, the Temperance Union convention voted so many rapid-fire resolutions that the clerk, unable to record them in order, stalked off in a rage and retired (claimed crowds outside) to the Senate for a refresher. One resolution announced an immediate move of "total destruction" against all the barrooms in Topeka; another favored Mrs. Nation's campaigns "in spirit and actuality"; a third denounced in villainous terms Governor William E. Stanley, who, it was said, "vacillated." Things were going so well, and the warm bonds of camaraderie had become so close that a Colonel J. C. Cook, an old Indian fighter with no history of fanaticism, jumped to his feet and proposed that an expensive medallion be struck off for Carry Nation. A group of detractors, later, put out the rumor that he was drunk and had wandered into the wrong building. Despite Mrs. Nation's sincere protests (she thought a trumpery bauble costing "about $1.50" might be ample), a purse of $117.50 was raised on the spot. The Colonel emitted what sounded suspiciously like a series of Comanche war whoops while Mrs. Nation tried to deliver the sum into the Union's treasury. She was refused, and in a few days presented with a splendid gold medal bearing the inscription, "To the Bravest Woman in Kansas."

The saloon people, far from idle as the storm clouds gathered, retaliated with a golden breast pin, in the form of a broom, for the redoubtable (and busty) Mrs. Myers. Observers of these events have since agreed that the jointists had been busy but stupid. They might well have subsided for a space, until the hot edge of Mrs. Nation's temper had cooled. Instead they flaunted their freedom and took measures that many regarded as bizarre. Not really wishing to kill a woman, three closely bunched dives organized a "seltzer-brigade," whose members, provided with the fizzy containers, would drive back invaders with streams of icy soda. At another place a bartender who enjoyed a reputation as an unsuccessful inventor rigged up several thick glass bottles heavily charged with pressured gas, on the theory that if she broke one, it might explode and cut off her head. Several saloons, more direct, employed patrolling Negroes armed with shotguns. A degree of indignation was aroused when a false report was spread that these sentinels had orders to seize all temperance women, strip them and fling them naked into the streets. Perhaps the foxiest precaution was that of four angry owners who installed trapdoors just inside their entranceways, with the idea of pulling a string and plunging Mrs. Nation to crunching death in the cellar. All these worthy devices were, of course, costly, but matters were eased when the Missouri Brewers' Association rushed six hundred dollars to the Topeka joints, with the promise of "as much more as may be needed."

The temperance convention over, Mrs. Nation decided on nuisance visits (she could hardly have been serious) to all the elective officials she could trap in their lairs. The overall total turned out to be zero. Among the dignitaries who found it convenient to be "out," or crouched in a back room, were State Attorney General A. A. Godard, Topeka Mayor Charles J. Drew, County Attorney Galen Nichols, City Attorney W. A. S. Bird and Police Judge Charles A. Magaw. The crusader was accompanied on these calls by Mrs. Anna Diggs, a Populist leader who enjoyed some local standing as a freak, and in the chambers of the absentee Magaw they struck pay dirt. The Judge was an admirer of art classics, on the order of Ingres' "Odalisque," a recumbent nude trollop featuring an elevated stern, and Rubens' entertainingly naked "Lot and his Daughters." Plump, pink reproductions of such cultural gems lined Magaw's walls, and Mrs. Nation sent up shriek after shriek of "Obscene!" The reformers raised a noisy stir, but it was not until a day or so later that they were able to have the pictures replaced with prints of "The Horse Fair" and "Whistler's Mother." (A wag's suggestion that they clothe the animals was discarded as frivolous.)

Rebuffs by these functionaries were more than offset by Mrs. Nation's immemorial confrontation of Governor Stanley, who the next day had carelessly let his presence be known. At ten in the morning, Mrs. Nation, alone, caught him in and walked contemptuously past the usual pickets, secretaries, sycophants, "advisors," lobbyists and hangers-on of a public-suckled office and greeted Stanley at his desk. He appeared startled. "Governor," she said, as if she were greeting a schoolboy, "I want you to arrest me. I am going to stay in Topeka until all the joints are closed." Confused he blurted out something like "Oh, boy!" or "Glad to have you, any time," but she charged on to ask him "if it was true he had said she was a lawbreaker." Then, curiously, she shifted into a minute and searching catechizing of Stanley about his duties as governor. She had seemingly swotted the subject up, and mentioned with familiarity two or three dozen items that had not yet come to his attention. Getting to the heart of the matter, she said, by the *Star*'s account, "You took your oath of office to support the constitution and if you refuse my request you are not only a lawbreaker but a perjurer." Here Stanley showed himself human enough to grow red in the face; then he blew up when the crusader, fancying her phrase, repetitiously chanted, "Lawbreaker and perjurer! Lawbreaker and perjurer!"

"You're a woman," Stanley yelled, "but I won't stand it. You'll have to leave if you don't mind what you say!"

"Look at my black eye and bruised face," she said. "You did that, Governor."

By now Stanley was so rattled that he instinctively began to present alibis, saying he was somewhere else at the time, and offered to prove it, but Mrs. Nation demanded that he call out the militia. When he refused, she suggested the alternative that he, personally, come out and help her smash some saloons, right now. "A general laugh followed," said a newspaper, and the antagonists cooled down; more than that, they became chummy. To give him credit, Stanley was not a man to shrink from a row, and he admired his tormentor's courage. "I'll tell you what I'll do," he said finally. "You get the county attorneys to convict the jointists and I'll see that they're not pardoned out."

This was a partial triumph for Mrs. Nation; another woman might have rested briefly on her laurels. She went directly to the office of State Attorney General Godard, shooed from his office an important lobbyist seeking some valuable concessions at the expense of Indians, and told him, "The Governor has just said for you to do your duty." In the loud, ensuing argument, Godard stood pat on his admonition that she badger the county attorney instead. She promptly did so, but the man in question, one Galen Nichols, had the ill grace to shout, "I don't care what the Governor said to you!" To this, Mrs. Nation replied that he "looked like a man who'd had a Mother," but she knocked the compliment apart when she added—she couldn't help it—"But then, after all, perhaps appearances are deceptive." The scene in Godard's office grew so heated that Sheriff Cook, for no valid reason, tried to strike a reporter named Charley Sessions. He quickly retreated on Sessions' willingness to fight back. All in all, Mrs. Nation's morning had been unproductive, aside from pumping up adrenalin in usually vacant officials, and at noon she went to a park bench where she ate a lunch from a paper bag. A crowd studied her every mastication, and when she was finished, she arose and harangued them, for a change, "on the evils of cigarette smoking."

In the next few days Topeka reached the boiling point. For all practical purposes, business was suspended; proprietors and clerks joined the sidewalk crowds to discuss Carry Nation's latest moves. The subject of their inquiry held a press conference in which she outlined a reorganization of the Home Defenders, previously a noncombatant debating society that deplored whiskey and held cookie sales. When she told of her plans to lead Defenders in armed assaults on saloons, questions were posed about the hatchet's standing as a defensive weapon. At a mass meeting in the Presbyterian Church, forty women joined up, many over the protests of their husbands, some of whom hinted at reprisals with belts. Other resistance formed when the Reverend Walter Scott

Priest, of the Christian Church in Atchison, raised a public bleat that Mrs. Nation was "acting the fool and bringing reproach upon the church, the temperance cause, and womanhood." One newspaper had the good sense to observe that the Reverend's voice in prohibition matters had heretofore been no louder than a bat's squeak, and he rededicated his energies to providing spiritual comfort for neurotic ladies of the congregation.

Mrs. Nation armed her group, distributing what she indicated were general-issue hatchets (obtained cheap at the Topeka Cash Store) and drilled in an empty lot, presumably coordinating hymns, making dummy runs while swinging the tools, etc. When Topeka papers announced that the wives of jointists had organized a competitive unit, armed with horsewhips, the crusader added the formation of a National Hatchet Brigade that would begin with "concerted attacks on saloons throughout the state." Appointed first lieutenants were the reliable campaign veterans, Mrs. Lucy Wilhoite, of Wichita, and Mrs. Mary Sheriff, of Danville (the latter a comparative newcomer but considered the most promising rookie of the year). The work of beefing up her unit was, of course, time-consuming, and Mrs. Nation lay dormant until February 4, when she advised her sisters that the occasion was ripe for a demonstration. Selecting eight women of commando quality, she led them—carrying new hatchets—out into what proved to be a blizzard so blinding that nobody could see where to turn the corners. Beaten back by Winter, like the Nazis at Leningrad, they waited for a letup; then they marched down Kansas Avenue, to "the most thunderous uproar of boos, jeers and abuse in all of Topeka's history." Police had great difficulty but succeeded in holding the crowd back. Things looked so ugly that Mrs. Nation settled for a secondary target, the drugstore of a Mr. Hobart, who had never been suspected of selling liquor except by the medium-shifty method of legal prescription. She bawled him out, consenting to let him off "this time," and proceeded to the similar dispensary of one B. F. Sims. Here she found three members of the legislature, possibly buying aspirin or mustard plasters but more probably laying in some therapeutic corn. Sims, badly agitated, rushed around his counter to demand, "Why did you come here, Mrs. Nation? This is not a joint"—only to absorb the usual ingenious insult. "I'd heard that the Legislature was to meet here at noon," she told him.

Though the Defenders, now bursting to smash, were persuaded away from Sims's, they slogged their way down the snow-packed street to Murphy's Unique Restaurant, a dive, and there the riot began. The truth is that a climax was overdue; Topeka was on the verge of explosion. "The crowds which followed her about the streets were becoming larger, and more boisterous and unruly," as one writer noted. For "a pore innocent restaurant," as the proprietor later descibed it, Murphy's had a marvelously guilty look. The front door was padlocked and a dozen oversized, club-toting guards—Negro and white—stood waiting before the facade. "Smash, women! Smash!" Mrs. Nation cried, and made a rush for the door. "There was a mist of rising and falling snow, humanity whirling and tugging, pushing and shoving, and the attacking party stopped stock still," said the *Capital*. "The line of defense had held." Pushed back, Mrs. Nation took a windup with her hatchet, hoping to heave it through a plate-glass window, but a croupier for the nearby "Big 803" gambling house grabbed the weapon and fled. It ended up, tied with a blue-ribbon bow, as the principal ornament over the Big 803's bar. "Another hatchet! Pass me another hatchet, women!" yelled Mrs. Nation, like Richard III bawling for a horse, and Murphy, cowed by the glint in her eye, flashed an appeal for reinforcements. In a few minutes "the gang of joint defenders was constantly increasing," reported the *Capital*, "and it was well organized. When about fifty big burly Negroes and white men were lined up in front of the joint, they pushed outward through the crowd, carrying Mrs. Nation and the women with them. It was football on a gigantic scale. The women struggled in vain to stay close to the joint.

"One drunken heeler [?] shouted 'Kill her!' and tried to strike Mrs. Nation. A Nation partisan biffed him between the eyes, and a half dozen fights instantly started in the crowd. It was so dense by this time that no man could do his neighbor much harm. Thousands of people were looking on. Sixth Avenue was blocked from Kansas Avenue to Quincy. Two street cars were marooned in the center of the street. The crowd climbed to the tops of buggies and wagons and stood on the backs of the horses. A fringe of heads hung from every upstairs window in the block."

Somehow Mrs. Nation's confederates were permitted to evade the guards, but she was grabbed by four Negroes and half-carried, half-dragged down Kansas Avenue. ". . . The occupants of a score of buggies and commercial wagons abandoned their vehicles as the mob swept down on them," noted a reporter. "Carry Nation was beaten, cuffed and kicked, and several times she was knocked down by frenzied men who penetrated the ring of Negroes, who were themselves unmercifully mauling their prisoner. Cries of 'Kill her! 'Lynch her!' and 'Where's a rope?' arose from the crowd. . . ." An ignominious end-of-the-glory-road appeared to be in sight for Carry Nation when City Police Officers McElroy and Boyle, revolvers drawn, courageously rushed into the crowd and warned her attackers back. Generally speaking, her head was bloody and slightly bowed, a condition that improved miraculously after she had been conveyed to police headquarters and placed in a rear "detention room." From first to last Mrs. Nation's physical and spiritual resilience was a source of admiration to her bitterest enemies. She had absorbed a beating that might leave one of today's heavyweight prizefighters boohooing in a hospital for a month, but the moment she'd scrubbed up, her belligerence revived like a bear emerging from hibernation. "The reporters followed her and a moment later the fragments of her army united at the station and were admitted to the room where she was held," said the *Capital*. This was a mistake on the part of the permissive Police Chief Stahl. In no time Mrs. Nation had burst from her detention and turned the place into a madhouse. She simply took the station over, rushing from room to room, greeting prisoners, consoling (and admonishing) drunks, giving tongue-lashings to protesting jailers. "She continued her arraignment of the saloons, the officers of the law and even the policemen who had arrested her," added the *Capital*'s account. "Her followers gathered around her. They clapped their hands whenever she gave utterance to a word . . . And all the time, hundreds of people tramped up and down about the police station, peeked through the windows, tried to work their way past the policemen who guarded the doors, yelled in encouragement and howled in derision."

While Chief Stahl (a thoughtful man) watched, possibly wondering whether it mightn't be better to free all his prisoners, resign his job and emigrate to Australia, Mrs. Nation organized a Chain Prayer in which her dozens of adherents did a kind of snake dance through the building and attempted to recite prayers in rotation. Failure of the project was ascribed to a fit tossed by an over-excited delegate who threw herself on the floor and "began screaming and kicking the planks," causing a splinter group of nine to defect for an independent "prayer circle" in a corner. "Mrs. Nation crawled on her knees closer to the excited woman," said the *Journal*. "The woman moaned and rocked until her head nearly touched the floor. Mrs. Nation laid a loving arm about her neck, bent lower and lower until her lips were near her ear, and whispered words of encouragement. Then they sang. . . ." It seemed odd to spectators that, while kneeling, the women sang the psalm (which the crusader always pronounced "sam") "Stand up for Jesus." Facing these conditions the authorities were stumped for a solution. After a series of conferences they summoned Mrs. Nation to appear before Police Judge Magaw, the former exhibitor of provocative but artistic nudes. To the wild applause of her group, she refused, explaining that they could either carry her or Magaw could come to her.

Judge Magaw cordially detested Mrs. Nation, but he was a prudent man, and he released her "on her own recognizance"—perhaps the least dependable recognizance in Kansas. She led an exultant procession back to the Coblentz home, where she found two cheerful surprises arrived via the U.S. mails. One, sent by a Kansas City saloon-owner named William Zimmerman, was a twenty-pound ax with an eight-inch blade; the other contained an offer, from Patrick Gleason, former Mayor of Long Island City, of a battle-ax used by an English knight during the Crusades. Gleason explained that the relic had a ten-inch cutting blade and "a very long spike," which he thought might be "useful in defacing bars and puncturing beer kegs." Women are known to appreciate such little attentions—the grace notes that make life worth living for the gentle sex—and Mrs. Nation sat down with a warm look of fulfillment. Taken all around it had been a stimulating day; she had collected a whole new schedule of bruises, her head was laid open afresh, she had lost a sirloin but gained two lethal weapons, she had sparked off a riot that continued all over town at the moment and she had focussed the conscience of Topeka, if not on temperance, at least on the dangers of intemperance. The crusader turned in early, determined to arise and strike while the enemy was still in his bed.

Promptly at six A.M. she trudged off toward the front in a heavy snowstorm. By her side were Mrs. John P. White, a tough proposition with a correspondence-course knowledge of judo ("baritsu"), and Miss Madeline Southard, an evangelist who had proved capable of fighting at the drop of a tract. All three women were armed with razor-honed hatchets. Dashing from the cover of storm, they fell without delay on the restaurant-cum-plank of E. C. Russam, only to find the guards somnolent but still ready. One, recovering nicely, was able to turn Mrs. Nation's hatchet back on herself, slicing a new gash on that small area of her head still unmarked. Repulsed, the reformers hesitated, brushed themselves off and scampered across the street to the Senate Bar, Mrs. Nation leaving a faint but trackable blood trail in the snow. In after years the crusader was frank enough to admit that, all along, her Topekan campaign had subtly been leading up to the Senate, which represented to her the symbolic sinkhole (or cesspool) of Kansas corruption. It was about the only place tacitly unbothered by the police. Here the legislators, the executors, the judges—the public servants of unimpeachable appetite and taste—gathered to drink the fine liquors they had voted to ban. The Senate's elegance has already been mentioned, and it was this, the splendor of an oasis proudly tended, that made so poignant the frightful demolition that followed. First off, the trio encountered bartender Benner Tucker, an amiable but nervous man who, pathetically, was singing as he polished glasses in preparation for the hot toddies required by the legislators for a rough morning session. His first premonition of an extraordinary day arrived with the tuneless jingle of breaking glass, as his long front window caved in. When he whirled around, stricken, it was to see Miss Southard wrecking a cigar case and Mrs. White chopping gashes in the gleaming cherrywood bar.

Tucker grabbed a revolver from a shelf and rounded the counter, where Mrs. Nation aimed a very realistic swipe at his head with her hatchet. All too obviously, she was prepared to kill him if necessary. Tucker panicked, fired two shots into the ceiling, and

tore for the rear exit, in the fashion of several saloonists before
him. Mrs. Nation takes up the narrative: "It was about daylight.
The bartender ran toward me with a yell, wrenched my hatchet out
of my hand and shot off his pistol toward the ceiling; he then ran
out of the back door, and I got another hatchet from a woman
companion. I ran behind the bar, smashed the mirror [it had cost
the Senate $500] and all the bottles under it; picked up the cash
register and threw it down; then broke the faucets of the refrigerator, opened the door and cut the rubber tubes that conducted the
beer. It began to fly all over the house. I threw over the slot machine, breaking it up, and got from it a sharp piece of iron with
which I opened the bungs of the beer kegs, and opened the faucets
of the barrels, and then the beer flew in every direction and I was
completely saturated." Other sources have filled in with details.
Mrs. Nation not only "picked up" the heavy iron cash register, she
lifted it "high over her head to smash it onto the street," said a
witness attracted by the shots. It was probably this single feat
of strength that most awed those thousands of curious who
later viewed the damage. A reporter wrote that "No average man
in good condition could have plucked the machine from its stand."

"The first beer keg she attacked seemed too stout for her," said
the *Star*. "She hammered at it for several minutes, but it resisted
every blow. Then she stopped a minute, said a little prayer, and hit
it a vicious blow with the blade of her hatchet. A stave of the keg
was broken, there was a hissing sound, and a foamy stream of beer
flew all over Mrs. Nation's face, hair and dress. She held her hands
out to let the beer drip off, blinked her eyes, laughed out loud." In
Mrs. Nation's own account she brushed lightly over her disposal of
the refrigerator, but the fact is that, with her bare hands, she
ripped its steel doors from their hinges; she also twisted open its
padlock. No comparable feat of destruction comes to mind except
(as mentioned earlier) Samson's when he disjointed the Temple of
Dagon in Gaza. (The two cases had other features in common; the
reformer, too, had lost some of her hair.)

Mrs. Nation's unique act of impertinence, done in the Capitol's
shadow, approximate to the state's leading lawmakers, was hailed
as the apex of her career to date. The newspapers, including,
again, the New York *Times,* abandoned their usual restraint and

excitedly bubbled over, many hitting the streets with extras. The Topeka *Journal* introduced its several-column story with ten scare-heads and sub-heads, establishing what was believed to be an all-Kansas record. In its account the *Journal* identified the Senate's defender as "Benner Jackson, colored," and had him uttering "a fiendish scream" as he "rushed toward her and seized her." No two stories agreed about the help situation in the Senate; in some, the bartender was aided by a porter, in others he was alone, called Benner Tupper, white. The New York *Times* stated that he was a Negro. Whatever the truth of this trivial point, the *Journal* verified that, after the opening swoop, "the smashers had the room to themselves. All that could be heard on the outside was the crash of breaking glass and the thud of beer kegs as they were rolled out onto the floor . . . Mrs. Nation in the scrimmage with Jackson had been struck on the temple with the hatchet, but this only served to nerve her for the work, though there was a lump on her head the size of a hen's egg when she was led out."

Years afterward, reminiscing about the Senate, Mrs. Nation paid tribute to Officer Graham (of the city police) who "sauntered" in and took her in charge. In a letter to a "Sister Martin," she generously observed that "it was one of the nicest arrests I ever had." It was a courtly remark, since by that period she was one of the most frequent and sought-after jailbirds in America. For a publication (and with a forgivable sense of pride) she reckoned up her score as follows: "In Wichita three times; sentenced December 1900, thirty days; January 21, 1901, twenty-one days and January 22 two days. Topeka, seven times; once thirty days; twice each eighteen days; then twelve days; fifteen days, seven days and three days; Kansas City once, part of a day; Coney Island once, part of a day; Los Angeles once; San Francisco once; Scranton twice, one night and part of two days; Bayonne, New Jersey, a day and a night; Pittsburgh three times, one night and part of two days; Philadelphia once, one night."

Many of these arrests (and others to come) were rough; Officer Graham was a hard nut of the old western school and he admired the crusader's gift to his city. "Well, Sister Nation," he said when he strolled in, "I guess we'll have to arrest you again." "All right," she replied. "You arrived just when I wanted you." Then she turned to her panting and beer-soaked companions, calling out, "Everything cleaned up, ladies?" Miss Southard, disappointed, said almost in a wail, "Sister Nation, there's nothing left to *smash!*" And, after that, off once more to the lockup, making what a newspaper called "an embarrassing procession" up Kansas Avenue as people standing in doorways went through the pretense of holding their noses (blocking off liquor fumes) and the unholy three brayed out "Bringing in the Sheaves." A waggish and irreverent reporter made the point that, if sheaves had reference to corn, then the ladies were certainly "coming home with the bacon," thus scrambling a metaphor and marring a small but tidy creative concept, the rare top-spin given a sentence by a man of lively mind. At police headquarters the ritual charge of Inciting-to-Riot was read Mrs. Nation while she continued to sing, her colleagues were dismissed and she was escorted briefly to the sanctum of Judge Magaw. He attempted to read the law in detail from a textbook. The interview was hopeless. "You might as well read me a novel as that stuff," she told him. "Do you plead guilty?" he inquired. "If you're trying to ask me if I smashed that joint, I rather think I did smash it," she said with a chuckle. This not being a recognizable plea in Magaw's experience, he adjourned the case until February 7, advising her to seek counsel. When she left, with a cheery shout of "Good-bye, Your Dishonor!" he was observed staring moodily at the spots where his unravished nudes once hung in quietness and slow time.

Chapter Fifteen

The great events, the weaving of its historic fabric, had only begun in Topeka. The city's tempo picked up sharply when Mrs. Nation left the chambers of the unhappy Magaw. Word flashed through the joints—*"They've set her free!"*—and newspapers reported that "large and turbulent crowds" formed, surged back and forth in the downtown streets, broke into smaller groups that fought each other, drank from bottles then smashed them in the gutter, made plans for mass lynchings and at last concentrated before the Senate. Meanwhile, the author of their woes marched back to her headquarters at the Reverend Coblentz's and threw herself into the chore of dealing with the incoming flood of congratulation and abuse. She gratefully pocketed a check for ten dollars from a J. B. Meredith, of the Badger Mining and Milling Co., Galena, who, it was discovered, had been having trouble with miners taking nips in the icy pits. She fired off a telegram, urging violent overthrow of the local government, to a newly formed society of Wichita women who had bought thirty hatchets and sharpened them in the public streets. To a man who wired assuring her that she was "the John Brown of Prohibition," she replied in a curt note that Brown was the Carry Nation of Abolition. According to the *Journal*, her letters were so voluminous that she finally "handed the ones to be answered to Mrs. Rose Crist [an apprentice felon], and distributed the rest among the crowd as souvenirs."

With plaster showing at various spots on her head (which part struck one reporter, further, as "looking lopsided with bumps, like a pickle") she offered the press a formal, printed statement, apparently with a nod to posterity, revealing that, "These jointists have the devil in their hearts. But I am not afraid of the devil. I give him a black eye every time I meet him. I used to see him in jail, and I always held up my Bible to him." Her reference to the contusion seemed incongruous when it was noted that she was wearing a fresh sirloin. During a lull, she gave out a "Proclamation to the School Children of the United States," composed somehow when she was detained. It read: "My Precious Little Children:—I send you greeting and ask you to help me destroy that which is on the streets and protected by the police and the city officials to destroy you, my darlings. I want every one of you little ones to grab up a rock and smash the glass doors and windows of these hell-holes. You will do your duty and enroll your name on the pages of undying fame, and place yourself on the side of God and humanity."

Local papers dutifully printed the broadside, which was picked up by the national press, and awaited the solicited wave of juvenile delinquency. But in the succeeding days, no mention was made that even a single unit of Junior Smashers had been joined. It was conjectured that school children, skipping ruthlessly past the national news, fixed their attention on the comics. Most papers restrained their urge to levity in this matter of Mrs. Nation and the young. Her love of children and lifelong record of taking in, feeding, caring for, educating and helping to raise strays—both black and white—as some people collect indigent cats, was well known throughout the West. Even the embittered David Nation, in a generally adverse report, gave her high marks on this score, telling of her work, mainly in Texas, in addition to forming the polyglot Sunday School in the graveyard. "She has a warm spot in her heart for little children," he said, reminiscing, "and we raised several orphans . . . I do not want to criticize her too much."

While Mrs. Nation was booming along, making friends and enemies in her easy, effortless style, the Senate arose like the Phoenix from its ashes, broken glass and spilled hooch. For a time it seemed that the proud old establishment was finished. After the proprietors, "Sheep" Lytle and Mike Kelly, arrived to survey the damage, it was feared that Lytle, for one, might break down. He was an emotional man, for a roughneck, and he had a trace of moisture in his eye. But when the partners saw the crowds bursting to get in, their natural greed reasserted itself. Plenty of liquor remained in the back rooms, and the place was declared open. What followed amounted to a stampede. Over the din of customers wrestling for a position at the bar (many of these new, and not a few in their early teens) Kelly's voice was heard, crying, "Get some more bartenders, men! We can't handle this alone!" Four extra bartenders were immediately put to work. Attention being focused on the wreckage—swept into mounds behind the bar—the management commenced to sell chips of wood and splinters of broken glass for five and ten cents each, depending on size and quality. The New York *Times* said that fragments of the fancy mirror claimed first priority among the collectors. When the market for rubbish eased (energies being more sensibly channeled into swilling) a porter named Bill was stationed outside the door, to yell: "Souvenirs free with each and every glass of beer!" The partners did not find it necessary to have as much as a bushel-basket of debris hauled away. Everything was sold or handed out to grateful passersby.

Lytle and Kelly, jubilant and approaching retirement status, were living in a fool's paradise. The incorruptible Chief Stahl stunned the city and confounded the politicians with a statement that began, "I do not care if Mrs. Nation smashes every joint in Topeka. I sympathize with her. I hope she will close up the saloons of the city. . . ." Then he ambled down to the Senate and arrested both partners, who were released on bail. The capital was thrown into such a frenzy that, next day, Sheriff Cook, bending to the wind, reactivated an old county commitment that imposed a $200 fine on Lytle and gave him a jail sentence of ninety days. Cook had tact enough not to make the arrest himself, and when he sent his deputies down they fell into a fistfight with the entire management. Carted off in the Black Maria were Lytle, Kelly, three bartenders, one Bernard Wagner (vaguely identified as a part-owner) and a drunk who climbed in by mistake and declared himself ready to confess everything. As the wagon went screaming up Kansas Avenue, fighting became general again in the downtown district. It seemed as good an excuse as any. After the brief, rather boring dead space during which it was feared Topeka might return to normal the city-wide tumult started up afresh. Arrests were held to a minimum, because the implacable Stahl, with his fine running start at the Senate, was busy charging forward to close other places. Topeka's politicians were in a pitiable state. Not only were they deprived of a rich source of graft but they no longer had a comfortable retreat in which to drink, and the wives of many—dry, snappish, powerful—had banned all liquors at home.

Stahl was in unusually good fettle at this point in the siege of Topeka. He gave out an interview that sounded like a herald of Armageddon. "I demand, as marshal of the city, that the joints close their doors, for the sake of the peace of the town, and for their own safety," he told reporters. "I believe that the situation is very serious. It is not from Mrs. Nation and the women that I expect the most trouble. Things are so guarded now that it is almost impossible for her to do any more damage. But I fear that danger is at hand from another source. I received a telephone message tonight from a very well-known and conservative citizen, telling me that men are ready to assist Mrs. Nation at a moment's notice. And I have heard the same thing from different sources."

The chief may or may not have had reference to a new unit that was shaping up under emergency conditions, like the Parisian taxicab army of the first World War. It was to be known, simply, as the Grenadiers and composed of ex-drunks. Details of the force were given by a dark and ominous letter printed in the *Journal* under a headline "Talk of Dynamite." George Moore (a prominent citizen) wrote, "I have it from reliable authority that because of threats to do personal violence to the crusader, an organization of victims of the drink habit is being formed, to be called the Grenadiers, for the purpose of wrecking every saloon and joint in Kansas. They will use a grenade in the shape of a percussion shell, the point being perforated and a fulminating cap inserted which will explode on striking. The shell is charged with a very high explosive, that will wreck any saloon. It can be thrown by hand against a door, or projected from a shotgun into upstairs windows, and is certain death and destruction to everything in the room. My informant says that companies of sixteen are already being formed in Topeka, Wichita, Kansas City and Leavenworth. The grenades have been made. . . ." The units were said to be efficient and steady and carried the comforting proviso that any time a member fell off the wagon he had to turn in his bombs.

Buoyed up by this support, Mrs. Nation took to the streets for intemperate speeches in front of the Senate, the Royal Café and other former spas, now locked at least temporarily. In a few, the employees could be seen scowling and shaking their fists, and she admonished them in terms that deserve recording. At one place she said, "I'm sorry for you, boys. You look so ashamed of yourselves! I'm not mad at you, boys. I'm not hating you a bit, even when I come around with my hatchet. I'm treating you just as I would treat one of my own boys if I found him with something that would do him harm. But, boys, you must not stay in this business any longer. I give you fair warning. You are harming yourselves and other boys, and I won't let you do that. If you don't get out of business, I'll be around in a few days and break up your wicked little shops for you. Mind me, now!" The conclusion of her remarks brought from inside such jungle howls of anguish that a reporter felt constrained to say, "They certainly don't *sound* ashamed." The reformer, herself, said she could tell that the saloon people were "deeply moved."

Midway in her tour, a man darted out of a candy shop and, instead of hitting her with a ballbat, as several had hoped, pressed into her hand a number of miniature pewter hatchets. He had caused them to be made up out of his private and skimpy purse. He said, "Sell these to the crowd, Carry, and you can pay your costs and fines this month." The incident proved to be crucial in Carry Nation's life. Thenceforward she would support herself and her causes principally from the sale of souvenir hatchets. The first pewter ware went like wildfire, at ten cents a throw, and she soon arranged with a Rhode Island manufacturer to keep her supplied. Seldom afterward was she to be seen in public without a satchetful of the toys. Her eventual price fluctuated between a quarter and fifty cents, according to the prosperity level of the center where she found herself campaigning.

In Police Court on February 7, Mrs. Nation heard the several city charges against her dismissed, but the state and county authorities ordered her appearance in Circuit Court on the fourteenth. After crying, again, "Good-bye, Your Dishonor!" to Judge Magaw, she led her faithful out of court while singing "Praise God from Whom All Blessings Flow" and, on a whim, dropped by the State Capitol, where she insisted on addressing the legislative bodies jointly (none of the reporters making a pun, or anyway none that survived the copy desk, on the adverb). Her intrusion was highly presumptuous in view of the fact that nearly all the lawmakers were in a condition of mourning, coupled with agitation, over the passing of the Senate. "An attack of nervous jumps seemed to strike the House of Representatives when Mrs. Nation made her entree," the *Journal* put it specifically. By a wild coincidence, the meeting was being presided over by her nephew, James Nation, a social coup largely offset a few days later in Chicago when Mrs. Nation found her grandson (another of Nation's line) tending bar in a dump. The nephew "recovered his equanimity" nicely, the *Journal* added, but a second member immediately leapt up and cried, "Let's adjourn!"

The crusader had charged in through the cloak room to establish her beachhead, and the solons' discomfiture was natural; the more timorous among them wondered if she was armed and her intentions pacific. The confrontation was not without humor. "At the desk the reading clerk lost his measured tone," said a newspaper, "and broke down repeatedly." He babbled like a lunatic. The legislation at hand was a fish bill. The *Journal* said, "It took him three valiant attempts to say 'fish hatcheries,'" but other accounts raised the figure considerably. For awhile, he dealt with "fitch hasheries," but under the storm of laughter he switched to "hash fisheries." Unstrung, he tried both "fash hitcheries" and "hass fitcheries"; then he threw the bill down and fled. There was evidence that he had burst into tears. The session voted whether to allow Mrs. Nation ten minutes; the affirmative won by a debatable margin, and she devoted the time to threatening the nays. At length, lashing herself to a near-smashing mood, she demanded that those who voted against her rise. Observing her expression, the opponents appeared reticent. "One intoxicated old man, who had wandered unsteadily in from one of the very dram shops she was lecturing against, stood up until pulled down by the member in the next seat," reported the *Journal*. She finally left, after trying to shake hands with each lawmaker and kissing all the pages, except a few who dived beneath tables.

A raid Mrs. Nation planned for that afternoon failed to come off, and she absorbed censure from some of her closest helpers. The historian must sympathize with their chagrin. About two-thirds of the Home Defenders had just bought new hatchets, and the students of Washburn College (of the Congregational persuasion) had turned out en bloc with crowbars, a device said to occupy a niche in the institution's heraldry, like the Masons' compass. The expedition was to sally out from the office of Dr. Eva Harding, a frosty old package whose Hippocratic oath had somehow become tangled up with whiskey. Unfortunately for the raiders there also materialized at the meeting one A. C. Rankin, a professional lecturer on temperance. He was not a member of the inner sanctum, and nobody knew how he managed an entrance. It should be noted that the Defenders, in this period, were using a password, without which admission to the councils was unthinkable, but Mrs. Nation, soon afterward, was to express an opinion that their number harbored an enemy agent. One way or another, Rankin wiggled in, with a proposition that quashed any notion of demolition fun for that day. His idea was to take the crusader on lecture tours, whenever possible, between her rapid-fire incarcerations. The first of these would begin as soon as they could conveniently catch a train out of town. There was money in it, said Rankin, and, further, she could spread the word in the states bordering Kansas, with some hope of starting a national revolution. Though the plan was endorsed with hosannas by the Reverend F. W. Emerson, pastor of the First Christian Church, the Defenders rose in their wrath. "Coward!" they cried when Mrs. Nation said she needed cash to pay off her fines, court costs, doctors' fees, butchers, hardware bills, and the like. Temperance, she added, had her up to her eyesockets in debt.

"I'm not a coward," the crusader then retorted (as recorded by the press). "Do you want to smash a joint right now?"

"Yes, I'm ready this minute!"

"Well, sister," she said, continuing to have the last word, "you must learn to conquer the sin of impatience."

Her remarks were directed mainly at the slavering Dr. Harding, who flung a stethoscope across the room and ripped out something brisk in pharmaceutical Latin.

This temporary defection by their leader caused an uproar in the ranks of the smashers. "The sudden departure of Mrs. Nation on a lecture tour is the cause of much comment," said the *Journal.* "Rev. F. W. Emerson and A. C. Rankin are receiving the burden of criticism. At noon today dodgers were distributed on the streets as follows:

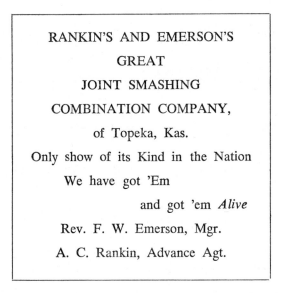

RANKIN'S AND EMERSON'S

GREAT

JOINT SMASHING

COMBINATION COMPANY,

of Topeka, Kas.

Only show of its Kind in the Nation

We have got 'Em

and got 'em *Alive*

Rev. F. W. Emerson, Mgr.

A. C. Rankin, Advance Agt.

The whiskey faction had run the bills off on a hand-press, and they entertained nearly everybody in town except Emerson, who gave out an interview so piously aggrieved that, though innocent of wrongdoing, he began to be an object of suspicion. The consensus was that he had a fist in the pot. His statement was in its essence incoherent, revolving (dizzily) around such words as "integrity," "my standing," "character," and "anyone so desiring can make an investigation if they wish." A request of the city attorney by three jointists to have the Reverend arrested on an open charge was denied, and he hastened off to join the tour.

In Iowa, Mrs. Nation was received by tumultuous devotees at Stuart, Atlantic and Adair, and then at Anita, Exeter, Earlham and Valley Junction, and the unrestrained adulation affected her judgment. At Des Moines, welcomed at the station by a swaying, surging, chanting, flag-waving, hatchet-brandishing crowd of five thousand, she let go and promised to "reward them with some smashing"—this despite the fact that saloons were legal in Iowa. The showiest greeting unit was a huge brass band that caused the reformer to exclaim in rapture, "Just *look* at it! Just look at the dears! God bless every one." The group was rendering a selection not yet identified with temperance, and many of its members were curiously off pitch, and it was several days before Mrs. Nation learned that the band had been provided by the Des Moines Bartenders Association in a spirit of careful mockery.

Of the historic precautions taken by saloonkeepers that day (February 9, 1901) none approached the brilliance of an A. Romani, owner, who rigged inside his doorway a towering wire cage filled with half-starved rats and mice and equipped with a trap-lift on a string that he meant to pull when Mrs. Nation made her entrance. It was a master-stroke, and unofficially, on the order of municipal prizes awarded for floats on the Fourth of July, it was agreed in Des Moines that he had distinguished both himself and his lounge. Among other things, he had capitalized on women's inherent fear of rodents, and he bolstered his position with a squib, in a local paper, wherein he described the special savagery and taste for human, "or near-human," flesh of the rare species which he had selected. The barricade proved effective. Mrs. Nation pulled up in front, as the proprietor urged her in with bows and Latin politesse, then passed on pretty fast. She might successfully have smashed the place, for the rats and mice had fallen on each other with gusto— as any two of the human species seem always eager to do—and were in process of absorbed self-destruction.

As the crusader's tour progressed, crowds began to dwindle. The reason was mechanical rather than philosophic. Despite Rankin's efforts to convert her to a prepared script, with a semblance of continuity and minus five or six dozen of the digressions that led her listeners off into a tangled thicket of syntax, she insisted on speaking offhand. In her autobiography she bragged about the habit, saying, "I never made a note or wrote a sentence for the platform in my life. I have spoken extemporaneously from the first and often went on the platform when I could not have told what I was going to say. . . ." For guidance, she'd consulted the Bible: "You shall not think of what you shall speak, but it shall be given in that same hour." Not infrequently in that same hour all that filtered through was a repetition of her curses against whiskey, tobacco, sin and the Republican Party. Word began to spread that Mrs. Nation's message was as conveniently obtained, free, on street corners during her visits. Too, there was trouble with hecklers. Many low fellows paid fifty cents for the privilege of trying to scramble her remarks. It was ridiculously easy; she was always happy to knock off and swap insults with anybody spirited enough to debate. A routine genealogical inquiry, such as [in Muscatine, Iowa] "Is it true that your grandfather was a mentally-retarded ape?" could lead to the dignified reply [same place], "Young man, step up here beside me and let's see if your knuckles reach the ground." This over, the crusader might sail into a half-hour's lambasting of the Masons, losing a couple of dozen members of her audience. It was good sport, but it often had little bearing on temperance.

In Chicago on February 12 Mrs. Nation had the bad luck to run into a competitive gala, in large degree inspired by her upheavals of the past. John Alexander Dowie was one of the most promising young cranks on the outlaw-lunatic scene. Many American fanatics expected him eventually to rise to the top of the heap, and already he had left his mark on Chicago. Dowie's curse of the moment was an animus against drugs as curative agents. He contended that prayer could fill the gap, and to prove it he'd recruited a female army outfitted with pitchforks, canes and umbrellas—these carried secreted beneath long capes. When Mrs. Nation hit town, Dowie's legions had just demolished four drugstores and held the employees of a fifth besieged though counter-attacking with thrown missiles of bottled drugs and, at last, several revolvers that turned the tide. Thus the crowds that might normally have attended Mrs. Nation's convulsions were partly seduced into Dowie's salient.

Even so, she gathered a number of excited spectators and estab-

lished a caucus before the obscure bar of a Henry McCall. Like
Judge Magaw, McCall was an art lover, and he had a nude statue
of a girl, splendidly candid, beckoning in his window. Spying it,
Mrs. Nation staggered; then she rushed in to scream, "Cover that
wicked and shameful object!" McCall was a peaceable man, and
he agreed to comply, waiting until his visitor was gone and then
tossing over the maiden a "flimsy pink netting" that left two peek-a-
boo nipples attractively thrust through the mesh. He had reckoned
without the crusader's dogged custom of following up on orders
issued in the field. On her return, an hour later, she screamed
much louder and demanded that he clothe the statue "as you
would your sister." McCall's mild reply that he seldom if ever
clothed his sister proving insufficient, he draped the figure in a
Mother Hubbard and slapped a sun-bonnet on her head. After
Mrs. Nation's second (and satisfied) departure, he slipped the
gown down to expose the girl's imposing left breast and tilted the
bonnet to provide an appearance incredibly wanton in sum. Overnight the bar's celebrity was sealed. "The statue justly became one
of the most popular sights in Chicago," observed a biographer, and
new customers fought their way in to make McCall a comparatively rich man.

The crusader's scheduled speech at the Auditorium defaulted
because the Chicago Press Club, arranging it, managed to sell only
twelve dollars worth of tickets. Upon investigation she was ab-
solved from blame. The journalists, following custom, had been
lounging in saloons instead of hustling to fill the house for a lecture
that might close them. Mrs. Nation's appearance at Willard Hall
was another matter; this function was sponsored by the W.C.T.U.
With the place jammed, the aisles in a condition of riot, and hundreds clamoring at the doors there occurred one of those psycho-
logical mass seizures that work periodic havoc at over-populous
meetings. Women began fainting in every section of the house.
Order was restored with difficulty, and guards pulled Mrs. Nation
to the platform through the swaying aisles. Her impact proved so
uproarious that, next morning, she decided to march on City Hall.
Even today it is not known precisely what she had in mind for
Mayor Carter Harrison, whom she had recently eulogized by saying, "I think he's the biggest devil in the land." Whatever it was, he

skillfully dodged it, leaving at his office a statement that began, "I will not see Mrs. Nation. I do not understand that the Kansas 'joint-smasher' has anything to impart to the city of Chicago. . . ." Nevertheless she climbed up on his desk, while municipal employees gathered, and unloaded about fifteen minutes' worth of abuse, mostly personal; then she undertook a tour of the rialto. To reporters in attendance she hinted that she might smash everything in sight—"no matter whether saloons are legal or not"—but she lost momentum when she entered the barroom of John Juertick.

Here Mrs. Nation suffered an embarrassing setback when "an extremely young man tending bar" came around grinning and cried, "How are you, Grandma?" The crusader was quoted as replying, after a heavy pause, "Yes, I know you"; then she turned and walked slowly out. The boy (son of David Nation's Lola) filled the glasses of two clients bawling for refreshment—specifically they wished to drink his grandmother's health—and dashed out in the street to catch her. "We had a long talk," she wrote in her book, "and while he returned to his job, he promised to quit and take up temperance work." Regrettably, no evidence has ever been uncovered that he did so. On the contrary, it seems natural to suppose the boy's employer hiked his wages and figured out some clever hook-ups in the way of special promotion, but there is no evidence that this happened, either. The press was surprisingly apathetic about the connection.

In an interview later in Topeka, Mrs. Nation gave an expanded, or different, version of the meeting, but she omitted this from her autobiography. She was quoted as saying, "God told me to go to Chicago, but Rankin wanted me to come back to Kansas. I told Rankin that I wouldn't stay away from Chicago if he gave me a roomful of $20 gold pieces . . . I met my grandson, Riley White, and he was running a saloon. He told me to go in and smash it if I wanted to . . . I had a meeting in his saloon. Nobody but saloon-keepers, reporters and lewd women were there. They treated me well and the women called me grandma. Poor women, they are dragged down by devils. It was the most remarkable meeting I ever held. Saloonkeepers and harlots have a much better chance of heaven than hypocrites who are in the church. I have no use for the women who are afraid they will soil their skirts in trying to lift up their fallen sisters." The day she put these remarks on the record, she also sent an "open" telegram to her grandson, curiously enough addressing it to the Chicago *American*. It was rapturous about a friendly, if debauched, city:

> "My Darling Riley:—I got here all right. O Chicago! Chicago! How fondly my heart turns to thee—the home of fond hearts that were so loving to me. To Eva Shontz and her colaborers who gave me all. The saloon men of Chicago treated me better than those of any city I have visited. I have never received such courtesy from any police force as was tendered by the police brothers of Chicago, whom I know but to love. Riley, my boy, tell that man who sang in your saloon that I never heard a voice so lovely. I expect to hear him sing in Heaven. Tell the dear girls that I met there that they are the sisters of Carrie* Nation. When I come to Chicago I want to meet them. I shall pray to God to open up the way that I may go to Chicago the first place after I leave Kansas, for I love that poor burdened city too well not to have an earnest desire to smash the hell-holes. Yes, sweet, affectionate Chicago, I love thee in spite of thy law defiance. There is a better day for thee. Riley, come to me as quickly as possible. I will be here until Tuesday morning at 11 o'clock, when I go to Medicine Lodge. Your loving grandmother,
>
> Carrie Nation

Mrs. Nation concluded her Chicago walking tour by having her hair dressed in an establishment on State Street, as spectators stared through the window. Then she visited a Turkish bath. In the latter place, told that the men's section was crammed with drunks drying out, she addressed them noisily (and scathingly) while she relaxed under the steam. Tortured howls from across the barrier suggested an adverse reaction. The lecture tour wound up in Chicago; she had an important engagement, in Circuit Court in Topeka, on the fourteenth. Rankin, the pushy booking agent, announced himself as being generally reconciled to the outcome. "It was an artistic success," he said, a trifle sourly.

* This was a curious spelling slip of the crusader's; she made many such.

Chapter Sixteen

If Mrs. Nation's tour of Iowa and Illinois seemed comparatively serene, the state she left behind had erupted into an active volcano. Topeka and all of Kansas were ablaze, with feelings running so high that Governor Stanley debated whether to call out the militia. Nearly everybody, on both sides of the liquor question, appeared to have gone berserk. The students of quiet, reverent, contemplative Washburn College were busily at work building a twenty-foot battering ram weighing 300 pounds, with which they hoped to introduce an added measure of light into the many saloons that reopened as soon as the crusader cleared the city. All stores were stripped of hatchets, axes, crowbars and ballbats—sold to members of the W.C.T.U. and the State Temperance Union who marched continually in the streets, singing, chanting, replying to taunts and breaking off to hear incitations to riot by ministers in the various churches.

For Carry Nation it had been a long uphill fight, but her philosophy at last was firmly implanted. *Smash!* was the catchword of the day, viewed as fondly, as wolfishly by the clergy as by once-horrified temperance groups, pacifists, theological students, children, the aged and infirm, strangers-in-town and the formerly sour and hostile husbands of trouble-making reformers. Under the leadership of the Reverend Dr. J. T. McFarland, of the First Methodist Church, and three other pastors, a hundred men were recruited for the nucleus of a male smashing group. Broken down into ten units of ten men each, they held drills in churches to acquaint themselves with lethal weapons and correct procedures for destroying saloons. Drillmasters in several cases were women, such as Miss Southard and Mrs. White, to whom the dreary, wet, beer-mired battlefields with their gnarled stumps of furniture were as familiar as the garden plots at home. A well-known and reassuring figure at the drills was Dr. Eva Harding, armed with a surgical saw, whose fighting spirit drove the men to prodigious outbursts in an effort to achieve the demolition standards of women. Of some use was a brief but expert manual-of-arms, largely the creation of Miss Southard with an unabashed bow to Carry Nation, "to whom we all owe everything." Indications were that Mrs. Nation had dictated most of the points, drawing on her deep knowledge of smashing, and that Miss Southard had refined them to readability. Most worthwhile were phrases like "For Cigar cases—flat side of hatchet, then lop off legs if any"; "Break beer faucets at top—better leverage"; "Tiny reminder—smash rungs from all chairs before leaving"; and "Do not hesitate to throw hatchets if bartenders armed." These kept high the morale of men who in the main were middle-aged and had never previously broken anything more resistant than bread at communion.

The attack cadre of one hundred was quickly augmented by three thousand volunteers at a mass meeting on February 10 in the capacious Topeka Auditorium. In advance of the unsettling rally, ten thousand circulars were distributed over the city; most were seized on and studied with pleasure, others were burned in public displays before saloons. They read:

THE JOINTS MUST GO!

MEN'S MASS MEETING

at the

AUDITORIUM

on

February 10, 1901

To Decide on Definite Action

AGAINST THE JOINTS.

The first speaker on that tension-filled night was Chief of Police Stahl, whose transition from peace officer to prohibitionist was almost complete. With each new threat to the statutes, his outlook toward temperance lawbreakers mellowed several degrees. To a deafening ovation, he declared that with any kind of judicial cooperation he could "close the joints for good in twenty-four hours." His utterance meant further annoyance for the artistically-bereft Magaw; after a wild melee the body unanimously passed a resolution demanding Judge Magaw's immediate removal by the City Council. Following this good start the meeting began to fire off resolutions like Fourth of July rockets, each a little more jarring than the last. They reached a climax with an ultimatum to saloon-keepers, to "close all bar-rooms before noon of February 11 and ship all bar fixtures and liquor out of Topeka before dusk of February 15." The vote here was not quite unanimous. Official consternation was expressed over the single dissident ballot, which then was discovered to have been cast by one Barney McMahon, a tool of jointists, who was attacked by volunteers carrying clubs and chased from the premises while shrieking for his life. He had cause to be worried; two habitually mild citizens—a draper's assistant and an elderly mercantile clerk—brutalized by the training under Miss Southard and Dr. Harding, were only a spring or two behind him with hatchets.

During these critical moves the saloon men had carried on in their flaunting and bullet-headed way, hiring hundreds more Negro guards, arming them with shotguns and leaving orders to "insult any female passerby who even looks like a temperance nut." Each fresh impertinence fanned the flames of the holocaust. The truth is that the jointists lacked leadership; in the high echelons they had scant depth and their tactics were outdated. The importation as military adviser of an A. Romani, whose rat-cum-mouse cage had turned the tide in Des Moines, might have spruced up an essentially rag-tag and mentally impoverished force. An attempt to reactivate the underworld Order of the Mystic Brotherhood—a terrorist society formerly given to hurling rocks through windows and booing down temperance chimneys at night—began, struggled and fell flat. The added Negro guards, plus dozens of reopenings, convinced the Volunteers that a gigantic smashing, a battle-to-end-all-battles, was shaping up, with Providence (promised the ministers) bone-dry and ready to stand on the side of the aggressors. Carry Nation's return from Chicago (on the fourteenth) was the catalyst that touched off the fantastic events of February 17. Beyond doubt, the city will never again see such frightening and well-organized violence, and a question has been raised why some arterial thoroughfare has not been named "Boulevard (or Avenue) February 17," in the French and Spanish manner. The date looms large in Topeka's liberation from sin.

Mrs. Nation alighted from her train, contrived to have her hearing adjourned and established herself downtown, renting two rooms of a building that she was later to buy. We have no evidence that the Reverend Coblentz turned her out, but he must surely have made mild, ministerial representations fervently endorsed by his wife. For an extended period that Mrs. Coblentz may well have seen as several years their home had been the focal point of plot and counter-plot, dissension, argument and backbiting. It had been trampled over by Amazons and men; it had been surrounded by armed crowds fired up with rage and inexpensive corn, and reporters had repeatedly tried to infiltrate all of the building's apertures, including a cellar crawlway and the upstairs windows. Reverend Coblentz was thinner and grayer. He was a good man, a sincere man, and his temper stayed high but his health had begun to wither. Short-sightedly he had equated himself with one of the phenomenal constitutions of all time.

Even the opposition papers paid homage to the spartan simplicity of Mrs. Nation's new quarters, permitting her the definitive word: "I covet the humblest walk. I will not have a piece of fine furniture. I have no carpets on my floors. The little cupboard I use is made of a dry-goods box with shelves in it and a curtain in front. My dishes all told, kitchen and dining room, are not worth five dollars . . . I used to delight in cut-glass, china, plush, velvet and lace. Now I can say vanity of vanities, all is vanity."

While the crusader arranged her *pied-à-terre,* a brief lull descended on the city. Business and ordinary life, but not death, were suspended in the breathless time that might be compared with 1939 in the struggle between Germany and Britain. A scrutiny of Kansas records in the period shows that, aside from temperance actions, little of note proceeded around the state. Frederick H.

Harvey, the English-born founder of Harvey restaurants in railroad stations, died at his Leavenworth home, to be eulogized by
William Allen White as "one of the great men of the country because he did so much for good cooking." Five thousand horses
were shipped to South Africa from W. S. Tough's barn in Lawrence for the British Army in its fight against the Boers. Winter had
been declared severe (as predicted) and the Armour Packing
Company was cutting "eight-inch" ice at Sugar Lake; for its refrigerator cars, the Missouri Pacific Railroad was cutting ice at
Downs. The last link needed for a transcontinental railway was
provided when control of the Southern Pacific passed to a syndi-
cate dominated by the Union Pacific (the deal represented a sum
of $70,000,000). "Pike's Pawnee Indian Village," near Republic,
was accepted by the state as a gift from George Johnson and Mrs.
Elizabeth A. Johnson; no mention was made that the Pawnees
were consulted about the arrangements. The almost solitary dissident voice of Reverend J. D. Ritchey, at the Wichita Episcopal
Church, spoke up to contend, bravely, that "the saloon is part of the
American social system and the best that can be done with it is
regulation"; he left his church uninjured. But a straw in the gale
that had commenced to howl over all of Kansas was seen in the
destruction of Arkansas City's celebrated Last Chance Saloon by a
hundred masked men armed with rifles and axes.

In view of Mrs. Nation's permanence, and the evident bloody
intentions of the Male Volunteers, most Topeka saloons now
started to close down. By February 15 only one joint was open,
and Chief of Police Stahl locked it that afternoon. However, an
investigation by the Volunteers' Sub-Committee on Deadlines revealed that, except for forty barrels of whiskey hustled out to Kansas City, all liquor stocks together with bar-fixtures and even a few
bars had been "temporarily" stored in barns on the outskirts of
town. There remained the grim, the inescapable alternative—war.
A hypersecret meeting was held the night of the sixteenth and a
plan of action composed. Since the password code had been cracked,
temperance elite were to be separated from guerrillas by the wearing of a white handkerchief knotted peculiarly about the throat.
Top strategy was set at the main meeting, and field-level tactics
were discussed at subordinate sessions in churches around town.

The rallying point, from which the central assault would be launched, was fixed as the east steps of the capitol, and here especially the white neckerchief was the *sine qua non* badge of identification, sleeve patch of Kansas' toniest corps.

Washburn brought its own separate password—the 300-pound battering ram—which was deposited on the capitol lawn at 6 A.M. on D-Day. It was a good, workmanlike job and appeared to consist of a peeled tree-trunk with oak pegs for hand-holds and a poured-concrete head about the size of a barrel. The ram forever removed the mild taint of denominationalism that clung to Washburn in some minds. A newspaper stated that the students were as "multi-skilled as theological figures from the Renaissance." A breathless hush settled over the reformers, bright with arms, pending the arrival of their commander-in-chief, Carry A. Nation, who overslept an hour and turned up at seven. For some time before dawn the fighters had streamed toward the State House from every part of the city, praying, cheering, singing hymns, bundled up against the cold, white neckerchiefs knotted in place. Topeka suddenly resembled nothing so much as one of the Himalayan religious shrines— Kadarnath or Badrinath—toward which pilgrims annually make their way in droves up Mother Ganges and across the Anaknanda. A difference spottable by an Indian child of four was the character of the bundles carried by the Kansas communicants. Most male worshipers had either sledgehammers or axes slung over their shoulders; a scattering were provided with crowbars; a paltry dozen—sedentary, hen-pecked fellows—carried hatchets. All of the women (who reporters thought were in the minority by a ratio of three to five) had hatchets, and Carry Nation, adding that splash of color so riotously in evidence at Spanish church functions, held aloft two brand new ones with red blades and white ribbons dependent from the hafts. Her first order was, "Get in line, men and women. We must be about the Lord's work!" Then she cried, "All ready? Follow me! Onward for Jesus!"

As the crusader wheeled toward Kansas Avenue, and the others fell in by twos, she positioned her weapons overhead to form a cross, and the question was raised, by heretics, whether this use of un-Christian ikons was not in fact blasphemous. Directly behind her stepped Dr. Harding (equipped now with a hatchet); and the

Reverend Emerson, whom Mrs. Nation had named chief-of-staff, marched third in line. The Washburn battering ram was carried well toward the front, and newsmen noticed that the porters were further armed with hatchets tied to their belts. There was some discussion, later, whether Mrs. Nation had a whistle; certainly there was a snarl-up in the beginning signals. Whereas she broke into the familiar and possibly suitable

> "Onward, Christian soldiers,
> Marching as to war,
> With the Cross of Jesus
> Going on before"

the Washburn contingent, led by pom-pom girls, chanted in cadence, "Rah! Rah! Carry Nation! Rah! Rah! Carry Nation!" all but smothering the battle hymn. The mix-up ended when the cadenced cry was altered to "Smash! Smash! For Jesus' sake, Smash!"

From excited newspaper accounts (whose details differed widely) it is not easy to define the structure of the crusader's force. One Topeka paper said, "At 6 o'clock [inaccurate] Mrs. Nation appeared and the line was immediately formed. In front was Company H of the secret law enforcement organization, composed of men; beside them were members of the Home Defenders. Behind these were college students and others favorable to the crusade. All were armed with revolvers, clubs, axes or hatchets. Four men carried an immense battering ram, 12 by 12 inches in width and thickness and 7 feet long. At each end handles had been made by boring holes and putting sticks or iron rods through them. This ram was operated by five men."

Not remarkably, windows flew up along the route, night-caps were thrust out in bewilderment, residents everywhere within earshot tumbled into trousers or skirts and rushed forth to join the sport. Mrs. Nation's army picked up further strength from early-to-work storekeepers, loiterers, several drunks sprawled in doorways and temperance-minded dogs, and by the time it reached Kansas Avenue, Topeka had mounted another raging mob, comparable in

temper to that howling outside the Bastille. The Volunteers' hard
core was marching under sealed orders, so to speak, for Mrs. Nation had not yet disclosed the nature of her primary target. The
matter was resolved when she announced that her aim was re-
venge. She had decided that vengeance was hers, not the Lord's, at
least for the moment. In short, she had in mind Murphy's Unique
Restaurant and Billiard Parlor, scene of a significant failure, and
here she hauled up, faced by four armed policemen before barred
doors and windows. Besides these, Chief Stahl had summoned a
posse for the ostensible purpose of maintaining law and order and
with the secondary duty of protecting the women from Murphy's
Negro guards. His action was futile. Mrs. Nation hesitated only for
a minute; then her trumpet-call rent the wintry air: "Don't pay any
attention to them! Smash! Smash!" She showed the way by taking
what one reporter called "a windmill swing" and hurling a hatchet
through a window. The melodic rain of splintering glass prompted
Washburn College to spring into action, but at the ram's first
crunching thwack the resistance proved so feeble that the students
(with ram) hurtled through Murphy's front door and almost ran
out of the rear. The engine was a success.

Thus given an ingress sufficient to accommodate a Santa Fé
wagon, the army poured through to mop up. Once inside, both
women and men delicately drew back to give Mrs. Nation the first
interior smash. She wasted no time in slamming her second hatchet
into the bar mirror, and after that the carnage became general. In
the recapitulations there was speculation about Washburn and its
battering ram. Apparently, almost suicidally, the students were
trying to knock the building down on top of the attack group.
"The whole structure shook beneath the impact," a writer noted.
Recent events have showed with what reckless courage certain
students are capable of throwing themselves almost under troop-
trains, manhandling draft cards, growing wispy beards, carrying
heavy signs and demanding post-graduate rights, and Washburn's
conduct in Topeka on February 17, 1901, was perhaps the herald
of worse things to come. Long after everything in Murphy's—mirrors, glassware, fixtures, all furniture, the bar itself—was little
more than history, the students continued to pound at the walls,
"but with scant success, for their excitement was so great that they

failed to coordinate their efforts, and seldom struck twice in the same place."

Mrs. Nation missed much of this immensely satisfying action. Some time during the first minutes she was seized by two police-men and, fighting like a tigress, waltzed outside and into a patrol wagon. The officers were "cuffed and pummeled" by women be-fore they made off up the street, bell ringing, horses galloping in acknowledgment of the prize. The anatomy of that February scene in Topeka has been expertly probed by a contemporary his-torian, who wrote, "From six o'clock in the morning until dusk the streets resounded to the thunderous tread of the embattled temper-ance hosts, the rush and roar of angry mobs, and the clanging gongs of patrol wagons; while the jangle of breaking glass and the thud of axes, hatchets, sledgehammers and battering rams against doors and interior woodwork scantily indicated the fierceness of the smashing multitude." When Mrs. Nation left, shouting over her shoulder what the *Journal* reported as "Keep on smashing! Keep on smashing! The Lord bless you!" Murphy's was already a shell. Booked and again released on her recognizance, she dived into a hansom and was back at the front in less than half an hour. By then only the main supports of the building remained; even so, Washburn continued to bong these with the same silent dogged-ness that had marked its first salute to the door.

February 17 in Topeka saw the establishment of records that any city could mention with pride. Before the day ended, Carry Nation had been arrested and carted to the station house four times, the effort surpassing her best embroilments in Kiowa, Wichita and Enterprise. Three diverse kinds of business firms lay in ruins, one largely by error, and the crusader had twice been extracted from the county jail by a Negro saloonist. On her return to Murphy's she found her cohorts helpless for lack of leadership. They were milling around pathetically looking for new worlds to conquer. Dr. Harding had attempted to rally the troops with drowned-out pleas to "form in line and check weapons," but the battering ram thud-ded dully on and nobody obeyed. Reverend Emerson had with-drawn to one side, for prayer, oblivious of his responsibilities as chief-of-staff. He seemed "paralyzed with indecision," said a wit-ness. Into this void Mrs. Nation strode with those unmistakable qualities of leadership—born in the favored few—that set apart a Napoleon, a Pizarro, an Al Capone. She cried, "Follow me! I know another place!" snatched two hatchets from a woman near panic, and darted up Sixth Street toward a livery stable where saloon fixtures had been stored. Here there occurred one of those trifling mishaps, an intramural dispute, that can happen in any army and to which impassioned reform forces are especially vulnerable. Histories, which never lie, say Washington's generals spent more time preening themselves for advancement than in fighting the Revolution, and the Reverend Henry Ward Beecher's attempt to snitch on his colleagues remains to this day a thorn in the side of good works.

The trouble began when a mob that collected to defend the stable, with clubs, fled before the oncoming array of axes, sledgehammers, crowbars and hatchets. Somehow—the precise details are lost—Dr. Harding and the Reverend Emerson hung up together in a doorway, both on fire to push inside and smash. One of the pair evidently jostled the other, and they squared off to mix it without delay. In response to a warm, rather unclerical observation, Dr. Harding called Reverend Emerson a liar, whereupon *Mrs.* Emerson leaped in to swing at the doctor. Had friends not intervened, a nasty mess might have followed, for the three disputants were heavily armed and anxious to put their weapons to use.

When Mrs. Nation emerged from the stable, after the fixtures had been smashed but the horses left untouched, she was re-arrested then carelessly turned loose again at Headquarters. This time she trimmed seven minutes from her first pinch, returning in a shade over twenty minutes to lead the Volunteers toward a cold storage plant in Polk Street. The establishment's only known sin, if it had one, was in supplying ice to saloonkeepers, but the crusader stated that, according to her private spy complex, the plant stored beer and whiskey to be parceled out as needed. Hearing this, the crowd—now of several thousand—began crying, variously, "Kill her! Lynch her!" and "Hooray for Carry Nation!" One voice rose above everything to suggest that, in Polk Street, Topeka had a fine opportunity to put Mrs. Nation in cold storage and keep her there. Greeted at first with laughter, the idea might have caught on, but Mrs. Nation smashed the plant in time to avoid being preserved.

The Home Defenders and Male Volunteers lost sympathy at the storage plant, which was owned by the brothers Moeser, Charles and William. For the first time a lot of costly smashing was done before any guilty evidence came to light. The hatchets were put into play on suspicion. As thousands cheered and booed, the reformers quickly chopped away windows and doors (though an entrance could have been managed without violence) then had the bad luck to find themselves up to their waists in butter. Tumbling through a door, they fell into butter vats where they wallowed in confusion for several minutes. After ruining the butter and scraping themselves partially free, they rushed into the ice chambers and scattered all the ice on the ground. This done, they looked about for the dreaded beer and liquor but failed to turn up as much as a bottle of bitters. The Moeser brothers, voicing dissatisfaction with the day's course of business, charged Mrs. Nation in a complaint that arrived a few minutes late, or seconds behind one rushed through by Edward Murphy, proprietor of the late Unique Restaurant.

For the third time that morning, the crusader was bundled into the Black Maria and hauled off with a rackety ding-ding-dinging through packed streets to Headquarters. The situation there was chaotic. Wholesale arrests had been made as independent fighting everywhere accompanied the main action. Some of this was to settle old scores, but the majority simply expressed western *joie de vivre*. In any case, a shortage of cells was reported, and Mrs. Nation counted herself fortunate to be given a single, with a half-bath. She was detained only briefly. For no good reason that anybody has advanced, a Negro saloon-keeper named Nick Chiles appeared to go Mrs. Nation's bail. It was an auspicious meeting; the two would tread substantially the same path, pulling in the double-harness, for months until disharmony and mutual suspicion ended their unlikely union. Chiles was more than a jointist; he was a big man in town—politician, hotel owner, publisher, dabbler in real estate, a normal, garden-variety reaper of business rewards from both legitimacy and sin. The publican enjoyed a professional and social position in Topeka, in 1901, that he could scarcely find in New York today, and Mrs. Nation was not much moved by his gesture except to promise, in leaving, "When I get time, I'll smash your joint for you."

Before she went free, her apostles of good works scattered to outlying church meetings; toward the nearest of these Mrs. Nation hurried only to face the legal bouquet arranged by the brothers Moeser. Trying to take her away, the arresting policeman ran into trouble when her followers threatened "to fall on and dismember him." By drawing his revolver and promising to shoot at the first hint of assault, he was able to restore the fire-eater to her familiar seat in the van. During most of that day, in fact, the patrol wagon simply followed Mrs. Nation around, waiting for the next pickup, but the allegation of a whimsical reporter that the initiative finally was left to the horse may well have been overdrawn. At headquarters the tireless Chiles still stood by, with the expectation of further calls, and he bailed her out again. Various theories, none of them sound, have been expounded to clear up Chiles' motive. It would seem that, as a jointist, he had everything to lose by Mrs. Nation's liberty, for she drew no distinctions between beneficent and malign whiskey-sellers. The best guess is that the Negro liked her style. He was a man of some stature, and Topeka beset by Mrs. Nation surpassed in interest the city of platitudinous solons and droning ecclesiastics. The alteration of Reverend Emerson, from psalm-reader to brawler-in-the-streets, was probably enough in itself to warp Chiles' commercial judgment. Emerson, incidentally, was injured some time later when, after a mass meeting had ignited several explosions, he took his place at the Washburn battering ram. The move was apparently a promotion, his hatchetation* and willingness to whip Dr. Harding having convinced everyone of his mettle. Fifty men with handkerchiefs that covered, this time, their faces—and armed with sledgehammers, crowbars and the ram—moved on Curtis' storage house in North Topeka and decimated thirty cases of beer. Police were forced to fire half a dozen shots, one of these grooving a Mr. Adams, a carpenter by trade and a Male Volunteer by preference. The Reverend Emerson hurt his hand when he tried to exhort his ram-mates into a fast canter with the engine. (It hit a pretty solid wall and bounced back, knocking the Reverend down.) Both he and a Dr. Mitchell were arrested

---

* "Hatchetation" was coined by Mrs. Nation in this period and used thereafter for the rest of her life. It denoted extreme skill with the tool, the work of an expert hatcheter, the 33rd degree of hatchet-wielding.

and carted off in the van, but all charges against them eventually were dropped.

Newspapers recorded the ebb and flow of Topeka's emotions in these crises with approximate impartiality, and the town's attitude toward its domination by women was genial. Nearly everybody except saloon-owners, a few policemen and several residents who previously had enjoyed sleeping late seemed grateful for the free recreation, and Washburn College had significantly expanded its curriculum. The Moeser brothers, honorable men, verified that they had occasionally stored beer for the jointists; they announced a cessation of the practice. The *Capital* printed their formal statement that, "after existing contracts are broken, we will not receive for storage any beer to be delivered to or received by jointists so far as we can prevent it."

"Summarizing the situation," added the *Capital,* "we would say that liquor sales have practically ceased; that liquors, bars and fixtures have been generally stored in the city; that the district court has granted eighteen injunctions against jointists, and other injunctions are now before the judge for action; that the Attorney General has appointed a prosecuting attorney for Shawnee County; that the police department is active and alert; and that the Legislature promises needed legislation for better law enforcement."

Locally, Mrs. Nation's triumph was all but complete, but not even the open-handed Chiles could save her from confinement when she showed up to answer the Moeser complaint. On the morning of February 18, Judge McCabe presided over District Court, but he broke down in three days and gave way to a replacement. The crusader's arraignment was tumultuous, attended by a room bulging with Defenders. The assistant county attorney, a Negro named Jamieson, strove valiantly to present his case but he was interrupted by hoots, howls, honks, cheers and song. Mrs. Nation's attorney now took the floor for an hour and a half to quote Scripture, none of it relevant. At this point, Mrs. Nation conceived the nuisance device of jumping up and opening windows, thus admitting icy blasts that drove official documents helter-skelter over the room. Even Judge McCabe abandoned his dignity and tucked up his skirts to join in a search to restore order. After this the crusader, refusing to stay seated, wandered about the chamber humming and conferring with her backers, shadowed by two ineffectual and frightened officers of the court. Then Mrs. Nation cried, "Somebody in this room is smoking!" and dismissed the case on grounds of nicotine poisoning. It was here that Judge McCabe went off for a rest, and District Judge Z. T. Hazen, a strong man of limited patience, cheerfully took over the reins.

Under Hazen's tenure, Mrs. Nation insisted on personally cross-examining all prosecution witnesses. Her intent was offensive. Newspapers reported her interrogation of William Moeser as follows:

C.: How many hatchets were used in breaking in?
M.: (Witness had no chance to reply).
C.: Who were the hatchets used by?
M.: (Ditto).
C.: What do you keep in your place?
M.: (Witness interrupted).
C.: Isn't it true that you keep all sorts of hell-broth?
M.: (Witness incoherent while waving his arms and trying to rise in his seat).

Judge Hazen released Mrs. Nation's three fellow Defenders in five hundred dollars bail each, but fixed their leader's price at a figure considerably higher. "You may be released on a peace bond of two thousand dollars," he told her.

"You mean I have to promise to keep the peace?"

"Yes, or you will be brought back to jail."

"I won't make any such promise."

"Then I remand you to the county jail forthwith."

"All right, Your Dishonor," Mrs. Nation called over her shoulder. "God will take care of me."

"From now on, this court will attend to it," observed Hazen.

Chapter Seventeen

At the county jail, Mrs. Nation insisted on crossing the threshold on her knees as the Home Defenders strung out behind intoning a dirge, like a double-column of nuns entering St. Peter's. She was given a large room, with a bed, two tables and several chairs, and she quickly made arrangements to begin publication of a semi-weekly organ of anti-liquor prejudice called *The Smasher's Mail.* The plan provoked from the Kansas City *Star* a shining small gem of an interview with Nick Chiles, the colored liberator and entrepreneur: "Topeka:—Mrs. Nation has announced that her new paper, *The Smasher's Mail,* will appear next week. 'Nick' Chiles, the Negro joint keeper and newspaper owner, who will manage the *Mail,* is holding frequent conversations with Mrs. Nation, and he says the paper will be a hummer. It will contain sixteen pages and will be in pamphlet form. The newspaper will be filled with temperance editorials and letters which the editor-in-chief receives. Each of the partners in the newspaper venture is a little suspicious of the other, as the following controversy between them shows:

" 'I believe, Nick,' said Mrs. Nation, 'that I have converted you. I believe you are going to forsake your evil ways.'

" 'I never had any evil ways,' said Nick. 'I have always been a good citizen.'

" 'Didn't you run a saloon?' queried Mrs. Nation.

" 'No,' said the business manager. 'I never did anything in To-peka but run a hotel and a newspaper.'

" 'Didn't you ever sell any whiskey?'

" 'I never sold a drop of whiskey in my life.'

" 'But,' persisted the senior partner, 'folks say you did, Nick.'

" 'Yes,' said the junior, 'and folks say you're crazy, too. But I don't believe every little bit of gossip I hear.' "

Financing of the new journal had been delicate, as Mrs. Nation admitted editorially. "All the money I had in the world," she wrote, "was from the sale of ten cows, which was two hundred and forty dollars." The money was turned over to Chiles, who had "talked very fair and promised to print my paper in a creditable way."

Volume One, Number One, of *The Smasher's Mail* made its de-but at the newsstands on March 9, 1901, its slogan at the mast-head: "A Newspaper for the suppression of the Rum Traffic." Over most of the front page was a gigantic picture of the crusader, clad in customary black, holding aloft a hatchet and looking tri-umphant. Below was the caption, "A Home Defender Who De-fends . . . Leader of the Greater Smashing Reform Crusade." In a spirit of equity, the *Smasher* also included a large picture of Chiles, on an inside page, that showed an impressive, good-looking man wearing a sporty suit of hound's-tooth check, a striped tie and a wing collar. The view in sum was striking but the clothes were perhaps more suited to a race-track than a journal of temperance reform. In a biography of unstinting praise, reeled off by the cru-sader at the top of her jailhouse form, Chiles was depicted as the offspring of decent, God-fearing slaves dwelling in South Carolina —a man who had fought his way up from humble origins through enterprise, integrity and a militant love of Christianity. Chiles was a popular fellow, with both black and white habitués of the saloon district, and this last came as a surprise to his cronies, who had no previous knowledge of his devotions. He was the owner, said Mrs. Nation, of "three large buildings on East Seventh Street," as well as several hotels, and publisher of the Topeka *Plaindealer,* a newspaper dedicated "to the interests of the colored people." Chiles was believed made uncomfortable by this naked parading of his interests, but he exploited the situation by running a hotel ad beside his photograph and life story. "Mrs. Chiles," it went, "is always pleased to see her friends at the Chiles Hotel, 116 East Seventh Street. Cuisine is perfect and guests receive every attention."

The paper's original price was ten cents, but after Mrs. Nation had weighed the critical appraisals, pro and con, she dropped the fee to a nickel. The first issue (which caught on immediately) was sprightly with the ignorantest kind of dispatches, all lumped together in the department, "Hell Letters," a designation later modified to "Letters from Hell."

As a cross-section of America's pro-liquor sentiment, the offerings were extraordinary, and may have provided an argument for Prohibition. An "M. Y. Bungstarter," of Dallas, Texas, wrote "To that Blockhead Carry Nation whose up in jail at Topeka: If you are so game, why don't you come to my saloon in Dallas you know better, ha ha. I will break a Colt's .45 over your head and let my dogs gnash your skull bones."

A remarkably kindred appeal arrived from "A Saloon-Keeper" in New York, who said, "If you will come to New York and lay a hatchet over the heads here as stated in the daily papers, I'll lay for you and put a bullet in your head." The advantages of eastern culture were evident in the writer's subscription, which was made after a punctilious "I am, Madam, Yours very truly," etc.

Ohio got on the record with a generally incoherent contribution signed by one "Deaf Gen," believed to have been an obscure nickname. It went: "Dear Carrie; I suppose you will come to Columbus and take a turn with my brother Roland. You are a lobster and that is no fable. I hope to see you soon dear and if you come I shall show you a good time."

The farthest corners of the nation were heard from. A man in San Luis Obispo, California, wrote, "Dear Madam: I once lived in Kansas but made my escape. I once knew Tiger Bill and Holy St. John, and the latest Jesus—'Sheldon' [?] and some lesser lights, you among the number. You have strength in your tongue and venom in your nails. I expect you'll be dead soon.—I. P. Standing."

The succeeding issues ran many notes in like vein, along with hard-hitting editorials and a scattering of lively advertisements that reflected the business life in that long-ago era. Also, Mrs. Nation, a tireless and imaginative editor, thought up additional features, all of them intemperate and the great majority libelous. Each brought fresh howls of anguish from Chiles.

Essentially the organ was strung together on threats—insights into the creativeness lying dormant in the lowliest bosom. "Dear Mrs. Nation," wrote a man in Chicago, scene of her joyous bout over the naked nymph, "If you know when you are feeling well you had better go back to Kansas and pick goose feathers out of turkeys awhile, because Chicago people will not stand for any of your monkey-doodling. Your loving friend—Nit." Illinois was the prime source of an early avant guardism that crept into the letters. A Taylorville man who signed himself Heinrich Katzenjammer—a name thought to be spurious—sweated out an elaborate and interminable piece of counsel couched in fake German. During the course of it he said, "If you aggsept my brobosal [that Mrs. Nation sign on as chief bartender of his establishment] I vill make you a present of dwo or dree pottles of de brandty vich I keep for my star customers. Now keep dis to yourself." Katzenjammer went ahead to explain about his bouncer, apparently a fellow German-American—Frits Sauerkraut, who would be glad (gladt) to "help you zell zooveneers on de side." It was a princely offer, but the crusader, in an editorial note, dismissed it as the work of a lunatic.

Present-day students of the *Smasher* are astounded at the painstaking research which supported some of the letters. A Massachusetts jointist displayed a minute knowledge of the Bible in a document that enlisted God on the side of the saloonkeepers. The offering was a *chef d'oeuvre,* brilliantly documented, and wandered on for several long paragraphs. Addressed to Providence and written in thee-and-thou style, it led off by saying, "Oh, Lord, we ask thee to take cognizance of the fact that a misguided wretch that calls herself a woman is seeking to raise a mob to commit crime against thy Holy Name by destroying our property and spilling our wines and liquors in the gutter. Oh, Father, we know this is against thy Divine Will!" Then the writer somewhat bumptiously reminded God that he had praised Lot after Lot had been "beastly drunk" and had "rebuked Ham for laughing at Noah when the latter was loaded with booze." God was also urged to remember "the drunkenness and debauchery of thy especial favorite, David, whom thou called a man after God's own heart." Jesus did not get off scot-free. According to the jointist, the Saviour's "first miracle was to manufacture three barrels of wine for a well-drunken wedding feast." After reciting other examples that made the Bible sound like a near-eastern liquor brochure, the author concluded with, "We ask thee to smite them [Carry and her sisters] in their unholy work and teach them to read carefully of thy servants Noah and David, Lot and Solomon, and thy good son Jesus, then go soak their heads in Budweiser until they become intelligent and law-abiding citizens."

It must have caused a strain, but Mrs. Nation printed the appeal without comment.

Against the prolixity of the above, capsule notes such as the simple "You are getting too windy, old woman," from Newport, Kentucky, attracted the readers' gratitude. Mrs. Nation's native state provided lots of advice, much of it invitations to come drink the new "Carry Nation Cocktail," one bartender assuring her that "you would hollow for more."

From the start of their partnership, Mrs. Nation and Chiles fought like wolverines. It was Chiles' not unreasonable belief that his possessions were apt to be stripped away through litigation. He and the crusader went to the mat on virtually every item in the paper. Usually Chiles had the last word, for he enjoyed the advantage of being able to hang around the shop, supervising the make-up, while Mrs. Nation's movements were limited to her cell. Among Chiles' devices—accompanied by injured innocence—was to pie, or scramble, the type of especially hot passages. Nobody except the typesetter ever found out, for example, the full burden of a letter that went, verbatim, "Why don't you mount your broomstick, you cackling old . . . Ch ta hw dafof eranugrswapble —J. L. Ward."

One of Chiles' strongest objections was to the department, called "Snapshots from Here and Everywhere," that featured uncredited news stories such as "The music at a New England funeral was furnished by a band of singers who had been refreshed for the occasion by six quarts of West India rum, one pint of brandy and a

gallon of cider, mixed; also cigars for everybody except the corpse.
The person responsible was named Lyman E. Belcher."

The publisher bewailed the editor's vivid assaults on railroads,
which had refused to transport the *Smasher* after Mrs. Nation
promised to end, by hatchetation, the practice of dispensing liquor
in the diners. Railroad cars of the period were wooden, and there
was little doubt by anybody, including the company presidents,
that she would make good when released. Her abuse of the carriers
became so all-embracing that she finally whaled away at the stations, writing, "I wish the Kansas City Union Depot was a decent
place for a woman to sit in; but I am obliged now to sit there and
like it." The attacks at last grew sufficiently sulphurous for both
the Santa Fé and the Missouri Pacific to begin running ads in her
paper; the roads also consented to transport it as baggage. Mrs.
Nation's gratitude took the form of printing, in its entirety, a popular temperance tract of the moment called the Black Valley Railroad, which set forth a schedule of way stops en route to hell. A
few excerpts will serve to capture its flavor:

> "Arrive Cigaretteville—7:30 A.M.
> Leave Cigaretteville—7:35
>   "   Mild Drink Station—7:45
>   "   Moderation Falls—8:00
>   "   Tipplersville—9:00
>   "   Topersville—10:00
>   "   Drunkard's Cure—11:00
>   "   Rowdyswood—11:30
> Arrive Quarrelsburg—Noon
> (Delay one hour to abuse wife and
>   children)
> Arrive Lusty Gulch—1:15
>   "   Bummer's Roost—1:30
>   "   Beggar's Town—2:00
>   "   Criminal's Rendezvous—3:00
>   "   Deliriumville—4:00
>   "   Rattlesnake Swamp—6:00
>   "   Devil's Gap (brakes all off)—10:00
>   "   Perdition—Midnight
> (Tickets for sale by all barkeeps)"

Many thought it a pity that, in the *Smasher's* department called "Letters from Honest People," nearly all the samples were piteous and tortured laments. "I am a broken-hearted woman and come to you for advice," wrote a "Mrs. N.," of Memphis. "My husband is a sot, my 13-year-old son loafs and works in these dives, and my daughter is engaged in what she tells us is social work—something called 'patrolling.' Frankly I never heard of it, and neither has my husband when he's sober, and nobody in the churches has, either. If you could help . . ." etc.

"A sister of mine married a drunkard," said another, "who went through a fortune of $150,000. This added to my bitterness. . . ." The correspondent wanted to know if Mrs. Nation could help her recover the money, whereupon they could both turn their attention to saloon-smashing with comparatively free minds. All in all, the Honest People's outpourings were so tiresome that readers generally flipped over to Letters from Hell, wherein they might be entertained to learn, for example, that "The Toddy Tossers of Sacramento are thinking of organizing a union to protect their interests. We most respectfully ask your opinion as to how to form the by-laws."

If the Honest People had literary strength, it probably lay in poesy. Some intricate and eye-catching verses arrived at the County Jail, and the occupant of Cell 43, perhaps repairing a laggard rhyme or bolstering a limp pentameter, shot them on to Chiles, who received them with well-bred confusion. What has been described as the best outstanding example of over-attention to the suffix "ation" (or, phonetically, "ashun") turned up in the form of an inexhaustible ode. It was entitled, starkly, "Mrs. Nation."

> "When Mrs. Carrie Nation
> Desires some recreation
> Or lively occupation,
> With due deliberation,
> And grim determination
> Against intoxication

"She scorns expostulation,
Ignores all explanation,
Puts ax in operation
At every liquor station
That comes in observation,
And there's no hesitation
Until the devastation
Has reached its termination.

"There's sudden agitation,
There's widespread consternation;
There's fiery indignation
O'er booze in percolation;
In fact her conversation
Is full of exultation."
(etc.)

Advertisements in *The Smasher's Mail* set the business scene of that day and place which, at least before Mrs. Nation, had been lazy and comfortable and shot through with harmless humbug and quackery. "The Electro-Medicated Ozone Treatment" was having a vogue, clearing up hypochondria in women, concentrating on "neuralgia, rheumatism, lumbago, malaria, nervous and blood troubles" as well as "all female diseases." The ads emphasized that, while the goo could be taken orally without immediate disaster, it was actually designed to creep in "through the pores of the skin."

The Star Grocery offered a weekend special—two pounds of coffee for a quarter, nineteen pounds of sugar for a dollar, twelve bars of laundry soap for twenty cents, twelve boxes of "parlor matches" for a nickel, twelve pounds of rolled oats for a quarter and a large can of salmon for a nickel. Foodstuffs on ordinary days were not out of sight in the markets: porterhouse steak sold for fifteen cents a pound; dressed spring chickens were 7½ cents; eggs sixteen cents a dozen; country butter fifteen cents a pound; apples twenty-five cents a bushel; turnips thirty-five cents a bushel; potatoes ninety cents a bushel, and cabbage $1.25 a hundred-weight. The Topeka Pantitorium and Howard Tailoring Company combined forces to cry, in bold type, "We don't care how many

joints Mrs. Nation smashes!" These moneymakers, though interesting, were dwarfed by a full-page ad for "The Nation's Water
Bottle—the Most Perfect Container in the World"—available in
its regular form at seventy-five cents and in the "engraved Carry
Nation edition" for a dollar. Of the many ailments treated in the
Smasher, gout led the list, and there was no lack of reference to
whiskey and wine as the original villains. A few ads touted products in distant places. The P. D. Nelson Company, in Wisconsin,
repeatedly ran an excited plug for "Patented Wood Sole Shoes,"
which were described as waterproof and "lasting twice as long."
(They were not, of course, fire-proof, but the time was antecedent
to the discovery of the hotfoot.) They cost $1.25—any size up to
fifteen. At least one Topeka establishment then represented in the
Smasher—Moore's Book and Stationery Store—has survived Mrs.
Nation and the succeeding decades of strife and peace, triumph
and disaster, lean times and plenty, and is prosperously functioning to the moment.

Editorially *The Smasher's Mail* was unique. Its message was not
so much critical as presented in a spirit of step-outside-and-fight.
Foremost target of Mrs. Nation's abuse was President McKinley,
who emerged as "the Brewer's president," "a profiteer from
booze," "a protector of the liquor traffic," "a crony or rum sellers"
and "a whey-faced tool of Republican thieves, rummies and
devils." *The Smasher* even accused McKinley of renting his wife's
Canton, Ohio, property to a jointist, an allegation neither proved
nor denied. Overall, the editorials were disconnected, blown by
whimsical winds. The writer was apt to drop in whatever came to
mind at the moment, regardless of whether it seemed apposite.
Midway through a diatribe against the railroads she was apt to
insert the observation, "It is horrible that a woman will consent to
kiss a walking spittoon." The reader's attention was wrenched
from this to learn, apropos of nothing, that, "We have no class of
men today as corrupt as lawyers." Many barbs were adorned by
idiomatic blossoms from the crusader's early life in Kentucky.
"Liquor is a bad thing," she wrote one morning after a night spent
largely on her knees, "but it seems that most people find it out like
hogs find hot slop—each one has to burn his own individual
snout."

Mrs. Nation was allowed visitors in her cell, and except for the sleeping hours she was surrounded by two or three dozen women choking with editorial support. Even so, the master's touch prevailed for the final form, the documents were handed out to Chiles (loitering in the hall with a look of profound suspicion) and a contribution was either argued, hurried off to the *Plaindealer,* or dropped into a refuse bin. Indefatigable, Mrs. Nation flogged the Republicans, their president, the Masons, all office-holders, vanity, attempts at personal beautification, drinking, smoking and dancing, "especially waltzing, which is nothing but a hugging school." As her editorial wrath rose, and her rhetorical skill deepened, the supreme, the final blow-up with Chiles became inevitable. The crusader made the error of pouncing viciously on Judge Hazen, author of her curtailed activity, and he responded with a calm but meaningful note to Chiles: "Dear Sir, I examined the newspaper issued by Mrs. Nation and yourself known as *The Smasher's Mail* and desire to call your attention to the fact that I am willing to pass this issue by, but if there is another edition of the paper about me I will certainly take steps to determine whether a man is compelled to submit to libel in a publication of that character. Very regretfully, Z. T. Hazen."

It could not be said that Chiles bowed out; he leaped out, and ran a public notice to prove it. The truth is that he had not been entirely comfortable about the prospect of taking on McKinley; the Negro had indicated to friends that McKinley, in his position, was bound to have leverage, whereas his (Chiles') influence was local and his patron's address lacked distinction. Generally unperturbed, Mrs. Nation made arrangements to have the *Smasher* published elsewhere and ran a strong editorial against Chiles. The division made her restless, however, and her thoughts turned to freedom, a prospect brightened by an offer from W. A. Brubaker, a prohibition lecturer, who wished her to speak in Peoria, Illinois, for a fee of $150; that is, Brubaker, personally, would cough up fifty dollars for the speech, and the Peoria *Journal* would pay her a hundred to edit the paper for one day. Needing the money, Mrs. Nation relayed word to Judge Hazen that she was ready for deliverance. To her immense indignation, he stood pat—she could fill the peace bond or continue to cool her heels. In what the crusader must have considered a seductive appeal, she informed the judge, by way of a note, that "I want you to stop your fooling and let me out of here. It is time for you to recover yourself, before the devil, your master, makes a clean sweep of you into hell. Let me out that I may go about my business of saving such poor devils as you."

The document proved ineffective, whereupon Mrs. Nation threatened to bankrupt Shawnee County by lawsuit, after assuring the Topeka papers—in approximately sixty-five letters of which they were safely able to print three or four—that "Personally I prefer to stay in jail. I need rest. I desire quiet for a little while. It is pleasant where I am, but I will not permit that the county shall confine me in jail." Supplementing these actions, she fired off an average of two threatening letters a day to Hazen while encouraging others to assault him physically if need be. He was inundated by abuse. Churchgoers in Russell County telegraphed their plan to tar and feather him unless his prize captive was immediately released. The most sobering news came from Douglas, Michigan, whence he was informed by previously responsible housewives that "We now propose, if Mrs. Nation is held longer, to raise the greatest army of women the world has ever known and wipe man out of existence. It it our intention to start with you."

During these frightening portents, Judge Hazen relaxed in his chambers, smoking a pipe to which the crusader had taken frequent exception. He seemed indifferent to tar and feathers and unmoved by the threat of male liquidation. It not being Mrs. Nation's nature to give in completely, she finally permitted several ministers to sign her bond *"with the provision that on my return I be locked up again promptly and the bond withdrawn."* If she had hoped for signs of penitence in Hazen, she was disappointed; his manner was brisk and impersonal, though somewhat screened by smoke, and he expressed the courteous hope of seeing her back in jail soon.

In Peoria the crusader faced a complexity of troubles. Brubaker turned out to be a snake in temperance clothing. He took the copy she tore off for the Peoria *Journal* and altered it so radically that its meaning was reversed. When the paper appeared, it was peppered with whiskey and tobacco ads, most of them welcoming Mrs. Nation to town and inviting her to visit the refineries for which

Peoria was famous. Saloon-owners asked her to drop in for free drinks at several well-known places. She had worked with fury on an editorial denouncing such places in detail, and her feelings were chafed. In the article she had scored many telling points, as her autobiography verified later. "For instance, there is a sign, 'Old Crow Whiskey,' " she wrote. "This is slandering the crow, for there is not a crow or vulture that will use a drop of this slop. There is not a dog or a bull that uses tobacco. There is the 'Royal Bengal Tiger Cigarettes.' This is taking advantage of these animals because they cannot defend themselves. There are the 'Robert Burns' and 'Tom Moore' cigars. There was not a cigar in England when Burns or Tom Moore lived . . . I never remember seeing the 'Grant Cigar,' by the way. His name is not used because he died with tobacco cancer."

Outraged by change and alteration, Mrs. Nation gave out a statement that "This man Brubaker was posing as a prohibitionist, but he was as loyal to the cause as Judas was to Jesus." After her speech, at the Peoria Opera House, she undertook a tour of distilleries and lectured reporters on the fact that, at the Great Western plant, the employees were restrained from drinking their own product. She asked her escorts, "What would you think of a dry-goods concern that wouldn't allow its employees to use what they make?" In the course of the crusader's ramble, a man named Weise, who ran a beer garden and dance hall, begged her to make a few remarks at his place, and she acquiesced; Brubaker then screamed and declined to deliver her purse for the Opera House speech. He also tried, unsuccessfully, to steal her fee from the *Journal.* Weise gallantly gave her fifty dollars to take up the slack, and she afterward said that she "addressed hundreds of poor, drugged and depraved men and women." "Mr. Weise treated me very politely," she added, but she forced him to throw a painter's drop-cloth over a nude statue of Aphrodite. He promised not to exhibit it further, acknowledging a catalytic effect it had on clients of both sexes, causing them to gulp beer disproportionate to their needs.

Back in Topeka, Mrs. Nation resumed her place in jail, according to her declaration to Hazen, and complained of inferior accommodations. The judge's disinterested remark that, like other prisoners, she'd "have to take pot-luck" stung her to the point of denouncing him afresh in the *Smasher*. During her absence she had delegated the management to her fast-tiring spouse, David Nation, and she admitted openly that she'd never committed a more serious blunder. As a temperance editor, Nation made Chiles look like a crusading publisher bent on financial suicide. Fearful of libel, he gelded every contribution handed him. Among other items, he ran a strong five-stanza poem in favor of hollyhocks; then he undertook the serialization of an obscure novel entitled *Oliver Chapman, the Story of the Hour,* since described as one of the few totally incoherent pieces of fiction published in the name of reform. The attorney took no chances.

After Chiles, the *Smasher* had continued publication briefly via *The Kansas Farmer* and then Mrs. Nation bought a second-hand press, but her lecture engagements became so demanding that she gave up after the thirteenth issue. In an extraordinary epitaph, she said that "The paper accomplished this much, that the public could see by my editorials that I was not insane."

Chapter Eighteen

After ten days of confinement, Mrs. Nation wearied of her martyr-dom and permitted her brother, Jud Moore, of Kansas City, to renew her peace bond. She stormed out of the Shawnee County Jail, snatched cigars from the mouths of three men smoking in the hall, denounced them for being Masons (though none was a member of the lodge and one had never heard of it) and marched off to a coming-out party arranged by the Home Defenders. In a sub-dued speech the crusader urged a prompt resumption of smashing but explained that Judge Hazen had insisted she lay aside her hatchet during the life of the bond. All agreed that the conditions were hard, and turned their attention to an exciting new topic of reform. The Reverend F. W. Emerson, himself lately released from jail for his battering-ram coup at Curtis's, had decided to run as an independent candidate for mayor. With his record of smashing, incarceration, incitement to riot and general contribution to anar-chy, he was believed to have a strong chance against two men of negligible accomplishments in felony. Emerson was not a natural politician, for he was a truthful, high-principled man with no twisted dreams of power, but he had a police record that many believed would go a long way toward offsetting his defects.

On this delicate political subject, the Topeka *Journal* soon

quoted the crusader at length in a piece that began, ominously,
"The Home Defenders and Mrs. Nation have quarreled." The
spat, at the office of Dr. Harding, began when a Mrs. Roudebush—
an acknowledged comer in the organization—challenged the wisdom of weakening the Democratic cause by throwing support to a
dark horse. In fact, she went so far as to classify Emerson, in the
Kansas racing jargon, as "a twenty-to-one selling plater." The real
trouble was, Mrs. Nation considered Mrs. Roudebush to have outgrown her breeches. Often of late the latter had appeared to forget
who was boss. When Mrs. Roudebush made the error of asking,
"Why don't you endorse one of the men nominated by the two
parties?" Mrs. Nation bounced back as follows (from the *Journal*): "My goodness! I reckon you are joking. You don't think we
would endorse that man Hughes, do you? I examined him and I
know what he is. He smokes cigarettes and drinks! We couldn't do
that. And the other man? Oh, my! Just look at that platform! A
man who will run on such a platform cannot receive the support of
any Christian. One is no better than the other and we must put up
a man of our own—the Lord will help us elect him. [This was
wishful thinking on Mrs. Nation's part; the Lord withheld endorsement, and Emerson was badly defeated.] I want to elect Mr. Emerson because he is one of us and is a good man."

As the argument developed, the *Journal* observed of Mrs. Nation that "she quoted from the Bible so rapidly that it was impossible to keep up with her. She quotes from the Bible instead of
swearing, as a man would do under like circumstances." The argument simmered down, Reverend Emerson entered the mayoral
lists, campaigning on his wound-stripe gained with the Washburn
battering ram, and Mrs. Nation tried without success to stir up a
fresh round of violence. For the first time since her arrival, Topeka
reformers fell prey to apathy. A few admitted to a temporary consideration of outside interests. A Mrs. Feigenbaum returned to her
interrupted hobby of hooking rugs; Mrs. Greene painted a long-
neglected kitchen; a pair of women—smashers both—began agitations to erect a hostel for indigent cats; one or two were even
reduced to looking after their husbands, who'd been dining on
crackers and cheese. Faced by these and other defections, Mrs.
Nation began an aimless program of travel in a mood ripe with

contempt. In leaving, she said, in effect, that she hoped to return when Topeka had recovered its guts.

After the passage of time, historians find it odd that the crusader could have been so ungrateful. Most emphatically, and with splendid help, she had lifted the curtain on the national temperance dispute. In the wake of her wrath, not only Kansas but the whole country rode a rising wave of hysteria. Mrs. Nation was neither a modest nor an immodest woman, and it is difficult to imagine that she could have failed to take note of the portents. Hysteria seems too weak a term in which to describe the violence now erupting in the unlikeliest parts of the land. In Oyster Bay, New York, a peaceable town suckled by shellfish and beer, a Negro named Benjamin Levy ran amok and obliterated a bar, advising police that Carry Nation had inspired his assault. In New York City, a waiter at the Waldorf-Astoria, shrieking Mrs. Nation's name, took a 1901 coffee-break to destroy the mirrors in O'Brien's Third Avenue Bar. When reporters inquired why he had neglected the Waldorf, he explained that "it would have been a pity, a nice place like that," thus recording a typical piece of dish-hustler snobbery. Simultaneously, McMahon's Bar on East 138th Street was kicked to pieces by a man who described himself as Carry Nation's brother. On Hudson Street a woman walked in with a poker, shouted that she was a "second Carry Nation," and beat a joint to flinders, leaving the bartender, with several clients, paralyzed beneath a table.

The rebellion took odd turns. At Harvard University students started a "Carry Nation Campaign" aimed to remove a fibrous and indeterminate edible, believed to be mutton, that was locally known (and detested) as "Old Bull." A gaunt youth named Shorey, stomach in full revolt, was named to lead the movement, and a thousand anti-Bull circulars were distributed on the campus. In Charlotte, North Carolina, a group of under-aged hoodlums of the kind now dosed with group therapy to correct murder, arson and rape entered Dick Bailey's Barber Shop armed with knives and revolvers and chanted that Carry Nation had released their inhibitions. Bailey completed the trimming of a customer's sideburns, wiped off his razor, removed his gun from a drawer and shot two of the youths dead. A sinister trend was seen developing in Secaucus, New Jersey, where a Mrs. Henry Wortansky marched to her husband's favorite saloon, smashed the barroom and dragged him home by the ear. One of the rowdiest events occurred in staid old Boston, where a Mrs. Mary Green, uplifted by the news from Kansas, charged into a saloon with a shout that "I'm Carry Nation and I'll leave no rum shops in this town!" Implementing her claim she hit a bartender in the face with a plateful of free lunch. Then she threw a billiard ball through the mirror and chased a customer into the basement; he was eventually rescued by police, his nerves shattered.

In Longview, Illinois, a newly-formed unit of "raiders," carrying pitchforks and scythes, swooped through a joint and left nothing recognizable as fixtures; in Dalton, Arkansas, five members of the W.C.T.U. cleaned out a pair of "blind tigers"; and in Milwaukee a contingent of wrathful (and curious) women tore through a red-light district, flushing several practitioners half-clad into the streets. Occasionally a saloon-man resisted. In Jacksonville, Indiana, Mrs. James Snyder and "one hundred members of the Carry Nation Club" fell tooth and claw (and hatchet) on the brand-new establishment of Dan Grimes, who seized Mrs. Snyder and tried hard to choke her to death. As she lost consciousness, he changed his mind and flung her into the street; her confederate, Mrs. Stephen Garrett, then had "the wind removed" by a thrown beer bottle that struck her in the region of the navel. Perhaps the most singular of these events took place in Louisville, where a Mrs. Effie Chase sprinted down a street yelling that God had instructed her to abolish the liquor traffic. In passing, she landed a haymaker on the jaw of Patrolman Joe Boutelier, but when he recovered to grasp her in a hug, she cried out—in what the papers described as "ecstasy"—"That's *nice!* Do it again!"

Meanwhile, the storm clouds of full insurrection began sweeping over Kansas; Governor Stanley's condition was described as "near-prostrate." He had taken a turn for the worse when his son, Harry Stanley, popped up at a meeting to eulogize Carry Nation and describe his father as "a witless aide of the rum-sellers." The adolescent's unfilial blast appeared in *The Orange,* student newspaper of Baker University, an institution of worship, corn-culture and sobriety situated in Baldwin City. In the spirit of most fathers today—in the age of pray-and-submit—the Governor neither cut off the boy's tuition nor put him witlessly to work, thus encouraging the tasteless criticisms to continue. When the French W.C.T.U.* (a minority group) dashed off a message of high approbation, hopefully aimed toward the migratory Mrs. Nation, the state-wide tornado struck. The gesture was only one of a series prompted by the crusader, but it went far toward fanning the winds of violence. The feeling was that if the French, red-faced and shrill with wine from noon to night, were turning anti-grape, then the time had certainly come to tear all hard-liquor joints apart. Most sections of Kansas proceeded to do so. Mobs ran the barrooms of Waubaunsee County out of business; and two in Clearwater, the county seat, were draped in mourning black. At Peck, south of Wichita, hundreds of both sexes marched behind a drum-and-fife corps then smashed two saloons that had previously been the sedate hub of village life, enjoyed by all. The day-long incident was not without its setbacks. About fifty of the raiders, exposed to unlimited hooch, got immediately drunk and fought among themselves for hours; also, the principal owner, George Hatter, made the bizarre complaint that the expedition's leader owed him a bar bill of twenty-two dollars.

Great emotion was expressed in Topeka, resting from past exertions, when telegraph keys started tapping out news from Winfield, the jewel of Cowley County. Significant events were going forward. The area had been regarded as a tinder-box because of its high number of churches and the presence there of Southern Kansas Methodist College, whose theological students bore a marked resemblance to the dogged contingent from Washburn. The fuse was lit when a New Testament major, Ernest Hahn, spied a barrel of whiskey standing on a platform of the Santa Fé depot. His reaction was a credit to divinity teachings everywhere: he grabbed an ax and knocked the barrel to pieces; then he rushed into the adjacent saloon and ordered it closed. The owner, Charles Schmidt, responded by creasing Hahn's skull with a billiard cue. The sight, at college, of the youth's irregular cranium set off a riot. In the

---

* Researchers have not to date fixed the precise name of the early Gallic organization but one source, possibly frivolous, has given it as "Les Dames Irritées de France qui se battent contre les Liqueurs spiritueuses qui excitent."

evening Schmidt's place was assaulted by shock waves of theology students, who broke windows with slingshots, for which a precedent had been established by David, and a meeting of women hastily convened at the First Baptist Church. In prayer they mentioned both God and Carry Nation, though not in that order, and set out carrying wicked-looking arms and led by the Reverend Francis ("Fighting Frank") Lowther. Schmidt's was dug-in, as the sight of two shotgun muzzles at portholes gave evidence, but the aroused temperance-ites pressed forward anyway. The opening blast felled the spinster Emma Denny, with minor birdshot wounds of the shins, and a second woman, similarly stung, joined her on the ground soon afterward; a third was felled by a beer bottle. The gage of battle thus far had been with the saloonists; this changed when Reverend Lowther landed a shrewd blow on Schmidt with his ax. The injury proved superficial, to Lowther's regret (and he apologized for it) but the jointists took to their heels, whereon the place was totally wrecked.

In Topeka crowds watched the bulletins in newspaper windows, and unrest began to rekindle. A partisan shout arose when the incoming news told of Winfield boozers regrouping, and there was jubilation when the town's United Brethren Church (which once had contributed a purse of $7.38 to Carry Nation) fell siege to hoodlums later that night. Its stained glass windows were destroyed, the organ smashed, and the pulpit (counterpart of the saloon bar) badly hacked; an anonymous note was left pinned to a cross: "We will show you how to treat the saloons, and will give you as good as you send. The next saloon in town wrecked means that some of you will be killed." By now the eyes of the world were on Winfield, and the succeeding violence disappointed no one. "This amounts to a declaration of war," said Lowther to the press, not bothering to go into the matter of provocation, and invasion plans were left to a quickly assembled new unit called the Vigilance League of Winfield. In a surprise move Lowther's League bought up all the five hundred shotguns and revolvers in Winfield and nearby Arkansas City; then it was hinted from the pulpit that some pretty special offerings, with an assist from the Lord, might be necessary toward the end of the month. Pickets were thrown around the churches and the college, and a posse of students undertook a fruitless search for the peppered Miss Denny's assailant.

By stealth, under cover of night, the jointists smuggled in guns by every unobstructed route, and sent out patrols of their own. The truth is, however, that the best brains in the joints were occupied in guzzling, singing, bragging, swapping lies, making windy threats, playing back (and distorting) attack and counter-attack, often falling into wasted intramural fist-fights—in short, having an all-around high old time, with serious damage to any hope of a skilled campaign. Even so, raiding parties of the factions met here and there, tangled, exchanging thunderous, poorly aimed fusilades (the jointists were drunk and the saints were unused to arms) and three hundred women and children sought refuge in the First Baptist Church. Thugs blasphemously swooped down on the sanctuary at midnight (contrary to ancient church custom) and pulverized five valuable windows. Fires were set at temperance homes over the city, and an imaginative patrol was interrupted while throwing rat poison into private wells and cisterns. A barrage shook the night, but the poisoners escaped without leaving casualties behind. Next morning, Mayor Albright warned that martial law impended, and urged all "right-thinking citizens" not to stir abroad unarmed. At noon two cannons hauled into the town square were manned by three clergymen and a deacon who quietly went about piling up barricades and cannonballs. All business was suspended, any persons seen on the streets bristled with guns, and sounds of skirmishing arose from outlying sections. Warned by an ornate but illiterate note that he would be shot on sight, Reverend John Hendershot (of the United Brethren Church) stuck tow pistols in his belt, then ventured forth looking for trouble. It failed to materialize as announced.

While an excited world watched, Winfield's private Armageddon roared on to its conclusion. The result was never seriously in doubt. What it boiled down to was the fact that the reformers stayed madder than the saloonists, who, intoxicated throughout, were in a joyous and even prankish humor. One of the latter, for example, dismissed the episode of the rat poison as a harmless and commendable (though risky) attempt to rid the religious element of rats. The League now slapped out what it described as its ultimate (and sixth) ultimatum: "Tomorrow at one p.m. if there is a saloon fixture to be found in town we will smash the same, and if any resistance is offered on your part we will injure the first man who attempts to stop us. We do not want any bloodshed in our community, but the saloons must go. The first man who strikes one of our members will be strung up to the nearest tree. We will stand no foolishness."

The whiskey faction cannot be blamed for receiving part of the message with raucous scorn. The pious disclaimer of bloodshed sounded hollow, they claimed, in the mouth of Reverend Lowther, who had tried to cut off Charley Schmidt's head, and the five hundred shotguns and rifles hit a false note in the emerging rhapsody of peace. When news leaked out that hordes of armed farmers—one of the nastiest breeds on earth, as any juvenile watermelon thief can attest—were streaming toward town in support of dessication, the saloonists tossed up the sponge. The situation appearing hopeless, they shut down and left, for good. In interviews, they affirmed that it was the church-sponsored lynch threat that had provided the margin of defeat.

In this period of 1901, when temperance excitements demanded such attention, little else of note transpired in Kansas. A rich deposit of snakeroot believed (by Indians) to be sovereign for snakebite (and later medically valuable for relieving hypertension) was discovered in Rooks County, where diggers were netting as much as $3.50 a day. Kansas University, taking the affirmative, won a debate against the University of Nebraska on the question: "Resolved, that the United States should own, control and fortify the Nicaragua canal." (The debate continues after a passage of decades.) News arrived that Colonel Frederick Funston, of Iola, under the command of General Arthur MacArthur, had captured the Philippine insurgent leader, Emilio Aguinaldo. A few happenings were indirectly related to Mrs. Nation and her firecracker-string of eruptions: F. O. Popenoe, proprietor of the Topeka *Capital*, left for Costa Rica; Dr. Oscar Chrisman, who told the National Mothers' Congress that men are "incapable of love," lost his job at Emporia Normal; "Carry Nation in Kansas," by William Allen White, was published in the *Saturday Evening Post;* and the Reverend F. W. Emerson finished a very poor third in the Topeka mayoralty race (it went by nine votes to the pro-liquor man). The Abilene Coursing Club opened with races featuring dogs from six states. At the Topeka Auditorium, Ernest Thompson Seton, the popular nature lover, gave a stereopticon lecture entitled "Wild Animals I Have Known" that was attended by several people who thought his subject was Carry Nation. There was much admiring comment about a jingle from the New York *Times,* that went:

> "There was an old woman, and what do you think?
> She lived on nothing but hatchets and ink,
> Hatchets and ink so long were her diet,
> That now the old woman can never be quiet."

The battle for Winfield obscured briefly the lawless rampages underway elsewhere in Kansas. "At Goffs, on Friday night," said the Kansas City *Star,* waxing slightly acid, "a band of women wearing masks like so many highwaymen broke into the Missouri Pacific depot and destroyed a lot of small packages of liquor addressed to private citizens of that town. There is nothing in the Kansas law to prohibit private citizens from shipping in and holding for consumption liquors of any sort . . . And an even more striking example of mob lawlessness is reported from Effingham, seat of the Atchison County high school. It is said that Effingham never had a joint, and that it had always been a 'dry' town. At one o'clock in the morning a mob, composed chiefly of students in the high school, and said to have been led by two teachers of that institution, went to the depot and smashed a case of empty beer bottles which were being shipped to Kansas City by a private citizen. Finding nothing more at the depot that might be associated with liquor, the mob went to a barber shop and smashed another case of 'empties' which were found in a shed at the rear. 'Longing to break something from which foam would run,' says a local paper, 'they then decided to break into the barber shop and smash the shampoo bottles. . . .'"

Students, dissatisfied women (history has seldom turned up any other kind) and ministers took the lead in most outbreaks. With their conceivably superior knowledge, and freedom from moral restraints, they steadily outmaneuvered the jointists, many of whom lived by the hard, upright code of white-collar felons. At Holton, where Carry Nation once badgered David Nation from a front pew of the First Christian Church, the matriculates of Campbell University collected some beldames and marched on the town's three saloons. They relished a satisfying spectacle when Edward Hicks, an owner, publicly begged for mercy from a kneeling position in the gutter. The new Christianity outweighing the crowd's possible sensibilities, he was badly trampled as the reformers swept on into his pub. At Garden Plain, Scott City, Chanute, Salina, Junction City and many similar centers, saloons were closed and their fixtures either destroyed or shipped away, often after combat that took strange turns. In Beloit the usual overwrought females insisted on inspecting joints even after the mayor had banned all sales of liquor. Surprising everyone, the mayor lost his patience. When the women tumbled into the third place on their list, the city sounded its fire alarm, by means of a siren's ululating wail, and a hose cart careened ding-dinging down the street. To the (for once) speechless wrath of the trespassers, its hose was unfurled and they were drenched with icy water. Dampened but not yet defeated, the ladies struck back by pulling revolvers on the hose company, setting off a free-for-all that resulted in five arrests.

At Florence a saloonist named Jack Webster, otherwise unsung, closed his place, went to Missouri and commenced construction of a barroom on wheels, made of boiler iron, with an iron door and a slot to shove drinks through. His plan was to hitch four armoured mules to this movable feast and tour Kansas in peace, barring a confrontation by heavy artillery. The first killing of the saloon wars took place at Millwood, near Leavenworth, when John Lochue's joint was set upon by twenty masked men reliably said to have been drunk. (Their church affiliation, if any, was never announced.) When the attackers began firing, in a pattern that pretty well boxed the compass, they sprinkled two of their own number; then they accidentally mowed down Mrs. Rose Hudson, the proprietor's daughter, as her father struggled to seize a shotgun.

It would be unrealistic to say that the disaster noticeably dented the reformers' resolve to pump Kansas dry. During the frequently bewildering turmoil, a portent noted by Carry Nation was the emergence, for the first time, of rivals. From Danville a rangy, grim-faced "biddy" named Mary Sheriff stalked out to challenge

Mrs. Nation's first-place ranking and to belittle her best work. Mrs. Sheriff's attitude seems bumptious when one considers that she'd only recently been named "chief lieutenant" of the crusader's important National Hatchet Brigade. The honorific merely tended to infuriate her, and she told the press, "I am the original smasher. I am sent from God to do this work, and not from Mrs. Nation. I will do more smashing than Mrs. Nation has done, and I will not talk so much about it. I intend to raid every saloon in southern Kansas, and that will be enough for one woman to do." The fatigued chagrin with which the jointists received this snarling advice may easily be imagined. "By God, it's just too much," the *Gazette* reported an owner as saying. "The woman sounds crazier than old Helen Damnation. I may close up and go to cattle rustling; they haven't got the machinery to torment a person so." Crushed, the man pulled down his shades, hung out a sign "Gone to Lunch" (though it was 8:45 A.M.) and stretched out on a billiard table for a rest.

High on Mrs. Sheriff's list for invasion was Medicine Lodge, Mrs. Nation's home town (where some joints had reopened), a piece of effrontery that could have touched off a full civil war. With a little difficulty (for Mrs. Nation's popularity was deeply entrenched) the lean, gabby scrapper of Irish descent recruited fifty women for her Flying Squadron of Jesus, an organization that she said would "not only smash but granulate" saloons. Today's students of military history, weighing the placement of Kansas temperance cranks, put Mrs. Nation in a class apart while acknowledging that Mrs. Sheriff had a bagful of tricks, surprises, dodges and devices. There were, however, serious chinks (that is to say, cracks) in her armor. At the town of Anthony she held a mass meeting, then, armed with an oversized pick-ax and followed by twenty-five men and women carrying hammers, hatchets and crowbars, swooped down like an eagle on the Klondike Bar, which had laid in weapons for a siege. The bartender, producing a six-shooter, fired several times into the ceiling when the Flying Squadron of Jesus breached the outer fortifications, but Mrs. Sheriff, ignoring the bullets, lit out after him and tried to bury her pick-ax in his head. Numerous witnesses verified the assault. The prudent fellow jettisoned his gun and dove out of the back door, continuing an established pattern of Kansas saloon raids. This episode was illustrative of Mrs. Sheriff's shortcomings in the field of smashing—not to mention those of the Flying Squadron as a whole —for in their insensate frenzy to destroy, the Fliers overlooked several cases of whiskey stashed under the bar. Within ten minutes after the group tramped off singing toward a church, the village of Anthony was inside the Klondike and going full tilt at the corn. A reporter wrote that the Squadron was hardly out of sight before "a score of drunken men and boys were reeling about the streets." Two early-teen-age children became so drunk that they were arrested and jailed until they could walk without support.

The name of Elk City, near the Arkansas line, has rung down the corridors of time, at once praised and reviled, for its gift to the world of Mrs. Myra McHenry, whose record of arrests (forty-one) in the line of both smashing and suffrage eventually provided Mrs. Nation food for thought. Among a multitude of advantages, Mrs. McHenry could boast a sanity better established than that of her counterparts. At each of the four trials to determine her sanity, she was given (after deliberation) a clean bill of health. And in another department she could claim a clearcut edge: throughout the history of American and foreign prisons nobody in Kansas had ever heard of a wilder inmate. She sang, shredded furnishings, shouted, prayed, assaulted the jailers, tried to chew through iron gratings and reduced fellow captives to quaking wrecks by deliberately scrambling their sleep. Mrs. McHenry's main thrust was directed at judges and jailers. In an Arkansas City court, threatened with a twenty-five dollar fine for contempt, she cried with a pitying laugh, "Better make it fifty, my lad!"

"Fifty it is," said the judge. "And thirty days besides."

In the Arkansas City jail her conduct grew so stormy that several jailors lost their appetites and developed nervous tics and twitches. On the twentieth morning of her duress, she found her cell door ajar and the inner and outer gates unlocked. Disgusted at this show of weakness, she demanded in vituperative terms that the staff return and tighten up security. Everybody in charge had pointedly left her free to go. Her rage mounting, she found the cell-block keys hanging on a peg, dropped them in her pocket, and charged into the street, where she spied a policeman who tried to hot-foot it down an alley. Mrs. McHenry overhauled him without effort and said, "Did you know the jail is wide open? The doors are all unlocked."

He replied, "Then why don't you escape?"

"Escape!" she cried. "I'm no lawbreaker. You come with me, my lad, and lock up this jail." When he protested, she dragged him back by the hair; then she lambasted the returning jailors for their slipshod program of custody, adding a few notes on their inability to take punishment.

The question of credits in general plagued Carry Nation. She sometimes fell prey to the delusion that she'd discovered temperance and smashed it into shape single-handed. Any mention of Dr. Benjamin Rush, who might fairly be said to have fathered the idea in America, rendered her vague and digressive. Rush was a signer of the Declaration of Independence and afterward Surgeon-General of the Continental Army. He was easily the best-known medical man in the United States, and when, after studying the Army's practice of ladling out a generous daily dollop of booze to soldiers, he wrote a pamphlet called "An Inquiry into the Effect of Spirituous Liquors on the Body and Mind," Rush struck the first telling blow in America against drinking. The work must have required careful thought, for it could scarcely be denied that a soldier's body, under the anesthesia of rum, was in danger of leaping heedlessly into a bullet, ending not only the body but any activities of the mind therein contained. Rush's approach, however, was more directly medical, and the brochure aroused interest, especially in a young physician named Dr. Billy Clark, whose excellent practice, in upstate New York, centered on the treatment of loggers for delirium tremens.* Rush had spelled out what he, Clark, had been wanting to say, and he jumped up straightaway to organize what came to be known as the Union Temperance Society of Moreau and Northumberland (the place-names represented towns of his area). Formed in 1808, the group is believed to have been the first and feeblest temperance society on record. Membership consisted of forty-three farmers who devised by-laws and fixed a fine of twenty-five cents for taking a "distilled" drink and fifty cents for

---

* Evidence is lacking that Clark had any more elaborate Christian name than "Billy."

drunkenness. Clark was congratulated on the common sense of his strictures. Any man feeling hard-pressed could ante up half a dollar and go ahead and get drunk; it would cause no serious pull on him financially and the society was glad to get the money. Better yet, the constitution permitted the drinking of wine "at public dinners" and, of course, contained a proviso that nothing should "infringe on any religious ordinance." At public dinners, while drinking wine, the members often read aloud some of Dr. Rush's conclusions, specifically that "Ardent spirits cause him [a drunkard] in folly to resemble a calf; in stupidity, an ass; in roaring, a mad bull; in quarreling and fighting, a dog; in cruelty, a tiger; in fetor, a skunk; in filthiness, a hog; and in obscenity, a he-goat." These were strong words, and the members needed plenty of wine to get them down.

The vivid barnyard of metaphor should have slowed drinking to a walk, but "There is no record that the Union Temperance Society had any appreciable effect on the use of distilled or other alcoholic liquors in Saratoga County," wrote one historian. Yet it provoked thought beyond the limits of its territory, and others began to take up the cudgel. In Connecticut, Dr. Lyman Beecher's much-applauded "Six Sermons on Intemperance," delivered and then printed in 1825, were perhaps vitiated by the lurid immorality and babbling pettiness of his son, the Reverend Henry Ward Beecher, and then sidetracked when his daughter, Harriet Beecher Stowe, started the Civil War. If the sermons accomplished anything, they put total abstinence on a decent social footing; theretofore, a man, or woman, who didn't drink had the standing of an underprivileged leper.

Students of the crusade have agreed that the Reverend Justin Edwards, pastor of the South Church at Andover, Massachusetts, was "the ablest organizer and promoter of the original temperance movement in America" and "the pivot on which all moved." Influenced by Beecher, Edwards rounded up sixteen prominent Bostonians and started the American Society for the Promotion of Temperance, a title that shortly shifted to "American Temperance Union." He was a tireless money-raiser, with the hide of a buffalo, and when he'd collected the impressive sum, especially in Boston, of $7500, he took to the glory road with various assistants. He held meetings tirelessly for years, organizing more than three thousand temperance societies in northeastern states; using these, he somehow managed to close fifty distilleries and persuade "upward of 400 merchants" to quit retailing booze—at least temporarily, or until he signed on as president of Andover Seminary in 1836.

In appearance Edwards was an astringent-looking beanpole with reproachful black eyes, a nose like a wedge, hollow cheeks, a mournful, tight-stitched mouth and a distrustful expression suggestive that somebody was about to plant a bottle of gin in his suitcase. His principal contribution to temperance—and here he was first in the field—was to align God on the side of teetotalism. Before he raised his Boston hue-and-cry, the emphasis had been on physical and moral decay in man, leaving God on the sidelines to drink or abstain according to taste. Edwards had positive word, he told listeners, that the Almighty was dry. This introduction of Mortal Sin (as if the human family hadn't been staggering beneath sufficient biblical guilt already) was a new departure for prohibitionists to use in the moist years ahead. Pushing his advantage, Edwards went to Washington and took to haunting the War Department, which finally surrendered and banned the liquor allotment for troops. Enlistments dropped sharply, but so, said Edwards, did desertions, so that nobody was seriously cut up by the loss. The pastor's other major accomplishment, widely considered benign, was to eliminate employers' work contracts that provided laborers enough whiskey to get drunk on before they started a day's job.

The oddest temperance movement of the middle 1800's was launched in Baltimore by a collection of men dangerously befuddled by grog. The group, eventually called the Washingtonians for no explainable reason, swelled and expanded and made its influence felt to the point where America literally tottered on the brink of prohibition. Six veteran soaks—two blacksmiths, a tailor, a carpenter, a coachmaker and a silversmith—were seated in their customary pew at Chase's Tavern one evening and conceived the ribald amusement of sending two of their number to a temperance talk. Theretofore they had been content, as the poet says, merely to sup and bowse from horn and can. Dice were tossed for the privilege of attending, and the losers, George Steers and J. F. Hoss, arose glassy-eyed to be pointed in the general direction of the fiesta. Amazing everyone, they returned sobered and convinced that abstinence made the heart grow fonder, and certainly much healthier. On the spot, at Chase's, as the landlord screamed imprecations at all reformers (for the tavern had never had better customers) the six drew up the articles of deprivation and signed the following pledge:

> "We, whose names are annexed, desirous of forming a society for our mutual benefit and to guard against a pernicious practice which is injurious to our health, standing and families, do pledge ourselves, as gentleman, that we will not drink any spirituous or malt liquors, wine or cider."

They had a drink on it, fixed the date for a meeting and vowed each to bring a friend, if they could find one sober after six P.M.

Inexplicably the grotesque whim caught on, spreading like wildfire, and by the end of the first year a thousand men had signed the pledge and agreed to straighten up. Chief among these was John H. W. Hawkins, a hatter, who by his own account had been continuously drunk for fifteen years. The allegation was supported by his daughter, who had apparently wrung the hatter's heart with a bleated, "Papa, *please* don't send me for whiskey today!" (This sob-wringer, true or false, came to be a popular dénouement of Hawkins' remarks from the stage.) All pertinent reports concur that the recruit turned out to be a speaker of almost mystical power. The rest of his life was dedicated to the cause, as Hawkins lectured in every state and garnered thousands upon thousands of signatures, the list only marginally repetitious. His sole rival in eloquence was John Bartholomew Gough, also a retrieved sot, who swept all before him with his fire and whose periodic relapses were indulged as the safety valve of a saint doing a wonderful work. Gough disappeared during a lecture trip to New York, and his friends, in some agitation, told police that the reformer had been done in by "the interests." For a week the nation's attention was focused on his fate, and when he was found, in a whorehouse, the relief was widespread. On recovering, Gough explained that he'd been slipped a Mickey Finn in a drugstore. "Everything went black after I drank a glass of soda water to condition my throat," he said. Quite a few people believed him. Among those who didn't was the New York *Herald,* which gave him no peace from the day police carried him intoxicated out of the brothel.

At the peak of its craze, Washingtonianism "spread across the United States like a plague," as an unconvinced critic put it. Hundreds of societies were formed, and drunkards rushed in to sign up like lemming headed for the sea. A few figures indicate the hysteria's scope: in Ohio, sixty thousand signatures; in Kentucky, thirty thousand; in Pennsylvania, twenty-nine thousand; in Nevada (around Reno and Las Vegas) thirty-two; etc., etc. A supplementary detachment was formed from juveniles and named the Cold Water Army; its tots carried banners exclaiming "Down with Rum!" and showing pictures of starved children, weeping women and Hawkins. Infant drunkenness was not at that time a serious problem in America, but implacable Washingtonians held that an ounce of prevention was worth two quarts of cure. Climax of the saturnalia-in-reverse was a monster march in Boston, featuring twenty-three sections each with a brass band, the Cold Water Army, a line of twelve thousand reformed drunks, a speech by Governor Briggs and six pieces of fire equipment that were never cleared up. The Boston banks closed for the day, possibly fearing raids, for there were some well-known former hellions in the parade, and business places dismissed their employees at noon. On Boston Common the women's auxiliary societies—curiously discriminated against in marching—provided organized cheers of "The Teetotalers are coming! The Teetotalers are coming!"—remindful of the time, some years previously, when the natives yelled, "The British are coming!" It was a gala day, and the Washingtonians seemed to slide gently into decline thenceforward. After Boston there were no new heights to climb; in a few years the members either returned to the jug or drifted into the less volatile but more permanent American Temperance Union.

Perhaps the most attractive figure of the period was the Reverend Father Theobald Mathew, who in 1849 arrived in New York from Ireland, where his success had been regarded as fantastic among a people from whom the separation of a bottle was apt to set off a donnybrook with critical results. The frail, gentle, elderly (he was past sixty) priest performed wonders among Catholics and Protestants alike. After triumphant labors in New York, he went to Boston and got into a marvelous amount of trouble over slavery. Invited to speak at a meeting celebrating abolition in the British West Indies (a pretty far cry from prohibition) he declined on the ground that he hoped as well to journey through the southern United States. Bigots like William Lloyd Garrison (whose intemperate yowls about slavery eventually became a nuisance to his family, his friends, the causes he professed to espouse and even to Negroes, most of whom preferred peaceful solutions) assailed Father Mathew as "a man without honor" and worse libels that caused him pensive, ecclesiastical dismay. But he stuck to his guns and made good on the trip to the South, where his exhortations against drinking inspired the formation of numerous Father Mathew Societies in alcoholic havens like Charleston, Richmond, Atlanta, Savannah and New Orleans, the last a riotous showcase of guzzling where he persuaded twelve thousand converts to sign the pledge. While the priest calmly pursued his line, careful to offend neither side about abolition, Garrison continued to abuse him as a conscious agent of the slave-holders. In the face of this senseless accusation, President Taylor pointedly invited the priest for a stay at the White House. In a temperance movement that dredged up a champion bag of cranks, fanatics, humbugs, opportunitsts and crooks, Father Mathew might reasonably have been described as the apostle of moderation; in the year when he returned to Ireland, Maine passed the first attempt at a prohibition law in the United States.

Not so moderate were the first ladies on the scene, arriving pretty much contemporaneously with Carry Nation. The ringleaders were Susan B. Anthony, who had led a splinter group of women away from the basically anti-feminist Washingtonians; Amelia Jenks Bloomer, who became sidetracked with her puzzling preoccupation over pants; Elizabeth Cady Stanton, who in 1874, in a Cleveland church basement, helped what a critic, borrowing from the Bard, described as those "secret, black and midnight hags" organize the Woman's Christian Temperance Union; and, most important of all, Frances Willard, a dogged and unpredictable rebel, who took over the group with the irrevocable finality of government-condemned land. In her youth, Miss Willard was engaged to be married, but she dismissed the idea as frivolous and spent her life egging on the W.C.T.U., directing her drive at legislators. After establishing branches of the body in the smallest hamlets of the land, she worked twenty years at forcing the assemblies of every state to enact "scientific instruction laws," that compelled public schools to include courses laying out the horrors of drink. It was a remarkable feat, and the fact that the laws have all been repealed in no way diminishes Miss Willard's personal triumph. "Millions of Protestant women have regarded her as at least semi-divine," wrote Methodist Bishop Asbury's descendant in *The Great Illusion*, "and since her death [in 1898] have addressed prayers to her as a Catholic pleads for the intercession of a saint." Part of the legend involved the case of a woman making a temperance address in Chicago, not long after Miss Willard died. The hall was jammed, the women eager, and the speaker succumbed to stage-fright, or buck fever. Her teeth audibly chattering, she suddenly cried, "God or Frances Willard help me!" and immediately received a mysterious but unidentifiable boost from Beyond.

Miss Willard was fortunate, when her career started, in securing the aid of a man since referred to as "the most improbable phenomenon ever cast to the surface of the temperance cauldron." He was named, or so he claimed in his fiftieth year, Dr. Dioclesian Lewis, but he was thought to possess other handles during earlier, murkier phases of his rise. Even the known areas of Dr. Lewis' history were brilliantly checkered. He had edited a "homeopathic" magazine in Buffalo, until his theories, mostly revolving around sex, so stimulated the authorities that they encouraged him to seek greener fields. As founder of the Boston Normal Institute for Physical Education, an abnormal cult resembling the Druidical, he provoked the conceivably unfair eulogium that it was "an arena of promiscuity," a tribute that he failed to incorporate into his catalogue. More positively, he urged the eradication of corsets and badgered all females to raise skirts as high as possible without being arrested. As a substitute for corsets the doctor advised women to adopt suspenders, so as "to take the strain off the pelvic regions and save them for worthier purposes." When his two books, *Chastity, or our Secret Sins* and *Our Digestion,* aroused little more than threats of tar and feathers, he relaxed and invented the wooden dumbbell. He also dreamed up a game that he chose to call "Beanbag." Lewis was a patriarchal figure with prematurely white flowing hair, a ruddy complexion, a large and robust frame, the ingratiating style of a check-kiter, and a booming, medicine-man's voice, and he became a focus of interest wherever he went, or was driven. After physicians had expressed interest in his sanitarium at Lexington, Massachusetts, he opened a girls' school in Boston, from which all students came out well versed in sex education (unusual in the day) and not a few with babies. Lewis was far ahead of his time, but he was never very far ahead of the law. In retrospect, it is hard to determine whether he was a mountebank, a progressive, an authentic evangelist or an outright rascal. He had an excellent sense of timing and never tarried too long with any one venture. A converted jointist who accompanied him on a tour wrote that Lewis was "a coarse man, beside whom you would not choose to sit, yet when he speaks of his experiences you cannot restrain your tears." In the period when he heard the call to temperance, he had achieved a measure of popularity with the slogan, "A Clean Tooth Never Decays."

Dr. Lewis' contribution to Miss Willard, and to temperance, was his organization of Visitation Bands (of females) which he said could sing saloons to death. He based his view on a synthesis of his past observations, and nobody could deny that the doctor had had a great deal to do with women. He knew them from top to bottom, inside and out, and felt certain of their musical incapacity. The campaign was trilled off in Hillsboro, Ohio, where half the housewives in town gathered and sang a druggist named Smith out of his place and committed never again to sell liquor in a little less than four minutes. The best estimates were that he had cleared the door and was begging piteously for a pen halfway through the first verse of "Give to the Winds Thy Fears," which the choristers chose as their standard punishment. Standing in the snow, working on the hymns, they cracked one place after another until they turned up a tough proposition in the Lava Bed, which enjoyed a reputation as being the foulest dive in Hillsboro and probably in Ohio. The women sang there all one day and most of the next, and then Joe Lance, the proprietor, a caricature of his old happy self, staggered out and said he was "going into the fish business." It was more than mortal ears could stand. Thus encouraged, Lewis and his Singing Bands, as they were commonly known, rapidly proliferated. Groups sprang up in Indiana, Michigan, Wisconsin and nearby states, and Lewis, toward the crusade's end (around 1874) claimed to have disharmonized twenty-five thousand saloons. Singing had not, however, proved a permanent answer. The last, mutilated note had scarcely faded away before most of the joints reopened with all their pre-hymn vigor. The city of Washington Court House, rendered bone-dry and practically tone deaf in 1873, reported a record number of saloons gratefully humming in 1875. As for Dr. Lewis, his thoughts suddenly turned to phrenology, from which he made a very good thing for nearly a year, or until he was reported occupying himself with a secret Choctaw nostrum (of which he alone had the formula) that was believed specific for pneumonia, lockjaw, hernia, aging and tuberculosis.

The foregoing galaxy of stars, together with luminaries of the Anti Saloon League of America—a semi-sinister organization formed in 1895 with the aim of forcing full prohibition on everybody—provided Carry Nation the bulk of her competition for credit in the domestic temperance movement. The League had first put down its roots in the vicinity of Oberlin College, then a masochistic center of yearning that had sponsored bans on nearly everything, including pepper, coffee, tea, white flour, reproduction and tobacco. As the new, militant outfit flowered and spread like poison ivy, it attracted strong support, outside the usual church groups, from wealthy industrialists who permitted themselves to be sold the idea that drinking—any drinking at all—slowed down production by the workers. The League's guiding lights were eventually Wayne B. Wheeler, its general counsel, who was said by a friend to have "a passionate sincerity that bordered on unscrupulousness," and William E. ("Pussyfoot") Johnson, its field representative, who described his work as "publicity and underground activities" and bragged that, in doing it, he had "drunk gallons of whiskey" and "told enough lies to make Ananias ashamed of himself; the lies I've told would fill a big book."

Leadership of this calibre was bound to bring results, and the League, planning, scheming, soliciting enormous sums, building a gigantic staff of paid employees and a propaganda machine that would have wrung tears from the late Joseph Goebbels, began the long series of chess-moves that finally accomplished the most disastrous legislation in American history. The Eighteenth Amendment, and Prohibition, were attributable most directly to the Anti Saloon League; it was Wheeler himself who wrote the enforcement act for the maundering Congressman Volstead of Minnesota, thus launching an orgiastic and prolonged era of hard drinking, merry-making, immorality, racketeering, gun molls, gang wars, political corruption, bribed police and judges, poisoned booze, speakeasies, irreligion, emancipation of women to fresh vistas of impudence, contempt for outfits like the Anti Saloon League, bobbed hair, short skirts, saxophone-tooting, the Charleston and additional decadence. On the night of January 16, 1920, the country had gone to bed fairly sober; next morning it awoke, grabbed a red tin New Year's Eve horn and blew it without interruption for the next fourteen years, or until President Roosevelt picked up a pen and revoked the unholy crusade. In a single "dry" year, victims of the grand experiment consumed nine hundred and ninety-seven million gallons of illegal booze, half of it smuggled in from abroad. Bootlegging had become the largest industry in the nation, employing eight hundred thousand persons and grossing an annual revenue of about four billion dollars.

Wheeler expressed himself as stunned; things had not developed in quite the manner he foresaw. As for Pussyfoot Johnson, he was obliged seriously to step up the tempo of his lying, to keep pace with the new air of spree.

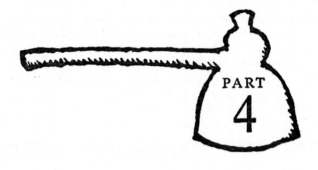

PART

4

THE AGING

Chapter Nineteen

Mrs. Nation's travels—interrupted by two confinements in jail at Wichita and Topeka—would take her over all of the United States, into Canada and abroad in the following years. Her life settled down to a generally unvarying pattern of wearisome train-rides in sooty coaches, stop-overs in dingy hotels, and lectures that frequently caused her arrest. Never once did she descend to the commonplace; her simplest acts were graced by extra dimensions of both insolence and humor. From her birth to her grave, nothing uncomplicated happened to Carry Nation.

During this long lonely period her fighting spirit never diminished, she confronted Sin without fear or favor, preserved her integrity in munificence and squalor and became without doubt the best-known woman in the world. It was a routine that might have destroyed a hardy male of iron mental balance, and which perhaps no other elderly woman could have survived. Continuous travel, unless done with the help of agents, porters, domestics and wealth, can be among the most exhausting of human pursuits; the gorilla, not often identified with weakness, covers an average of two hundred yards a day, cut up by frequent naps, in its wanderings after food. Mrs. Nation—alone, in the beginning making her own plans, toting her unraveling carpet bag together with a black satchelful of small pewter hatchets, copies of *The Smasher's Mail* and a normal-sized hand-ax for emergencies—bloomed like a desert flower in a hostile and improbable setting.

From Topeka the crusader headed for Leavenworth, wooed by a letter from an inmate of the Old Soldiers' Home:

> For God's sake come to the Old Soldiers' Home and save the Old Veterans. Bring your hatchet along and clear out the canteen in the Home. Congress recently passed a law for all saloons to be closed on United States reservations, but officials of the Home claim the law does not apply to the Old Soldiers' Home . . . Come at once and clean out the joint in the Home. We are to be paid in one week. Over seventy half-barrels of beer are sold in one day in the Home on Pension Day.

Mrs. Nation arrived in Leavenworth the morning of March 24, to be greeted by a hooting mob that had somehow been tipped off about her intentions. Paying little heed, she strode up the street to an empty lot, where she turned and delivered a brief, savage address while every policeman in the rough-and-tumble town (that lately had been selected as the site of an outstanding prison) held back the curious and the challenging. When she thanked them, they gave assurance that their role was to prevent her from smashing. The crusader then relieved a surprised deputy of a half-smoked cigar and proceeded to the Home. Her reception there was better; a number of aged and creaky veterans, a few ornate with bullet and arrow scars, appeared in formation to quaver a feeble but soldierly recital of hymns. Still singing, they escorted her into the mansion, where some younger veterans of more recent wars pounced out from behind a door and threw her into the street. This was the first time it had been brought home to Mrs. Nation that there are veterans and veterans. On her departure, many of the two contingents joined forces and spent the rest of the day drinking beer.

As for Mrs. Nation, humming with anger, she hurried downtown to the, appropriately, National Hotel and burst into its bar, crying, "Look out for me, you hellhound, rum-soaked rummies!" Here she encountered a saloon-keeper of diabolic cunning. Ferdinand Mella, who also owned the hotel, a man far above his guild in guile, dropped to his knees and asked her to join him in prayer.

She inquired, apropos of God knew what, "Are you converted?"

"Not yet, but I want to be," Mella replied.

While customers, police and a crowd outside watched, mesmerized with wonder, Mrs. Nation and the owner piously intoned *en duet* for nearly an hour, or until Mella sprang up, contending that he'd seen the light. His first action of the abrupt conversion was to buy several small hatchets, a Home Defender's button (which he affixed to his lapel), a souvenir picture and numerous copies of the *Smasher*. Then, with an air of deep penitence, he locked his saloon, ushering out its clients, and walked the crusader to the depot. A reporter wrote that "her face bore a look of moving rapture." When her train (bound for St. Louis) cleared the platform, Mella ran back to reopen his saloon. Then he arranged his trophies for display on a shelf, and engaged three extra bartenders to handle the tidal wave of new business. Witnesses of Mella's recent reformation were forced to conclude that he'd backslid.

In St. Louis, Mrs. Nation debarked and roundly abused a group of women whose hats were concocted of feathers. Reporters offered to convey her to the Tenderloin, but she tarried to snatch cigars and cigarettes from a dozen or so men in Union Station. She was quoted as yelling, "I want all you hellions to quit puffing that hell-fume into God's clean air!" The remark was regarded as piquant in a city where soft-coal smoke was the principal ingredient of God's clean air for generations, where the downtown lights often burned full on at midday, but the victims of her petty larcenies (as so often the case before), taken by surprise and dumb with western chivalry, made no protest except to step around baggage trucks and light up fresh weeds. The correspondents finally persuaded Mrs. Nation to visit the beer joint of Joseph Sauerburger, at Sixteenth and Market Streets, in an area of trumpery pawnshops, pool halls, taxi dances, saloons and flophouses. She was thunderstruck to behold Sauerburger's prominent and well-lit sign, "The Carry Nation Bar," and she plunged in to demand that, "You take that sign down before I come back to this town, my man, or I'll use a little hatchetation on you!" The proprietor meekly agreed, and the crusader left for Cincinnati, where she'd promised an agonized mother, by mail, to extinguish the red-light district. In Jake Pittner's relaxed "Concert Hall," with a firm police escort, she heard a seedy rendition of "Glide on, Silver Moon" by a burlesque queen who conducted a better business on the side and whose act, at the end, featured a kick that suggested a shortage of underdrawers. Mrs. Nation was sufficiently stirred to break into tears, though whether the result of the singer's morals or an outraged musical sense none of the papers made clear.

In this phase of her travels, when she was yet unattended by a manager, and therefore sporadically ballyhooed, the crusader's spoor is hard to pinpoint after the lapse of years. Her autobiography, some editions of which drift into incoherence supported by lengthy and irrelevant biblical advices, presents an inconsecutive picture of her movements. It is known that, after leaving the bare-bottomed chanteuse in Pittner's, Mrs. Nation crossed the green, ice-choked Ohio River to Kentucky, her choice and native state. It was either on this trip or afterward that she ran into a fellow countryman of remarkably like disposition. He may have been a kinsman. The man, a saloonist, was reading a newspaper at his bar when Mrs. Nation entered with the purpose of kicking up a row. He looked up, smiled courteously, laid down his paper, picked up a chair and smashed it over her head. The reformer was not inclined to make allowances for his dark-and-bloody background; she complained bitterly about "illegal methods." Then, after a period of convalescence, she returned to Ohio, somewhat disillusioned about Kentucky, lectured on street corners, peddling hatchets and other souvenirs, and hastened back to re-check Sauerburger. (Among Mrs. Nation's deadly attributes was a memory that never left loose ends dangling.) To her dismay, the St. Louisan had failed to remove the noxious and unauthorized sign. She was recognized the moment she stepped off the train, and a crowd collected to follow her meaningful march toward the dive. The crusader reeled when, once again, she spied "The Carry Nation Bar" blinking away in the murk. Tucking up her skirts (and collecting the principal assault tool from her bag) she rushed shrieking into the saloon and raked her hatchet along a bar loaded with bottles and glasses. But the canny Sauerburger was armed, with a pistol, and he drove her out as a streetful of ill-wishers howled with pleasure. "God will smite you, you rummies!" she cried, shaking her fist; then she scuttled to a nearby, safer joint to sing "They Who Tarry at the Wine Cup." In the end, a squad of policemen took her to Union Station, and Market Street simmered back to normal.

Mrs. Nation's outlook was not improved, on her re-entry into Topeka in mid-April, to be greeted by a limerick of dubious worth in the *Capital:*

> There came to our town an old pelican,
> Whose manner was scarcely angelican;
> To a man who sold beer
> She said, "Say, look here!
> If you want me to save you from helican."

In an emergency conference with her sisterhood, she proposed a horsewhipping of the publisher, but he was discovered (as previously mentioned) to have left for Costa Rica. Enthusiasts proposed the substitution of Judge Hazen, or Governor Stanley, and, as a last resort, President McKinley, but the ideas were vetoed by moderates in the group. Holed up in her small office-dwelling, Mrs. Nation dashed off any number of articles for *The Smasher's Mail,* borrowing items of violence from whatever newspaper she could lay hands on and adding, usually, the gratuitous: "The man had been drinking." Thus the account: "Nowater, Indian Territory: Plaas Childers, one of the best-known farmers in the Indian Territory, shot and killed his step-daughter this week and fatally wounded his wife. He had been drinking heavily." Nearly everybody pictured unfavorably by *The Smasher* had been drinking, and generally smoking heavily as well.

On April 15 the crusader went to Kansas City, Missouri, to visit her brother and was immediately arrested on a trumped-up charge of "blocking traffic and causing a crowd to collect." Next day in a hearing she presented the curious allegation that she had been "waiting for a streetcar." It may have marked the debut of a saying that was to take on an evergreen blush in the following years. A patrolman testified that he had seen eleven streetcars go by "without the woman trying to git [sic] aboard none of them." Singing out, "You're a liar!" she was fined five hundred dollars, the sum to be remitted if she cleared the city limits by six P.M. For some time most of Mrs. Nation's funds had been plowed into fines that reaped no harvest but inconvenience, so she hurried across the line into Kansas City, Kansas. The kangaroo proceedings had a beneficial result, however, for the Law and Order League of the unfriendly metropolis rose in its wrath, starting a storm of protest and resistance, and closed every saloon in town by Sunday, May 5.

Mrs. Nation left behind a city in turmoil, but she breathed a sigh of satisfaction and proceeded to Wichita, where she promptly found herself jugged on an old warrant. Now, at last, she confided to a friend that the incarcerations were "becoming tiresome"; she was "spending about as much time in jail as out." Though numerous of her cronies, including a collection-plateful of clerics, offered to stand bond, she refused and remained confined (tiring a little more each day) until April 28 when she left to attend the obsequies of a brother, J. W. Moore, who'd died in Louisburg, Kansas. The death appeared to affect her critically, her reason being in serious though temporary doubt for the first time. For several days she nipped about on her knees, praying, gnashing her teeth, and calling loudly for the Lord, and she continued the lamentations after her restoration to jail, on May 1. Late one night she knee-hopped out of her cell (accidentally left unlocked) and awoke a dozing jailer to say, "Let me out of here! I've been elected President of the United States by the Smashers' League and it's time to go to Washington for the inauguration." In a crafty political move, the jailer attempted to persuade her that the Constitution had been revised and that the inaugural was scheduled to take place in her cell. When she recognized the ruse, she yelled bloody murder and floored the man with a heavy right to the jaw. With several assistants, he succeeded in wrestling her back into place.

Once she'd calmed down, her brother in Kansas City prevailed on Mrs. Nation to accept bail, and she went to Topeka for trial before Judge Hazen. It is impossible not to admire the crusader's practical sense, for with her Wichita gyrations fresh in everyone's mind, she blandly entered a plea of insanity. Hazen, a man not easily stampeded, instructed the jury to ignore her contention; he came dangerously close to hinting that it would be insane to consider her insane, and the twelve-man panel found her guilty of the "malicious trespass" on February 17. Sentence was deferred, and she was released on bail, again to take up the sawdust trail.

On the Fourth of July Mrs. Nation made headlines with her stellar performance at Crawfordsville, Indiana, where she was the main attraction of an out-of-door gala sponsored by the Elks. Before an audience of eight thousand, prancing back and forth on a jerry-built platform, assailing rum, judges and Republicans (and there was scarcely a Democrat in the Hoosier crowd), she became so energetic that the platform collapsed, causing her to sprain an ankle and injuring numerous other persons. For a few moments she tried to continue her remarks while lying on the grass, holding aloft the twisted limb, but police forcibly removed her for treatment. The incident, wholly Mrs. Nation's fault, appeared to fire her with fresh rage against whiskey, which was innocent. Trussed up, one leg installed in a kind of splint, she rampaged out of the doctor's office, using a stick for a crutch, or cane, and recruited twenty small boys and girls into an army of rebuke. She had a tow sack partly filled with miniature hatchets, and she catechized the tots on questions and answers. Then she invaded the rialto, attended now by sightseers far down the road in celebration. The day proved to be Crawfordsville's most memorable Fourth of July.

Before each saloon (and they seemed numberless) the reformer stopped to cry, "Look, children, what is that place?"

"A hell-hole!" they replied dutifully.

"Anything else?"

"A murder shop!"

"What do they sell?"

"Hell-broth and devil-soup!"

(This utterance was regarded as unfortunate from the mouth of a child whose father owned the place at the moment serenaded and was standing in front with an unmistakable woodshed expression.)

"What do they do?"

"Murder souls!"

"What must we do to a place like this?"

"SMASH IT!"

Maneuvers here were beautiful, but, apparently, too fast for the press to follow precisely. The children wheeled to fall in two abreast, grabbed up full-sized hatchets* from Mrs. Nation's bag (amply provisioned on this tour) and prepared for an assault that was delayed briefly when the crusader discovered one boy, of around eleven, to be smoking a pipe. She snatched it away, threatened to spank him, dropped for a moment in prayer, then shouted, "Come, children!"

The carnage that followed would have done credit to criminals thrice the young avengers' age. Yelling with synthetic hate, they swarmed into a saloon, crawled like monkeys over the bar and other furnishings, smashing everything in sight including (as always) the great bar mirror, hacking to bits the bar itself and breaking all bottles and decanters. The only fly in an otherwise perfect ointment, as a reporter put it, was the fact that the juvenile army became thoroughly saturated with fumes and, unused to intoxicants, began to stagger around starry-eyed. Then, suddenly, it was borne in upon the children that they would be obliged to live on, here in Crawfordsville, with their folly, while Mrs. Nation might probably disappear unless collared by the law. To do her credit, as her brood scattered for cover, she stood outside and yelled, "Arrest *me!* Arrest *me!*" Presumably the owner was insured, for he refused to sign a complaint. No follow-up stories ever appeared to detail the children's eventual reception at home. It is presumed they were permitted to grow up to a badly chastened adulthood.

The next day in St. Louis (a city that attracted her hypnotically, perhaps as being too tough a nut to crack) the crusader was arrested and then released for trying unsuccessfully to wreck the Oheim Brothers Bar and she left, ruffled, for Terre Haute, from which a traveling salesman had written her a heart-wrenching letter of despair, temptation-wrestling, reform and indecision—a document now believed to have been bogus. Among the fellow's complaints was that, after contracting "the indulgence of drink," he had fallen so low as to become a "slave to lewd women." Though currently occupied as a part-time temperance lecturer, he felt an occasional twinge of the old, wild hungers. Mrs. Nation

---

* Over the past months, Mrs. Nation had eliminated brickbats and rocks and had replaced them with what might be described as the Mark Two, or modified, hatchet, a model in nickel-plate obtained from a special hardware store, with a grip and heft suited to her style.

tried to fly, or ride a train, to his side, but she failed when the address given proved to be a particularly gamy saloon.

Back in Topeka for the sentencing, on July 24, Mrs. Nation heard the immovable Hazen fine her a hundred dollars and sentence her to thirty days in jail. From his expression she was able to gather that, for any act of contempt, he was prepared to make it thirty years. She was led away, silent for once, but at the Shawnee County Jail she registered another protest about her quarters. The frequency of the crusader's visits to the Topeka lockup had given her a proprietary feeling, like that of a traveling salesman who expects specified accommodations at a dingy hotel on his route. Her complaint this time was based largely on the fact that she was assigned a double room, compelled to share quarters with a female bootlegger. As was characteristic in all her personal contacts, even with the underworld, the crusader soon found reason to defend her fallen sister, whose demeanor changed rapidly from dismay to bewilderment to shock to a lingering apathy and then to the apostolic. (She left the establishment with a raging bias against beer-sellers, especially females, and with the stated intention of picking up a hatchet on the way home.)

"When I was put in jail I told Mr. Cook [the sheriff] to send the milkman to my cell," Mrs. Nation wrote. "He came and was very kind. He agreed to bring me some bread and milk, ten cents worth a day. This I lived on for eighteen days. In the cell with me was a woman named Mrs. Mahanna, who was put in for selling beer.* She did not happen to have a government license. Poor creature! She had been the mother of fifteen children; had a broken hip caused by the kick of a drunken husband. She was very ignorant but kind-hearted. The heat was intense and we were next to the roof. Sometimes I would feel as if I was suffocating. The windows slanted so that but little air came in. One pane of glass was partly out and we would sit by that to get a breath of air. [There is reason to believe that Mrs. Nation punched the pane out.] While in this jail I had many offers from different theatrical, circus and museum

* Mrs. Nation in her writings was notoriously slipshod about names; she seldom checked spellings or the triviality of surname-or-Christian-name. The earliest Topeka directories do not list a family of Mahannas; the woman's correct name could have been McHanna, Mrs. Mark Hanna, Manning, or, possibly, Smith.

managers; one as high as $800 a week, with a palace car and a maid. I never for one moment thought of taking any of them until two managers came from New York City. Mr. Cook brought their cards up. I said, 'Tell them to wait until morning.' I prayed over the matter nearly all night and before day all seemed settled. (This was a test to try my faith.) The cloud was lifted and I told Mr. Cook to tell the men that 'a million a minute would not catch me.'

"My dear friends, especially Mrs. Goodwin, Dr. Eva Harding and others, used their influence to have Stanley, the governor, pardon me; this he refused to do; the joint-keepers were those he favored. I had never thought of going before the public as a lecturer. I knew those people only wanted me as they would a white elephant . . . At this time I was entirely out of money; I was in debt and the dunning letters I got while in jail were a terrible trouble to me. The ten cents I paid for my bread and milk came in almost daily for copies of my papers. I paid my milkman sometimes in stamps. I never wanted to get out of jail so badly in my life, as I did at this time, when the offers of lecture engagements were so many. Two days after the New York managers were there, I got a letter from James E. Furlong, a Lyceum Manager of Rochester, New York, who had managed Patti and many of the great singers. He told me if I would give him 'some dates,' he would assist in getting me out of jail."

When the crusader's friends again confronted Stanley, with an unsubtle hint that he was in danger of being exterminated, he consented to remit the sentence of thirty days. Simultaneously, the Shawnee County Commissioners permitted Mrs. Nation to pay off her fine at the rate of five dollars a month, like a Sears Roebuck icebox. Further to speed her into the field, Dr. Harding collected a purse of seventy dollars. Furlong was informed, and Mrs. Nation led a shouting crowd to the Santa Fé station. After several affecting speeches, which had the effect of bewildering a large group not involved in the movement, the Defenders left before Mrs. Nation went to buy her ticket. Reduced by the payment of some bills, she lacked fifty cents of having enough to see her to Clarksburg, Ohio, scene of Furlong's opening date. Hard-bitten veteran that she was,

Mrs. Nation borrowed half a dollar from the station's fruit vendor and climbed aboard both flat broke and starving. She settled weakly into a seat, dusk fell, she slept, dawn broke and she arose in an attempt to struggle to the water tap, the only source of nourishment left available. She fainted, sprawling across the plush. Then (she wrote) "a dear, sweet-faced woman turned to me and said, 'Will you have a lunch?' I answered her the best I could. The lunch seemed manna from heaven. Nice beaten biscuit sandwiches."

In the next days, as Mrs. Nation's strength improved in the trains, passengers cursed the circumstances that had given her sustenance. She took to exploring the cars, directing her attention to the smoker and ordering everyone to discard the weed. Then, returning to the day cars, she cried, "Plenty of room in the smoking coach, ladies. I've made those hellions stop blowing poison all over. Come right with me, ladies!" On this occasion (near Columbus) several women accompanied her to the smoker, where she seated them with ceremony, saying, "Make yourselves at home, ladies, and don't let anyone puff hell-fume at you. There is whiskey on this train, and I am going to find it." While the explorers, spurred on by such high caliber of leadership, placed themselves about like pickets, the crusader poked into the smallest corners of every car, including the higher-priced Pullmans (from which the conductors gave up trying to extricate her); she confiscated a good deal of both tobacco and liquor. Then she crashed into the lounge of a Pullman men's room and found three noted midwestern horsemen en route to the impending and much-heralded duel between the champion trotters, Croesus and The Abbot. The contest was an early, similar forerunner to the great flat race between Man of War and John P. Grier. The train ride being in itself boring, the fans, H. F. Allen, Michael Reardon and James Scanlon, deep in speculation, were consulting a whiskey bottle from a nearby washstand. Mrs. Nation recognized them from photographs, but she smashed their bottle with a single stroke of her hatchet before nodding; then she remarked, "You infernal sots!" "This is cold tea, Madam," said Reardon, a gentlemanly fellow like most people of the horse-world. "It's very good on a hot day like this," and he poured her a tumbler-full from another bottle.

No doubt the oddest of Mrs. Nation's traits was her lifelong naiveté. Despite the harangues, the rampages, the assaults, her extremest forms of violence, she could never actually bring herself to believe that anybody was bad, with the result that she found herself tricked over and over again. She accepted the cup, knocked back a mouthful, then screamed that she had been poisoned and tossed the remaining drops at an opened window. When they blew back onto her dress, she said in a suddenly resigned and sepulchral tone, "I am annointed with iniquity!" The crusader remained naive, but the quality that set her apart from all temperance cranks past and present was her warm, down-to-earth gift for making herself companionable with people of diverse origins. From her beginnings in the ghostly, affection-filled slave shanties of Kentucky to the sad, forlorn finish at Leavenworth, she was absolutely unaccountable, a paradox of fury wrapped in an enigma of love. After drying her dress, she returned to the lounge with no show of embarrassment, though another rider was occupied in the lavatory, and entered into the friendliest possible chat with Allen, Reardon and Scanlon, who were charmed, beguiled, made captive by the most hypnotically compelling woman of her time; and they never ceased to recount the adventure to the ends of their lives. "I don't like your whiskey," she confided, surprising nobody, "but I like good horse racing, and I wish you men luck. If I wasn't in this hatchet business, I'd go to New York for that race myself. I think Croesus will win." Thereafter for upwards of an hour, she talked horses, about which she knew a great deal (like any rural Kentuckian of her class) and convinced all three that the horse she favored (and apparently had studied in the sports sections) was a prime choice on which to lay money.*

Astute followers of Mrs. Nation's life may have deduced that her union with David Nation, the potential lawyer, editor, farmer and cleric, lacked closeness. More properly, it had degenerated to exchanges of public mutual detestation at long range. Nation gave out a scurrilous interview about his wife whenever he could corner a reporter, and the crusader frequently struck back with her usual lack of inhibition. "My life has been made miserable by this

---

* Croesus won the race, run August 15 at Brighton Beach, New York, and set a world's record for three consecutive heats.

woman, who means no good in this world," he now told the Topeka *Journal*. "She has robbed me of all my happiness, and
dragged my name, along with hers, down to the mire of notoriety.
She is a great woman for prayer, and is continually praying that I
may die, so that she can lay claim to the small pension that I draw.
I will state that my health is good, and that I have every prospect
of outliving her. . . . She smashed all those saloons against my advice and she alone is to blame for the punishment she has received.
I want nothing more to do with her. I am done with her."

The statement, uttered in safety during one of the reformer's
incarcerations, is a curiosity from several standpoints. To begin
with, Nation's pension amounted to twenty dollars a month, approximately the sum his wife took in from the sale of hatchets on
any prosperous street corner. Moreover her record shows no slight
evidence of venality at any point. On the contrary, she had a notoriously lax viewpoint toward money, and seldom spent as much as
a dollar on herself. Also, friends who should have known said that
the notion of Mrs. Nation's praying for her husband's death was
absurd—she lacked any such personal feeling for him—and one, a
minister in good standing, at liberty (though with a trifling court
date to be kept by and by), uncharitably contended that, in Nation's case, only the county coroner was in a position to say
whether he was officially alive or dead. As to the lawyer's complaint that she had "dragged down" his name, he had been permitted, by Mrs. Nation's God, seventy-odd years in which to establish
his name as lustrous and had failed, through laziness, at everything
he undertook. His pleasure was to loaf around, complaining, in his
frayed uniform from the Civil War. He once told a reporter (as
mentioned in Chapter Five) that his wife's management of Texas
hotels had made him "rich," a careless and blowhard appraisal of
his financial posture. In a magazine piece, a fellow Kansan, Arch
W. Jarrell, told how, in the wake of Gloyd's alcoholic death, the
crusader prayed for a loving successor, and added that "David
Nation was the answer to the prayer, but evidently his appearance
on the scene was in the nature of a divine joke. . . ."

Whatever his faults, Nation's life with the world symbol of tem-
perance-wrath had not been easy, but the agencies that sprang to
his support were without exception composed of persons who

never knew him personally. Now, in August, as his bride, train-bound, nosy, happy in her new work, steamed eastward over the bursting fields of the republic, the New York *Times* reeled off a frightened and waspish editorial in which it said, among other things about her, "It seems that her husband, who might be described as Stag Nation, has applied to the courts of Kansas for a divorce upon grounds that the partner of his bosom has subjected him to odium, ridicule and contempt. The plaint indicates that the perceptive qualities of the man are better developed than his combativeness. 'A quiet life was all his joy.' But tranquility is apparently impracticable within sight or hearing of this energetic female." Nation had indeed filed for a return to his solitary, un-nursed state, wisely delaying his action until his wife was halfway across the country, and she, from Columbus, telegraphed back the machinery to oppose him.

In the improbable relationship between mates, few divorces spin out their tired, bitter tale without acrimony and squalor, or, at the best, rueful humor, and the Nations put forward some enjoyable counter-accusations. First of all, it was true that Nation, in To-peka, in his latest role as interceptor of letters and wastebasket custodian for *The Smasher's Mail*, had accepted room-and-board money from the crusader, and the condition had curdled his normally sour disposition. "She not only exposed me to ridicule and humiliation," he said; "she took my featherbed and nine hundred dollars out of my bank account." The clumsiness of his wording inevitably brought astonished queries of why he kept his featherbed in a bank, and Mrs. Nation retaliated by saying, "Those are all lies. He didn't have nine hundred dollars, and the featherbed was always mine . . . I thought I loved David when I married him, but he was a fleeting fancy. David isn't a bad fellow, but he is too slow for me." Whoever was right, the divorce went through (on November 27, 1901) the case resting on the incontestable grounds of desertion. Mrs. Nation (for whom scores of witnesses flocked in to volunteer testimony) was exonerated from all charges of "cruelty" and given the home at Medicine Lodge. If the division caused any emotional upheavals during her long, long tour of the lecture spots, she kept the fact carefully concealed.

Chapter Twenty

The eastern part of the United States was flinched against Mrs. Nation's arrival in late August of 1901. New York City was particularly apprehensive, having been made the butt of bloodthirsty threats, and many saloons hired billy-carrying guards, even as the Topeka jointists had done. At the Hoffman House Bar, on Fifth Avenue, burly representatives of a detective agency were posted to protect the famous and irreplaceable painting, "Nymphs and Satyrs," a quasi-pornographic variation on a theme sportif, the whole rendered classical by high technique and a brief, convulsive vogue of the artist.

En route, Mrs. Nation told a reporter that she was in "top trim" for the encounter—mainly from exercise taken in dashing up and down the train aisles, dodging conductors—and at Watertown she stopped off for an unofficial, non-Furlong-sponsored preliminary. This appearance may have removed some of the thrust from the reformer's eastern invasion. In responding thus to one of her hundreds of mailed appeals for personal help at conspicuous trouble spots, she had failed as usual to check references. She was greeted by men whom she remarked as outstanding in politeness and accommodation (two of them wearing black arm bands for reasons never explained); she lashed out (in a Chautauqua tent) at drink and its minions, expressed amazement at the predominantly male aspect of the crowd, took the pledge of everybody in the place—to a man—and then learned that the meeting had been sponsored by saloonists. They saw it as a species of diversion. She seemed too deflated to protest, and she declined a courteous invitation to step round to the rowdiest dive in town and have a few on the house.

The crusader's spirits revived before she stepped off her train in New York City. She had gone so far as to re-outfit herself, an un-heard-of innovation. She was wearing a new poke bonnet with white ribbons tied under the chin, a new and shiny dress of black alpaca, and—in deference to the season—a white linen duster that reached to her shoes. From one shoulder dangled a satchel bulging with miniature hatchets, copies of the *Smasher*, photographs and memorial buttons; and strapped to her waist—unconcealed for all to see—was a hatchet of extraordinary dimensions, "almost as large as a small broad-axe," wrote a biographer. On her entrance she was greeted by an army of reporters and police, a crowd wildly cheering and a New York *Times* editorial that appraised the affair limply. "It was not Alexander the Great who wept because there were no more saloons to be smashed in Kansas," the paper said in a vein of moral astringency. "It was the female Alexander whom we are at present entertaining, not unawares, though possibly un-willingly . . . in our midst. As an exhibition of what may be done by a woman unsexed largely by nature and still more by habit, her performances are of a somewhat revolting interest. But there is no reason why anybody, except a policeman, should take Mrs. Nation seriously."

These were pretty harsh words, and they inspired the crusader to promise a visit ("all spraddled out," as the term went back in Kansas) to the Tenderloin. In the lobby of the Hotel Victoria, at Fifth Avenue and Thirty-seventh Street, she signed the register "Carry Nation, Your Loving Home Defender, Kansas," with a flourish that used up the better part of a page. Then she spied a naked statue of Diana leaning sexily over a fountain. "Look!" Mrs. Nation shouted. "She ain't got a thing on!" and dispatched three aged and rheumatic bellhops after the manager, who turned up wringing his hands as if he'd suddenly realized a great mistake. His manner descended to the abject when his guest unfurled her hatchet, shook it like King Arthur brandishing Excalibur, and cried, "Look here, my man, you cover up that nasty thing or there'll be a little hatchetation around here!" Bawling for his staff, the unfortunate produced a piece of cheese cloth, which he threw over the tilted huntress, and Mrs. Nation announced a press conference in her suite. There her mood changed, and she sang a song of her own composition, with an assist from Mother Goose:

> "Sing a song of six joints,
> With bottles full of rye;
> Four and twenty beer kegs,
> Stacked up on the sly.
> When the kegs were opened,
> The beer began to sing,
> Hurrah for Carry Nation,
> Her work beats anything."

The reformer's mention of beer kegs was opportune, for saloon-keepers in the theater district had been busily erecting signs that said, "Welcome all Nations but Carry," concocting drinks in her name, and publicly soliciting a visit, with promises of unlimited (empty) beer kegs and bottles to smash. Several establishments had hired press agents, who stood by to see that their patrons received full notice in the papers. Late in the morning she came downstairs prepared for her courtesy call to Police Commissioner Michael C. Murphy. (Acting Mayor Guggenheimer had described himself as preoccupied with the demands of office and confided to friends that "Nothing, *nothing* could persuade me to let that lawless creature in here!" On the record, he told the policeman stationed before his door: "Kennel, if Mrs. Carry Nation comes down here she is not to be admitted. The Mayor's Office is public, but it is not intended to serve as a medium of advertising.")

In an "open barouche drawn by a team of spirited black horses," Mrs. Nation proceeded down Fifth Avenue ostentatiously carrying her outsized hatchet over one shoulder like a rifle. And she further embarrassed her escorts by arising whenever a saloon hove within sight to shout, "Rummies! Murderers! Hell-holes!"

Her confrontation of Commissioner Murphy marked a memorable milestone in New York political welcomes. With high glee, the newspapers described the event as follows:

The reporters in attendance were put at about twenty; with these, Mrs. Nation "bustled" into Murphy's office, "sporting" her new costume and a new pair of glasses. She leaned over his desk, cornering him in the manner of bull-baiting, making it difficult for him to arise; then she shook hands and sank into a chair, where (said the *Times*) "for some minutes she beamed at him over her gold-rimmed spectacles."

The crusader's opening utterance appeared to strike the wrong note. "Mr. Murphy," she began. "you and I are fellow travelers to the Grave. Time's a-comin' when we've got to give an account of our stewardship and—"

"Yes, yes," said Murphy, understandably annoyed. "What are you trying to say to me?"

"Don't you think New York is an awful place?"

"There is no bad condition in New York, and I have no time to discuss things," he told her, starting to rise. "If you have anything to say, put it in writing and I'll read it—maybe!"

"You refuse, then, to discuss the crime and murder-shops in the great city—now mind, the time's a-comin'!" (again probing a sensitive nerve, for Murphy was elderly, a Civil War veteran, erect, soldierly and proud of a military bearing preserved to a great age).

"I must ask you to cut this interview short," he finally managed to say.

"Well, why don't you close the saloons on Sundays?" inquired Mrs. Nation.

"Because the citizens of this city believe in drinking when they please, and because the law so allows under proper circumstances."

"And it's your business, too," said Mrs. Nation. "And mind you, the time's a-comin'! The time's a-comin'! You still have an opportunity to be good. 'By their works ye shall know—' "

Here the Commissioner became just slightly malicious, for the news of David Nation's action had recently been published: "None of that, Madame! Don't quote Scripture at *me!* Go back to Kansas and get that off on your husband."

"Tell me, do you think I'm crazy?" she asked, with the beguiling look of an alienist about to examine a psychopathic killer.

Murphy told her he was glad to be able to answer promptly, and he did: "Yes, I do."

"That's what all the vicious rum-soaked creatures in Kansas thought also, but they're wrong. I've shown them things, and I'll show you a few before I'm through."

"Let me assure you, Madame, if you break a law in this city you will be very quickly apprehended. I shall have a close watch kept on you. I'll lock you up at the least provocation," and the *Times* added that "Colonel Murphy raised one long thin finger and wagged it under the woman's nose."

Mrs. Nation's next question has long puzzled students of her inexplicable mind. Until now, the Commissioner had maintained an edge, on points, according to the reporters' scorecards, but she had apparently divined the enemy's weak spot, in her usual canny style. She said, softly, "Are you angry with me because I want the rum-holes closed, *father?*"

On this note Murphy blew up. "What the devil do you mean, Madame?" he shouted, red-faced, rejecting the lineage. "I'm not your father!"

"I know," said Mrs. Nation, happy at last. "But you look it. You're old enough to be my father. I'm fifty-five, and you're eighty-five if you are a day. But there is no shame in being old, my *father*."

By now Murphy was able to make no coherent noises that reporters could set down as speech. He was reactivated when Mrs. Nation, having exposed his Achilles heel, said, "Father, don't you think a little hatchetation would be good for New York?"

"If you violate the law here, I'll have you locked up!"

"Now, father," and she patted his shoulder condescendingly, as he drew away in horror. "Don't be upset, father. Good*bye*, father!" *

And now, inevitably, the *tête-à-tête* fell into the broad, action-filled pattern of Mrs. Nation's other official visits. The *Times'* story explains the dramatic severing of diplomatic relations:

---

* The exchanges quoted are a synthesis from the *Times*, the *Tribune* and other New York papers. Altogether, the reporting was wonderfully varied.

" 'Madame, you are evidently looking to be thrown out of this office!' cried the Colonel savagely, springing [or escalating] to his feet. 'I know of nothing with which it is easier to accommodate you. *Sergeant!*' and a minute later the sergeant on post and two policemen entered. The policemen took hold of each side of Mrs. Nation who, smiling and beaming all over, was led out of the office and the building to the sidewalk."

In any comprehensive scrutiny of the crusader, the interview is important, for in a sense she had won again, having reduced to savage bad temper a man previously noted for iron self-discipline and graceful good manners.

New Yorkers relished Mrs. Nation's sprightly bow in town, savoring the detailed newspaper accounts the next morning with their breakfasts. It measured up to their expectations. The truth of the matter is that nothing else of much account was going on. The season was high summer—the "dog days"—and the city marked time until autumn and the theatrical and operatic openings. On the inside pages, removed from the blunders of front-page politicians, several news items sounded depressingly timeless. Under a headline, "Neighbors in Dispute," it was revealed that "Spite fences and the color line figure prominently in a squabble that has developed among Tremont property owners, and a bitter fight is in progress." The principals were "Wolf Boylin, a wealthy collar-button manufacturer; Mrs. Mary Blanch; and Lester Harrison, a colored man who for years has been connected with the Singer Manufacturing Company." In a nutshell, Boylin, objecting to Harrison moving in, raised the question of Harrison's roof projecting eight inches over Mrs. Blanch's line, whereupon Harrison bought the offending piece without demurrer—an action viewed as insolent—and the Boylin-Blanch axis raised a high wooden fence. The big news came when Mrs. Blanch, finding that Harrison "was not an objectionable person," took down her part of the fence, and Boylin retaliated by cutting off Harrison's drain pipe. At last report Mrs. Blanch (white) had joined forces with Harrison against Boylin, though without concrete plans for a counter-offensive, and "residents of the vicinity are anxiously expecting developments."

In Brooklyn, then as now the scene of the unlikeliest metropolitan events, a battle had been joined over the corpse of a Mr.

Goudge, who, lying in church, patiently awaited even a token ceremony that might hasten him toward the graveyard (for which he was several days overdue at an awkward time of year). Trouble was, Goudge had been a vociferous Odd Fellow, and his former brothers wished to hold the Lodge service over his dead body. The church rector, the Reverend Dean Richmond Babbitt, had informed the men, in effect, that they would do so only over his (Babbitt's). He aimed to plant Goudge, he said, using ecclesiastical rhetoric, according to the funeral prescription of the Protestant Episcopal Church. Trotting out the headline, "Trouble in Brooklyn Church" (a slug of type that may have been lying around the shop, ready for emergencies, since the days of Henry Ward Beecher) the *Times* seemed convinced that the situation, as well as Goudge, was hopelessly deadlocked.

August or not, conditions were livelier along the rialto. The immortal Weber and Fields were appearing in a skit called "Hoity-Toity," at Broadway's Music Hall, and offered as an encore what a writer of temperance biographies would give a good deal to have seen, called "Burlesque of Diplomacy." At the Casino, the Flora-dora Girls, perennial favorites of New York's artistic and healthfully salacious, were on view with crotch-high kicks and well-exhibited bottoms, and any number of burlesque shows were booming along the twinkling street in that realistic era before church pressures squashed earthy fun and replaced it with pornography, prurience and sex crimes. (This was in the time of entertainment for its own sake—before an absurd and hypersensitive delicacy about races put such incomparable storytellers as Lou Holtz out of business.) At Manhattan Beach, John Philip Sousa and his band were providing non-cool music for the already cooled-off bathers; the great marches—"Stars and Stripes Forever," "On the Mall," "El Capitan,"—were a few years away from the drawing board. For the theatrical serious, John Drew was drawing crowds at the Empire with his production of "Second in Command;" and William Faversham, at Charles Frohman's Criterion, had settled down to a success with "A Royal Rival."

In its front-page coverage of the crusader's first day in New York, the *Times* condensed things neatly in its lead paragraph: "Mrs. Carrie Nation arrived in New York yesterday morning. Before the day was over she had attended St. Patrick's Cathedral, made an effort to penetrate the interior of the Democratic Club, toured the Tenderloin, been arrested on Eighth Avenue, and delivered a lecture at Carnegie Hall on the subject, 'The Lord's Saloon.' "

The papers, and the city, were impressed, but the introduction fell short of Mrs. Nation's usual first visit to any metropolitan center. "Police hostility," she said (intimating that it was immoral and probably illegal) prevented her from carrying out anything worth comment in the way of smashing.

The newspaper was, of course, unable to include everything in its short first paragraph. The visitor caused a mild, routine uproar in the streetcar that conveyed her up Fourth Avenue to the cathedral. She was accompanied by the Furlong Lyceum Bureau's representative, Robert Grau, plus as many curiosity seekers as could jam into the vehicle and hang onto its sides. Despite the crush, she succeeded in snatching away the cigars of four somnolent men minding their own business, or trying to, and one of them, bouncing up, cried out, "See here, that was a good cigar!" "My friend, tobacco is your worst enemy," she said. His answer, provoking cheers and a brief scuffle toward the rear, was, "But we are told to *love* our enemies." For a second, it looked as though the car might explode into riot, but the church hove into view, and Mrs. Nation alighted without injury. In St. Patrick's she was a model of deportment (after she had made an entrance like a heavyweight prizefighter's, mitted the crowd, and seated herself [with retinue] in a front pew). Her appearance aroused "considerable attention" as the papers said, but there were no open outbreaks. She observed the mass carefully and went through the ritual with precision, watching her neighbors. When the service was over, she arose and remarked loudly, "That was a good sermon!" There was no indication that the padre seemed grateful; on the contrary, his face assumed a look of heavenly peace when the doors clanged shut behind her.

On Fifth Avenue, pointed to the nearby Democratic Club, Mrs. Nation came to life and tried to storm the unhallowed cupboard in which all the skeletons had historically been male. She surprised reporters with an intimate knowledge of New York City politics.

Theretofore her insults had been directed more specifically at Republicans, concentrating on Roosevelt and McKinley, and, of late, William Jennings Bryan, the metallurgist and perennial candidate for president. (Bryan, in Mrs. Nation's opinion, had become a legendary bore, and besides, she suspected him of smoking.) "Is this Richard Croker's hang-out?" she inquired of a doorman whose brogue and hauteur implied an aspiration toward lace curtains. His answer, finally, was to try and pitch her out, but she sidestepped like a halfback and pushed through as far as the clerk, who told her (again) that ladies were not admitted. The usual pro-and-con mob on the sidewalk enjoyed the encounter, and when the crusader called, loudly, "You ought to be ashamed to have a place where ladies can't go!" the question was inevitably raised: "Is Mrs. Nation a lady?" It appeared so, for she was given an un-violent bum's rush, which she took sportingly and nipped into a saloon on Seventh Avenue in which four sailors from a "man-of-war" were sipping an unidentified beverage from mugs. The crusader went into a paroxysm of lament over the tragedy of young men "in defense of their country" fallen to such a low estate, but one (the youngest) said with a mature look, "Why, Ma'am, this is what we're fighting for!" "Well," she continued, what *is* that you're drinking?"

"Lemonade," said a second gob, and took a deep swallow.

"Ha!" she cried, and grabbing his mug took a draft of her own; then she spat it across the room. She screamed, "Poisoned malt!" but when the bartender reached into his demesne as if for a ballbat or a bungstarter, she retired to a neutral corner and began a lecture on the evils of all drink including beer. During its course, several remarked the improved tempo of the sailors' guzzling; they were stowing it away, wrote the *Herald* reporter, "as if it might be their last day ashore for years."

Journalistically, the word "Tenderloin" was then in currency, and the papers harped gleefully on Mrs. Nation's probe of this lively and perhaps blasphemous section of town, aglow with alcohol and bright lights, pockmarked with iniquitous dens, protected by police and politicians. But those among her tumultuous following who expected the usual smashing were disappointed. Other, subtler souls marveled over the incident at the Apollo Music Hall, a basement dump that carried the preposterous legend: *Entrée Libre—Café Chantant*. The place was unlit and looked vacant, but below stairs Mrs. Nation found the two partners of the dive—a man and a woman—seated at a dim table and locked in business dispute. The Apollo, with chantant, was about at the end of its rope. The crusader sat down and joined them, trying (and her managerial skill had been praised by the ungenerous David Nation) to help get the establishment back on its feet. Among other things, she suggested that the Continental come-on seemed empty, for the cafe had approximately the same French aspect as Dublin. The partners thanked her, offered her a free shot of whiskey (which she declined) and she returned to the street, where she was arrested by a timorous and probably hen-pecked policeman who refused to give reporters his name, preferring to identify himself by his badge number: "3769." The equivocation was believed without precedent in the annals of New York's finest.

The crusader made no objection to being arrested (for "blocking traffic," "disturbing the peace," etc.—the usual grab-bag of charges into which the authorities often dipped in her case) but she boiled over when 3769 shooed some children out of the way. "Don't hurt those children!" she cried. "They aren't bothering anybody." 3769 now seemed baffled how to proceed, for the crowd, aided by Mrs. Nation, suddenly realized that he was a kind of modern King Herod, and a kindly reporter stepped forward to urge that the visitor be permitted to board a streetcar and proceed to the hotel, where she could cool off (the naked Diana being draped). In the lobby, to importunings of "Speech! Speech!" she expressed the following sentiment: "There is just one thing I want to say to you. New York has the neatest children I have ever seen. You men are all smokers, using poison. But the little children are good and clean, and I'm proud of them." *

That night at Carnegie Hall, she addressed herself mainly to women in the audience, which was about half male and had paid the then thumping fee of $1.50 a head to get in. The papers quoted her at length, stressing her dressier phrases, such as one describing

---

* The crusader was nearly correct in this. Only a handful of the tots had been smoking, and several of these politely discarded their scavenged cigar-butts.

men as "nicotine-soaked, beer-besmeared, whiskey-bloated, red-eyed Devils," and paid solemn attention to her advices against the wearing of corsets—"they deform women out of all shape." Her feeling that Paris (France) was an instigator of fashions incalculably evil was noted, and two writers, at least, were edified that she equated herself with Moses: "he was a grand smasher" (golden calf, idols, etc.). One difference was recorded as between her New York reception and those in Kansas and elsewhere. Carnegie Hall at times rocked with laughter, and it did not come at exactly those moments which the speaker might have wished. The audience exhibited symptoms that would have gone down better at the Apollo. A unanimous point of admiration—a perplexity to historians—was the crusader's untypical costume. For the speech, she wore a white linen dress, this marking her fourth change of raiment in a single day. New York may not have been unduly impressed by Mrs. Nation, but she appeared to have been impressed at least by the prospect of New York. And nobody, to this moment, is certain where she managed during her travels to lay in the fancy clothes. One reporter at Carnegie Hall wondered if she might not have been influenced just slightly by Paris.

By now, Mrs. Nation's adventures at Coney Island, for ten days beginning on September third (Labor Day) are familiar to any serious student of reform. They presented some singular features. In general, the appearance fell below the style expected by enthusiasts of Mrs. Nation's campaigns; that is, it was lively but different. While world temperance-ites awaited news that New York, like Topeka, lay prostrate, another victim of hatchetation, their idol held forth as an "attraction" at George Tilyou's Steeplechase, focal point of the best-known amusement park extant. She was exhibited like a two-headed calf. Certain criticisms were aimed at James E. Furlong, of the Lyceum Bureau, but he was in the business of reaping what he could, regardless of the antics required to exploit what, in this instance, the *Times* chose to describe as "the Island's particular freak of the day." The reformer had beguiled respectable numbers into Carnegie Hall, giving Furlong a fat purse for that stand. Labor Day morning dawned bleak and showery, as well as unseasonably cool; the beaches were emptied of their normally impeccable bathers; hotel honeymooners were glad to remain abed, getting their rest; a scant handful of shills turned up to tout the bars, cafes and dishonest games of chance; pickpockets (according to police) were in thin supply on that traditional fall vacation—and, as a result, the price for hearing America's noisiest woman was dropped from fifty cents to a quarter. It was a poor start.

It is disappointing to report that nobody took Mrs. Nation's evangelical mission to Coney Island very seriously. Furlong, however, had not been idle in his pre-game tactics. He had dressed a local hayseed as a Kansas farmer, provided him with a billygoat and a "mangy" (the papers agreed on this) dog, fitted heraldic signs to both man and beasts and sent them strolling along the promenades. The ballyhoo proved dubious. The animals wasted no time in squaring off with expressions of mutual distaste, and when this was solved, the goat butted a large, solid woman who'd stooped over to pick up a penny. She threatened to sue. Then the dog ate all the frankfurters displayed on a hot plate. The public's reception of this triumvirate was more ribald than devout; it had almost nothing to do with reform. "Many seemed to see in the goat an inspiration," said the *Times*. "Suggestions to the farmer were frequent that Mrs. Nation ought to add the goat to her equipment as a smasher. There were others who inquired whether Mrs. Nation intended to come out for Bock Beer." Furlong had, besides, any number of men selling miniature hatchets, using a vague threat as a sales talk: "Right this way and get a Carry Nation hatchet—*protect yourself!*" People who arrived as the weather brightened bought souvenirs in the spirit of small shopkeepers hoping to avoid a bombing by gangsters. Inside his park, Tilyou helped drum up business with barkers who shouted Mrs. Nation's attractions (all violent) in extravagant terms.

The crusader's contract called for two lectures a day, with an aftermath, or "Olio," in which she would answer questions and perhaps dodge a few deviled eggs and stuffed fish. On Labor Day, her first spiel was scheduled for four P.M. and she arrived, at three, pretty well spent. Aboard the "iron steamboat *Pegasus*," she had fought throughout the trip from the Battery. The melee was triggered when she began removing cigars from amazed mouths and snatched one from a dozing man who woke up and objected. He did not just quite manage to put her overboard. Then she spied a waiter passing with a tray of beer. Voicing a strangled cry, she lit out in pursuit, as he jettisoned his load and fled below, perhaps to study his union contract. Stimulated, Mrs. Nation approached the bar, where an excursion crowd in white flannels, striped blazers and straw hats were preparing themselves for the long evening to come. It made a pretty scene, the carefree, yet undefeated champions of free enterprise thronging the ornate iron tub as it smoked down a harbor still white with sails that seemed like pennants flown to celebrate an end-of-summer fete day. A shout rang out at the bar, "Here comes old Carry!" and there formed a line of defense, not dissimilar to football's flying wedge. Scattering the merrymakers right and left, she seized all the glasses from the bar, held them aloft, then dashed them to the floor. "The Captain of the boat," said the *Times,* "who had been keeping an eye on her, stepped up and informed her that he would put her in the hold and keep her locked up if she made any further trouble."

When Mrs. Nation debarked, she climbed into a horse-cab and proceeded slowly along Surf Avenue, shaking hands with throngs that pressed around her carriage. To the chagrin of both Furlong and Tilyou, she showed no immediate interest in her duties. She had decided, she said, to enjoy herself at the attractions. Her starting visit was to the "House of Too Much Trouble," a nest of booby-traps that offered potential fractures, then she took a turn at the See-Saw. Before the distorting mirrors she lingered for several minutes, seeming drawn to one called "Intoxication" that showed her head thirty times larger than her body. "I always thought the drunken state was hell," she told reporters, "and now I know it." "The Loop the Loop, the Flip Flap, the Jolly Razzle Dazzle, all the vertigo-producing machines could not compete with Carry Nation," wrote the *Tribune.*

The *Tribune* man had painted things in colors a trifle rosy. When, at 4:30, the crusader consented to cease swinging, flying through the air, barking her shins on snares and gazing at herself in mirrors, she appeared on stage to a mere handful of curious. She was radiant (if disheveled) in a white dress made with a cape, she held a Bible in one hand, and had a hatchet strapped to her side. The truth is that, while she had excited Coney Island's attention on the outside, the fee for her lecture—a quarter knocked down from fifty cents—struck the proletariat as stiff. Rides cost a dime each, a gigantic stein of beer (with free lunch consisting of cold meats, hard-boiled eggs and potato salad) was a nickel, and one could dance with the buxomest kind of girls in festooned gardens for the bare price of the drinks. Cooch shows that featured naked (and even tattooed) bellies were within reach for twenty cents, and it was possible, for a dime, to win a handsome gold-washed watch without works. And, of course, to stroll the boardwalk and study the Laocoön groups on the sand was a diversion available without charge. As a competitive entertainment, Mrs. Nation at the start, was a dud. Furlong fell into a sulk, but Tilyou, the honky-tonk king (who would forever be her *beau ideal* of the good and proper knight) remained sporting through lean times and good. As her years grew long, and the days of her years became bitter—while her minister friends, so daring when her ideas seemed popular, succumbed one after the other to opportunism and self-protection —she thought of Tilyou as the symbol of what a male ought to be. Writing, not long before the end, she said, "Mr. Tilyou is one of the few men you meet in this world who is able to be pure amidst all kinds of debauchery. God bless that man! I like to know such men are living."

Mrs. Nation's idolatrous view of Tilyou did not prevent her, between talks, from trying to smash the bar in his Steeplechase Auditorium. Her life credo may well have been stated by the pronouncement, in her autobiography, that, "I never saw anything that needed a rebuke, or exhortation, or warning, but that I felt it my place to meddle with it." She was "repulsed and disarmed," and her rage enabled her to pounce on a thriving cigar stand at the end of Steeplechase Walk. First she braced Charles Wallenstein, the young, rather ineffectual fellow in charge, who could only stammer in reply to the shouted question, "Is not tobacco an abomination to the human race?" Luckily the crusader did not at that moment possess an edged weapon. As a substitute, the youth's indecision brought her satchel down on his head, together with the puzzling scream, "Answer me, you rummy!" Since there had never been a suspicion that the establishment dispensed booze, Wallenstein stood bewildered, as well as stunned, while Mrs. Nation smashed his cigar cases and tossed out Havanas by the double-handful, thus providing a windfall of nicotine to dozens, including children, who swooped in beneath her skirts to grab what they could. In a few minutes the neighborhood resembled an industrial complex fired by bituminous coal. In due course the police arrived, but when Mrs. Nation was advised to enter the Black Maria, her resistance grew so marked (she called the officer "purple and bloated from beer drinking") that she suffered a whack on the knuckles from a nightstick. It broke a small bone in her right hand. In protest, she lay down on the sidewalk, to avoid entering the vehicle—an action believed to have been the first forerunner of the sit-in. The crowd was amazed that she ignored the pain, and instead yelled, "Never mind, you beer-swelled, whiskey-soaked, saturn-faced man! God will strike you!" For whatever it's worth to Duke University's toilers in the field of extrasensory perception, the patrolman fell dead of a heart attack six weeks later.

Tilyou bailed out his contentious freak on her promise to pay Wallenstein a hundred dollars, and she went on to worse disasters. It has been mentioned that no living male had yet bested Mrs. Nation, but President McKinley did so posthumously. On September 6, at Buffalo's Pan American Exposition McKinley was shot in the stomach by the anarchist Leon Czolgosz, who said, "I did it for the people." The President lingered in agony until his death eight days later, on the fourteenth, and as none of the people for whom the assassin performed the service stepped forward to verify his assertion, Czolgosz was hanged, both by and for the people. Mrs. Nation detested all politicians, but she reserved a special virulence of feeling for McKinley. It was not remarkable, therefore, that when a member of her Coney Island audience demanded, "What about the President *now?*" she stood stubbornly steadfast. The previously mentioned principle of *de mortuis nil nisi bonum* has always confounded morality students. Why anybody—paragon, plain citizen or villain—should become officially sanctified by the simple act of his demise, immune from criticisms of what may have been monumental treacheries and blunders, remains a mystery. In a sense, the mossy old practice is tantamount to saying that the only good human is a dead human.

"I have no tears for this McKinley," courageously stated Mrs.

Nation, whether right or wrong in her views. "Neither have I any for his assassin. I have no sympathy for this friend of the brewers." It was the wrong thing to say. Republicans and Democrats alike— though they might have loathed McKinley up to the moment of the shot—were wallowing in bathos, and there was talk (in case he died) of renaming in his behalf Lake Superior, Pike's Peak, the Potomac River, Cape Cod, Ohio (where he was born), Florida (where he had visited) and Washington, D.C.* In boxing argot, the roof fell in on Mrs. Nation. Her Coney Island audience ex- ploded with catcalls and hisses, and not only men but demure- looking women commenced to jump up and down as if demented. "Shut up, you sots!" shrieked the crusader, laying the disturbance mainly to whiskey. Then, marvelously, in this region whence all tolerance begins, there arose horrid, Kansas-like cries of "Lynch her! Lynch her!" and two men tumbled outside in search of hemp. They collared an Indian fakir trying to do the rope trick, but he seemed unwilling to part with his property, and besides, the upper end was hooked to a wire. Those persons who stayed in the audito- rium now loosed a bombardment of what reporters identified as bags of peanuts and popcorn, popcorn balls, a pink kewpie doll, a cane, a blond wig, a corset, the remnants of several hot dogs (a confection that came to be known as a Coney Island), a box of crackerjack, and numerous wads of newspaper. Some of these mis- siles struck Mrs. Nation, already crippled with a broken hand, and she tried to scramble off the platform and out, yelling, "You sots and hell-hounds! You'll all go to hell! God will strike you!" Sud- denly the crowd—as inexplicable in its way as the lecturer— wheeled and ran outside, where it paused and organized "three cheers for President McKinley!" Not unexpectedly, Mrs. Nation in- sisted on finishing her speech to an empty hall. Later, when she ap- peared on the sidewalk, she was charged, but not seriously dam- aged, by groups of persons chanting in favor of William McKinley.

Fearing for her life, Furlong broke the crusader's Steeplechase contract and next day whisked her into upstate New York. The manager had good stuff in him, usually obtained in the best bars in

---

* On the President's death, good sense finally prevailed, and no more than one mountain, two small towns, and a scattering of public buildings were re- christened.

town, and he meant well by his mule-headed evangelist, often in the face of skimpy gates and embarrassing run-ins with the police. To his dismay, however, in Rochester, with a sell-out crowd apparently poised to hear an attack on booze, Mrs. Nation again touched on McKinley, and the place lost all holds on reason. Wild shouts of "Lynch the old hag!" exceeded anything in her experience to date. The ticket purchasers had evidently come prepared, and stones "as large as baseballs" rained down on the stage. For a minute the elderly reformer stood, defying the world; then it suddenly occurred to her that she could either fly or join McKinley on the critical list. With a last snort of contempt, she skipped nimbly into a rear alley, where two scared policemen scooped her up and took refuge in the back room of a saloon. "I'd rather die than accept protection from a jointist!" she cried. When the officers, crouching, uttered the equivalent of "O.K.," and "Your business," she subsided, listening in awe to the wrathful mob in the streets. "Well," she said, incapable of giving up entirely, "I can at least wreck this saloon," but the policemen pinned her down and the owner locked and barred his doors. She had been overheard, though, and the searchers bashed in the front windows—one of the things she herself had hoped to do, so that she gained at least a partial victory. In the end, the policemen spirited their unruly self-destructive charge by some underground route into a hotel next door and guarded her room all night.

From then until October 27, Mrs. Nation lectured in cities of northern New York and collected a rich variety of denunciation on each appearance. In her autobiography, she saw only a single experience of this period as worth noting in detail, and it took place during her off-hours. When she was attending high mass at St. Joseph's Cathedral, in Buffalo, one of the assistant priests, a Mr. Percell, made the mistake of sticking a collection plate under the crusader's nose. She looked up and said, in a carrying voice, "You smell *so* bad from cigarette smoke!" Well-trained or not, the young cleric cannot be blamed for giving the customary startled response: "Who, me?"

"Yes, you," said Mrs. Nation.

Mr. Percell then fell off the celestial wagon, so to speak. Orders were orders, but he was still only human, and he blurted out, "You're a liar."

"No, I am not," said Mrs. Nation. "You do smell bad."

"I will have you put out of this church!"

It was an attractive offer. The reformer had been put out of nearly every other kind of building in America, and she thought it over, eventually saying, "I dare you! You are the one who should be put out."

Here Percell may have received signs from his Superior to cool off, for he withdrew the plate from Mrs. Nation's presence (she hadn't contributed as much as an anti-whiskey button) and continued up the aisle, grumbling. When the mass was finished, she hurried to the "house of the priests," in search of the collector, but she was cordially received by two other priests in a room smoldering like a city dump. Coughing, and then wrenching at a window, she had the fathers' assurance that smoking was general with God's agents everywhere. "What a shame for a man to dress like a saint and smell like a devil," she said, and left.

During none of her New York visits did Mrs. Nation suffer a serious injury. But she had a good many narrow squeaks because, perversely, she incorporated McKinley, by one means or another, into all of her lectures on drink. The fact is she got off miraculously well. In Casper, Wyoming, during the over-emotional crisis, a man named Hans Wagner praised Czolgosz and was tarred and feathered and ridden out of town on a rail.

Chapter Twenty-One

"When I began lecturing [Mrs. Nation wrote] I tried to get into churches, but only a few would open to me. I had many inducements financially to go on the stage, but I refused to do so for some time. Like a little child I have had to sit alone, creep and walk. I paid my fines by monthly installments and in December of 1902, I settled with the court at Topeka for the 'Malicious destruction of property,' when, in fact, it was the 'Destruction of malicious property.' "

As 1902 got under way, the crusader severed her connection with Furlong and managed herself, accomplishing little except notoriety that provided enjoyable headlines wherever she went. Her energies continued high, and her spirit had never been stronger, but many of the old campaigners, the comrades of raid, jail and battering ram, had taken on a new sanctimony that included a horror of extremism. Left, of course, were the hard-core fanatics, and to these Mrs. Nation addressed herself by any method available. It is distressing, again, to record that her course was much eased by saloonists, who began to regard her as their special pet and protégé. When she arrived in a town, the reformer made inquiries whether her presence was *grata* or *non grata* in the churches, and when, commonly, the latter condition prevailed, she tried to rent an empty hall. This failing, she spoke either in a vacant lot or on any street corner from which the police were not apt to seize her for a jailing (with the resultant fine so badly needed by the municipal coffers). After a talk, if she found herself at liberty, she sold souvenirs. All in all, it was not a perfectly rewarding life. Of her old associates, the saloon men were by far the most sympathetic, and at last they provided her a podium that she would come to accept as standard—an empty beer keg gay with ribbons and surrounded by placards bitterly deploring liquor. On these incongruous stumps, in many a town of the Middle West, Mrs. Nation held forth with vigor, and the custom she drew to the pubs was incalculable. After her departure, the kegs were prominently displayed by their owners, and a few, to this day, are to be found in regions where the crusader was particularly active.

Mrs. Nation's unexpected quality was never more obvious than in June of 1902 when she made the return trip to Topeka (mentioned in her paragraph about lecturing) and chose to sit out part of her fine in jail. When she emerged, old friends and the public were stunned to hear her announce that she had become a "Christian Catholic Apostolic Zionist"—that is, a follower of the health crank (her one-time competitor in Chicago) John Alexander Dowie, who had taken on the added moniker of Elijah III, without briefing anybody on what had happened to Elijahs I and II. Dowie had a blistering bias against curative drugs, along with an ambition to become known as top-crank (Mrs. Nation had once mentioned his "lust for power"). To reporters she said, mysteriously (for Dowie was nowhere near at hand) that the self-professed prophet had "appointed me to proselytize for him in Kansas and the adjacent states, also empowering me to practice faith healing." Historically the art, since the Middle Ages, had meant "laying on of hands," together with voodoo babbling, or incantation, aimed to hypnotize the sufferer into casting off his misery.

Faithful to the new call, Mrs. Nation began her campaign by assuring fellow Topekans that, over the years, the Lord had cured her of numberless ailments, all serious, not to say critical, though she refused to name any specifically. Then she went to work. First she laid hands on an elderly ruin limping along State Street, but he had sprained an ankle in a saloon fight and he reciprocated by laying his right hand across her jaw. Next she tried some cures among the progeny of friends (down with trifles like measles and chicken pox) but they complained that she tickled and bounced out of bed to romp and hide, giving her a series of pretty rough house calls. After Mrs. Nation had unsuccessfully treated for tumor a maiden lady who turned out to be pregnant, she blew up at Christian Catholic Apostolic Zionism and denounced its founder not only as a charlatan but "a spawn of Satan," and said, further, that his teachings were "the hellborn brother of Masonry and Christian Science." Charitable in the face of adversity, she saw her last patient through the delivery, then said, in effect, the hell with it; she had fulfilled her professional oath, and she added a few of her own to go along with it.

Mrs. Nation's flirtation with Dowie had scarcely faded from the papers when she commenced her long and baffling encounters with collegians, the merriment reaching its peak at Yale. This phase of her work had its genesis at the University of Missouri, at Columbia, when she consented to address a student group headed by a W. B. Burrus, known to his intimates as "Bottle Bill." She delivered a smashing tirade against intoxicants and then, en route back to her hotel, learned that Burrus was using the considerable gate receipts to buy champagne. When her confidence in students revived, Mrs. Nation went to the University of Michigan and addressed the Woolley Club, which gave her "a banquet and a heartfelt reception." Naive always, she wrote that "God will bless the Woolley Club of Ann Arbor and their kind," but disinterested spectators contended that the "heartfelt" gala was stimulated to a level remindful of Henry the Eighth, and that not much benefit was apt to accrue from her remarks. Mrs. Nation's geniality persisted toward the University of Michigan, but she finally compromised by modifying her attitude about Ann Arbor as a whole. "I have been to all the principal Universities of the United States," she said. "At Cambridge, where Harvard is situated, there are no saloons allowed, but in Ann Arbor the places are thick where manhood is drugged and destroyed. Also Yale, the latter being the worst I have ever seen."

As between Harvard and Yale, it seems odd that Mrs. Nation should have singled out Yale; her experiences at both centers could hardly have been more crushing. At one time or another, she indeed visited nearly all the colleges in America, with uniformly negative results, but it was the Ivy League that produced the hyper-cultured antics that were building the select guild's repute. Nowhere on earth could undergraduates have displayed invention more diabolic than that shown at Yale on September 29, 1902. Mrs. Nation's setback at Missouri and Michigan had brought a mixed bag of appeals from eastern colleges, a lot of the anguish sounding sincere and to all of which she paid credulous heed. From Yale came a suspicious bleat (faithfully reproduced in the crusader's book): "Here are eight-hundred shining young souls, the cream of the nation's manhood, on the broad road which leadeth to destruction. God help us. Assist us, Mrs. Nation; aid us, pray for us . . . Publicity will do it." Another Yale youth, who refrained from identifying himself among the cream of the nation's manhood, sent her a dozen menus from the college dining hall and emphasized that several dishes were goosed up with champagne and brandy sauces. (Reading them over today, one can feel a vicarious nostalgia for university life in that era: "Roast Ham and Champagne Sauce"; "Apple Dumpling and Brandy Sauce"; "Wine Jelly"; "Cherry Wine Sauce"; etc. etc.) Her communicant, however, wound up by stating that the concoctions were "starting us on the road to hell." The revelation was sufficient to start Mrs. Nation on the road to Yale.

She arrived in New Haven early in the afternoon and for some reason went to the office of Mayor Studley, where she found his secretary, C. E. Julin, a recent Yale graduate, sprawled in an easy chair and smoking a cigar. Municipal business being slack, Julin had been adrift in a dreamy, Yalish reverie when suddenly he was clouted on the back by a large, strong woman who cried, "Throw that nasty thing away!" It is a credit to Yale, and to Julin's training there, that he didn't jump up and hit her in return; instead he convinced her that the mayor was powerless to mend Yale's ways. As a graduate, he seemed sad about it. Mrs. Nation then headed off toward the campus. Her familiar garb quickly recognized, she was taken in tow by a student club known as The Jolly Eight, composed of the most determined boozers in Yale's history. The members deposited her on the steps of Osborn Hall, where she started to make a speech, while the enrollment hastily gathered. Every time she opened her mouth she was drowned out by organized cheering of the "Osky Wow-wow! Carry! Carry! Carry!" species. Cheerleaders in turtle-necked sweaters spanned the gamut of Yale's sporting yoicks, with mentions of bulldogs, Eli, etc., and when these commenced to trickle thin, a choral group undertook some tortured renditions of anti-liquor songs that included "Down With King Alcohol" and "Goodbye, Booze." In forty-five minutes, the crusader had failed to fling a single word above the din, and she lost her temper. "What's the matter with these rummies?" she demanded of the Jolly Eight-er nearest at hand. He was able to give her a lucid reply. "They're drunk," he said. "They had ham with champagne sauce for lunch and they haven't gotten over it yet."

Clutching her hair, Mrs. Nation ran—literally ran—down the steps and away in the direction of the administration building. There was disagreement later whether President Arthur D. Hadley, informed of the approaching Kansas tornado, tried to get out of a hall window and climb down a drain spout. The student newspaper was inclined to whimsy and hyperbole, and the reader occasionally finds it difficult to separate the chaff from the wheat. It appears unlikely, as stated, that his "academic robes caught on an umbrella stand and prevented his escape." In any case, whether Hadley tried to retreat is irrelevant. Mrs. Nation cornered him for a showdown, in his office, about which he forever maintained an official silence. The reformer was not so reticent in her book, though, and she said that, braced about the swilling, he "described the intoxicants as fruit juices." So they all were, of course—champagne, cherry wine and brandy; fruit juice in an advanced state of decay—and Dr. Hadley may have outwitted his adversary with an honest subtlety that she failed to perceive. She then switched to the subject of tobacco—many of the choral group, and others, had been smoking even as they sang and cheered. Here the writer must place Hadley's remarks in a framework of levity. Presumably straight-faced, he told Mrs. Nation that he "was taught it was wrong in America, but when I went to Germany and saw that everybody smoked there, I thought better of the vice and am now teaching it to our boys." At the very least, it must stand as one of the most singular academic credos on record.

Much of the bland fall afternoon remained, and the crusader spent it tramping back and forth across the campus, often stopping to make disastrous efforts to speak above the clamor. Despite these failures, she collected useful data from individual students who volunteered case histories. One youth said he was so dizzy all day from the over-active food that he was "unable to make high marks"; the stimulants were all that kept him "off the dean's list." Another said the alcohol choked him at each meal, and he would cheerfully have foregone eating entirely, "out of respect for my mother," but he was afraid he might starve to death. A third claimed he was considering suing Yale for contributing to the delinquency of a minor. An upperclassman assured her that the seniors of Sheffield School always engaged "a whole beer wagon for their annual wrestling procession" and generally drank it dry before sundown. On the other hand, a freshman recounted to her *his* class's principal recreation: "Upon appointed evenings they will meet at a select hotel," he said. "They take their places at a table, then each 'sets them up' for the rest. If there are twelve at the table, every freshman gets twelve drinks. You can imagine the 'games' after such a debauch." Mrs. Nation noted down the complaints, then agreed to pose for photographs at Mory's Restaurant, a traditional undergraduate hangout. There she was tricked into helping produce an enduring work of art. Surrounded by students of bilious and funereal mien, she stood beside a table, holding aloft a glass of water, but before the camera snapped, the saints all produced beer mugs and broke into leers of "drunken abandon." As for Mrs. Nation's water glass, it miraculously changed over to a foaming stein at some point in the process of dark-room development. This photo is the memorial, mentioned in Chapter One, that today either graces or disgraces, depending on one's attitude toward spirits, the bar of the excellent Yale Club in New York.

The reformer's day in New Haven should not be dismissed without a mention of her tribute to Yale students, uttered to reporters that night in New York. Looking a bit defeated, she said (and her experience had been vast): "They're the toughest proposition I ever met."

Her visit to Harvard, equally sapping, differed only in its details, and these were uniquely sprightly. In a sense, Harvard's hospitality exceeded that of Yale, for the moment Mrs. Nation entered the campus at Cambridge, on November 14, swarms of undergraduates rushed forward to press into her hands both cigars and cigarettes, free. She tried to throw them away but quit when the academicians misunderstood, crying, "No, no! It's all right. Keep them —won't cost you a penny." En route to the Mather family's mossy old lyceum, she had learned that its victuals, like Yale's, were swimming in tonics, and she fought her way to Memorial Hall, where the one o'clock shift was busy at lunch. Poised dramatically in the doorway, she cried, "Boys, don't eat that infernal stuff! It's poison!" To her immense gratification, the diners tossed aside their plates and rose as a single drunk, but instead of dropping in prayer, as ordered, they burst into a song of growing popularity in the now reform-conscious East: "Good Morning, Carrie." Then they swooped the crusader up with a howl and hustled her across Harvard Yard to Randall Hall. She was propelled inside and courted with shouts of "Speech! Speech!" This was what Mrs. Nation had come for, and she expanded her lungs to begin, only to hear the audience, as if by prearrangement, launch into what struck reporters as an inapposite and generally senseless ditty:

> Ain't it a shame, a measly shame,
> To keep your baby out in the rain?

If the aria had other verses, the students never got around to them, and the reformer finally went berserk, shrieking, running about the room, grabbing at cigars and cigarettes, and slapping faces. In fairness to Harvard, it should be said that the undergraduates took it sportingly, showing the highest regard for academic freedom and, in short, accepting her actions as a form of musical criticism. When she finally slumped into a seat, panting, she was whisked up again and borne to the Sanders Theater in downtown Cambridge. Finding its doors locked at the awkward time of day, the visitors kicked them in without delay (smashing one) and conveyed Mrs. Nation to the stage, as Harvard scholars tumbled over and into seats. It appeared at long last that she was to be permitted a few censorious remarks about American college life, of which she had perhaps been given a specialized view, but once again she ran into the same troublesome roadblock:

> Ain't it a shame, a measly shame,
> To keep your baby out in the rain?

It was too much; the song was plainly of intellectual depths beyond the reach of Shakespeare-quoting Kansans. By main strength, Mrs. Nation fought her way through the wings to the street, where she gave out the opinion that Harvard students were "demented." In this she found a measure of agreement among both the police and the theatre owners, who were eyeing the doors with the familiar expression of townies trying to reckon up costs and penalties. Late in the afternoon, Mrs. Nation ventured more-or-less quietly across the campus, and on this second round she drew attention to herself only by trapping a quartet of professors furiously smoking. They seemed disinclined to surrender without a struggle, so she asked, virtually in civilized tones, "Why do you smoke?" She regarded their reply—"More important, why don't you?"—as impertinent, but she resisted the urge, if she had one, to assault them physically, and an hour or so afterward she elected to let Harvard become stewed in its own fruit juice. In conversation, she remarked that the place was too depraved to admit of possible salvation. For her newspaper (and eventually in her book) she touched on the institution, saying, mainly, "While I was at Harvard I saw Professors smoking cigarettes . . . These same Professors are the followers of Huxley and Herbert Spencer, who did far more to make the world ignorant than wise." Then she dismissed the Ivy League universities by observing that "The great controversy between Yale and Harvard now is which shall excell in brute force, and foot-ball seems to be the gauge. Colleges were founded for the purpose of educating the young on moral, intellectual and spiritual lines. The test of these is oratory, debate, intellectual contests. It used to be conceded that the mind made the man; now the forces of the mule and the ox are preferred." To her surprise, the words brought in a rich crop of sincere congratulation, much of it from Harvard and Yale graduates.

Mrs. Nation's worst enemies noted that she shrank from playing favorites, and in this period of her college uplift she struck the University of Texas a quick, glancing blow. Notwithstanding the Ivy League's reputation, there was little to choose from as between the thoughtfulness of her treatment there and at the southern center of learning. At the depot in Austin, she was met by students who sought to escort her, as they said, "to the main building of the campus," but they steered her instead into the saloon of Alderman William Davis, who ordered her out with frightful threats. For years Mrs. Nation had listened to such cries in the rowdier state of Kansas, so that her natural response was to draw her hatchet and, Texas-like, prepare to remove the T-bone, sirloin, tenderloin and any other cuts she could reach. She implemented her intentions orally, saying, "Do you know who you're talking to? I'm Carry Nation, and I was never known to leave a saloon until I got good and ready." (This was something of an exaggeration; she had been hustled from dives too numerous to count.) In the present case, she got ready at once, for Davis ducked under her swing, seized her by the shoulders and pushed her through the door. Mrs. Nation saw the position as strategic for an address, but her words became incoherent when Davis shoved a sickly phonograph horn out of his window and played a record that was nothing but scratches. As the reformer made another gesture toward her hatchet, police stepped in, and this time the students actually took her to the campus. Everyone appeared glad to see her, and the organized cheers approached in volume the ones up north, but the noise subsided when she began her speech, which was promptly interrupted by "an official of the University who came running up white with excitement."

"Madam," he cried, "we do not allow such."

"I am speaking for the good of the boys," she answered.

Curiously enough, he said, "We do not allow speaking on the campus," but the shout of disappointment that followed his words caused a nearby postman's horse to bolt, heaving the postman onto the turf and demolishing his wagon against a telephone pole. It was at approximately this low point in her education that Mrs. Nation decided to drop out of college.

The proper beginning of Mrs. Nation's lecturing life took place in Springfield, Massachusetts, midway through the final act of a burlesque show. The first engagements with Furlong had been tentative and desultory, at a time when, her finest frenzy past, she was wondering what to do with the years that lay ahead. As many churches banned her tirades, she found her best forums at theatres, street carnivals, county fairs, flea circuses and chautauquas. At times she moved over the county with traveling troupes, and the money she made—often important sums—was laid aside for unusual charities that she conceived one by one. Even in this nadir of her career she clung faithfully to her creeds, and kept intact both her dignity and her good humor. Neither did she apologize for taking what might be described as the low road to prohibition. "Gradually I saw the light," she wrote of her multiple invitations to tread the boards. "This is the largest missionary field in the world. No one ever got a call or was allowed to go there except Carry Nation. The door was never opened to anyone but me. The hatchet opened it."

Her relationship to her new associates—chorus girls, burlesque strippers, carnival cheats, tricky vaudeville managers, fleas—was always excellent. She never stopped trying to convert them (aside from the fleas) but she had the common sense to enjoy their company in spite of certain failings. As a rule they called her "Mother Nation," and the most degenerate among them came to attend seriously her incongruous public pleas—sandwiched in between, say, the popular burlesque song, "Oh, How I'd Like to See My Old Gal Flo Again" and a *double entendre* explanation of bull-fighting that told how, at the finish, the torero flung his montera up into the Queen's box. "The Shed-house Four," a seedy quartet that clergymen thought might make better music in jail, caused her sincere grief, but she was able to laugh through her tears. Broadly speaking, her sudden appearance before a burlesque crowd resembled the entrance of an over-dominant trainer into a cageful of starving lions. Many had thought that the first things to hit her would be fruit; the truth is that she attracted an uncommon number of vegetables, these being cheap in the metropolitan centers. Usually she could make herself heard only by out-screaming her hecklers, and when they subsided, as they always did, for her address contained features of interest for everybody, she often stepped over to a box, where she talked conversationally with its occupants. As a general thing, her spiel proved the hit of the show.

Since her harangues were ad-libbed, the crusader had much of her day free, and, being hyperenergetic, she sought devices to fill in time. Toward the start of 1903 she began work on her autobiography, *The Use and Need of the Life of Carry A. Nation,* but as she warmed to the writing she divined that she had tapped a rich vein, and she attacked a temperance play called *The War on Drink.* She won the battle—completion of the work—but lost the war, for she failed to find a publisher willing to risk wooing customers inside a theater to be argued into dropping amusements like drinking and attending plays. Mrs. Nation's second unsuccessful drama— *Hatchetation*—was never finished, but she sold the title for a special dramatization of *Ten Nights in a Barroom,* in which she appeared personally, at Elizabeth, New Jersey. The producers hitting on a clever means of tailoring the presentation to the reformer's notoriety, had written in a saloon-smashing scene, but it turned out to be a financial disaster. Settling into the part, Mrs. Nation felt the old blood-lust rise and very nearly demolished the theatre. Next day in the reviews it was stated that, in all, she not only smashed forty-four goblets and twenty-nine bottles but banged up four chairs and three tables. The play had a short run, with diminishing props, and was not revived in the new form.

A strange facet of Mrs. Nation's later years was that, while she quarreled with the former smashing set, her general celebrity grew, the legend adding depth and color. Like any good folktale, her story lost no flavor in the telling, and she was eventually given credit for most recorded destruction since the collapse of London Bridge. She continued to interest the civilized world, and her name remains familiar even to schoolchildren today. She never permitted the demands of her honky-tonk schedule to collide with other duties, and late in 1903, for example, we find her raising cain in the United States Senate. The dignitaries on the chamber floor were dozing through a clerk's rendition of a bill for the "relief" of one John Carter, an Arkansan whose contribution to the land had not yet been divulged, when raucous cries of "Saloons are anarchy, conspiracy and treason!" rang out from the startled ladies' gallery. The slumberers awoke, rose and turned around, and the easily recognized figure of Mrs. Nation was seen, standing with a satchelful of souvenirs, and preparing to add further observations. Laws in those days were enforced, the Senate had an efficient machine for the suppression of bomb-throwers and other irritants, and Mrs. Nation was quickly seized by a policeman and a door-keeper who carried her into the corridor.

In police court, where she cheerfully disgorged twenty-five dollars supplied by carnival- and vaudeville-goers who had paid, no doubt, to see naked women and snake charmers, it was learned that the reformer had arrived in Washington quietly, planning to call on President Roosevelt and give him a piece of her mind. At the White House, turned out without that ceremonious protocol reserved for foreign moochers soliciting a loan, she had strolled off toward the Capitol. In the ladies' gallery (according to the press) she had first "done a thriving business for several minutes, selling probably ten dollars' worth of little tin hatchets at 25 cents apiece." Then, before the Senate convened, she descended to the Marble Room, where she asked to see her "old neighbor," Senator Cockrell of Missouri. The bemused fellow rushed out of the cloak-room with every intention of greeting a well-known constituent and nailing down a few votes, but he ran into such a hornet's nest of abuse that his nerves were affected for months. Each time he essayed a stentorian bray that his influence was being exerted in behalf of Progress and against Sin, Mrs. Nation demanded to know what he specifically meant to do about saloons. Moreover, her manner was "bullying." Cockrell moved repeatedly, though feebly, to detach himself, saying, "I am a member of the Senate, and it's my business to be in my seat." "At this," wrote a Washington reporter, "Mrs. Nation broke into a fierce and prolonged tirade against the liquor interests. She said some bitter things of men who come to Congress, and used several words that were hardly suitable to appear in print." After the exchange, she climbed up to the gallery, where she scrambled the session as related.

A favorite game of the day was to guess where Mrs. Nation might pop up next. She was on hand, in a gallery seat to which she remained fixed only briefly, for a gala opening of the horse show at Madison Square Garden. Her complaint of the moment was the

341 VESSEL OF WRATH

over-gorgeous and under-cut attire of the ladies present, and she singled out the Vanderbilt box as the worst offender. The horses (with riders) had been twinkling about the sod, clearing jumps, changing pace, pleasing everybody, when hoarse shouts of "Jezebels! Drink is a curse!" etc. floated down from the darkened balcony. Mrs. Nation was making her way toward the focal points of fashion—the box seats on the lower levels. Halfway down, a *Tribune* reporter joined her to point out the notables. The papers said that, once descended, she started "scrutinizing closely the occupants of the boxes, until she came to the aisle opposite the end of the show ring, where she halted directly before the box held by Reginald C. Vanderbilt and occupied at the time by the holder and by Mrs. Alfred Gwynne Vanderbilt." Also in the box were two emphatically toothsome girls, including a Miss Nielson, fiancée of the gilded Vanderbilt, and it was Miss Nielson's inadequate bodice that lent eloquence to the crusader's words. Even so, as writers have observed, it was an era of plumply exposed bosoms, and besides, Mrs. Nation's first suggestion was not only silly but illegal.

"You think you are well dressed," she said, leaning close to the young ladies, "but you ought to be ashamed of yourselves for wearing such disgraceful clothes. Take them off at once."

When Miss Nielson and companion declined to strip for the horse show, Alfred Vanderbilt, who had been "stretching his legs in a cleared space," sprinted back to the action. The Vanderbilts were somewhat noted for knight-errantry—Commodore Vanderbilt, the former Staten Island costermonger, once threatened to break down to fireman a conductor who'd pinched a nurse on a rattletrap railroad Vanderbilt acquired in a stock deal—and Alfred now suggested to Mrs. Nation (in what the *Times* described as an "undertone") that she leave the Garden. Instead, she rapidly flashed a handkerchief, causing the women to shrink back in fear of a hatchet attack, and "gesticulating wildly, flourished [it] toward the Vanderbilt party." Horse-show officials were nonplussed; like many a saloonkeeper over the land, they lacked experience at handling the situation. Nothing of the sort had happened before at the normally impeccable function. Even the horses appeared shocked, for they halted their performance and stood gazing at the outrage with liquid and lugubrious eyes. Unable to provoke a fight,

Mrs. Nation turned away, but "a large crowd had collected, and, as she moved on, the crowd followed." Near the exit she ran into an acquaintance, George Kessler, a socialite (and horse loving) champagne salesman whom she denounced in a voice that carried to the gallery, crying, "George, if you don't stop selling the devil's wares, you will be eternally damned!"

Kessler grinned but made no promises, and various of the happy crowd pressed forward with ideas. It came as a surprise to the officials that their audience included many not exactly of the elite. Some of the merrily shouted offerings were more suited to a medium-caste saloon. One man assured Mrs. Nation that all the riders (a number were in their early teens) had been drunk since lunch, and another said he could produce affidavits that the best horses, the champion hunters, or jumpers, were spurred onward and upward by a daily "quart of bourbon mixed in with their fodder." The only person Mrs. Nation heeded was a fellow, with an unfrivolous face, who suggested that she had here a priceless opportunity to wreck the notorious pub on the corner of Twenty-third Street. Thither she hastened, to find a tableful of oddities sitting near the door, ostentatiously sipping mineral water. She praised them with gusto and gave each a souvenir hatchet, which one carelessly used to stir a drink he had sitting on the floor. Then she discovered that the group was window-dressing and that everybody else in the place was swilling cheap gin, a *specialité de maison*. Mrs. Nation broke whatever glasses she could reach (the place was too crowded for easy traffic), hurled vituperation at the clients, and called for the manager, James Villepigue, who crept out from a kind of priest's hole in the rear, wringing his hands. He had commenced begging, wailing, that she leave when a police sergeant and a detective showed up and two-walked Mrs. Nation to the street.

In this time of her unpredictable rambling, the crusader became the feature-writers' darling, the chief and willing subject for reporters who had to let themselves go a little or explode. The scores of sensational papers—later called tabloids and worse—bore down creatively on her doings, and even the *Times* and *Tribune* put her in a journalistic class apart. The finest sample of this latter dispensation was an account, in the *Times,* that today might get the entire editorial staff imprisoned by the United Nations Committee for Human Dignity with Special Attention to Minorities. It dealt with Mrs. Nation's unheralded appearance at the annual New York ball of Chuck Connors, a shifty but plausible political bounder who described himself as the "Mayor of Chinatown," meaning that he extracted a living by systematic thievery from frightened and gullible Orientals. Among other felonious dodges, Connors gave a yearly "ball"—referred to by most newspapers as a brawl—for the benefit of himself. It was held at Tammany Hall. The function that Mrs. Nation crashed was a trifle out of the ordinary, for it featured the "debut" of Connors' new girl friend, a semi-professional prostitute identified by the *Times* only as "Pickles," who the paper said was "escorted to the hall by Ling Quong, the Chinese interpreter, whom she met coming out of a hop parlor in Pell Street."

Apropos of little except that the *Times* man was off and running, and meant to stay that way, the story proceeded to add, "Mr. Ling explained that he had only 40 cents, as he had just dropped three dollars in a fan-tan game, and needed a quarter of what he had left for gate money at Chuck's ball." The reporter came out especially strong on dialects, and gave the debutante's reply as follows:

"Tush," said Pickles, "you pay me fare up on de automobile, and I'll git in de ball all right, even dough I ain't got no coin."

The story then offered a handsome paragraph about a mob trying to push inside Tammany Hall without paying, and noted that "Ling forced his way through the crowd to the box office where he learned that the price of admission was fifty cents."

"Tloo blad," he said. "No takee twenty-five centee, play fiftee."

(The *Times* generously gave Ling further substance when it confided that he was planning to run for office on "the Laundry Ticket.")

"Hey," shouted Pickles, addressing the ticket seller. "I'm a fren' of Chuck's, see? And if you tell him dat Pickles is down here at de door, he'll send a escort to bring me in."

The ball was swinging into high gear, while Connors, as host, busied himself circulating in his easy style, levying petty blackmails here, taking bribes there, when Carry Nation burst in. Her first act was to grab cigarettes from the mouths of perhaps two dozen girls who responded in the warm, ripe idiom of the streets. Then she began forcibly to separate dancers who had effected what seemed like a permanent amalgam. At the start, Connors was inclined to be lenient, telling the crusader, "Sure you can come in. Der are udder automobiles in here wid loose wheels. Just step in an help yourself to a twist." (An uptown interpreter translated this to mean that, although she must certainly be crazy, she was welcome to enter and dance like the cheapest hooker in the joint.) Connors' mood changed when Mrs. Nation yelled, "I came here to stop this ball. I received a letter from a broken-hearted mother about it, and she said her son lost his job by attending it last year. I'm going to break it up." In the traditional style of musicians faced with a crisis, the band struck up, "Bedelia, I'd like to Steal Yah," but the reformer, failing to kick over a table at which some ward-heelers and pimps were drinking, climbed quickly up onto the stage, where she adjusted her gold-rimmed spectacles and plunged into a noisy reading of the "letter" (which the Ball Committee later decided she had written herself).

"Put her out!" yelled the crowd (in the *Times* version). "Fire her! Rats! Shut up! Hey! Hey!"

The papers spoke admiringly of Connors' tact when he persuaded Mrs. Nation to step down and "meet a nice little girl who ought to be home in bed"—Connors' bed—but this turned out to be Pickles, who diminished her fiancé's high social tone by telling the crusader, "If yer don't git downstairs in a minute I'll push yer nose through de back of yer neck!"

"Then," said the *Times*, "Pickles caught hold of Carrie, and Chuck caught hold of Pickles, and three Committeemen caught hold of Chuck, and all moved downstairs to the outside door."

In a surprise tactic, Mrs. Nation returned to Topeka in December of 1903 to "take elocution lessons." She had some notion of embracing the stage as a second career, her hope being to play the main roles in temperance plays she would write, spinning them out "at the rate of three or four a year." Why she selected Topeka over New York, the theatrical hub of America, was never explained, but the decision proved costly. Back in the heady environs of smash, riot and siren, scene of her salad days, she succumbed to a small, token explosion. Unannounced, she entered a drugstore and emptied out three kegs of legal prescription whiskey. The proprietor, helpless, stood gaping in disbelief. And once again, after the long passage of time, Mrs. Nation was hauled before her ancient nemesis, Judge Magaw, the devotee of nude art, who fined her twenty-five dollars, alternative to the usual incarceration. Despite the many shabby defections, the disillusion of rats leaving the sinking ship, one of the most resolute men of his age, selfless (and slightly combat-worn) wielder of ax and battle hymn, the Reverend J. T. McFarland, now dean of the First Methodist Church, came hurrying to her side. No slanderer of the Cloth could describe McFarland as a fair-weather friend; he was the kind of clergyman— fearless, clear-headed, patriotic—that throws today's National Council of Churches into such stealthy and questionable contrast.

McFarland arrived as sentence was being pronounced on his old trench-mate. "This is an infernal shame!" he cried, close under the judge's nose. Magaw countered with, "I will also fine you twenty-five dollars for contempt."

"You may make it a hundred," replied McFarland coolly, suggesting that his contempt had been gravely underestimated.

"Very well, I will make it a hundred."

In the cheeriest (and most defiant) spirit, though he was far from a rich man, the reverend paid up and left, and he shortly managed the release of Mrs. Nation as well.

Chapter Twenty-Two

It was heart-warming to Mrs. Nation that, after the noble McFarland had sprung to her aid, other old friends and champions called to heal the breaches cleft by an over-active hatchet. Mrs. Myra McHenry, the crusader's one-time chief rival, and, it was believed, the recipient of more rotten-eggings than any other reformer in history, publicly promised that anybody who dared lay a hand on Carry Nation would have her (Mrs. McHenry) to whip; and Mrs. Lucy Wilhoite, once described as "the second-worst woman in Wichita" (a printed estimate that she framed and hung in her parlor, where it was taken down, she said, seventeen times by her husband before they reached an understanding), declared that, as a smasher, Mrs. Nation ranked first and the rest nowhere. (The three, with a couple of others, would further close ranks for one last convulsion before they were finished.)

Such words were, to be sure, manna for Carry Nation's travel-weary soul. In these the doldrums of her uphill campaign against liquor, the confidante of tarts and tumblers, target on stage of many a squash and cabbage, somewhat bitten by fleas, she found vindication sweet. The ladies persuaded her, however, that a professional actress, to be successful, must be in a position to answer the curtain and that this was awkward in jail. Since hardly a month went by that she was not locked up in one hamlet or another, she saw the wisdom of their counsel and resumed her helter-skelter odyssey. The dramatic stage, she implied, could shift for itself. In Canada, in the spring of 1904, she was lyrically received, the visit not much marred by an unimportant arrest on Cape Breton Island for an attempt to wreck the Hotel Belmont. She wrote that, "I sold all the hatchets I had in three meetings." This meant, of course, profit, and she felt herself ready to proceed with her life's dream of a charity—the establishment of her "Home for the Wives of Drunkards." Mrs. Nation had erected a large brick building in Kansas City, Kansas, and sold it when the Salvation Army, for some obscure military reason, defaulted on a promise to use it for a mission. Using these proceeds, plus savings from the burlesque circuits, she made a down payment of $5,500 on a nearby mansion and incorporated the Associated Charities to handle its management. In the first years, when the idea seemed novel (and the quarters regally comfortable) wives flocked in by the score, many wearing wedding rings and clutching documents claiming matrimonial union. Most of these waifs from the stormy seas of life wandered off in time, looking bored with an establishment that ran strong on virtue and short on recreation. In 1910, the haven was closed for lack of victims, and the crusader took it as a trend toward respectability.

No single volume, of course, could cover all the appearances that Mrs. Nation made in those otherwise quiet years after the turn of the century. A few were outstanding, however, and should be mentioned. A repeated complaint of her employers was that she exceeded the bounds of her contracts. At the Chutes, in Los Angeles, a glorified beer garden that featured a dizzy boat ride down a long slide into a pool, the crusader became restless after two speeches and led a W.C.T.U. expedition toward the red-light district. To transcribe their stories, it was said, she meant to flush the toilers out of their "open-door cribs." Naturally enough, the police were horrified, for the area had been a prime source of graft; one of their number was rushed ahead in a feeble effort at camouflage. Among other homey and asinine touches, several samplers—"God Bless our House," "Hard Work Never Killed Anybody"—were hung, and some Bibles scattered around. Shades were drawn, and five or six inmates produced darning materials, but Mrs. Nation pulled the girls out anyway. Most of them were Mexicans—early forerunners of "wetbacks" who had been slipped across the border for better-paying careers among the gringos—and it made an exotic scene, the half-naked, mystified visitors to the new land standing around in the street asking questions in pidgin: "Who thees woman?" "Mehico was never like thees," etc.

Next morning, according to custom, Mrs. Nation called on Chief of Police Yelton for an explanation. "If we close the joints," he told her, "those degraded girls will be all over the town." When the crusader assured him that she would be happy to close them over his dead body, city officials trumped up a charge having to do with her advertising, and shot her north to San Francisco. But the aroused ladies of Los Angeles galloped ahead and nailed up the cribs in less than six months.

Mrs. Nation's best blows in the arena of harlotry—the provocation of an all-out riot—were struck in Denver, after a speech she made to the Juvenile Improvement Association. A scattering of headlines will serve to set the tenor of the evening: "Thousands of Screeching Auditors"; "Scenes of Lust"; "Clothes Ripped, Bare Shoulders Slapped"; "Denver's Wildest Night"; "Stampede"; "Carry Nation Jailed"; etc. Before proceeding to her contribution, the writer must praise Denver's unique degeneracy of the period. The city was widely acclaimed. Even at a time when an attitude of *laissez* completely *faire* marked the operation of municipalities, Denver stood out in the brilliance of its saloons, brothels, gaming halls and dives of broad range; and the corruption of its authorities was a model for duller centers to study. To the righteous, Carry Nation's arrival was a godsend (as all of the churches conceded) and her reception was triumphant. The Salvation Army provided a band reinforced by two hired trombones and a volunteer piccolo, and the crusader marched beaming to the Midland Hotel, thence to the People's Tabernacle. In her address, she spoke feelingly about masturbation, a subject she had lately boned up on, and passed to the larger problem of prostitution. Excitement mounted in her audience when she cried, "Women, let's attack these dens of iniquity!" and plans were shaped in a hurry. As field commander, Mrs. Nation suggested an assault cadre of a hundred females, "as many as possible carrying babies," who would immediately invade Market Street, which an unchauvinistic paper had said was given to "open and flagrant vice of the blackest character."

Students of the Denver holocaust have expressed dismay at the temper of Mrs. Nation's force. Her progressive address, plus the inflammatory surroundings of the dens, provoked reform over-tones that may have bordered on the salacious, after the manner of Reverend Davidson administering to Sadie Thompson, in Mr. Maugham's play. Whatever the cause, a crowd of seven thousand gathered, the whores tumbled belligerently out of their lairs, a howl of joy burst from the Tabernacle Juveniles (conspicuously unimproved) and all hell broke loose. One need rhapsodize no further on Denver's imaginative sin than to observe that the youth-ful trollops were about equally divided among the Anglo-Saxon, Arapahoe, French, Italian, Japanese, Mexican and Negro. In this, the city had done a bang-up job, and there was restless comment about it afterward from persons of sheltered lives. Precisely what sparked the violence remains controversial, but one account de-clared that the polyglot workers "in abbreviated skirts, red stock-ings and high-heeled slippers collected and fought to get at her [Mrs. Nation] . . . Boys and men emboldened by the confusion threw their property to the winds and engaged in unbridled licence, tearing the scant clothes off the women and slapping their bare shoulders. Many women were bereft of their garments, and a few appeared to be almost nude."

Sirens (mechanical) were screeching, and when the reformer scrambled into a large, occupied crib, crying "Shame! Shame on you! Have you no modesty before all these lewd men?" (receiving the equivalent of "Not an ounce" in about six different tongues) police crashed through and tackled her. "One of these days you'll get into jail and never get out," a patrolman snapped. "And one of these days you'll get into hell and never get out," she replied, kick-ing out at a vulnerable spot. She was jugged, after a prolonged and casualty-filled battle with the crowd (which was just warming up) and a reporter visited her cell to say, "Mrs. Nation, I expect this will go pretty hard with you; they have brought a state case—sworn out a complaint that you were raising a riot. That's a penal offense." She gave her ritual reply: "God will take care of me," and in the morning she faced Mayor Speer, who was caught up in mixed emotions. While Mrs. Nation had turned the town upside down, she had also drummed up business and notoriety. Nearly all the world was reading with pleasure about Denver. When word arrived that, in the wake of the orgy, well-heeled farmers were streaming in from the outlying sections, Speer decided to release her after an affecting fatherly chat—this despite the fact of his being her junior by approximately thirty years. "Showing tears in his eyes," in the presence of police high brass, he tore up her bond and threw it into the wastebasket. This paradoxical, almost mercenary viewpoint by city fathers arose to confront Mrs. Nation on several occasions. Perhaps the most cynical of these took place at Hot Springs, Arkansas, where, after her penetration of "gambling dens and other disreputable houses," she was "arrested and dragged to jail by a miserable, cruel policeman. I was put in the cell with three desolate-looking, cigarette-smoking magdalenes." In this low condition, the crusader received a chatty social note from the mayor, who said that, if she would attend an auction of lots the next day, he would send a carriage to her present domicile (jail) and give her fifty dollars. "Of course I accepted it," she wrote, "and I sold $60 worth of hatchets to the crowd."

Continuing to swirl over the land, Mrs. Nation was ravaged by bedbugs in Wheeling (whose detention facilities were archaic); lost her skirt in Houston, where a saloon door banged shut behind her; swallowed her false teeth after being struck in a Colorado joint (she restored them to the open, broken, when a bystander pounded her back); paid a fine in New Jersey for joining a "drunkard's wife" in trying to drag a reluctant lounger from a saloon; was knocked down four times by a Mr. Chapman, manager of a hotel that sold beer in Bangor, Maine; and bulldozed the gigantic captain of a Fall River cruise boat who said, when she disembarked, "Madam, I was told you would raise the devil, but if anybody thinks you are a fool, they are very much mistaken." Informed (by the State Department) that a cousin was insane in Mexico, she dropped everything, made the long, arduous, expensive trip, brought the boy back and placed him in an institution at St. Joseph, Missouri, and she never bothered to chide his closer relatives for their neglect.

The reformer's career rolled ahead on its high plateau of fines, lumps and bruises, and, jolting the world, she nipped back to Wichita for a last, definitive smashing in Kansas. Though busy speaking (and being jailed) Mrs. Nation announced herself as touched by an anxious letter from the ravening Lucy Wilhoite, who said, in summing up an ornate materialization by the Lord, "Immediately, like a great scroll reaching across the sky, these words appeared, written in letters of gold: 'Spill it out!' Then He showed me the very place I was to attack—Mahan's Wholesale Liquor House!" There had never been any question in Mrs. Wilhoite's mind where to turn; mediocrity knows nothing higher than itself but talent always recognizes genius.

Evidence is lacking that any of the sorely tried Mahans retired to an asylum on hearing the news, though such a move might have been logical. Back in the beginning, dark days, their Hotel Carey had been splintered, and others among their properties had felt the heavy hand of reform. Importuned in a postscript to "lead the expedition," Mrs. Nation canceled all appointments and hastened to the once-riotous cow-town, locale of her first really large-scale depredations. She arrived on September 28, 1904. In advance of her return, she dispatched a note to the Topeka *State Journal:* "I ask all women over the state and elsewhere to meet me at Wichita on September 28. Bring your hatchets with you. I will pay the railroad fares of those not able. Now [she had the audacity to add, evoking a rash of sarcastic Wichita curses] this appeal is made to the gentle, loving, brave Christian women whose hearts are breaking with sympathy for the oppressed."

Through a need for tactical preparation, the raid was postponed until the next day, when, early in the morning, Mrs. Nation filled a gunnysack with stones and freshly honed hatchets and half-walked, half-ran to the Methodist Church. There she outlined an attack of such savagery as to leave her audience gasping. The leaders selected, however, offered credentials not to be matched in the western world. The city regarded Mrs. Wilhoite's bile as a staple nuisance of the community; Mrs. Myra McHenry was a woman whom no policeman cared to face without sidearms; Mrs. Nation's own celebrity was now sufficient to have her arrested anywhere on sight and the fourth member, Miss Blanche Boies, while a comparative upstart, had made her mark when, not long before, she had inavded the office of Wichita's then Mayor Parker and given him a going-over with a horsewhip. It was a well-balanced group, and optimism ran high as it headed off toward the warehouse. Three armed guards stood sentry-go, and the crusader greeted them in tones deceptively genial. "We are going to destroy this den of vice," she said, "but first we want to go in peacefully and hold gospel services . . . Please stand aside." The guards refusing to comply, Mrs. Nation cried, "Women, we will have to use our hatchets!" The nearly forgotten cry echoed down Wichita's streets with awful familiarity—"causing people to bolt their doors, babies to cry and dogs to howl in anguish."

Stepping back, she flung her first stone, but Mrs. Wilhoite rapidly followed by kicking in a panel of the door. The old, stimulating crowds formed, pushing, shouting and striking out, and the guards then fell realistically upon the reformers. Unofficial counts put the number of times that Mrs. Nation was knocked to the pavement as seven, and a man thought to be an onlooker tried to dash Mrs. McHenry's brains out with a length of gaspipe. When she dodged, he dropped the tool and began hauling her back and forth by the shoulders. "Help!" she cried, then, neglecting her grammar in the crisis, explained that, "I'm being shook to pieces!"

"Bite and scratch!" Mrs. Nation shouted, and Mrs. McHenry, breaking loose, left a deep teeth-wound in her attacker's hand. Swarms of police suddenly arrived to hustle Mrs. Nation, Mrs. McHenry and Mrs. Wilhoite into the van, while the younger Miss Boies fought free after smashing two windows with her hatchet. (She went to earth in the basement of a church but was bagged when, with a splendid lack of prudence, she appeared at jail next morning to visit her colleagues.) "We were driven through the streets," wrote the crusader, "amid the yells, execrations and grimaces of the liquor element. I watched their faces and could see that Satan was aroused in them beyond their control, making diabolical faces and sticking out their tongues. There never was such a sight. Angels wept and devils yelled with diabolical glee."

A jail-delivery crowd was dispersed when police tossed buckets of water out of windows, and the prisoners, for security reasons, were transferred to a stronger lockup in Sedgwick County. At a preliminary hearing, on October 6 before Police Judge Alexander, the four women acted as their own lawyers, with Mrs. Nation leading as "senior counsel." The arrangement perfectly illustrated the maxim: Anyone who acts as his own attorney has a fool for a client. The trial's hectic and undisciplined air was not markedly different from that of the crusader's burlesque engagements. As an opening gambit, the ladies moved for dismissal on grounds that the prosecution had stolen their briefs from a table; Judge Alexander nervously turned the request down. In a legal way, the defense staff sought to substitute the Bible for the Kansan statutes. When Mrs. Wilhoite arose and said, "Now I'll read from Ecclesiastes," Sam Amidon, who still was County Attorney, inquired, "Is there anything in Ecclesiastes about this case?"

"Shut your mouth, you perjurer," cried Mrs. Nation. "We're trying this case by divine law, not by Kansas law." Higher authorities took a divergent view, and in District Court, in April of 1905, some curious and arbitrary penalties were assessed. Mrs. Nation was fined two hundred and fifty dollars and sentenced to four months in jail; Mrs. McHenry got two months and a hundred and fifty dollars; Mrs. Wilhoite twenty-five days and a hundred and fifty dollars; and the elusive Miss Boies wriggled off scot-free. The jail terms were all suspended, and Wichita's hatchetation was finished forever.

In reduced circumstances, for the heavy fines were threatening to draw her stinger, Mrs. Nation moved to Oklahoma Territory soon after her trial. She wished to be where the action was, as the Broadway saying goes. (Besides, Wichita had proved itself an ingrate and false friend.) Guthrie (later to become the state capital for awhile) was the center of a fuss over Prohibition, the question being whether to incorporate sections against sin in a charter when Oklahoma applied for statehood. Overnight the crusader took a leading role in the turmoil. She organized the Prohibition Federation which, had it prevailed, would have kept Oklahomans playing croquet and singing psalms for years. Paradoxically the region was about as lawless as any part of the country, the refuge of gunmen and rustlers, a place beyond the reach of state and federal marshals, a jolly haven for everybody with a tendency to avoid strangers and keep a buttoned-up lip about his past. In essence, Mrs.

Nation's new group aimed "to oppose in every way the use of intoxicating liquors, making it a crime to manufacture, barter, sell, give away, export or import the same into the United States for any purpose." But the platform had additional plans. It hoped to "elect a Prohibition President (Mrs. Nation), recommend compulsory education, see that the Sabbath was observed, ban public games on the 'Lord's Day,' provide imprisonment for 'blasphemous language in any public place,' " make the selling or using of cigarettes a misdemeanor, regulate strictly those saloons already legally operating, and oppose all jointists seeking new licenses. Both the W.C.T.U. and the newly formed Anti Saloon League offered assistance, and the crusader felt the joy of being in harness again.

Mrs. Nation's Elysium (if so loose a term may be applied to the Oklahoma Territory) was short-lived. As the action swelled, she decided to reactivate her old newspaper, the deceased *Smasher's Mail*, the new version to be called, simply, *The Hatchet*. She installed presses in the Harvest Home Mission, a collapsed refuge she had bought for a campaign headquarters, and laid out a format that presented a large, well-drawn hatchet on the front page; its blade was scribbled over with such mottoes as "To Cut Out the Evil," "To Build up the Good," and "Your Ballot is Your Hatchet." Subscription price was a sensible twenty-five cents, and local financiers—saloonists, procurers, thieves, political foes—predicted the paper's failure, but Mrs. Nation made it the official organ of her Prohibition Federation, causing business to boom automatically. At this point the crusader had things running smoothly, and prospects were bright for her elderly future—too bright, for she had never been able to endure an entirely unclouded horizon. As previously mentioned, she had decided to deal with self-abuse among the young (who in that day were warned about lunacy, the onset of vile and crippling diseases, biblical corruptions like boils and festuring pustules, hell, and other abominations) and she sailed into the frankest discussion of the subject thus far published in English. The results exceeded her most hopeful expectations. Not only was she denounced on the streets, but weird and protesting letters flooded in to be printed without rancor in *The Hatchet*.

One man went so far as to describe the article as a "blueprint for masturbation." Another wrote, "I have always been one of your admirers, helping you all I can, but I cannot endorse your letters to 'the boys.' I have one boy ten years old. If I saw him reading anything like that, I would take it from him. It was unfit even for me to read and is a hindrance to the good cause for which you stand [and signed—'A. Stephens']." One unfortunate, possibly the victim of ministerial lectures, wrote in a different vein, saying, "I want to encourage you to continue your Private Talks to boys and girls. For want of knowledge on this very sex question—horrible to relate—I am a victim of this secret vice; and I would give all I am worth, and gladly, too, if my past life could be forever blotted out and I could be a real man. I am a man in age but not in strength, and I feel that I would be many times happier if I had a life partner; but I dare not marry, though there is one I love more than anything else on earth."

Upshot of Mrs. Nation's worthy campaign was to see her arrested, during a brief trip to Cleburne, Texas, by United States Marshal R. A. Walden, of Dallas. Quite evidently, Walden's sympathies lay elsewhere, for Mrs. Nation wrote, later, "I was never arrested in as respectful and elegant a manner as by Mr. Walden." This was high praise indeed, for the crusader had been taken into custody practically every place and under all kinds of conditions, and it would be interesting to know if her words furthered Walden's career, but the records are incomplete. The charge was "dispatching obscene material through the U.S. mails," and, to his everlasting credit, a federal attorney dismissed it curtly, observing that the material was no more obscene than many passages from Holy Writ. His face showed deep disgust over the whole silly incident.

Even so, Mrs. Nation transferred her newspaper, with her person, to Washington, D.C., and out of the half puritan, half miscreant Oklahoma Territory in 1907, when, imitating her gamble of years before, she opened her Bible and placed her finger on a passage from Genesis. It read: "And I will put enmity between thee and thy woman, between thy seed and her seed; it shall bruise thy head. . . ." She felt that only a dummy could fail to detect this clue; Washington was clearly the head of the nation, and selling her chief Oklahoma properties she made her move. Then, in the

Capital, she announced by handbill that she was available for free lectures. In doing this, she declined any number of lucrative professional chances, among them one, at the Eldorado Theater in Atlanta, that involved a payment of five hundred dollars. By good fortune, the Washingtonians who recently had shunned Mrs. Nation as a dangerous freak now flocked in to sponsor her free engagements, prompting her to hike *The Hatchet*'s subscription price and buckle down to take over the city. She tried again to beard President Roosevelt but failed, this time, to get even as far as his secretary, a Mr. Loeb (who, after the prior visit, had lain down on a sofa for a period of recuperation scrutinized by a physician).

Now it occurred to Mrs. Nation that throughout her career she had been under-armed. From a hardware store, as a large crowd watched, she selected three new hatchets and named them (with indelible pencil) Faith, Hope and Charity, and she found herself in jail before nightfall. Released, and planning larger strikes, she went on tour to replenish her funds and had a notable encounter, in Cleveland, with one Mike Goldsmith, "walking delegate" of the Bartenders' Union. Before a noisy audience, they joined in debate for a purse of $320, and when it was over, Goldsmith seemed stunned when the crusader pocketed the whole amount, refusing to divide according to plan. The incident is believed to have been one of the few times in history when a union leader failed to get part of his own way. To assuage his chagrin, Mrs. Nation gave Goldsmith a free copy of her *Four Rules for Longevity,* which recommended spring water as a refreshment and advised the snubbing of bartenders.

Back in Washington, she caused everybody, including President Roosevelt, a great deal of embarrassment by the kind of mulishness that had marked her actions for sixty years. Standing in the post-office lobby, she objected "in a threatening manner" to the use of tobacco there, whereupon several wags made little darts and dashes to blow smoke in her face. It was ill-considered conduct. She grabbed one youth and hurled him about thirty feet, after which she in turn was seized by a policeman. For some reason, on this occasion, Mrs. Nation determined to make life exactly as difficult as possible for the authorities. At the police station, she was asked to pay a twenty-dollar fine. Normally the levy would have raised no trouble; it was the sort of thing she faced every week. This time, however, she replied, with a sunny smile, "I have paid my last fine." The situation was awkward. Nearly everybody in Washington attended the crusader's work, usually in the morning papers, and many of the Capital's best-known residents knew her personally. Still, the authorities, if they wished to remain in authority, had little choice except to lock her up—in the "drunk cage" (because of crowded conditions) with a collection of "Negroes, cigarette fiends, two morphine addicts, and two drunk-and-disorderly men with cut heads." Washington, but not Kansas, was astonished when Mrs. Nation, calling all the captives "Mothers' boys," bustled over them, giving physical aid, peremptorily summoning guards to make their wants known, chatting and fraternizing on the friendliest basis.

In the morning, during her appearance before Judge Bundy, she described the situation in the tank, made urgent recommendations, and then, ruining his day, refused to post bond. Bundy's spirit at the start had been high, for Mrs. Nation had promised to cite some decisions of "the Supreme Court," but she fished a Bible out of her dress and cited several cases from that. Helpless (though he tried hard to dissuade her) Bundy sent Mrs. Nation to the Workhouse, where she was ordered to strip, bathe and put on a starchy Mother Hubbard. She complied happily and pitched into the assignment of sewing buttonholes for overalls. It became clear that she enjoyed being a Workhouse inmate, and she wrote that, "When the day arrived for me to do my scrubbing, I got my bucket, scrubbing brush, soap and cloth and got down on my knees like the rest . . . I never allowed myself to murmur and complain at anything . . . for my fellow prisoners were in a worse position than I." In quick order she became established as Leading Trusty, but her influence threatened to convert the place into a continuing revival. Eventually, after much persuasion (which residents hinted came from "the highest quarter") she let the Holiness Association of Evansville, Indiana, pay her fine, and temporarily resumed her rounds of the lecture circuit.

At the National Prohibition Party's convention in Columbus, Mrs. Nation met a desiccated Briton named Scrymgeour (later to be a perennial election opponent of Winston Churchill) and at his insistence agreed to convey the good word to Europe. Accompanied by her niece, Miss Callie Moore, an apprentice smasher, she sailed for Glasgow on November 28 aboard the steamship *Columbia*. She made a pleasant voyage, somewhat enlivened by her destruction of the bar mirror and the tumbling about of several dumfounded waiters carrying drinks. The Glasgow *Times* made a several-column story of her arrival, and described in detail the "dense crowds who alternately booed and cheered" her on the dock. For the enthusiastic, she performed about as gratefully as usual, the account saying that, "While Carry was making for the exit, a compatriot squeezed forward to the lady, and, after shaking her by the hand and giving her welcome, exclaimed—'Wal, Carry, I guess this is a stiffer proposition than Kansas.' With a smile, Carry replied—'I'm afraid so. Scotland is much nearer hell than Kansas.'" Mrs. Nation's first talk was in Dundee, a sewer of inebriation, and it went down badly. To offset it, she called on Lord Provost James Urquhard, who beguiled her into tranquillity with old-world charm and articulation; the two—leaders of exceptional force and intelligence—became good friends. Despite this victory, the reformer was spun out of a Scottish bar several days later, and she continued to be booed and cheered, praised and damned, feted and snubbed during the following three months that she spent lecturing in Scotland, England and Ireland. A Scottish poet who signed himself "Shem," was inspired to cough up an eight-stanza panegyric entitled "To My Charmer, Carry A." that nearly all papers treated seriously, one suggesting that a dry reincarnation of Tennyson might be hovering in the wings. The first stanza went:

> "I have read of all your capers,
>   As reported in the papers,
>   Since you came to dear auld Scotia on the Prohibition
>   lay,
>   And my feelings have been welling,
>   And my stricken heart is swelling,
>   All with love for you, my Carry! Oh, my charmer,
>   Carry A."

Crowds even more populous than those in America attended her meetings, and she was everywhere pressed to stay on as an immigrant. At Newcastle-on-Tyne, arrested for pub smashing, she paid a niggling fine, and proceeded to Cambridge University, where the intensely cerebral students expressed surprise at her "accent and vocabulary." Late in 1909 she signed for engagements at the London Music Halls, and it is painful to note that the vegetables which greeted her exceeded her best efforts in New York. Her discontent was underscored when, in a subway, she broke her umbrella on a sign, advertising Players Cigarettes, that showed a youth and a maid sunnily puffing while occupied in a garden swing. Mrs. Nation took her arrest sportingly and complimented the judge on the sensible amount of her fine—five shillings.

Of the European countries she had seen, and been locked up in, the crusader spoke with highest warmth of Scotland, which she eulogized by telling an eager (American) reporter, "I never saw men of any nation superior to Scotchmen. They impressed me with their sincerity, generosity and chivalry. I attribute this to their knowledge of God's word, as the Bible is the best authority in Scotland. One cannot help but notice the difference between Scotchmen and Englishmen." She specified her distaste, adding that, "Britain is cursed with the House of Lords. To call it the House of Frauds would be more truthful." It was a peculiar utterance from a descendent of the Dukes of Argyll and a fantasy Queen Victoria.

As her attacks on whiskey waxed increasingly fruitless in England, the crusader decided to jump on tea as well. She sought to join forces with Lady Emmeline Pankhurst, Britain's squalliest feminist, whose record of incarcerations matched the best in America, and wrote her a letter opening the door to an international axis against the morning reviver. For some years, however, Mrs. Pankhurst had lived on little more than tea and mayhem, and she elected not to make a reply that might have proved suicidal. Mrs. Nation took the snub calmly and sent along a copy of her autobiography for general use.

En route home, aboard the *Baltic,* she took exception to the spectacle of female passengers drinking, and, in mid-ocean, made the ship's captain order his stewards to stop carrying alcohol to ladies. From there on, in the eyes of one passenger, the voyage seemed to take a "rather sullen course." The niece, Callie (who later married a Mr. Blum, in the contracting line), expressed herself as "mortified," in recollections afterward. She set down the surprising news that, for the trip, her aunt had designed a special costume consisting of a one-piece dress that hooked all the way up the side. "She explained that she couldn't wear a shirtwaist and skirt," said Mrs. Blum. "They'd pull 'em off of her."

A month after her return, Mrs. Nation bought a tract of Ozark Mountain land in Boone County, Arkansas, using sums derived from parcels of real estate, still owned in Oklahoma, that had inflated in value when the wild and colorful Territory had achieved statehood, almost sorrowfully, in 1907. She built a cottage that was to be her base for the brief time remaining. A few final spasms of disorder, in New York, in Washington, and elsewhere, told of her still-flaming spirit, but her strength was on the wane, and her last, ineffectual try at a smashing—aimed at a sprightly nude in a Montana dance hall—saw her battered by the young, feminine owner. In 1910, as a complexity of European alignments marched the world toward history's costliest disaster, she attempted a speaking campaign on which she had trouble finding words and constructing meaningful sentences. Acutely aware of the deficiency, she gave up and returned to Arkansas. The crusader was sixty-four. By the standards of ordeal, punishment and expenditure of energy, she had lived, if we may believe the physicians, about three rigorous lifetimes. On January 13, 1911, in feeble health but showing a resolve that makes one wonder if today's willingness to give in, compromise, cringe before an enemy, gear progress to the weakest and worst, can assure the country's survival, she rose, at Eureka Springs, Missouri, to face her last mortal audience. In the beginning, her words came distinctly and she looked encouraged. Then she stopped with an expression of confusion; her forehead knotted in what seemed to be terrible effort; and she lifted one hand to her cheek. Nevertheless she refused to be helped from the platform, and after a few moments she said, in barely audible words spaced out slowly: "I—have—done—what—I—could." As several men sprang forward to support her, she collapsed in the arms of a friend.

Early the next morning she was taken by train to the Evergreen Hospital at Leavenworth, Kansas, but a stroke that left her listless and inert, for the first time in a career of unparalleled turbulence and drive, ended her life five months later, on June 2, 1911. With her when she died were only a nurse and a doctor, who told Mrs. Nation, a few moments before her death, that her time was near. Her consciousness apparently reviving for awhile, she "smiled gently" at the news but made no attempt to speak. Such, on occasion, is the selfless fidelity of Christians that she was buried, beside her mother in Belton, Missouri, in a grave that nobody bothered to mark until 1923. Then outraged friends identified the weed-covered mound and subscribed funds for the erection of a granite shaft that now bears the legend:

CARRY A. NATION

Faithful to the Cause of Prohibition

"She Hath Done What She Could."

Over the years other memorials have risen to offer homage, as people of stature in both America and Europe have come to realize, that, with all her faults—the extremism of her methods, her Kentucky love of violence, the inflexible determination never to yield—she fought what thousands considered to be the good fight. Wichita's Hotel Carey, Topeka's Senate Bar, the nearby pleasure-domes that once ran ankle-deep in liberated booze, were long ago rolled under by reform, for Kansas, aside from beer and wine and because of Carry Nation, remains dry. Medicine Lodge, the old home from which Mrs. Nation emerged to slay the dragon, has grown to be a community bustling with tourist attractions and a Chamber of Commerce, but an odd western stillness lingers on to remind the visitor that hardened desperados stopped here. Taut-faced young cowpokes wearing Stetsons sit unsmiling in restaurants like "The El Rancho Cafe," eating good Mexican and American food and talking in the laconic phrases of a calling that must rely on the companionship of sky, plain and scattered, shifting herds. The cattle country, the real ranches aswarm with longhorns and white-faced Herefords, begins a few miles farther along on Highway 160, in the direction of Denver, but Kansas early adjusted to the economy of visiting Texans, and Medicine Lodge still busies itself with a mixture of stock, wheat and coby milo. To accommodate the tons upon tons of grain that grows over prairies stretching endlessly toward a hazy, mythical horizon, chalk-white elevators tower high in lonesome and improbable spots to shimmer, break apart, vanish and reappear during any hot summer day.

The First Christian Church, where David Nation strove to speak above his wife's tart directions, is rebuilt in gorgeous yellow brick—the principal building in town—but the rickety bridge that spans the muddy winding stream known then and now as the Medicine Creek Bottoms seems no less rickety than on the circumstantial afternoon when Mrs. Nation whipped up Old Prince and headed for Kiowa and international fame. Long ago the red-clay lane was superceded by a better route, and the bridge, for all anybody seems to know, may be the same one from beneath which devils carrying three-pronged forks boiled out to "grimace and make obscene gestures"—understandably trying to halt an ill-omened crusade before it gained momentum. The low-lying, overgrown swamp has an air of brooding decay—a place in its season murmurous with locusts and gloomy with the sad-voiced croaking of frogs—a believable haunt for emissaries from Below.

Near some stockaded "Indian villages" that offer aboriginal bracelets and ear-fobs to sightseeing eastern dudes, Mrs. Nation's old home is preserved by the local chapter of the W.C.T.U. A soberfaced (male) caretaker crippled in a mill accident about which he carries clippings steers the visitor around for a modest sum, and appears willing, though not anxious, to sell commemorative dinner plates adorned with pictures of the smasher. Set off by crossed hatchets, a red and white sign hangs outside, urging students of reform history to "See Carry A. Nation Home—Highway 160, Medicine Lodge, Kansas." On entering the faded yellow-brick structure, one is struck by its near-miniature size, as if it once had been inhabited by a different race altogether, a diminutive people playing at imitating grown-ups. A few curios laid out for inspection—the crusader's gold hatpins, one of the trusty hatchets (now reinforced by wire) that may tell of some dark act in the years when Mart Strong ran the town's leading pub, a tuneless melodeon, a small maple rocker, some holograph letters, a dusty and peeling leather valise—are all that survive after seven decades of warfare over liquor. "Father used to hire his physician by the year," Mrs. Nation wrote to a friend, and a neighbor recalled that "I have been in Carry Nation's home several times. Dined in the basement with her; ate cheese and vegetable soup." (In the pursuit of coolness, most Kansas kitchen-dining rooms then were set in deep-dug cellars.) A cracked and yellowed photograph shows the crusader—fresh-faced, curiously eager but somber, enveloped in the hideous garments of the day—with a group of church friends before the trouble started. The unmistakable look of a person determined to establish a special identity sets her apart from young ladies to whom the discovery of a new recipe for muffins might nourish the ego for a week.

Mrs. Nation placed her faith in the goodness of people, the buried common sense of a race that year by year struggles against the nervous accretions of a civilization turning in desperation to the balm of anesthesia. She traveled a long, hard road from the slave huts in the backwoods of Kentucky, and recognition, the unabashed honors for which everyone yearns, eluded her until long after the lonely ending in Leavenworth. But humanity has a belated way of righting the slights and rebuffs of its giants, and grateful temperance-ites are yet building monuments to her memory. Only a few years ago a handsome inscribed fountain was erected on the spot where she suffered her first arrest in Wichita, a testimonial not long afterward knocked down and smashed by an errant, oversized beer truck.

(THE END)

Sharon, Conn.
January 18, 1966

Index

ACKNOWLEDGMENTS

The author is greatly indebted to Robert W. Richmond, of the Kansas State Historical Society in Topeka, and to Nyle H. Miller, Mrs. George Hawley, and Mrs. Elsie Beine, who preside over archives admirably bountiful and well-organized. Hundreds of newspaper clippings, magazine pieces, letters, scraps of conversation, and recollections of neighborhood gossip provide a full background to a life minutely chronicled during most of its course.

At New York City's Public Library, the Black Temperance Collection offered a vast field for exploration into the irreconcilable viewpoints on liquor-drinking in the past; and at Medicine Lodge, Kansas, both the library and the W.C.T.U. have faithfully kept account of Mrs. Nation's residence there around the turn of the century.

Martin Lewis Taylor (the author's son), a resident of Chi Psi fraternity, focal point of social life at Stanford University, assisted with prolonged and hawk-eyed tracking over much of Kansas and Missouri; and Judith Martin Taylor, formerly of the Vassar *Miscellany News*, performed in her usual, generally thankless role of copy reader, editor, and repository for skull-cracking lamentations over a period of years.

Special mention should also be made of Dexter Loeb, for his tireless researches among the vagrant files of often long-deceased journals in centers where the crusader visited; and to Roosevelt Hayes, the brilliant young graduate student (and great-grandson of Aunt Kitty Hayes, a saintly slave once owned by a branch of the author's family) whose inquiries into some aspects of Mrs. Nation's Kentucky life proved invaluable.

Among the many volumes consulted, some were of outstanding interest as source material. Preeminent among these was, of course, Mrs. Nation's book, *The Use and Need of the Life of Carry A. Nation;* others included: *Women Torchbearers,* by Elizabeth Putnam Gordon; *Carry Nation,* by Herbert Asbury; *Dreamers of the American Dream,* by Stewart H. Holbrook; *Cyclone Carry,* by Carleton Beals; *The Great Illusion,* by Herbert Asbury; the *Annals of Kansas* (Vols. 1 and 2); and *The Real Stories Behind Carrie Nation* [sic], *American Reformers and the Liquor Question,* by Morton T. Frisby, Jr. (suppressed in 1924).

ABOUT THE AUTHOR

Robert Lewis Taylor was for some years a staff writer of profiles and articles for *The New Yorker* magazine; his work has also appeared in *The Saturday Evening Post, Life, Reader's Digest, Esquire* and other magazines.

Vessel of Wrath is his twelfth book. His previous books include *W. C. Fields: His Follies and Fortunes; Winston Churchill: An Informal Study of Greatness; Center Ring: The People of the Circus; Adrift in a Boneyard; Professor Fodorski*, a novel that was made into a Broadway musical; and a long work about the gold rush, which many critics called an American classic—*The Travels of Jaimie McPheeters*, winner of the Pulitzer Prize for fiction in 1958. He is also the author of the bestselling *A Journey to Matecumbe* and *Two Roads to Guadalupé*.

Mr. Taylor was born in southern Illinois in 1912, was graduated from the University of Illinois in 1933, and achieved the rank of lieutenant commander in the Navy during World War II. He lives in Sharon, Connecticut, with his wife, Judith, and two children, Martin and Elizabeth.